CHINESE RED

CHINESE RED

by E. Howard Hunt

ST. MARTIN'S PRESS
New York

PUBLISHER'S NOTE

This novel is a work of fiction. Names, characters, and incidents are the product of the author's imagination, and any resemblance to actual persons, living or dead, is entirely coincidental.

Production Editor: David Stanford Burr
Design by Paul Chevannes

Library of Congress Cataloging-in-Publication Data

Hunt, E. Howard (Everette Howard).
    Chinese Red / E. Howard Hunt.
        p.   cm.
    "A Thomas Dunne book."
    ISBN 0-312-08157-X (hardcover)
    I. Title.
PS3515.U5425C48   1992
813'.54—dc20   92-26156
                                                                CIP

First edition: November 1992

10 9 8 7 6 5 4 3 2 1

To Laura:
through the tough times and the good

... there lay upon the hearts of the people of the last few generations a constant and wanton feeling of catastrophe, which was evoked by an impressive accumulation of indisputable facts, some of which have already passed into history and others still waiting accomplishment. . . .

Aleksandr Blok,
"Nature and Culture"

PROLOGUE

ROME

The messenger from Moscow was a young man with the rank of lieutenant in the KGB.* His Aeroflot flight from Helsinki had landed late because a ground crew strike at Rome's Leonardo da Vinci Airport had kept the big Tupolev circling for more than an hour above the Mediterranean. The delay added little to the lieutenant's tension because he had no fixed schedule. No one in Rome was expecting him, and only a very few of his countrymen even knew where he was.

Ignoring strolling whores of both sexes, he stood in the shadows of the Villa Borghese and gazed down at the garishly lighted Via Veneto. The ancient street was jammed with vehicles; only loud motor scooters maneuvered freely up and down the hill.

The driver of the airport bus had recommended a small, inexpensive hotel near the Foro, where earlier the lieutenant had taken a room. Three nights, he had said, but now he was less sure how long his business would take.

Final briefing had taken place in an obscure Moscow café three days ago: *Your mission is not only of the highest state secrecy, but personally dangerous. Act with the utmost discretion and attract no attention. Our enemies are alert and will stop at nothing to keep you from reaching your objective.*

My objective, he thought. A guarded building, whose location he had found in a street guide. Would the embassy guards let him

---

*Komitet Gosudarstvennoi Bezopasnosti—Committee for State Security.

1

enter? He had only his diplomatic passport to convince them. And once past the guards, whom would he talk to? Would his message be believed? Doubts flooded his mind. The lieutenant shrugged off a male whore and moved out of the shadows.

He walked partway down the hill and got into a taxi parked in front of a hotel. He used the guidebook to show the driver his destination. The taxi moved out and turned sharply in to an alley that continued for several blocks before joining a broad street. When he could see the embassy two blocks away, he tapped the driver's shoulder and indicated that he wanted to stop and get out. The taxi pulled over to the curb and the lieutenant pressed a wad of unfamiliar money on him. The driver took it with a smile.

The lieutenant let the taxi disappear before he began walking toward the embassy. As he neared the grilled gates he felt the cold thrill of action just begun. Now came the most dangerous part. He looked around to see if he was followed, glanced ahead and saw only the poorly lighted street. Two police guards stood beside the embassy gate and the lieutenant decided to walk past them and turn back as though to ask directions.

He crossed the intersecting street and gained the curb. From nearby shadows a man appeared. He said something the lieutenant did not understand and held up a cigarette indicating he wanted a light. The lieutenant hesitated. Do nothing out of the ordinary, he thought; he stopped and reached into his pocket for a match folder. As he held it out the lieutenant became aware of a second man behind him. Whores? he wondered. Thieves? He glanced around.

In that moment the cigarette man pushed him backward. Even before the lieutenant could cry out he felt the strangling wire tighten around his throat. He tried to kick, to run, but they dragged him back into the shadows and plunged a stiletto into his heart. As the lieutenant died, his bladder and bowels gave way.

In Russian the strangler said, "Ah, how he stinks. Let's get it over with." Expertly they went through his pockets, extracting passport, billfold, and money. They felt clothing seams for stitched-in paper, found nothing. The cigarette man opened the diplomatic passport, glanced at the name, and put it in his pocket.

As they walked away the strangler said, "Well done, Alexei. Whoever is next won't be coming to Rome."

"But they'll keep trying," the other man said. "There's a café over there—I'll treat you to a drink." The *spetznialniy* intercept men walked off toward a neon-lit doorway framed with decorative paintings of garlic strings and long sausage chains.

In front of the Chinese embassy the two police guards were complaining about the boredom of guard duty. Nothing ever happened to liven things up.

Around the corner a stray dog sniffed at the young lieutenant's corpse, scented the foulness of death, and padded on into the tranquil Roman night.

BOOK ONE

ONE

WASHINGTON

Those who met Quinn Chance in social circumstances often later agreed that, aside from his quiet charm and old-world manners, his most unusual quality was his power of observation. Chance, they said, noticed *everything.* Whether the subtle change of a lady's evening scent, new contact lenses, a tush-tuck, false pearls, imitation diamonds, an elusive accent, a concealed liaison, a suppressed mood . . . it was uncanny, they said, weird, awesome. And to some, off-putting. Not everyone was comfortable around Quinn Chance. He was charming and intelligent but, well, disconcerting.

Most women were impressed by his masculine presence; others were captivated by his deep-set gray eyes, his preference for listening over talking. One renowned Georgetown hostess remarked to her consort, a nationally syndicated columnist: "Chance is the most marvelous dinner guest one could desire. But imagine—I spent an entire evening at his side and I haven't the faintest idea what he *does.*"

"I think I heard he lectures somewhere," said the columnist. "Or writes for some think tank. He's at home in several languages—maybe he's one of those international conference interpreters. Whatever he does, dear, I'll bet he's pretty good. Shall I look into it?"

"Oh, please don't. You know how I *adore* a mystery."

In his thirty-five years Quentin Ransome Chance, Jr., had done many things, and all of them well. For in addition to his powers of observation Chance had been endowed with a remarkable memory. His mind accumulated information as a magnet draws iron filings. Chance had learned early on that he did not always need to write down homework assignments; at home he usually *recalled* what he was required to do, and did it without prompting from his parents or the nanny who organized his daily life and that of his younger brother, Roger.

Memory combined with powers of observation propelled Chance almost effortlessly to the head of his school classes, and when in his penultimate year at Hotchkiss Chance took the College Board examinations he scored 1590 of a possible 1600. Chance later remarked that gambling on the true-false portions had helped, though there was more to it than that. He had *observed* how each question was framed, detected any minuscule bias in the wording, and chosen accordingly.

Chance enjoyed memory games and was a hands-down winner at Trivial Pursuit. He entered a national trivia contest and won the runner-up prize, lamenting later that his opponent had known Marlene Dietrich was the star of *The Garden of Allah*, not Greta Garbo, as Chance had confidently proclaimed.

He had a musician's ear for tonality and languages. Using a chord-chart booklet and Andrés Segovia recordings, Chance had taught himself to play classical guitar. Then he set aside guitar, deciding that his hands were too large and powerful for the delicate strings.

Early on, his Austrian-born mother had enjoined her elder son to be modest about his talents and abilities. They were gifts, she told Chance, genetically acquired, and not evidence of personal effort and accomplishment. He was, of course, to make full use of his talents but without attaching importance to them. So self-effacement became part of Chance's charm.

In his senior year at the University of Virginia, Chance was interviewed by campus recruiters for business and government, and opted for a career with the Central Intelligence Agency. During his training Chance unknowingly became an object of contention between the directorates of operations and analysis, each directorate finding Chance admirably suited for its specialized requirements. In the end the director of operations presented a more persuasive case to the DCI, whereupon Chance entered the clandestine world that he was not to leave for a full decade.

During those years he met Carla Francine Hobbs, who had come to Buenos Aires on a month's TDY to reorganize the station's counterespionage computer bank. Attracted to her at once, Chance had introduced her to small, choice restaurants along La Boca, took her sailing across the Río de la Plata, and taught her fly-fishing for trout and salmon in the icy streams that fed Lake Llao-Llao in the high cordillera of the Andes. They stayed in a Swiss-style chalet overlooking the lake, made love abundantly, and before returning to Buenos Aires decided to get married.

Other foreign posts followed, then a period at headquarters, where his assignments were increasingly less satisfying. That and two deeply felt tragedies caused Chance to resign from the Agency and return to Charlottesville to enroll in the doctoral program for Asian studies. He took on a teaching assignment in nineteenth-century German literature so that Carla could be treated at the university hospital, where encouraging advances were being made against Alzheimer's disease. Not quite three years ago Carla had become increasingly disoriented and forgetful. The physician who made the dreaded diagnosis had commented that so early an onset was aberrant but not unknown. It was now a year since his wife last recognized him, and though he visited Carla on Sunday afternoons he was always shaken by the way her physical disintegration kept pace with the obliteration of her mind. Her entire body was shrunken, doll-like, her mouth a perpetual teeth-bared grimace, skin yellowed and parchment-dry. She had become a sorcerer's effigy of the young woman he had married eight years ago and still loved.

Because his mind required diversion as well as challenge, Chance had listened attentively to the assistant director of training who came to his off-campus apartment with a suggestion that he enunciated between sips of Chance's *solera* sherry. "I speak," said Harold Kappler, "for the Department of State as well as the Agency. As you are probably only too well aware, the Agency has posted abroad a number of senior officers who proved inappropriate to their situations and had to be recalled."

"Why?" said Chance.

"Why did we assign them? In-house politics is an obvious reason, but the underlying problem has been disorganization at the upper levels, thanks to congressional harassment and personnel turnover. Continuity has been lost. No one knows anyone anymore. So we've been sending out regional reps who not only lack language qualifications but haven't the faintest idea of the country's political background or local customs." He sipped thoughtfully. "They come off as crude and uninformed, which they are. Unintentionally they insult a cabinet minister or his wife, are unable to mingle in local society, and lose any potential usefulness." Harold Kappler frowned. "They are brought back and a replacement sent in, an officer probably no better prepared than his predecessor. It's a very discouraging cycle, Quinn."

"I can imagine." Chance tilted the decanter and refilled their small crystal glasses. "Same problem at State?"

"Even worse. You know how ambassadorial appointments are made—a certain number reserved for presidential patronage, the rest divided among Foreign Service careerists? The secretary can nominate those, but he's powerless when it comes to White House designations. Not all of those ambassador-designates come from, let us say, the best-educated levels of society. During confirmation hearings senators make sport of them; some unfortunates can't even pronounce the name of the country's capital or its president, let alone its trade partners, religious and political history, the mores and no-no's." Harold Kappler sighed. "The Foreign Relations Committee loves to needle and taunt them, and that reflects on the judgment of our chief executive."

"Can't do anything about that," Chance said, noticing that Kappler's front teeth bore crowns added since their last encounter four years earlier.

"Well," said Kappler, "we hope we can," and eyed Chance penetratingly.

The new crowns were not nicotine-stained, leading Chance to conclude that Kappler had given up smoking. "What do you have in mind?"

"At a high-level State-Agency meeting it was decided to try to establish a sort of prep school for outward-bound ambassadors and station chiefs."

Chance smiled. "You mean a finishing school."

Kappler sipped sherry. "*Polishing* is the preferred term. Well, names were kicked around, computers consulted, and your name came out as the ideal candidate to brief these people, try to shape them up sufficiently that they won't embarrass us or the diplomatic service."

Chance said, "I have a pretty full dish right now, Harold. I lecture three mornings a week, take two graduate classes, and spend additional time in the libe. Even if I had spare time, I don't know how I could absorb all that ought to be conveyed about some exotic country."

It was Kappler's turn to smile. "You've always been modest about your abilities, Quinn, but it's a simple fact that you're a lightning-fast study, and what you absorb you don't forget. Too, you were largely raised abroad, you speak a variety of languages fluently, and your service in three foreign posts was distinguished. I know you enjoy private means, but everyone can use a little extra income—right?"

"How little?"

"The secretary and the director have discretionary funds; the agreement is to compensate you at a rate of a thousand dollars a day."

Chance said nothing.

Uncomfortably Kappler said, "That's less than a good down-town lawyer earns, I know, but it's a hell of a lot more than a cabinet secretary makes . . . and you'd be doing our country a rather large favor."

Chance said, "I'll think about it, Harold. But if I should take it on, I require anonymity. The university, you know."

"No problem. Fake papers, phone backstop, whatever you require." He drained the rest of his sherry. "When can you let me know?"

"Tomorrow," Chance told him. Harold Kappler stood up. As Chance walked him to the door Kappler said, "Satisfy my curiosity, will you? Your Christian name is Quentin. How come you've always been called Quinn?"

"When my younger brother—my late brother—Roger was four he couldn't handle Quentin. It came out Quinn, and the name stuck. I'll call you tomorrow."

"My number—," he began, but Chance said, "Unless you've changed it. . . ."

"Of course," Kappler said resignedly. "I should have thought of that."

Chance had agreed, which was why, on this Saturday afternoon, Chance sat at a glass-topped table in a Washington hotel suite whose walls and drapes were of soft pastels, attractively setting off the French provincial furnishings. Across from Chance was a plump, balding man with button eyes, who had been designated by the White House for an ambassadorial appointment. His name was Wesley Monkton and he had made a considerable fortune distributing plastic toys from South Korea, Taiwan, and Hong Kong. A part of that fortune ambassador-designate Monkton had contributed to the president's reelection campaign, and at his wife's urging he had asked a political intermediary whether, in the president's good judgment he, Wesley Monkton, might not embellish the administration by representing the president abroad. The reply had been affirmative, but the assigned post was not London, Paris, or Rome, as Mrs. Monkton had hoped, but a small sub-Saharan republic whose citizens' per capita income averaged out at forty-two dollars a year. This and other relevant demographic facts Chance had already relayed to ambassador-designate Monkton, who took notes on a long yellow legal pad. His scrawl, Chance noticed, was childlike. Undoubtedly his pupil was more accustomed to writing Arabic numbers and signing checks.

"It's unfortunate that you're left-handed," Chance continued, "because in that part of the world the left hand is considered dirty. It's used in excretory functions. Don't ever attempt to shake hands with your left hand or be seen touching it to your mouth. That would make you *impaii*, which means polluted or unclean, and you would be shunned despite your high position."

Monkton shook his head slowly. "My wife isn't going to like this," he muttered. "Felice won't like it at all."

Restraining a smile, Chance said, "Is she left-handed, too?"

Monkton gave him a withering glance. "No, she's not, and she wanted a nice post in Europe, Brussels even, but *this* place. . . . After a week she'll be telling me we should have stood at home."

"Regarding homes," Chance went on, "never enter a home or

12

hut unless invited—don't even peek inside. The senior medicine men, or witch doctors as they were called in the Tarzan movies, paint their faces and bodies in particular ways for particular reasons. Don't stare at them and never, *never* laugh at their antics. Chieftains customarily carry an ebony rod topped with the tip of a lion's tail. Don't touch it or point at it—very bad form." Monkton was writing hurriedly. Chance paused a few moments before saying, "Lion testicles fried in elephant fat are likely to be offered a dignitary such as yourself. Don't try to avoid eating what's offered you, close your eyes and swallow. Same with the *chuka* ants in wild honey—dessert. When you've consumed your portion, use a napkin or mango leaf to wipe your mouth—with your *right* hand." A wave of nausea whitened Monkton's already pale face, but he kept gamely on, recovering himself as Chance began to review the country's rural transportation system and the river routes that served as highways for produce, and mentioned the Soviet consulate in Kabiri at the great river's mouth.

Monkton swallowed. "I've never met a real Russian, I mean a Communist. How do I act with the consul?"

"Well, as ambassador you outrank him, but don't pull rank. Be polite and remember that the Sovs are very popular because they, not we, helped the present rulers take power. Don't do anything to offend the Soviet consul, Andrayshev by name. He'll make a protocol call on you, which you don't have to return. Don't bug him and he won't bug you." Chance allowed himself a slight chuckle at the double entendre which escaped Monkton completely.

So it went for the balance of the afternoon, until at six o'clock the timer rang and Monkton relievedly closed his notepad.

Chance stood up. "I think you should study your notes over the weekend. The committee hearing is only a few days away."

"I know, I know." He inserted his pad in a gold-trimmed brown calfskin briefcase. "You're such a bright guy, how'd you like to go in my place?"

"I'd hate it," Chance said candidly, and showed him to the door.

Alone, Chance went to the bathroom and removed the thin, purposely distorted dental plates from his even teeth, peeled away the brown mustache, and took off the horn-rimmed nonrefractive

13

lenses. Then he shaved, took a shower, and changed into clean clothing from the bedroom closet.

The suite was rented by the Department of State on a monthly basis; its only visitors were Chance and his students. Chance seldom stayed overnight because he had a comfortable pied-à-terre in Georgetown off Wisconsin Avenue that contained a PC word processor, a selection of professional books on loan from Charlottesville, and a cache of unclassified Post Reports supplied by the Foreign Service Institute.

Before leaving, Chance opened his attaché case and placed in it his items of physical disguise, and the billfold whose contents documented him as Herbert F. Aylward, an assistant librarian at the Johns Hopkins University in Baltimore. From the attaché case he recovered his own wallet and placed it inside the pocket of his jacket. His true identity back in place, Chance locked the door behind him. As he rode down the elevator he adjusted his mind to real life and his schedule for the next few hours.

First, a workout and swim at the University Club on Sixteenth Street. Dinner in Georgetown at Chez Nous, a small three-star restaurant on M Street that held a table for him every Saturday night at eight. By nine-thirty he would be settled comfortably in the library of his one-bedroom apartment, immersed in a survey of Philippine regionalisms. By midnight he would have entered the distillate in his PC and would be ready for sleep.

He would rise at six-thirty and begin preparing Monday morning's lecture on the transition from Romanticism, as exemplified by the Schlegels, into the Realism of Börne, Heine, and Freytag. Wednesday and Friday mornings he would cover the Naturalism of Holz, Sudermann, and Hauptmann, ending that week's teaching. Friday afternoon would find him back at the hotel suite indoctrinating his next student, a chief of station candidate for Algiers.

At a lobby pay phone Chance dialed an unlisted District telephone, said, "Herbert F. Aylward," and listened.

"Thank you for calling to confirm, sir. The pupil will meet you next Friday at thirteen hundred hours. His instructional name is Ben Adem."

"May his tribe increase," Chance intoned and disconnected.

As he stood waiting for the doorman to attract a taxi Chance summed up the results of sixteen months' work in the polishing program. Nine ambassadors confirmed by the Senate and none recalled. Twelve chiefs of station dispatched and none expelled from their duty countries.

Each month Chance mailed time sheets to a post office box in Petersburg, Virginia, and within three working days a cashier's check for the precise amount was credited to his wife's account at the University of Virginia Hospital. The funds paid for a private room and a licensed therapist who saw to all of Carla's needs. Tomorrow afternoon he'd visit and confer with the doctor and therapist. Not that there was much hope of restoring the vitality of her mind and body, but as the young physician said, "There are those who would be alive today had we known then what we have learned in the interim."

After that he would stroll the campus with its graceful buildings and serpentine wall, perhaps stop by his old undergraduate society, the Jeffersonian, and chat with some of its young members. All to clear his mind of remembered tragedies so that he could get on with his own life and make it useful to others.

When a taxi pulled over, Chance tipped the doorman and got in. He rode wordlessly through rush-hour traffic until the taxi steered into the club drive where he got out and paid the driver.

Before going in, Chance glanced at the adjacent building, tall, gray, and topped with radio and microwave antennae. It was the embassy of the Union of Soviet Socialist Republics. Within it, unknown to Chance, a secret meeting was taking place that would soon and forever change his life.

TWO

Had the Soviet officials who were meeting privately known that Chance was exercising on a Nautilus machine a scant fifty yards away, they would have been jolted out of their usual taciturnity. Instead, the three high-ranking intelligence officers, dressed in civilian clothing, sat at a small table in the embassy's soundproofed "secret room." Constructed in the geometric center of the chancery building, the chamber was windowless, padded, ventilated by a noisy air conditioner, and swept frequently for probe mikes and related electronic devices. Each officer had been supplied with a glass of heavily sugared Russian tea.

Major General Nikolai Petrovich Berlikov was the KGB "legal" *rezident* in Washington. His GRU* (military) counterpart was Major General Pyotr Andreyvich Chavadze, and the senior officer present was Lieutenant General Yevgeni Lubovich Sobatkin, who had arrived that morning from Ottawa where he exercised overall direction *(operupolnomochenniy)* of Soviet operations against the North American target.

Sobatkin was a thin-faced man of spare build. The top of his head was bare, the side hair closely trimmed. His skin was mottled by liver spots and white patches where actinic keratoses had been removed. Sobatkin's most distinctive feature was his nose; its downward curve, like a raptor's beak, enabled him, it was said, to thrust into everyone's affairs and tear flesh.

---

*Glavnoye Razvedyvatelnoye Upravleniye.

Stacked on the table were the dossiers of a dozen Americans, nine from embassy files, three brought in by Sobatkin traveling under diplomatic immunity. One of the twelve files was captioned: CHANCE, Quentin Ransome, Jr.

General Sobatkin was neither KGB nor GRU. He was the North American representative of the Tsentralnoye Byuro Politicheskoy Informatsii—the Central Bureau for Political Information—which had been created by and reported directly to the Central Committee of the Communist party of the Soviet Union. The Byuro executed special high policy tasks for the Central Committee, tasks that were never known outside Kremlin walls, and to only a select few Soviet officials within. So the unexpected arrival of General Sobatkin distressed the two major generals, who viewed him apprehensively.

Ignoring the stacked dossiers, General Sobatkin gazed penetratingly at the Washington-based officers. "Pyotr Andreyvich, Nikolai Petrovich, some years have passed since you spent time in the Motherland. Correct?"

Chavadze said, "Two years for me, Yevgeni Lubovich."

"And for me, nearly three years," said Berlikov, adding wistfully, "I miss our homeland more than I thought possible."

Sobatkin grunted. "Be that as it may, you are nevertheless aware that vast changes are taking place, monumental changes in the structure of our government, our Party, its political orientation, possibly even our ultimate goals as a great power."

"Well," said Chavadze with assumed diffidence, "I listen to Radio Moscow and read all newspapers that arrive by diplomatic pouch, so I am generally aware that certain reorientations are being debated."

"I, also," said Berlikov. "What particularly did you have in mind, Yevgeni Lubovich?"

Sobatkin looked at them with suppressed contempt. "Have you lost the ability to read between the lines of *Izvestiya, Trud,* and *Pravda?* Have you forgotten that only thus is authentic information conveyed to the masses? Were everything to be stated directly in black and white, our enemies would know as much as our loyal Soviet citizens." He lifted a pocket flap and took out a package of Chesterfields. Lighting one, he blew out the match and dropped it on

17

the flooring. It was a thick sheet of Plexiglas, transparent to eliminate the possibility that any electronic devices might be concealed in the base concrete. "Is it possible?" he asked rhetorically, "that both of you are suffering from senses dulled by constant swilling in this American *kormush?* Are you so preoccupied with your wives' luxurious purchases that you have forgotten to pay keen attention to the progression of events in the Socialist Homeland?"

GRU chief *rezident* Chavadze said, "In my case, Yevgeni Lubovich, that suggestion lacks even the threads of reality." Nevertheless, it worried him that Sobatkin had referred to the normal custom of buying abroad for sale at home. It was *amoralka*—illegal, of course—but everyone involved considered such black-marketing one of the perks of foreign service.

Berlikov said, "As always, Yevgeni Lubovich, because of your superior position and intimate ties with high Party officials, you are much better informed than those of us who serve the Motherland so far from home."

"Precisely," said Chavadze, inferring that Sobatkin had come to brief them in anticipation of some important government change that could be crucial to their welfare and careers. "Is it that you refer to the radical changes accompanying *glasnost* and its handmaiden *perestroika?*"

"Even beyond that," said Sobatkin puffing smoke at the air conditioner's exhaust screen. "There is a general loosening of controls in our society. As you will have observed, previously proscribed Jewish authors are now permitted to publish their foul anti-Party scribblings. Iosif Vissarionovich* is being derogated far beyond the denunciations of Khrushchev. Critics say in public that Koba, far from being the military genius whose decisions won the Great Patriotic War, was a cowardly madman. These dregs of socialist society boldly call him the Cannibal."

Spiritedly, Chavadze said, "What rubbish!"

"More," Sobatkin continued. "In certain quarters the inspired writings, policies, and directive genius of Vladimir Ilyich* are being brought into debate and contention."

---

*Iosif Vissarionovich Dzhugashvili—"Stalin." Aka "Koba."
*Vladimir Ilyich Ulyanov—"Lenin."

"Impossible!" Berlikov exclaimed. "What you describe is nothing less than a revisionist nightmare!"

"Nevertheless," said Sobatkin, "things are not at all what they used to be. For example, our press boldly mentions the name of that Jewish wrecker, Trotsky, almost as though he had been a Hero of the Soviet Union whose passing is to be lamented. Moreover, the cult of personality, so long deprecated, is being revived and restored in the person of our premier, Mikhail Sergeyevich."

Berlikov, for personal reasons, thought it best to say nothing. Chavadze shook his head in seeming despair. Sobatkin went on, "When I was in Moscow recently, I smelled the stench of right-wing deviationism—it was enough to make a soldier vomit in the street." He drew in a deep breath and straightened his back as though to ward off nausea.

Berlikov asked, "Do you perceive a fundamental reason for all this . . . reorientation?"

"Let me put it this way," Sobatkin replied soberly. "The premier is a man of personal charm—in public. That he has applied this charm abroad—successfully—is beyond dispute. I have only to cite the fact that our NATO enemies have, in effect, surrendered their arms to him. De-coupled from America. Moreover, America, our once principal adversary—*glavni vrag*—has agreed to reduce its nuclear stockpile and to withdraw its most menacing missiles from Western Europe." He shrugged. "No one is complaining about *that* inside the Kremlin."

"Then what—?" Chavadze began, but Sobatkin's wave silenced him, and the visitor continued, "Within the Council of Ministers, though not yet within the Secret Defense Council, there is sentiment, even plans, to alter the direction of the Soviet economy. Beefsteaks in place of missiles, stylish dresses in place of uniforms, refrigerators and all manner of consumer appliances to take the place of tanks and machine guns. In short, abandonment of the Communist vision before it's realized worldwide." He stopped to let the effect sink in.

For a while his listeners said nothing; both realized that Sobatkin's words could be interpreted as treasonable. Berlikov decided to alter the subject slightly. "Yevgeni Lubovich, you used the

19

phrase 'our once principal enemy.' Does that mean the United States is no longer *glavni vrag?*"

"The imperialist attempt to encircle the Soviet Motherland has fallen apart—one has only to examine a map of Europe. The United States lives its bourgeois consumer dream and will neither come to the aid of an ally nor defend its own interests. That direction is one that certain ministers see as the collapse of the Soviet Union. *If* it is pursued." He drew on his cigarette and exhaled slowly. "Other ministers apparently welcome the relaxation of state controls, privatization of industry as in Great Britain, giving our citizens a bourgeois life-style never contemplated by Marx, Lenin, or Stalin. They argue that the impotence of the United States allows such a reorientation—and indeed it might, were the United States the *only* enemy to be taken into account."

"Ah," said the KGB *rezident,* "you refer then to the unreconciled enemy. China."

Sobatkin grimaced approvingly. "China indeed. A country whose population soars geometrically. A country bordering ours, whose crimes of left-wing deviationism have yet to be adequately punished. A country that has achieved sufficient rapport with the West to bring itself out of the nineteenth century by technological means—and in so short a time as to be almost unbelievable. What its armed forces may lack in advanced weapons—and they may lack little—can be more than compensated by their sheer size. China," he said dramatically, "has become our number one enemy. China must still be reckoned with."

Chavadze swallowed. "Are we to consider ourselves in a potential state of war with China?"

"Worse," said Sobatkin. "A potential state of *peace.*"

Berlikov studied his hands, his fingers interlaced. The subject had become unbearably delicate. His stomach had shrunk and his throat was dry as sand.

Finding that his declaration evoked no response from his listeners, Sobatkin said, "As one who fought shoulder to shoulder with Brezhnev during the Great Patriotic War, I am not willing to stand idly by while misguided rulers cede world domination to the yellow hordes." His gaze fixed on Berlikov, then Chavadze. "Are not the interests of the Motherland supremely dear to you? Do you not accept the historical mission of the Soviet Motherland?"

"Yes," said Chavadze.

"Unquestioningly," said Berlikov, who knew that Brezhnev had been a political commissar in the Great Patriotic War, and that Sobatkin had been another, though younger and much lower ranking than the late premier, whose once-heralded wartime deeds were already being dissected and downgraded. And he wondered how Sobatkin would dare boast of comradeship with Brezhnev unless . . . unless Sobatkin enjoyed support within the Kremlin that transcended his association with the denigrated Brezhnev. Yes, that was possible. More than possible. So Sobatkin had come on a mission directed by the Council of Ministers or by the Secret Defense Council itself, despite its incompatibility with the policy of Premier Gorbachev.

What treacherous ground, he thought. Why the devil did this old sycophant have to come? Berlikov himself had been a partisan operating behind German lines when he was only thirteen, and he felt contempt for the wartime political commissars. They were propagandists and executioners, meddlers who interfered disastrously with command decisions. Yet this Sobatkin, who had probably killed Russian soldiers instead of armed Nazis, had risen to high position and exercised undeniable authority.

The question, Berlikov reflected, was the source of Sobatkin's authority. If he could find out, he could appraise the validity of Sobatkin's mission. Berlikov's thoughts were interrupted by Chavadze, who said, "Comrade General, although I would never be so impudent or disloyal as to question the information you convey, how is it that neither Nikolai Petrovich nor I was informed of your coming? Nor briefed to act according to your instructions?"

To Berlikov's surprise Sobatkin did not take offense. "A proper question, Pyotr Andreyvich, and the answer will be found in what I am going to confide to you.

"The policy changes—actual and proposed—that I have summarized have both their advocates and their opponents within the Council of Ministers. For convenience's sake let us refer to those ministers who prefer our customary way of doing things as the Conservative group—traditionalists who hold unwaveringly to the teachings of Marx and Lenin." He ground out his cigarette and lighted another. "For the present, the Conservatives are in the majority. Their outnumbered opponents—so-called Liberals—are advocates of new freewheeling policies, which would bring only ruin to our Motherland. One of the Liberal goals is to bring about an understanding with our principal enemy, China, a rapprochement that would turn Soviet interests inward while allowing China to expand outward."

"And who are these Liberals?" Berlikov asked. "Is it possible to mention names?" Already his mind was running down a short list of likelies, but he wanted Sobatkin's confirmation for the record.

"Why not?" Sobatkin replied, "inasmuch as we are three soldiers dedicated to the preservation of our Motherland. Minister of Culture, Ruminov, as you might surmise, is one. Kirilenko, education, another. Minister of Technology Fedotov is also on the side of rapprochement." He blew smoke at the air conditioner's exhaust. "Who would be the fourth?"

Berlikov looked at Chavadze and shrugged. Hesitantly the GRU rezident said, "Possibly the minister of Economic Planning, Kalinikov?"

With an indulgent smile Sobatkin said, "Wide of the mark, so I will surprise you with the name of our agriculture minister."

"Grachev!" Berlikov exclaimed.

"Yes, Grachev. He would dismember collective farms and give land to the peasants. Imagine, private ownership of lands that belong to all. Land stripped from the czarists, the discredited nobles, the defeated Whites." He shook his head. "Well, there you have it, comrades. Factionalism when there is room only for unanimity of the collective will." His hooded eyes lifted. "Worse, comrades, far worse. We have learned that at least one of these Liberals has been seeking direct contact with the Chinese leadership. Confidential intermediaries have been dispatched to Chinese embassies abroad—Paris, Rome, London—but in each case they have been . . . intercepted before overtures could be made."

"Who——?" Berlikov began but broke off at a wave of Sobatkin's hand.

"Who they were is unimportant. What *is* important and concerns both of you as a matter of the highest priority is that a fourth attempt to contact the Chinese is under way." From an inside pocket he drew out a color photograph and held it under the light. "You recognize this face?"

Chavadze and Berlikov peered and shook their heads.

Sobatkin laid the photograph on the table. "The fourth emissary," he said. "Pavel Vasilyevich Sosnowski." His gaze turned accusingly on Berlikov. "Major, KGB."

Berlikov gasped. "Incredible!"

"Nevertheless," Sobatkin pressed, "entirely true. This villain must be prevented from reaching the Chinese embassy in Washington. And Sosnowski must be liquidated in such a way that our hand is undetectable. Blame for his assassination must fall elsewhere—and where better, comrades, than on the limping, gut-shot CIA?"

A fabulous concept, Berlikov thought. But how to bring it off?

Sobatkin said, "Now let us consider these dossiers. What have all these CIA agents—or former agents—in common? No response? Then I will save time by telling you that each of the twelve, at one time or another, has had some manner of contact with Sosnowski in a foreign country. Each has a record of prior contact, enmity, animosity." He dropped ash on the clear flooring. "Both of you are schooled in these matters, skilled even. You know what has to be done, and I leave the details to you." He riffled the file edges with a thumbnail.

Chavadze stared at the stack of dossiers. "Is it important that the American survive? Be tried? Perhaps in court he could establish his innocence."

Sobatkin leaned forward and glared at the questioner. "It is up to you to thoroughly incriminate whomever you select. It is as important to your futures as the interception of Sosnowski."

Surround the Chinese embassy? Berlikov thought. Impossible. Sobatkin acts as if we were operating in Moscow.

Sobatkin drew a typed card from his inner pocket. "Through his Liberal principal Sosnowski was issued travel orders from Moscow to Helsinki, Stockholm, Paris, then Washington. His passport is in his true name. As you see by his schedule, he arrives here next week via Air France."

"Should he be interrogated before . . . ?" asked Berlikov.

"By all means," Sobatkin replied brusquely. "I suspect one minister of being Major Sosnowski's principal, but I and Marshal Yaroshenko will welcome Sosnowski's confirmation of the fact. By his voice, or in his own handwriting." He looked at his wristwatch. "I have a little time, comrades, so I will remain while you select from these dossiers the name of the American agent."

THREE

The maître d'hôtel led Chance to his customary table. "Your usual vodka martini, sir?"

"Please." Chance took the leather-bound menu, glanced at the handwritten pages, and closed it. Small salad, he decided, double lamb chops, medium, *pommes de terre rissolée,* and *petits pois.*

The small room was two-thirds filled with early diners. Second seating at ten. His tablecloth and napkin were spotlessly white, the silver polished to perfection. A single red rose in a thin crystal flute adorned the setting. Presently his martini arrived, so chill and crisp it set his teeth on edge. Chance savored it lingeringly and was about to order dinner from the waiter hovering nearby when he saw Rony come in.

Veronica Talbot was a tall, slim woman with high cheekbones, pale complexion, a small straight nose, determined mouth, and dark hair. She was wearing a perfectly fitted black sheath with a wide white belt that matched her gloves. As she drew them off she looked around the room and caught sight of Chance. Breaking into a smile, she waved and headed toward him.

As Chance rose he recalled their first meeting during their counterespionage training. Rony had been an intense young Radcliffe graduate, eager for her first assignment in the field. They became friends, then lovers, until Rony left for Rome. There she had met and married the then counselor of embassy, a divorced, older career officer named Pennington Boyce III, who had soon gained ambassadorial rank. The sight of her made Chance's pulse quicken as memories kaleidoscoped through his brain. She looked, he thought, as desirable as ever; no, more so. Perhaps—

"Quinn!" she exclaimed, giving him her hand. "How marvelous to see you! Penn's to join me after an endless meeting at State, but I've time for a drink. You?"

"By all means." He drew back her chair and signaled the waiter. Kir was her choice. "Lord, how long has it been?" she asked. "Two years? Three?"

"Two years ago, July," he said. "You and the ambassador were back home on leave. We met at a dinner party, at the Indonesian embassy."

"Of course—still infallible, aren't you?" She smiled fondly. "How've you been keeping?"

"Reasonably well."

"Did you actually go to grad school?"

He nodded. "Oldest in the program."

Her face sobered. "And Carla—I don't suppose. . . ."

"She's—what can I say? Doing as well as can be expected."

Her hand covered his sympathetically. "I'm *so* sorry, Quinn."

"So am I. Well, Rony, still enjoying high-level diplomatic life? Do you miss the Agency?"

She shrugged, took her kir from the waiter, and sipped. "Pluses and minuses," she admitted, "like everything, I suppose. Penn and I separated for several months—we may do so again." She put down the glass. "If so, it'll be permanent."

"Should I say I'm sorry to hear it?"

"Don't. Penn's—well, stuffy, Quinn. Not at all as I remember you." She smiled. "We had some fabulous romps, didn't we?"

"Terrific," he agreed, pleased that she remembered. "Are you here for long?"

"So far, two weeks. Penn's considering whether to take an assistant secretaryship. So he's very tense right now, because nothing else has been suggested." She paused. "The alternative is early retirement, which he doesn't want."

"And you?"

"If he got UN Affairs, it would mean a lot of time in New York and Geneva." She shrugged. "Speaking of Geneva, we were there last month and came across . . . guess who, Quinn."

"Charlie Chaplin? Judge Crater?"

"Seriously. Paul Valcour, of all people. Apparently he made it very big in the international financial community, has all sorts of Arab and Oriental clients. And when OPEC doubled the price of oil, they all became hugely, inordinately wealthy."

"What's his business?"

"Investment banking—I thought you would know. After all, he *was* your regional controller before he left the Agency. I had the idea he was sort of your rabbi, as they say."

"I respected his brains and ability," Chance acknowledged, "but he was considerably my senior."

"Even so, Paul asked about you."

"Oh? And what did you tell him?"

"That you'd departed the Agency for academia." She eyed him. "Shouldn't I have?"

He shrugged. "There was this African project called Brigand. Paul set it up and held it very close to his chest. It involved subsidizing an East African resistance movement and its leader, Nzdwali. Paul took over the first payment personally—two million in gold bars. Nzdwali's plane exploded over Dar, and that was the end of Brigand." He sipped his drink.

Rony glanced over her shoulder at the entrance and turned back to Quinn. "So?"

"During the last two years of my decline at the Agency, I was given a variety of odd jobs no one else wanted. One was a final wrap-up of Brigand. Information had come in that two of Nzdwali's aides had searched the plane wreckage and found no gold bars. They suggested their leader's suitcase had contained a bomb instead. When the comptroller and I asked Paul to take a polygraph he became bitterly resentful, wrote out his resignation, and disappeared."

"Fascinating," said Rony. "So maybe Paul used Nzdwali's gold to set himself up in business? No wonder you have reservations about him. And I suppose he's angry at you?"

"Why should he bother? There was no evidence, and Paul got away with it."

"Just one of those things," she mused. "And planes are exploding over Africa all the time."

Chance finished his drink and decided against a second. "Paul

27

was an inspiring leader," he acknowledged, "and I learned a lot about the intelligence business from him."

She laughed lightly. "Including how to become an instant millionaire."

"But nothing about murder."

Rony sipped her kir. "I don't suppose the rumor's generally known."

"Couldn't say."

"Any reason I shouldn't pass the word around?"

"Why not? It's the truth."

She smiled. "The truth, Quinn, is what you always sought. That trait made people uncomfortable, you know. Telling the truth inside the Beltway is limited to the impregnables, the Big Rich."

"How rich is that?"

"Harriman rich. Your father left you, what—Medium Rich?"

"Comfortably fixed," he said.

"Which isn't enough to tilt at windmills with impunity," she chided. "If you hadn't left the Agency, you'd have been let go in the big purge. The admiral's gang would have seen to that pronto."

"I suppose." Quinn shrugged. "Anyway, there were more important things on my mind at the time."

She nodded. "I often think of your brother. Did they ever find out?"

"No," he said sharply. "Hard to put a name to a masked terrorist, I guess they never will. Roger's widow, Judy, remarried in less than a year. Her husband adopted my nephew, Sean, and I never hear from any of them. It's as though that part of my family never existed." Quinn's tone had turned bitter. After Carla's three miscarriages, they were preparing to consult Hahnemann, until he noticed her forgetfulness, her unsteady gait, her open-eyed gaze into some world of her own, one that excluded him. . . .

"Here comes Penn," Rony said, and Chance turned to see Ambassador Boyce bearing down on them, flushed and unsmiling. Stopping beside her chair, he stared down at his wife. "What are you doing here, with *him?*"

Before Rony could say anything, Chance said, "Penn, she was just telling me how happy she is with you."

"Really?" the ambassador sneered. "I know all about you and my wife."

"Then you know very little," Chance said mildly, "because there's not much to know."

"Stay away from her," said the diplomat in a strained voice, "I'm warning you." His hand thrust downward and seized his wife's wrist. "Let's go," he said, and pulled. Rony's white face turned up at her husband's, and Chance saw her fingers curl into claws. The nails dug into the underside of his wrist. Boyce gasped in pain and dropped her arm, stared disbelievingly at welling blood. Rony rose, smiled tautly, and said, "Mind your manners, Penn. Let's reserve these scenes for our little love nest. Thanks for the drink, Quinn." She strode past her husband and after a moment the ambassador followed her to the doorway. A few heads turned, and Chance saw Boyce wrapping a handkerchief around his wrist.

Grist for the gossip mills, he thought. Boyce must not have landed that UN post. Well, Rony could take care of herself, married or not. For the ambassador and his lady there would be no candlelit dining à deux tonight.

Chance nodded at the maître and ordered a Châteauneuf du Pape from the sommelier's extensive list.

During dinner Chance put the Boyces out of his mind and thought about Paul Mazarin Valcour: tall, suave, impeccably tailored. Never married, of course, but his much younger sister Antoinette's marriage to an Arab princeling had generated international publicity. Toni was probably much wealthier than her brother, with royal jets at her disposal and sumptuous residences in half a dozen capitals and resorts. Why not? It was the sort of life Paul would have planned for her.

Chance ordered strawberries in kirsch and began thinking about the considerable amount of reading that awaited him.

While Chavadze and Berlikov reexamined the twelve dossiers in the secret room, Sobatkin pushed back from the table to stretch his legs. Smoking in silence, he watched them with half-closed eyes and wondered if the two officers would prove adequate to the assignment. Far from being authorized by the Council's Conservative faction, the entire mission had been conceived by Defense

Minister Yaroshenko. According to the marshal, not even Shevard-nadze, the foreign minister, had been informed. Much less the technocrats Rhyzov, Kalinikov, and Carnovsky, ministers respectively of transportation, economic planning, and trade and industry. So, the marshal's initiative had to be developed with meticulous care. Any foul-ups or premature revelation would finish Yaroshenko—and himself.

Sobatkin was well aware that he had to carry out the marshal's orders—if possible without implicating himself inextricably—and also, like any intelligent soldier, prepare a means of retreat. In the event of failure, Berlikov and Chavadze would take the fall, unable to verify that he had ever spoken to them about the China problem. They would end their lives in the same kind of strict-regime labor camp where he'd been a *zek* for two years until amnestied by Brezhnev, a rehabilitation ratified by Premier Andropov, who had been an especially vicious chairman of the KGB.

To the current premier, Sobatkin had no ties at all, and he was mindful that Gorbachev could be replaced overnight. So long as he, Sobatkin, enjoyed Yaroshenko's trust and confidence, his position was reasonably secure. And the marshal had a strong grip on the armed forces, so he was the one to follow. The only one. Still, Sobatkin mused, he had to extract some permanent benefit out of this scheme of Yaroshenko's.

Inevitably, the relationship between the U.S.S.R. and refractory China was going to change; whether sooner or later would depend upon the success of Yaroshenko's intrigue. Eventually, accommodation and stability would ensue, enabling China to satisfy its thousand-year dream of seizing Japan, an ambition that required Russia's assent.

Within the Chinese Politburo, Yaroshenko had mentioned an ideological and philosophical division that echoed that within the Kremlin. Sobatkin remembered the old post-Yenan lineup: Mao, Chou, Teng Hsiao-p'ing, Chu Teh ... but they were all gone now, and he had no acquaintance with today's Chinese leadership beyond their names. They had done well, he considered, in restoring China after the long years when Mao had liquidated so many leaders, like Stalin's purges.

Sobatkin reflected on the possibility of establishing personal links to some element in the Chinese Politburo that could find him useful in the future, perhaps as a go-between. That path was perilous indeed, Sobatkin reminded himself, but not impassable. First he would have to choose the target, then the least dangerous approach. Finished, Major Generals Berlikov and Chavadze looked up expectantly.

Rousing himself, Sobatkin said, "Well?"

"Comrade General," Chavadze proposed, "from these dozen dossiers two candidates emerge as the most plausible."

"And who are they?"

"One is Marvin Charles Bruder, now under instruction at the Naval War College in Newport, Rhode Island. Bruder met Sosnowski as though by chance in Ankara, where he suggested that Sosnowski defect. Sosnowski correctly reported the approach to his rezident, who then arranged with Turkish officials to have Bruder declared persona non grata and expelled. Grounds for resentment, certainly, even revenge."

"Not bad," Sobatkin mused. "But you say Bruder is in Rhode Island. What would he be doing in Washington?"

"Every three or four weeks Bruder drives down to visit his family in Oxon Hill, Maryland, not far from here."

"And the other agent?"

Berlikov said, "Quentin Ransome Chance, Jr. Ostensibly resigned from the CIA not quite three years ago but is believed to have at least a contract relationship. In that capacity he briefs chiefs of station and ambassadorial candidates on the customs and political circumstances of their assigned countries. Reports from Brussels, Buenos Aires, and Cairo evaluate Chance as an agent of high intelligence with a prodigious memory."

"Where did he and Sosnowski connect?"

"In Cairo, Comrade General. Chance and his new wife were attending a Foreign Ministry reception. Sosnowski, fired with liquor, made suggestive remarks and pawed Mrs. Chance. When Sosnowski refused to apologize, Chance dragged him into the garden and beat him senseless."

"I like that," said Sobatkin. "Both men would remember the episode, as would everyone attending the reception." He fingered his narrow chin. "Chance is in Washington?"

"From time to time. Mainly he is a doctoral candidate at the University of Virginia, in Asian affairs, with an apartment there and one in a fashionable part of Washington."

"These CIA people," Sobatkin said witheringly, "they sound like eternal students. A weakness, eh? Why was it arranged that Chance appear to leave the Agency? Preparing him for a deep-cover assignment abroad? A sleeper teaching at some foreign university?"

"That is, of course, a possibility," said Berlikov, "but his dossier indicates two personal tragedies that may well have inclined him toward a more contemplative existence. First was the death of his younger brother, Roger Herz Chance, a copilot for TransAfrica Airlines. During a refueling stop at Khartoum the aircraft was infiltrated by Arab guerrillas attempting a hijack. Roger Chance resisted and was shot dead."

"These 'Arab guerrillas'—supported by any of our organs?"

"Several had trained at the Black Sea camp, but the hijacking was their idea."

Sobatkin nodded. "This Quentin Chance might know or surmise who trained them and avenge his brother's death by killing a Soviet official. This gets better, Kolya. The second circumstance?"

"Carla fell ill of a deadly disease."

"And Sosnowski had insulted her in their days of former happiness. All adds up, does it not? What else is known about this Quentin Chance?"

"His familiar name is 'Quinn.' Now thirty-five, he was born in Philadelphia. He attended a Quaker school in that city, the Vienna *hochschule,* the lycée in Paris, and graduated from this country's Hotchkiss School before enrolling at the University of Virginia."

"Was his father a diplomat? Or agent?"

"It appears not—unless it was during army service in Austria, where father and mother met. The mother came from an aristocratic background . . ." He consulted the file more closely. "Erika Herz zu Waldober was her name. The father was a brilliant research chemist who worked for General Aniline until, privately, he developed a special ultrahard synthetic resin that is used in automobiles, aircraft, space vehicles—"

"Missiles?" Sobatkin interjected.

"Undoubtedly, as well as in various consumer products such as ovens and refrigerators. From that patent the chemist became quite wealthy, and the surviving son continues to benefit from royalty payments."

"Both parents, dead then?"

"The chemist was piloting his private aircraft from Florence to Geneva. During the cross-Alpine portion of the flight bad weather closed in, and the plane crashed into a mountain peak. Quentin Chance was fifteen at the time." Berlikov returned the newspaper clipping to the file.

His conspiratorial mind at work, Sobatkin said, "Was the plane perhaps sabotaged?"

"There was never that suggestion, Yevgeni Lubovich. No one gained from their deaths other than their two sons."

Sobatkin was silent for a while. When he finally spoke he said, "So this Chance has no relations who would press to clear his name?"

"None that we know of, Comrade General," said Chavadze, who had been quiet until now. "Chance has no children, no siblings, and his wife appears to be incompetent."

"Very well," Sobatkin said, "let us agree upon Quentin Chance as the murderer of Comrade Sosnowski." He stared at them both. "Agreed?"

"I agree," said Berlikov. Chavadze nodded.

"As to the arrangements, I leave them in your hands. I also leave you with two important considerations. One is that you will in no way communicate the subject of this meeting to anyone. Not to the ambassador or even your most trusted subordinates. You will not communicate with me or with your centers in any fashion on this subject. I will read about your success in the press; if you fail, I will know about that as well." He selected the three files from Ottawa and set them aside. "It would be better—much better—if Chance did not live to be put on trial. He is intelligent enough to realize that he was framed and would undoubtedly say so. Perhaps overcome by remorse at his crime, he turns a gun on himself, ending an unhappy life?"

Sobatkin rose and fitted the Ottawa dossiers under his arm.

"We'll meet again, perhaps in Moscow, where your reception will reflect your loyal service." He left the table and unlocked the flush-set padded door. Chavadze and Berlikov followed him into the dark, narrow corridor where they shook hands and parted company. Once Sobatkin was out of sight, Chavadze said, "Kolya, I'm not comfortable with this special assignment. I want to discuss it with you."

"Yes," Berlikov agreed, "but not now. Tomorrow, when we can be alone."

Berlikov climbed the staircase and entered his empty office. Aside from desk and chair there was a straight-backed chair facing the desk, no other furniture. His desk held English and Russian-English dictionaries and a photograph of his wife and children. The old wallpaper was worn and spotted; near the ceiling, parts of it curled downward revealing mildewed patches. The blinds were in place to prevent electronic eavesdropping by the FBI. He locked the door and hung his coat on a hook. Then he unbuttoned his shirt and removed the miniature wire recorder he had taped to his thorax earlier in the day.

He was to have recorded a report from a Norwegian diplomat over a discreet dinner. Then Sobatkin had called them into the secret room, where Berlikov had remembered and activated the device. Assuming it had functioned properly, he now possessed a record of everything that had been said inside the soundproof chamber. He opened the recorder and withdrew the small wire reel. He would cache it securely in his home and decide later how best it could serve his interest. He buttoned his shirt, adjusted his tie, and drew on his coat.

Using the tape against Sobatkin was not a priority, Berlikov mused; it was really a negative. He would prefer to exploit the recording in the interest of personal advancement and security among the *nomenklatura*—the ruling class.

Meanwhile, he must focus on the liquidation of two individuals: Pavel Vasilyevich Sosnowski and Quentin Ransome Chance. Nikolai Petrovich Berlikov did not intend to bloody his own hands in the matter, nor would it be necessary.

* * *

Chance signed the credit card slip and added a generous tip for his waiter. The maître escorted Chance to the door where Chance thanked him and unobtrusively passed a ten-dollar bill. "Until next week."

Outside he strolled north on Wisconsin Avenue, past boutiques, trendy shops and specialty stores, ethnic restaurants and saloons that catered to Georgetown University students. At Volta Place he turned west toward the two-story apartment building. He unlocked the front door and climbed the stairway to the second floor. His apartment, number four, was to the right. Number three was across the hall. Its long-term renter was Mrs. Evaline Crolius, an elderly Southern widow of a cavalry colonel who had spent much of his career in the Philippine Islands. Now vacationing in Barbados, Evaline Crolius had left her door key with Chance for the cleaning woman they shared.

Chance shot the security bolt behind him. In his kitchen Chance started the percolator and got out a thick pottery mug. Then he went into his small study and turned on the classical FM station. He recognized Tchaikovsky's Sixth Symphony, and as he located his sourcebook on Philippine regionalism he recalled that the composer had died of cholera only a few days after conducting the great Sixth in its premiere.

Coffee mug steaming on the stand beside his easy chair, Chance opened the book and began to read. His receptive mind synthesized and stored each bit of information as readily as a computer.

For later retrieval.

FOUR

Pavel Vasilyevich Sosnowski was enjoying his Paris layover. He had a large room in a two-star hotel on the Boul' Mich, in the fifth arrondissement, which embraced a considerable area of the Left Bank. Documented as a Hungarian student, Sosnowski found himself quickly at home in the university milieu. There was an abundance of good food, wine, vodka, and girls. Thérèse, a student at the Faculté des Sciences, slept, half-covered in his bed. As he shaved he watched her in the mirror, admiring her slim form and good legs, so unlike the bulky, starch-fed figures that typified his homeland. And Thérèse was intelligent as well as sexually innovative. Her appetite matched his own, and as she stirred, the sheet slipped away revealing her firm young breasts.

For more than a year Major Sosnowski had drifted in the backwaters of the KGB. Then an astonishing proposal had been made to him by a comrade so influential and highly placed that he could not possibly have declined. He expected to be appropriately rewarded, and now he'd decided to request Paris posting, perhaps as KGB *rezident*. If not then as cultural attaché. In either position he would be able to enjoy Thérèse or any of the hundreds of her kindred spirits, for he had no intention of bringing along his wife and three children, who spoke no French. Saying good-bye to Paris would be made easier by the prospect of return.

The mission seemed relatively simple: Contact a senior diplomat in the Chinese embassy in Washington and inform him that certain members of the Council of Ministers desired rapprochement and would meet Chinese emissaries secretly in whatever venue they desired. Further, Sosnowski was authorized to explain that the U.S.S.R., having achieved its goals in the West, sought enduring peace, friendship, and mutual accommodation with China so that both countries could turn from external concerns to internal development. Beyond that, he was instructed to say that additional matters would be addressed when the authorized representatives of China conferred with their Soviet counterparts.

What was so difficult about that? One obstacle was physical: eluding detection and reaching the embassy. The other was ideological: ingrained Chinese distrust of the Soviet Union. Suppose he was not believed, and the overture publicized as a Soviet provocation? That would finish him, of course. And he must remember not to let slip that the Eighth Chief Directorate had long ago broken Chinese diplomatic codes and was reading their most secret messages as easily as a page in *Pravda*. Sosnowski intended to insist that their communications with Peking be verbal or via special courier, for he also knew that the *rezident* in New Delhi had access to the Chinese diplomatic pouch, whose photographed contents were translated and disseminated in Moscow.

He counted on Chinese respect for conspiracy to keep their diplomats from phoning the Soviet embassy to authenticate Pavel Sosnowski, but it was a risk. He could only hope that the Chinese conducted their secret affairs in Washington as discreetly as did the Soviets. They should, because their revolutionary cadres had been trained in intelligence procedures by the legendary General Berzin in the years before the Great Patriotic War.

Sosnowski was glad that the secrecy of his mission precluded contact with his embassy in Washington. The ambassador would want to know why he was there, as would Generals Berlikov and Chavadze. Even were they incurious, which was unlikely, the inevitable meetings and dinners with the SK—the Soviet Colony—where he would be expected to pass along all the latest news and gossip from home, would leave no time for private pleasures. But by the time he left Paris he would have pleasured himself sufficiently to avoid temptation in Washington. Two days there, three at the most, then the polar flight to Tokyo, and onward to Moscow to file his report.

Sosnowski rinsed shaving cream from his face, enjoying the

dependable hot water, and dried with a fluffy towel. The West may be decadent, he reflected, but they know how to treat travelers.

Turning, he saw that Thérèse was awake, sprawled voluptuously and regarding him with expectant eyes. "Good morning, Lalo," she said. "What time is it?"

"About eight," he replied. "Hungry?"

"Not yet, lover." Sitting up, she handed him what remained of last night's vodka bottle, took the wine bottle from the nightstand, and drank deeply. Sosnowski drank, too, and wiped his lips appreciatively. Thérèse sat on the edge of the bed and tilted the wine bottle so that wine flowed over her breasts and brimmed the dark patch of her crotch. "My first class is at ten," she said silkily, "and I don't really want breakfast. What I want is you." She lay back receptively. "First, you must dry me."

Setting aside the vodka, Sosnowski knelt on the carpet and gazed at the damp plateau of pale flesh. "I have this unquenchable thirst," he said softly, and with mouth and tongue avidly set to work.

FIVE

It was a cool, breezy Sunday afternoon in Charlottesville. Chance drove down early while the roads were clear, keeping his Mercedes at sixty-five most of the way. Until noon he worked at home, had brunch at the Colonnade club, then drove slowly to the university hospital. Now, in the glassed-in pavilion, Chance sat beside his wife's wheelchair and looked at the shrunken hands resting quietly in her lap. Her eyes had shown no glint of recognition when the therapist wheeled her to him, and Carla seemed not even to notice when they were left alone.

He had kissed Carla's cheek, touched her hair. "Hello, darling, I'm Quinn, your husband."

She had not reacted, nor had he really expected her to. Yet, as always, his mind filled with rage against the disease. Why was someone so young, so beautiful, so life-filled . . . doomed to this repulsive fate? Why, why, *why?* He had an impulse to gather her small form in his arms and rush outside, hold her on his knees and beg the God of the universe to make her well, to restore her. Instead, he had turned his face and wept silently, oblivious of other patients and their visitors.

His gaze lifted to the green lawn and trees. A robin glided past the pavilion's glass. Life, he thought, how precious it is, and cursed the hours, the early days when duty had kept him from Carla. They had lived the illusion of the young, and when he recalled how thoughtless he had been, how carelessly they had passed their time together while both assumed—*assumed,* for God's sake—that nothing would ever change, it shattered him. His wife, in sickness and in health. . . .

Chance dried his cheeks and eyes, breathed deeply. At least Carla was beyond suffering—that was reserved for him, to deal with as best he could.

Her cheeks were waxy, yellowish. The lost flesh made her eyes pathetically large, but they were dull, all animation gone, even their color faded. The therapist had applied makeup once, but Chance had asked her not to do it again. It had looked as though cosmetics had been laid on by Carla's embalmer.

He took her hand and felt its small bones and sinews. Against his palm her flesh was cold. He drew it to his lips and pressed it there, eyes closed to help him recall her sparkling smile, the echo of her easy laughter. We were more than husband and wife, he thought, much more than lovers. We were friends. I never had a better friend than Carla, never wanted another. She was my world.

When he could bear it no more, he kissed Carla's cheek and whispered, "Good-bye, darling." Then he turned her chair so that she faced out over the lawn, the trees, the blue sky with its puffs of cotton wool, and walked away as he had come.

Seeing him, the therapist rose. "I'm so sorry, sir. Every day I keep hoping there'll be a change."

"So do I." He dried his eyes. "Is the doctor available?"

"He was called to another patient, but he asked me to tell you there are increased indications of systemic weakening, and—"

"What does that mean?"

She glanced away before answering. "The vital organs lose their ability to function—it's not always immediate."

Chance swallowed. "And then?"

"Artificial life-support . . ."

Slowly he shook his head. "Life . . . in human terms it's gone. Her heart beats, she breathes, but her brain, her mind . . ." He choked.

After a while the therapist said gently, "As next of kin you have the right to decide—if it comes to life support."

"I know," Chance said, grateful that soon after marrying they had jointly signed so-called living wills that expressed their resolve not to prolong their lives by artificial means. Carla had relieved him of at least that dreadful burden. "I'll contact her doctor," he said.

Outside, patients and visitors strolled along flower-bordered walks. On a bench sat a large elderly man in a gray topcoat, his bald head glistening under the sun. His eyes were closed behind thick spectacles, and his prominent nose gave him the appearance of a benevolent turtle. Chance walked over and sat down. Hearing the bench creak, Jan Abrams opened his eyes, blinked, and cried, "Quinn!"

They shook hands warmly. Abrams said, "I hoped I'd see you, Quinn. It's good to see a friend afterwards." Chance knew what he meant. Jan's wife had terminal cancer and Jan came down from Washington to be with Sarah as often as his duties with the national security adviser permitted.

When Chance joined the Agency Abrams had been a senior reports officer who periodically lectured trainees, and Chance had been deeply impressed by Abrams's intelligence, linguistic precision, and analytic abilities. A Dutch Jew, Abrams had been scooped up late in the war by the Nazis and transported to Dachau with his family and young fiancée. Only Jan was alive, but barely so, when the American Eighteenth Regimental Combat Team entered Dachau. Once, in the Agency's medical office during annual physical examinations, Chance had glimpsed the gray-blue numbers on Abrams's bare arm.

Against what must have been appalling handicaps Abrams had learned English and gone to work for Army Intelligence in Germany, then Washington, where he joined CIA when the Agency formed. After retirement Abrams became a special assistant to the national security adviser, who appreciated Jan's abilities and rock-hard refusal to tamper with the truth. Chance admired Jan as much as any man he had ever known. He had admired Paul Valcour, too, but there was a considerable difference between Jan Abrams and Paul Valcour. Jan was forthright, humble, and honest.

"Beautiful day," Abrams remarked. "A little while ago I saw a cardinal and two orioles. It's that kind of day, isn't it, when you're glad to be alive."

When Chance said nothing, Abrams put a hand on his arm. "Sorry, Quinn, I should have thought before I spoke. A failing of age, I'm afraid."

41

Chance managed a smile. By tacit understanding they never spoke of their dying wives.

"Things going well for you, Quinn?"

"I keep busy, Jan, and that helps a lot."

"I know. If I weren't working as hard as I've ever worked, I'd come apart. We have to keep our minds engaged, challenged."

"I have a year to finish," Chance said, "most of which will be taken up with writing my dissertation."

Abrams smiled. "I can't wait to call you Doctor Quentin Chance. And I've learned you're conducting tutorials for outbound officials. Must be quite a challenge, considering the prevalence of ignorance and stupidity."

"Means a lot of reading," Chance said, "then spewing it out."

"If you're ever short of students, let me know," Abrams offered. "I have a few candidates in mind; quite a few, in fact. Incidentally, since you're involved in Asian affairs, I suppose you know we're exchanging intelligence with the Chinese. We even have ELINT installations targeting the Russians."

"So I've heard."

"Limited basis, of course, where our interests coincide—as with the Soviets. But ten years ago who would have believed such a relationship possible? I see it as a great watershed, Quinn, dividing past from future. The Chinese exist, they're a nuclear power, and their population alone means we can't ignore them. I've been advocating getting into bed with them wherever possible."

"Despite Tiananmen Square?"

Abrams sighed. "That was yesterday, this is today. We have no enduring friends, Quinn, only enduring interests. And they have to be protected."

"If only those interests could be defined," Quinn said wryly. "And from what I can glean, our policy has a Soviet tilt. The Sovs, after all, have pretty well dismantled their empire, but the land mass of China hasn't essentially changed. Politically it's where the U.S.S.R. was, say in the thirties."

"Well, that's so, but they're emerging, Quinn, developing, though China's years from anything resembling *glasnost* and *perestroika.*" Abrams paused. "Can you conceive a scenario in which

Peking, encouraged by the U.S.S.R.'s new weakness, attacked the Soviet Union?"

"Only if some crazed element in their geriatric leadership decided it was the way to go."

"Hitler committed that error," Abrams mused, "despite the advice of his general staff, and the error was fatal. Perhaps the Chinese will remember that."

"Let's hope," Chance said. They left the bench and strolled the grounds until Abrams looked at his watch. "Afraid I have to start back now—early morning meeting to brief the president." From his wallet he took a card and wrote a telephone number on it. "Quinn, it doesn't look as though I'll be coming here many more times. So if there ever comes a dark night when you need someone to talk to, call me—I'll be there."

Taking the card with its blue-and-gold executive seal, Chance said, "Thanks, Jan—I'll remember."

Well before they reached the waiting limousine, a marine driver got out and opened the door. Stopping out of earshot, Abrams said, "We never know about life, do we? I thought perhaps I had suffered enough to be spared this too, but that's not how it happened. So I try to focus on the happiness I shared with Sarah." He glanced away. "It's hard, Quinn, terribly hard for me."

"I know," Chance said, "believe me, I know." He watched the White House limousine pull away down the long drive.

Chance looked at Abrams's unlisted home number, memorized it, and put the card in his billfold. Then he went to his car and drove to his apartment where he studied and wrote until dark.

His microwave oven was heating a frozen casserole of beef burgundy when Chance heard his telephone. He recognized Rony's voice, tightly controlled. "Quinn? Forgive me for interrupting, I need to hear the voice of a friend."

"Rony—you okay? Where are you?"

"I . . ." She paused so long that Chance said, "Rony you there?"

"Yes, I'm here—sorry . . . my nerves . . . It . . . it got to be too much, Quinn, too damn much. I've left my husband."

43

He considered possible responses and said, "If that's what you wanted to do, it was the thing to do."

Her laugh was thin and bitter. "It's what I *had* to do. Penn's frustration was destroying me, I couldn't keep feeding his ego. As you might have guessed, he didn't get that UN job, and he didn't even particularly want it, which infuriated him even more. That rejection and seeing me with you last night set him off, and he's been half crazy ever since. There . . . there's no future for us, Quinn. I can't cater to a big spoiled child the rest of my life and said I wasn't going to. Penn began hitting me and there was a very ugly scene, lamps broken. . . . You can imagine the rest."

"Unfortunately, I can," Quinn admitted, his tone worried. "Now, what can I do to help? Do you need a doctor?"

"No, but I've a bronze cheek and an eye that's turning very dark. Guess I was lucky, eh? I called my lawyer, but he's in Cancún at a bar meeting, won't be back till midweek. I want to stay clear of Penn till then. I'm calling from the Mayflower lobby—I was going to check in, then I realized I'd be seen coming and going—I do have to eat now and then. But my face—Quinn, you keep a place in the District, don't you?"

"Isn't that the first place Penn would look for you?"

"Where would he look? You're not in the phone directory." Her laugh was brittle. "Tradecraft precautions?"

"Maybe. At least it's saved me from computer solicitations." He thought for a moment. "I won't be there until Friday night, Rony, so until then the apartment is yours." He gave her the address. "I'll phone the building super, tell him to let you in. Name's McCrory. There's food, liquor, and no one will bother you."

"I'm terribly grateful, Quinn."

"You'd do the same for me. Besides, Penn might not have been so savage if he hadn't seen me with you." He paused. "You could stay indefinitely, except that if you're heading for divorce, it wouldn't look good to be sharing a place with a man."

"Right," she agreed. "Well, one step at a time. I'll get over to Volta Place. See you Friday, right?"

"Right. Washer and dryer are just outside the kitchen. I've got a couple of shirts in the hamper—toss them in when you wash, will you?"

"Gladly. But I'm no good with an iron."

"Who is?" he asked. She laughed and broke the connection.

The oven timer bell had sounded. Chance drew out his dinner to cool while he phoned the building superintendent. Mr. McCrory listened to Chance's description of Rony and returned to his TV program.

During dinner he sipped wine, ate slowly, and resolved not to let Rony's marital difficulties affect his own life. Letting her use the apartment was a small thing—when they were lovers he'd stayed frequently at her place—but they were both married now, and the equation had changed. They were old friends, nothing more, and that's the way he wanted it.

As he rinsed his plate and set it in the dishwasher it occurred to him that Rony might not want it either, at least not as long as there was the chance of a reconciliation. Even so, seeing her last night, hearing her voice just now brought back memories long set aside. The sloping curve of her breasts, the small mound of her belly, the dark fleece that led to the softness of her thighs; her voice, husky with passion, urging him to come with her; the surprising strength of her arms holding fast . . . It would be better if she were gone when he returned to Georgetown, Chance decided.

He went into the library, found the page where he had left off, and continued reading until his eyes watered and it was time for bed.

Defense Minister Yaroshenko strolled with a fellow cabinet minister in a small Kremlin courtyard whose paved walks intersected with geometrical precision. Most of the grass was still winter brown, but the flower borders had been cultivated to receive the warmth of an occasional sunny day. This was not such a day. It was gray with low-hanging charcoal clouds and there was light mist in the air from the nearby Moscow River. They had chosen this open place because they did not want their conversation overheard. With a tug at his gray mustache Yaroshenko began, "I have heard from Sobatkin. Full arrangements have been laid on in Washington. I thought you'd want to know."

"I appreciate it."

Marshal Yaroshenko reached down and plucked an early crocus and set it in his lapel. "In your opinion," he asked, "will your colleagues continue dispatching messengers after losing a fourth?"

The minister considered. "At this point I sense discouragement, but whether they will persist depends on many factors. I can, of course, suggest that they cease and desist."

"Then I suggest you do so." He stopped and faced his colleague. "Don't look so glum, Comrade Minister. Bear in mind that were it not for this intrigue of ours, we would be in danger of losing our jobs to those who have forgotten where the Motherland's true interests lie."

The minister nodded. "Your logic is indisputable," he conceded, "but what about security? Does Kryuchkov know of our design?"

Yaroshenko smiled condescendingly. "The chairman of the Committee for State Security is a mere apparatchik. If he knew, he would be the first to run yelling to the premier. No, be confident that Kryuchkov knows nothing."

"Yevgeni Sobatkin knows."

"He knows only the little confided to him, and he is a man who has never known great dreams," Yaroshenko said. "His aspirations, such as they are, would be to replace me. You, as the next premier, could prevent that, but I have already decided that Sobatkin's long career has come to a close."

"You mean—?"

"Ottawa is his final post." Yaroshenko plucked another flower, smelled its blooms, and tossed it away. "You understand?"

The minister nodded. "That is perhaps the best way to seal his lips." He licked his own and studied the marshal's impassive face. "My own life is in your hands. I often think of that."

"We have trusted each other," Yaroshenko said, "and we must continue to do so. Otherwise"—he shrugged—"we will have risked our lives for nothing. So think of it another way: Our lives depend upon each other's silence and cunning. I have demonstrated that I can be relied on to get things done. You must carry out your role within your faction."

"I've done all I could."

"And you will continue to report, will you not? Of course you will, Comrade."

The minister's feet shifted uneasily. "If Sosnowski is somehow not intercepted . . ."

"But he will be, and in a way that incriminates the CIA."

The minister brightened. "That would indeed be a masterstroke."

"You may depend upon it. When next you hear from me it will be to confirm the deaths of two enemies of the Motherland."

Arms linked, the two officials resumed walking the courtyard, turned in at the doorway, and went off to their separate offices.

As Marshal Yaroshenko strolled down the long, spacious corridor with its gleaming parquetry and immense red-draped windows, he reflected that there might be further use for Lieutenant General Sobatkin. And Sobatkin was a man who never questioned orders, however bloody they might be.

SIX

Major Generals Chavadze and Berlikov had driven separate cars to an evening rendezvous on the Virginia side of Great Falls. From the railed overlook they watched the falls spilling into the muddy Potomac River, where two boys were fishing for perch and catching small writhing eels. Free of electronic surveillance, the two *rezidents* smoked and exchanged small talk, finally broaching the subject of their meeting.

Chavadze said, "Kolya, to be frank, I'm queasy about this Sobatkin-inspired operation. If anything goes wrong, it's your neck and mine."

Exhaling, Berlikov watched breeze carry his smoke away and noticed a family arrive at a picnic table. FBI surveillants? he wondered and turned to Chavadze. "I don't like it myself," he admitted, "but orders are orders, are they not? Besides, I foresee no difficulty in intercepting Major Sosnowski at Dulles airport, which is our primary goal."

"Leaving the other part," Chavadze observed, "which is the more difficult. Laying blame on the CIA is excellent in theory, but I don't see it as essential, as Sobatkin does. Washington is a violent city, after all; Sosnowski could be mugged and killed. I'd leave it at that without going to all the trouble of framing this Quentin Chance. That's where things could go wrong."

"Does Chance go about armed?"

"No license was issued to him in Washington or Virginia. But even if he carries an illegal weapon, he won't be expecting trouble."

An eel had wound itself around the line of one of the boys. It flopped on the sand like an angry snake until the line was slashed. The boy kicked the eel back into the current. Once Chance was hooked, Berlikov thought, no one was going to free him.

"So," Chavadze said, "Sosnowski arrives—when? Tomorrow night?"

"On the Air France flight from Paris."

Chavadze flicked his cigarette into the current below. "Do you trust Sobatkin?"

"It's not a question of trust. Yevgeni Lubovich has rank, prestige, and influence. I can't afford such an enemy, and neither can you, Petya."

"Still, I've been tempted to use my back channel and ask Moscow Center if Sobatkin should be obeyed."

"But you haven't?" Berlikov asked apprehensively.

"No, I haven't gone that far. But I'm not accustomed to acting on verbal orders alone. We're responsible. To Sobatkin as well as our own centers if anything goes wrong. I don't like it at all, Kolya."

Berlikov thought of his wire recording safely cached in his home and hoped he wouldn't need it. Besides, why anticipate failure? "Let's think positively, Petya. We'll interrogate Sosnowski and learn who sent him to contact the Chinese. Sobatkin should be more than pleased with that information."

Chavadze lighted another cigarette. "Our ambassador called me in and asked what Sobatkin's trip was all about. I said it didn't concern him, and he should forget it."

"That's what I told the pompous old shit," Berlikov said spitefully. "Always trying to pretend he's boss. I'm sick of him."

Chavadze chuckled agreement. The picnicking family had a charcoal fire going and its flames lighted the narrow beach. Berlikov was reminded of picnics with his family beside the little lake at Makino beyond the Automobilnaya Doroga, the hundred-kilometer highway that circled Moscow. Those were happy days, he reflected. Taking Irina and the children on a picnic outside Washington would only raise eyebrows among watchers in the *Sovietskaya Kolonia*—the Soviet Colony—which regarded picnics as a collective outing. Everyone in the SK attended, or none. And he found himself envying Americans their freedom to come and go without interference or criticism. Well, those counterrevolutionary thoughts should be erased from the mind of a loyal servant of the state. And he was determined to be just that, for not without reason was the KGB termed the Sword and Shield of the Revolution.

He heard Chavadze saying, ". . . nosy bastard, the ambassador. Thinks cocktail parties are where his work is done, when you and I know where the *real* work is done, eh, Kolya? *Our* work."

"He's not one for *konspiratsiya*, that's certain," Berlikov replied. "Full of himself, he and that fat peasant wife of his, but they're all the same, those stuck-up diplomats of ours. I have no use for them."

"Snitches," Chavadze said, scornfully. "They do nothing to advance the cause of socialism, just snoop for scandal and send back reports on workers like you and me."

"Well, so far this one hasn't given me any trouble—knows I don't take *gavno* from anyone, whatever his rank. I made that clear the week he arrived."

They lapsed into silence, lost in their own thoughts, lulled by the hiss and rush of the water below the falls until Chavadze said, "So when do I see you again, and Sosnowski?"

"As soon as he's secured in the *yafka*—safe house—and ready for questioning."

"You need anything—drugs, implements—I'll bring them."

"I've got everything needed," Berlikov said, "so expect a call after midnight. I'll say something about meeting for breakfast at the Hilton—that'll confuse those FBI bastards. Only don't come direct, Petya. Make sure you're not followed."

"Naturally I'll take normal precautions," he said with a trace of irritation. They shook hands, and Chavadze left the overlook.

The sun was hidden behind the rim of trees bordering the river. In the near darkness, the water below was chocolate brown. Berlikov gazed at it, wondering whether he ought not to protect himself by getting a message to Moscow Center via secret writing—a conventional letter addressed to a "friend" in Kuncevo with his query about Sobatkin's orders laid invisibly between the lines.

But no, it was too late. Such a letter should have gone out right

50

after meeting with Sobatkin. By the time the message was developed and read by his controller, Major Sosnowski would be dead, and Quentin Chance along with him. Better say nothing and trust to his wire recording if it turned out that Sobatkin was acting on his own. Berlikov heard Chavadze's engine start and looked at his watch. Beltway traffic would have thinned by this time, and if he left now he could still have dinner with Irina and read a story to the children before they went to bed.

SEVEN

Under the vaulted ceiling of Dulles International Airport straggled lines of ticket-buyers, visitors, and others waiting for plane arrivals. Two among the waiting crowd sat apart from others, occasionally glancing at the flight arrival board and conversing softly in Arabic.

Born in Palestinian refugee camps, Yusuf and Hamid had been given weapons instruction at ten and infiltration training at eleven, and were then assigned to assault teams. Their fearlessness and savagery against the Zionist enemy brought them to the attention of Soviet advisers and the two young men were detached from their PLO units for specialized training by the KGB. Yusuf spent three years at the Semiferopol Academy in the Crimea, while Hamid was trained at a special camp near Varna, Bulgaria. As elite graduates of insurgency and terrorist schools, they came under the KGB's Thirteenth Department. With Jordanian passports they were dispatched as illegals to the eastern United States and covered as coffee merchants in downtown Washington.

Two or three times a year they executed special assignments whose details were brought them by a scruffy, shabbily dressed cutout. Their controller, the KGB official who originated their orders, was Major General Nikolai Petrovich Berlikov.

As they waited for Pavel Sosnowski's Air France flight, Yusuf and Hamid smoked thin, dark cigars and silently reviewed their preparations. Both men were short by American standards, and dark-skinned. Yusuf was scrawny, had irregular, nicotine-stained teeth, and a trimmed black beard. Stretching, he said, "Our business is going so well I'm thinking about a two- or three-week vacation this summer."

"Where?"

"Arizona. Anyplace without this cursed Washington humidity."

Hamid, the more heavyset man, stroked his mustache thoughtfully. "If you like it out there, maybe I'll go after you get back. I need a change anyway. Where I'd really like to go is Damascus or Cairo, be with our own people for a while. I came here hating this Jew-infested country and now I'm beginning to enjoy it. That means I've been here too long."

"Well, we were sent here for a purpose, to serve. Remember that."

"How can I forget it? But after four years I should be allowed to go back for a month or so."

Yusuf exhaled heavy smoke and shrugged. "Won't hurt to ask."

"You'll back me up?"

"After we deliver this defector. That's a good time to ask the chief."

"Whoever *he* is." Hamid dropped cigar ash on the floor, ground it under his sole.

"Look, the plane's landing." Yusuf pointed at the electronic announcement board. "In half an hour, forty minutes, he should be out of Customs and Immigration."

Hamid smiled wolfishly. "We'll have a drink at the bar and work our way down to the exit door."

Pavel Sosnowski had expected the Americans to examine his documents more thoroughly, but they passed him through the arrival area without comment. If he had been traveling on a Soviet passport, he told himself, then he'd probably have been taken off to an isolation room where he would have been secretly photographed while his passport was subjected to a battery of technical tests—after which he would have been rigorously interrogated concerning recent travel and the purpose of his visit. The officials had shown no interest in a Hungarian student properly visaed for language study at George Washington University.

Sosnowski allowed himself a thin smile as he blended in with fellow travelers, mostly foreigners, who were moving toward the exit door. It was so pitifully easy. So much for the first hurdle.

Waving off porters, Sosnowski carried his bag through the exit doorway. At the curb passengers were shoving baggage into taxis. In the Soviet Union he would have pushed to the head of the line and demanded immediate service—his KGB epaulets gained priority in such situations. But he was too well trained to draw attention to himself, and so he stood in line breathing the cool night air, glad that the end of his unorthodox mission was so near.

He was aware of clusters of oriental faces among the moving crowd. Chinese? he wondered. More probably Japanese commercial travelers. The airports of the world were jammed with Japanese businessmen and tourists, even Sheremeteyvo Airport was hard put to receive and process the slant-eyed hordes. But, he thought in satisfaction, one day they too would bow to the Kremlin and offer up their incredible manufacturing capacity to socialist direction and priorities. Without a credible army and nuclear warheads, Japan would be an easy conquest. And a neutral China gave Japan no ally to turn to.

It occurred to Sosnowski that he hadn't stopped at the foreign exchange office. But he had been supplied with enough dollars to get to his hotel in downtown Washington. Doubtless the room clerk could give him advice tomorrow.

He moved a few steps ahead and was setting down his bag again when a heavyset man appeared at his side, tapped his elbow, and said in Crimean-accented Russian, "No need for taxis, Comrade Major, give me your bag and come with me."

Startled, Sosnowski said, "But my orders—" He looked around apprehensively. "I—," he began.

With self-assurance the stranger interrupted. "There are additional orders for you. Just follow me." Taking the bag from Sosnowski's hand, the man strode along the walk and stepped out between two taxis to where a black Toyota was waiting. Uncertainly, Sosnowski followed, glanced at the mustached driver and got in. The stranger placed his bag in the front seat and slid in beside Sosnowski. As the car moved ahead, the major asked, "Why wasn't I contacted in Paris?"

The man shrugged. "Who can say? Like you, Comrade Major, I follow orders. In a little while everything will be explained to you. Don't worry. Our bosses will be glad I found you among so many."

The car was rounding a wide curve that led out of the airport area. Slowly, Sosnowski's apprehension was evaporating. After all, the man knew his rank, his arrival flight. . . . What was there to worry about? He sank back against the cushion. He hoped the mission hadn't been canceled; perhaps altered instructions would make it easier to carry out. But if the mission were to be canceled, then he could not look forward to the Paris posting. Thérèse, he thought, don't forget your Lalo while I'm gone. Sweet little slut, I'll come back to cover you with kisses if it's the last thing I do.

Vaguely, he was aware of the man shifting beside him—getting out cigarettes, probably. The car was leaving the airport area and joining the main highway, through the lush Virginia countryside. As the car turned up the entrance ramp, Sosnowski felt the man lurch heavily against him. He was about to rebuke the man's clumsiness when he felt a sharp pain in his thigh. His first reaction was to push the man away. Then he reached toward the door handle only to find his arm too heavy to stretch. From his thigh an icy chill was spreading and he knew then that he had been poisoned. He opened his mouth to cry for help but his constricted throat produced only a croaking bark. His head rolled to one side and his eyes stared blindly at darkness beyond the window.

EIGHT

In his Charlottesville apartment Chance was studying late. His eyes burned, and when he found himself rereading sentences he closed his eyes. Leaning back in his chair, he began thinking of his brother.

It was more than three years since Roger had been shot in the cockpit of his plane and no agency, U.S. or foreign government, had put a name to any of the murderers. That they still lived and were committing other outrages Chance had no doubt. But he doubted that any of them would be brought to justice for killing Roger Chance.

He remembered taking Roger on their first ibex hunt in the Atlas Mountains, the dusty, bumpy ride in the guide's Land Rover, Mannlicher .270s cradled in their arms, sun glinting from the barrels' bluing, the heavy scent of the oiled receivers, their dry mouths and throats, their lungs laboring as they climbed steeply from boulder to rocky crag until they could sight the herd three hundred yards beyond the deep gully, browsing along a narrow ledge. They had calculated range and windage carefully, adjusted their scopes, and selected the two largest males. Firing simultaneously, they dropped both goats, but Chance's had staggered up and he'd had to put a second copper-clad bullet into its dun body.

It had taken them an hour to reach the far ledge, another hour to sever the heads and skin out the capes. Chance remembered Roger's exultation when his trophy's horns outmeasured Chance's by four centimeters. Chance had been amused and pleased for his sixteen-year-old brother.

Then there had been a spring vacation at Bariloche, in the Argentine Andes, where they fished for cutthroat trout in snow-fed mountain streams, and twenty-kilo brown trout in the deep, icy lake. They stayed at a chalet whose proprietors were supposedly Swiss but whose unmistakable German accents led Chance to believe them to be fugitive Nazis.

Years later he had gone with Carla on that memorable first vacation to the same chalet. He remembered gulping stream-chilled white wine in the meadow below El Tronador while their guide in worn lederhosen grilled silvery trout over white-ashed embers. And how they had picked the flaky white flesh with their fingers and eaten it with chunks of bread baked before dawn. . . .

Roger had met him at Zürs one Christmas vacation for skiing in the Vorarlberg. Together they had skied morning and after-noon, tanning under the reflected mountain sun. One evening they took the lift's last ride together and started down the longest run as the sky was growing dark. Roger had taken the lead, flashing ahead down the funnel trail and vanishing in lengthening shadows. But Chance's left ski had struck an exposed root and flung him off the trail, breaking a ski against a tree trunk. Dazed, alone, unable to make headway through the hip-deep snow, Chance had begun to think, as his feet and fingers numbed, that he was going to freeze to death. But after an hour he heard his name shouted from below; he yelled back, and after a while Roger was there with brandy and spare skis, and they hugged each other and tears froze on their cheeks. Climbing skins covered Roger's skis, sealskins snatched from the ski shop when no one else would join the search for his missing brother. . . .

That summer, shortly after Chance had joined the Agency Roger entered the Air Force Academy and they saw each other less frequently. And as Chance thought back on how brief his brother's life had been, he regretted bitterly the circumstances that kept them apart. As he regretted the weeks and months his work had kept him from Carla's side.

He turned out the reading light, mixed a stiff drink in the kitchen, and carried it to his bedroom where he drank and un-dressed slowly. He felt prepared for tomorrow morning's lecture, and for his own class that followed. In late afternoon he would drive up to Georgetown and deliver Rony wherever she wanted to go, maybe have dinner together somewhere her husband was not likely to appear.

Rony was as well-fitted for diplomatic life as Penn, he reflected, for her father had been a four-star general and then an ambassador at two Class-A posts before retiring. Chance wondered if she and Penn would reconcile, decided it was none of his business, turned out the light, and got into bed.

After his dissertation was accepted and he had passed the orals, what would he do? As he lay in darkness he realized that he had not given much thought to the future. Study had been the anodyne to pain and he had embraced it without reservation. So let the future take care of itself, he thought, and as his mind cleared of sorrow he fell into shallow sleep.

In his dream he was in an all-white room with Carla. He saw her rise from her chair and walk toward him, arms outstretched. It amazed him that her face and body were restored and she was young and beautiful again. Gliding toward him, she said, "Darling, I'm so sorry for all the sorrow I've put you to, but I'm well now and we can go on living." He tried to speak, but no words came, and when he tried to take her in his arms there was only a wraith with no more substance than smoke.

Chance woke and his face was wet with tears. He turned on the light, went to the kitchen, and drank deeply from the bottle, gasping at the burning liquor. He drank again and stumbled back to bed, leaving the light on while the dream dissolved, until he finally surrendered to healing sleep.

NINE

In the basement of an isolated farmhouse a few miles south of the Beltway, Major Pavel Sosnowski was tied to a chair beneath a powerful light. He could not see Yusuf and Hamid in the shadows behind him, but he recognized the face of General Berlikov from a time when Berlikov had addressed his tradecraft training class. The man with him was unknown to Sosnowski, but he assumed it to be another high-ranking officer, since they addressed each other as equals.

They sat in chairs facing Sosnowski, whose mind was filled with confusion. He was fearful, too, afraid of the unknown and unable to rationalize how it was that while carrying out a delicate mission for an important personage he had suddenly become a victim of his own service, the KGB.

"Comrade Major," said Berlikov in a casual voice, "I feel you should understand that it is in your best interest to cooperate. At present no criminal blame attaches to you for having accepted a task pressed on you by a high-ranking official whom you could not refuse. Whether you are tried for high crimes against the Mother-land will depend entirely upon the degree of your cooperation. Do you understand?"

"Yes."

"After all, you did not conceive this mission, did you, Comrade Major?"

"No."

"We can say then that you are an innocent victim of a conspiracy constructed by others, can we not?"

"Yes, Comrade General."

"Good."

While Berlikov lighted another cigarette, Sosnowski considered his situation and found it almost hopeless. He had been betrayed and intercepted. If he was to emerge with his life and the remnants of a career, he would have to shape his answers with extreme care.

"Having comprehended the gravity of your position," said Berlikov, exhaling, "it is essential that you withhold nothing."

Sosnowski was silent. General Chavadze said roughly, "Your life is at stake, and the lives of your wife and children. Is that clear?"

"Yes," Sosnowski said dully, "I know very well what can be done to them." Having myself carried out such reprisals against others, he reflected.

"But it is premature to touch on so unpleasant a finale," Berlikov pointed out, "because by now it is entirely clear that it would be unpatriotic and futile to try to protect those who embarked you on disaster."

Sosnowski let his words sink in before replying. "Although at first I was hesitant to accept the mission, the ease and speed with which I was supplied false documents, exit visa, and money persuaded me that the mission was fully official. How can I be blamed for that?"

"An illusion was created," Berlikov replied. "A show in which you played obedient puppet. So it would be unjust if those who manipulated the strings escaped judgment. Is that not so?"

"It is how I have come to view the matter," Sosnowski agreed. "Nevertheless, I daresay few comrade officers would not have fallen into the same trap. Imagine yourselves in my position—a mere major summoned to the Kremlin for what turns out to be a private interview with a member of the Council of Ministers—"

"That's how it began?" Chavadze interrupted.

When Sosnowski nodded, Berlikov said, "Who arranged the meeting?"

"It was an officer I had seen in uniform at the Lubyanka. When he approached me he was in civilian clothing."

"His name?"

"He told me to call him Sasha. On the fourth of last month I was to report to a particular office in the Kremlin, without informing my *sektor* chief. I agreed to appear, and to keep the matter secret."

"And when you got to this particular office . . . ?" Chavadze inquired.

"Sasha was there. He led me into the presence of the minister."

"And he remained while you talked?"

"No, Comrade, Sasha withdrew. There was only the minister and myself. I was awed and flattered. I had never even spoken with a minister before—who has? And this one extolled my background, my language abilities, my reputation for circumspection. The comrade minister told me I had been selected for a mission of the highest importance to the Motherland. He impressed me with its secrecy because it was necessary to carry out the mission outside diplomatic channels, without the knowledge of the Ministry of Foreign Affairs. He informed me that the premier himself had instigated the mission, that its purpose was to bring about a peaceful understanding—rapprochement—between our Motherland and the People's Republic of China. He gave me to understand that this was greatly in our country's interest and cautioned me that if the overture became known, it would die stillborn." Sosnowski paused, throat dry. "He then asked if I was willing to travel secretly to Washington and make contact with the Chinese embassy."

"And you," said Chavadze scornfully, "agreed to go."

"As you know." He tried to shrug, but he was too tightly bound to the chair back. His wrists ached, his arms were numb. Well, all this would be over with soon. After he named a minister they would release him. He said, "It will not be possible for me to return to Moscow, of course. Please consider the alternative—let me remain in this country working for you."

"Well," said Berlikov, "I appreciate your predicament and we will find a solution. Now, Comrade Major, which minister was it who embroiled you in his private plot?"

Sosnowski hesitated, gaze fixed on Berlikov's impassive face. With a sigh of resignation he said, "It was Comrade Kirilenko, minister of education." And hoped they would believe him.

TEN

Rony glanced around the apartment, lifted her small Hermès bag, and said, "I don't believe I've left anything behind, Quinn. That's one virtue of traveling light."

He took the bag from her hand. "Decided where to perch?"

"Uh-huh. Sally Bevins, a Radcliffe classmate, is taking me in while her husband's in Tokyo. Their place is in Potomac, out River Road." She opened her purse. "Here's your neighbor's key the cleaning lady gave back to me. Fresh sheets on the bed, shirts ironed, kitchen clean. Now, what about me? How do *I* look?"

"Much better," he said. "Hardly a mark on you. Any contact with Penn?"

She sighed. "Not directly, but I had a feeling I was being watched, or the apartment was, at least. And a couple of late-night phone calls upset me. I answered, but no one was there. Could have been Penn or his detectives. Or maybe I'm paranoid. I asked the super if he'd seen anyone lurking around, but he hadn't. On the other hand, he stays pretty close to his TV."

"You're not kidding. Well, shall we move along? Since we're heading for Potomac, let's eat at Canal House."

"Love it."

As they drove there, Chance considered her fears and decided they were groundless. Rony was still, understandably, in an emotional state, with heightened sensitivities. It seemed highly unlikely that Penn knew where she'd been staying, much less set detectives on her trail. Nor, Chance mused, was there any reason for him to be under surveillance of any kind. The whole thing was irrational.

They dined in the old canal-side lodge with its open fireplace, rough-hewn beams, and smoky, dimly lit atmosphere, sharing a rack of lamb and a bottle of good Beaujolais. Inevitably, Chance thought back to other long-ago evenings with Rony, and the nights of lovemaking that followed. Her glance told him she remembered, too, and he felt relieved that she was out of his apartment and on the way to friends. "Things go well with the lawyer?" he asked.

"I guess. I signed papers this morning: They have to be served on Penn or his attorney." She took a deep breath. "Ending a not-very-satisfactory marriage. Thinking back, I realize that almost from the first I had doubts, but I determined I was going to be *one* Foreign Service wife who was happy in her role." Her hands parted. "So it went." She looked away. "You and Carla were right for each other, weren't you, Quinn?"

"Just right—and I have that to remember. Under the circumstances, I feel very fortunate."

"I'm glad."

They drove up the winding hill to River Road and west through white-fence country until Rony told him where to turn in. Half a dozen horses clustered in the front pasture a hundred yards from the white two-story house. Chance parked on the gravel drive and carried Rony's bag to the door. Before ringing the bell, Rony turned to him. "I can't thank you enough for helping out. You're a good friend, Quinn. I hope you'll always be that. And if there's ever anything I can do . . ."

"I'll let you know." Before he could turn away she took his arm and kissed him lightly on the lips. "For old times," she said, and let him go. As he got behind the wheel he saw the door open, the profile of a woman welcoming Rony. He waved good-bye and drove to River Road, passing Canal House on the way back to Georgetown.

For a while he thought about Rony, then forced his mind to tomorrow's briefing session and the pupil, whose instructional name was Ben Adem, the outbound Algiers station chief. So far, he had known none of the Agency students, but all seemed to come from the same mold: careful, uninspiring bureaucrats, more interested in cultivating their ambassadors than in undertaking covert operations, their nominal raison d'être. The era of risk-taking was dead as the dodo bird.

He parked behind the apartment building, unlocked the front door, and took the staircase to the second floor. At his doorway he fitted key in lock and pushed inward.

He and Rony had turned off the lights. Now one at the far end of the room revealed a man standing beside a chair in which another man slumped. Before Chance could back up, the door closed behind him and a pistol bored into his ribs.

At LaGuardia Airport, General Berlikov left the shuttle plane and hailed a taxi. He had decided to visit his counterpart in the Soviet delegation to the United Nations for the next few days. General Chavadze was en route to the Soviet consulate in San Francisco to confer with a vice consul, who was in reality a lieutenant colonel in the GRU and Chavadze's subordinate.

Berlikov and Chavadze had agreed that it would be a good idea to be away from Washington when the killings took place.

ELEVEN

Burglars? Chance thought. But, no, they were waiting for him. The man in the chair moaned and moved his head sluggishly. The one behind him reached down, grabbed hair, and pulled back showing the upturned face. "Know him?"

Something familiar even in the dim light, but Chance shook his head. "No."

The gun in his ribs prodded him closer. "Now?"

Cairo. The garden fight . . . "Never saw him before," Chance said. Why were they here? What were they going to do? The man in the chair—*Sosnowski,* that was his name—was obviously drugged.

The man beside him drew away and Chance saw the silenced muzzle pointing at his heart. His eyes registered the flash before his ears heard sound a millisecond before the slug slammed into him with sledgehammer force. The scene shattered into slivers of colored lights. Unconscious, Chance dropped forward.

Pain was his first awareness, silence the second.

He was dying . . . yet he could still move. He lifted his outthrust hand and a weight slipped from it. Opening his eyes, Chance glimpsed the remembered lighting, the man in the chair.

Sosnowski.

Pavel something. Mik—no, Vasily—Vasilyevich. Rank: Major. Service: KGB. That he could remember was evidence his mind was functioning. His left side was a mass of pain. He rolled over, groaning between set teeth, felt his jacket for blood.

Fabric dry.

Blank cartridge? No. A bullet *had* struck him. He must be bleeding internally, inside his ribcage. *Telephone for help.*

Slowly he got to his knees, rested while dizziness passed. Probed his shirt for bleeding.

Nothing.

Something inside his left breast pocket was heavy against his knuckles . . . his wallet-checkbook. He drew it out and saw the spent slug still in it. Evil-looking, flattened against the metal mini-calculator that had saved him. He breathed deeply, gratefully. He really wasn't going to die.

What about the Russian? He went slowly to the chair and looked down. Sosnowski's chin rested on his chest. Bright blood stained the shirt beneath it. Sosnowski's open eyes stared vacantly. Chance touched the pallid temple. No pulse.

Looking down, he saw a revolver in Sosnowski's hand.

So that was the setup, a scene of double murder. He looked back where he had fallen and saw the weight that had slipped from his hand—a pistol. His prints were on it, had to be. Nothing he could do for the dead KGB officer, but he could save himself.

Who were the men who shot them both? Why? Whose orders?

He looked at the telephone, saw the cord torn from its connection box.

His mind computed: the killers would call the police, probably had. He listened by the window, heard nothing. When police arrived, would they believe him? How could he convince them he'd been framed?

He needed time to think. A voice in the back of his mind yelled: *get out, get out!*

Chance started for the door, remembered the fallen pistol and picked it up. Wiping it clean, he realized he had a choice of leaving it to be found or taking it with him.

He shoved it into his coat pocket, heard the muzzle grate on metal.

Faintly, a siren rose in the distance above the night hum of traffic. His hand slid down along the pistol, retrieved a bit of metal. A key. The key to Mrs. Crolius's apartment.

After a final glance at Sosnowski, Chance walked to the book-shelf, took down a thick volume of *Contes drolatiques,* and opened it. From the hollowed-out interior he lifted one hundred fifty-dollar bills. Five thousand dollars. He pocketed the currency and returned Balzac's merry tales to the shelf.

He had cached the emergency fund for weekend money when banks were closed, a traffic accident, say, when he'd need bail or a lawyer. Well, this was the emergency, and he needed a lawyer.

The siren wail was higher, closer, more insistent.

He left the apartment, stepped quickly across to the opposite door. The key opened the widow's apartment, and without turning on light he made his way to the corner telephone stand. Through lace curtains he could see the flashing lights of a patrol car.

Chance was deciding whom to telephone when heavy steps pounded down the hallway. McCrory's voice called, "Take it easy, officers, there's a lady in there. Don't bust the door, I got a pass-key."

"Okay, hurry up. You din' hear no shootin'?"

"Nah, had a movie on. Besides, way down there in the base—holy *God!* Lookit *that!*"

"Yeah."

Footsteps softer now as they approached the seated corpse. Then: "Call the meat wagon, Homicide."

Chance pulled off his shoes and went quietly to the kitchen where he gulped two glasses of water. As he wiped the glass dry he heard pounding on the door, then McCrory saying, "No one there, officer. She's outta town. Miz Crolius."

"You sure?"

"Hell, yes, I'm sure."

"You said there was a lady in Chance's place—all we find is a body, male."

"There *was* a broad there, all week. I seen her."

"Describe her?"

"Sure. About five-eight, -nine, kinda skinny—"

"Save it for later. Tell the other tenants to stay put, there'll be questions for them." Footsteps receded.

Chance went into the bathroom, closed the door, and turned on the cabinet light. Inside he found a bottle of codeine tablets for the widow's arthritis. He swallowed two with another glass of water and stretched out on a sofa near the door, where he could hear what was going on.

The rib pain was stubborn, the slug could have cracked bones. But he couldn't let pain keep him from making decisions.

Review: He was ex-Agency; Sosnowski KGB. The facts would surface and make a nasty combination. He could almost see the headline: SOVIET OFFICIAL SLAIN BY CIA AGENT. And the old Cairo fight would surface, increasing circumstantial evidence against him.

He didn't intend to flee, just stay out of sight until he could get legal advice. Meanwhile, he ought to let the Agency know that he'd been framed. By persons unknown.

His wristwatch dial showed 9:14. Law offices closed. Where were lawyers when you needed them? At the Agency there'd be a night duty officer, but he'd log the call, be wary and generally unhelpful.

Who?

Vince Stainbeck had been an area chief with whom he'd been on good terms; worked the Soviet target, too. Call Vince?

Not yet, there were men in his apartment; even speaking softly, he might be overheard. Chance took the phone directory into the bathroom, looked up Stainbeck's number, and memorized it. And he ought to warn Rony to stay away. The super could identify her, cause needless trouble, embarrassment.

The directory provided Sally Bevins's number and he filed it in his mind.

Rony had a lawyer who could recommend another to advise him.

He turned off the light, left the bathroom, and replaced the directory beside the telephone. Then he lay down on the sofa to wait.

Lying on his back relaxed chest muscles and reduced pain. Another hour or so, he thought, and police would be gone from his apartment. They might leave a patrolman guarding it the rest of the night, then seal it in the morning. To Chance it seemed a waste of law enforcement manpower badly needed on the street.

As he stared up at the ceiling he reflected that he was not yet officially a fugitive from justice. But that proclamation would be made unless he was able to find a competent criminal lawyer who could explain matters in a persuasive way. Chance had seen both killers and committed their faces to memory. His mind focused on every aspect of their faces, their clothing, their unfamiliar accents. Details that would aid the police in tracking down the killers—unless they preferred to settle for him.

He recalled Rony's concern that she was being watched. He understood now that they had waited for him to arrive—how long? Not quite three hours—no problem with a sedated victim.

But who would kill a major of the KGB and lay it on a man who had known Sosnowski briefly, though violently, long years ago? It was his Agency past, he figured, that had stood out in the plotters' minds. But who were they? The killers were not ethnic Russians—their faces were too swarthy, their builds too slight. Besides, their accent was not Russian.

He'd barely looked at the pistol, but now as Chance considered its proximity, he drew the weapon from his pocket and thumbed out the magazine. Ejected the ready shell from the chamber into his hand. As though field-stripping blindfolded, Chance slid the ejected cartridge into the magazine, replaced it in the hollow handgrip, and set the safety. That done, he returned the pistol to his pocket and heard the door of his apartment open, low voices, the creak of gurney wheels under the corpse's weight. Sosnowski carted off to the District morgue.

The door closed with a loud noise, footsteps moved away.

He felt detached from everything, as though he were no more than a distant observer, an onlooker; yet he realized that his freedom, his future depended on the next few hours.

What angered him most was that the three of them had managed to enter unseen and had simply waited for him to return. They knew his movements. And surveillance took time. How could he not have noticed? Because he had long ago stopped checking for surveillants, assuming that in his own country it was needless.

And because when he had left the Agency, he'd abandoned tradecraft forever, that very day. How naive I was, he mused, and how I'm paying for it now.

He got up slowly and painfully and listened, one ear against the apartment door.

He could hear muffled voices in the first floor corridor as police talked with other tenants. His own apartment was silent. Now was the time to use the telephone.

He was walking toward it when he heard steps outside the door, the scrape of key on lock.

He bolted for the bathroom as living room lights went on. Chance stood behind the door, gripping the pistol and listening to the heavy footsteps of a man moving across the living room.

Hamid and Yusuf had waited in their car behind the apartment building. Keeping low on the front seat, they had seen police cars and ambulance arrive; now the ambulance pulled away, siren growling to part the crowd of onlookers.

"So," said Hamid, "it's over with. Job done." He turned the ignition key to start the engine.

"What about his car?" Yusuf gestured at Chance's Mercedes, dark in its numbered slot.

"What about it?"

"We could sell it—*he* won't need it again."

"You take his keys?"

"No."

"Forget it. Could lead back to us." He steered out of the lot onto Volta Place before turning headlights on.

"There's light in the apartment."

"You expect a cop to sit in the dark?"

After a while Yusuf said, "I'm hungry, how about you?"

"I could use a bite. The Lebanese joint, El Djazair?"

"Why not? Some drinks. A little music . . . We deserve it. We do good work, brother."

"The best."

The car headed east to Wisconsin, down to M Street and across the bridge. Away from Georgetown and their perfect crime.

TWELVE

The narrow doorframe separation gave Chance only a few degrees' scan of the apartment's main room, and he had been concealing himself behind the door when the man passed through. He was still there, though, invisible in the dining room; Chance heard the clink of glass at the sideboard. Policeman? Thief?

Again the sound of glass on glass, the faint murmur of liquid, then nothing until Chance heard a grunt of satisfaction. Presently, footsteps went into the kitchen, lights went on, tap water flowed. Lights out, the man returned to the dining room and moved out where Chance could see him plainly.

Building super McCrory, wiping lips on the back of his wrist.

Chance felt his muscles relax. The super had used his passkey to cop a drink from Mrs. Crolius. He wasn't there to steal the silver or search for Quentin Chance; just a small-time chiseler taking advantage of the widow's absence.

McCrory belched, patted his stomach, and strode to the door. He turned off the lights and went out.

Chance left his hiding place.

With McCrory likely to come in from time to time to satisfy his thirst, Chance realized he would have to find another refuge. He thought of an alternative, but that one had its drawbacks, too. In any case, it was too soon to leave, and he had calls to make.

He dialed the Bevins number first, and in a low voice persuaded Sally to bring Rony to the phone.

When she answered he said, "Phone discipline—don't mention my name."

"Oh—I'm *so* glad it's you. . . . I was afraid it was Penn, after—"

"No time, Rony. I came back to the apartment and found a bad scene—I was being framed for a killing—" He paused at the intake of her breath. "Penn wasn't watching you, the killers were watching my place. You'll read details, but right now I need a lawyer, badly. Can yours provide a name?"

"I—I suppose so, I'll call him, but this is so sudden, so terrible—"

"It is, but there has to be a way out, a way to clear myself. I'm depending on you."

"Yes, of course. Are you okay? Where can I phone you?"

"I'll call back. Fifteen minutes, okay?"

"That's fine."

"For your own sake, stay away from my apartment building—the super can identify you."

"Oh, God!"

"Fifteen minutes," he said, and hung up.

After a glance at his watch Chance dialed the McLean home of Vince Stainbeck. After six rings Chance was about to hang up when he heard Vince answer.

"This is Quinn Chance, and—"

"Quinn! What the hell—?"

"Listen, Vince, a Soviet KGB officer was killed in my apartment and I was left for dead by the two killers—"

"This some kind of joke, Quinn? If it is—"

"No joke, Vince, I'm dead serious." Fingers touched aching ribs. "An old connection between me and the dead guy is going to be made, and that brings in the Agency. I'm calling you because I was framed and the Agency should know it."

"Jesus, Quinn, if you're not joking, it sounds awful." He paused. "What do you want me to do?"

"Pass the word to Security because the press will be yammering for a statement. If the KGB wanted to settle some old score with me, they could have knocked me off any time in the last four years; they didn't have to kill one of their own men for that."

"Seems logical. But, why . . . ?"

"God knows."

"Listen, you want I should phone Security now?"

"By all means. I'm getting a lawyer, but I could use some help from headquarters along the way."

"Ummm—don't count on much, Quinn."

"I'm not, but because I worked for the Agency I was picked for the fall. The link is there."

"Sure, I understand. . . . Where are you?"

"I'll call later, check with you."

"Quinn." His voice was bleak. "Why'n hell you have to pick me?"

"Because you know how Sovs operate—and not everyone in that big, beautiful building does. Why didn't I phone the duty officer? Because he's probably some Mideast petrochemical specialist who's never seen a Russian. You'll pass the word?"

"I will."

Replacing the phone, Chance looked down through the window and saw that the street crowd had dispersed, then wondered if the killers had stayed around to check the results of their handiwork. If they had seen only one gurney loaded into the ambulance, they would wonder why. But if they merely saw the ambulance drive off, they could assume both corpses were gone.

Until the morning paper said otherwise.

Whatever the case, he would have to leave the building unseen. Fortunately, there was a fire escape leading down from the kitchen doorway, and if he went quietly, his chances of leaving undetected were good.

While waiting to call Rony, Chance went to the dining room sideboard and saw a bourbon bottle, whose inner neck was still wet. McCrory liked bourbon. Chance did not. He uncapped a bottle of Old Grouse and drank to steady his nerves. Mrs. Crolius wouldn't mind, he told himself. Consider it payment for his caretaking.

Because rib pain was returning he swallowed another of her pain tabs—three so far; more would risk impairment.

Sitting beside the telephone, Chance wondered if he should risk driving his car. If he saw cops around it, obviously not. But it might be less risky than a taxi—this hour of night he would be remembered by any driver.

Time to call.

Rony answered the second ring. "That you?"

73

"Any luck?"

"Think so. The name I got is Wilson Jones." She gave him a phone number and an apartment address out Massachusetts Avenue. "He's near American University, and my lawyer says he's very good; he'll know how to handle things."

"Did your lawyer phone him?"

"He did, and Jones is expecting you. Call, or just go."

"I'm grateful, Rony."

"One good turn . . . What else can I do for you?"

"Nothing," he said, "except avoid the apartment—and me."

"It feels I'm turning my back on you," she said unhappily.

"You haven't. And the less Penn knows, the better."

She was silent for a while. "After this is over, straightened out, will you get in touch with me?"

"I will," he promised, "and I hope things go smoothly for you."

"So do I. . . . Dinner brought back a lot of memories—"

"I know."

"I've missed you," she said softly, "and what happens to you is very important to me . . . so take special care of yourself. Good night."

For a moment he gazed at the telephone, then tore his mind off Rony. From a kitchen window he looked down into the building's parking lot: slots for eight cars and turnaround space. A board fence screened it from the service alley. The lot had gone unlighted for at least three weeks because of McCrory's delay in replacing the burned-out floodlight. For that procrastination Chance was now grateful. With care he might be able to reach his car unseen.

He returned to the telephone intending to call Wilson Jones and Stainbeck, decided he'd used this phone enough and would call Vince later from another location. Wilson Jones was expecting him, no call needed.

Chance carried his shoes into the kitchen and put them on. He unlocked the rear door very quietly and looked out on the parking lot. No cops visible. Five cars, all empty. He could see no surveillance vehicles, police or otherwise. Unforeseen circumstances were forcing him to resurrect skills that for years had been routine.

So be it, he thought, as he tiptoed down the rusty iron steps, but staying alive is only part of the picture. I have to know why I was set up, why Pavel Sosnowski was killed. Otherwise I'll have fear walking with me down whatever street I go, for the rest of my life.

He stepped onto the asphalt parking lot, crouched over, and made his way to the Mercedes. Music blared suddenly from one of the first-floor apartments, died away. The night air was cool, misty, the moon blurred, out of focus. He unlocked the car and pushed it to the street with an effort that made his left side ache.

At the corner, he turned downhill and got behind the wheel. As the car gathered momentum he released the clutch and the engine started. He drove out Wisconsin Avenue to its crossing with Massachusetts, found Wilson Jones's building, and rang the bell.

THIRTEEN

To Chance, the lawyer's study resembled a side conversation room in a good men's club. Paneled walls hung with sporting prints, built-in bookshelves, indirect lighting, and leather-upholstered furniture in green and muted red. A large desk was set near the tall window and on it lay open legal books and written-on yellow pads illuminated by a green-shaded brass lamp.

After listening to Chance for twenty minutes Wilson Jones lighted a cigarette, got up from his high-backed swivel chair and walked around it to the window. Parting heavy drapes, he looked at the avenue three stories below and smoked silently before turning back. "That's quite a story, Mr. Chance. Anything to back it up?"

Chance rose and removed his jacket, pointing out the heart-level bullet hole, then opened his shirt. For the first time he looked at his injury and saw a blue-purple swelling the size of his open hand.

The lawyer stared. "Hurt?"

"Enough."

"Anything else?"

Chance laid the pistol on the desk. "When it was used on Sosnowski it had a silencer, like the one used on me. They took the silencers with them."

"Men you'd never seen."

"That's right." He looked at Wilson Jones and saw a man in his early forties, five-six or -seven, pale face, thinning blond hair. Chance buttoned his shirt and pulled on his jacket, wincing.

The lawyer sat down again behind his desk. "You'd recognize the men if you saw them?"

"I can do better than that. With a police Identikit I can come up with two good likenesses." He eased back into his chair.

"And you may have to." He exhaled thoughtfully. "Of course, it would have been better if you'd stayed there to talk to the police; that would have made things easier."

"The frame was too good," Chance said. "I'd be phoning you from jail."

"Possibly." He looked away. "One of the problems is that the Agency hasn't enjoyed too good an image the past few years. All sorts of wild things are charged to it, some true, most not. Point is, it's credible to the public that a CIA man—"

"*Ex*-CIA man."

"Right—would shoot a KGB officer who happened to be an old enemy."

"Hardly that," Chance said. "He pawed my wife, I resented it."

"Enough to beat him up." Jones nodded, thumbed his plump chin. "Any other violence in your past?"

"No."

"Armed service?"

"Wouldn't take me." He touched the flattened bridge of his nose. "Hockey puck—I was seventeen."

"And never had the nose repaired."

"My wife liked me the way I was, said it gave character to my face." He managed a wry smile.

"It also makes you identifiable in a crowd. Look, Mr. Chance, protecting you isn't going to be easy. By now the police have probably built a circumstantial case against you, and the Soviet embassy will be hollering for blood and retribution."

"It serves their purposes," Chance said. "So what can you do for me?"

The lawyer looked down at a heavy gold ring on a left-hand finger. "I should notify the police that you will surrender in the morning for questioning. I'll accompany you and try for bail. I'm not sure it will be granted, but we'll certainly try. That doesn't sound too good to you, does it?"

"I thought you could represent me without my having to appear and risk jail. Explain what happened and say I'll cooperate in describing Sosnowski's killers."

"That could be for later," Jones said, "but my advice is to accompany me to headquarters and let me do the talking. I'll file an appearance for you, and try to avoid an indictment."

While Chance was considering the proposal, Jones said, "Apropos my representing you, Mr. Chance, I'll need a retainer."

"How much?"

"Five thousand."

He had the cash in his pocket, but he got out his wallet-checkbook and set it on the desk before Jones. While the lawyer watched, Chance pried out the flattened bullet and removed the smashed computer. "In case you were wondering." He used the least damaged check to write out Jones's retainer and laid it before the lawyer, who was turning the bullet between thumb and forefinger.

Jones said bluntly, "I suppose you could have shot yourself."

"That's what the police will assume, and that's why I'm not eager to surrender. Once they have me in jail they won't have much reason to look elsewhere. And they won't want to get involved in the Soviet angle; that would bring in the FBI, and the D.C. cops would hate that."

"Still, an FBI investigation might be your best hope."

"Possibly," Chance conceded, "but let's not allow things to get that far."

Jones laid down the bullet, picked up Chance's check, and slipped it into his desk drawer. "So we understand one another, I am going to presume you've told me a straight story. I don't know you, you don't know me. In fact"—he stubbed out his cigarette—"I have no knowledge that any crime has been committed, much less that you may be a fugitive. What I have is a melodramatic tale by a walk-in client, a tale I will, in due course, try to establish as truth or fiction. So for the present I am under no professional obligation to contact any law enforcement authority."

Chance shifted painfully in his chair. "Good."

"But if it is brought to my attention that Quentin Chance is wanted on suspicion of murder"—he glanced away—"I will take certain required steps to protect myself, and you. Is the position clear?"

Chance nodded, impatient with the legalistic boilerplate.

"What about your own people, the Agency? What's their attitude?"

"I told you I made a preliminary call. I'll call again for reaction."

Jones slid the telephone toward him and Chance punched Vince Stainbeck's number, activated the speaker phone. When Vince answered, Chance said, "What's happening, Vince?"

"Like you firebombed the building, Quinn. Everyone's panicked—where are you?"

"So nobody appreciates my early warning?"

"Frankly, no, but Security wants to hear your story as soon as possible. After that, the Firm will decide what position to take."

"I'm not asking for a position. I mainly want the Agency to stay out of it."

"Like, how?"

"Abstain from prejudging the situation."

Stainbeck sighed wearily. "Jesus, Chance, you have a genius for mixing in the wrong things."

"Like what?"

"Paul Valcour . . . Brigand. Didn't win you any friends."

"That's long over with," Chance said thinly.

"And of course you had to damn near kill Sosnowski in Cairo."

"My fault he couldn't use his fists? C'mon, Vince, don't be so damn righteous."

A pause, then, "Walt Stillman wants to talk with you right away, try to sort things out. Quinn, we feel it's in your interest to see him."

"Where?"

"Wherever you say."

"I don't know Stillman."

"He doesn't know you either. So what? He's number two in Security, liaises with the D.C. cops and the Bureau."

"What's his background?"

"Treasury—Secret Service. Office of Naval Intelligence. Talk to him, Quinn."

Chance looked across the desk at Wilson Jones, who nodded. "Can't hurt, might help," he said quietly.

"All right," Chance agreed. "An hour from now." He thought for a moment. "Across from the Senate Office Building there's a café called the Hunters Lodge, with some outside tables—"

"The place'll be closed," Stainbeck objected. "Hell, it's going on eleven."

"Even better, no eavesdroppers. Tell Stillman no coat, no tie, just his shirt—I'll recognize him."

"I'll pass the word." Silence . . . then, "Hope things work out for you, but do me a favor, Quinn. Don't call me again, it's out of my hands. Stillman is point man now."

"Hell, Vince, I wouldn't embarrass you for the world. Tell everyone I contacted you because of your sterling qualities." He broke the connection and looked at Jones.

The lawyer shrugged. "What do you expect? They're hustling to cover their collective ass. You've become an embarrassment. Still, you ought to go and tell your story, for the record."

Chance took back the pistol.

Jones frowned. "Think you need it?"

"Six hours ago I'd have thought it absurd, but things have changed. You heard the arrangement with Stillman. If I disappear, you'll know what to do."

"Surely you're not anticipating—"

"The way I see things now, anything can happen." He pocketed the pistol and left the lawyer's apartment.

As Chance rode downward in the ornate old-fashioned elevator, he wondered if Wilson Jones was the right man to help him. The lawyer's quick grasp of the situation had impressed Chance, but then Jones seemed to waffle and grow cautious, apparently more concerned about his own vulnerability than his client's. Well, Chance mused as the doors opened, I didn't have a world of choice, and he's taken my money, so all I can do is hope for the best.

From the apartment building he drove down to the new mid-town hotel where his classes were held, parked underneath, and went up to the training suite, confident it was not surveilled. One, it was leased by State, so CIA Logistics would have no record of it. Two, his salary and expenses were paid by the Office of Training, so there was no internal locator cross-reference, as there would be if he were paid by Ops. Three, a simple matter of legal authority: CIA could neither bug the suite nor arrest him, that was the law. Four, even if that legal barrier were overridden, there would not have been time to summon the troops and deploy them in and around a downtown hotel. But he had no intention of pushing his luck by wasting time.

Inside, he double-locked the door, stripped, and took a hot shower. The warmth felt good on his lacerated ribs, but he dried off with care. After shaving, Chance changed and applied the physical disguise that converted him into Herbert F. Aylward. He added the Aylward ID to his damaged wallet and checked the time. Thirteen minutes, ample time to go down half a dozen blocks. He studied his disguised features in the mirror. Only his indented nose was unchanged.

He turned off the lights as he left the suite, realizing that tomorrow Ben Adem would wait in vain. Unless Harold Kappler could find a substitute briefer, the program would be dissolved, its instructor irrevocably tainted.

And what about Charlottesville? he wondered. My dissertation, my teaching? All of it could be down the drain by tomorrow, even after I'm cleared. If I were accused of Communist sympathies, they'd circle the wagons to defend me, Chance figured wryly.

Waiting for the elevator, Chance decided to taxi to the Hunters Lodge. Walt Stillman was an unknown quantity; no point in showing him the car.

There were plenty of cabs in the rank, and the doorman was off duty. Chance got into the nearest cab, got out a block away on a side street, and made his way through a narrow service alley that ran alongside the dark café.

From the shadows where he stood, Chance could see the street and the awninged front, the wooden tables stacked with chairs. He touched the pistol in his pocket, looked at his watch. An hour had passed since his call. Where was Stillman?

Chance heard a car approaching on the dark street. Its headlights became visible as it veered toward the curb near the café entrance. The car braked, lights went out. The driver opened the door and stepped to the sidewalk. A tall man, he wore neither tie nor jacket. His shirt was open at the collar. For a moment he looked around, then strode under the awning. He took two chairs from a table, righted them, and sat down. The man got a cigarette from his shirt pocket and lighted it. Breeze ruffled his hair and collar, gave his cigarette tip a crimson glow.

Chance moved.

FOURTEEN

"Mr. Stillman, I presume." Chance had come behind him, and his words startled the man. Quickly he looked around, managed a smile in the near-dark. "You don't look like your photo."

"Faces change under stress," said Chance, "as you may have heard." Before sitting down he looked around. "You came alone?"

"I assumed you wanted it that way."

Chance seated himself so he could watch the street. He felt edgy, knew he had to calm down. "How much did Stainbeck tell you?"

"Not much, really. I expect you'll want to round it out."

"That's why I'm here," Chance said, "and to make clear I'm not begging for help. Even though I wouldn't be in this mess if I hadn't been with the Agency."

"How's that?"

"I've had time to think things over," Chance told him, "and to me it's clear that someone wanted Sosnowski dead, for reasons we may never know. The killers needed a scapegoat and I was chosen because of a tangle with Sosnowski in Cairo years ago. And because I'd left the Agency, I wasn't expecting trouble. Or prepared for it," he added.

Stillman laced his fingers and flexed them. "But somehow you escaped death." The tone was condescending, held the trace of a sneer. Chance didn't like it but decided he had to make the best of this contact. Stillman didn't impress him as a man ready to do violence but as a timeserving bureaucrat. An empty suit unwillingly dragged into a situation whose parameters he couldn't comprehend.

83

To bolster his story Chance showed Stillman the smashed calculator. "My lawyer has the bullet," he said, "and if you're wired, it's fine with me."

"Who's your lawyer?"

"Why?"

"It's possible the Office of General Counsel might decide to cooperate with him."

Chance named Wilson Jones and told Stillman everything he had related to his lawyer. When he finished, Stillman was silent, though he craned his neck and looked around.

Chance said, "Expecting someone?"

"No . . . oh, no, we're quite alone. Ah—you'll admit the story does sound . . . fantastic?"

"Fantastic? That's not a word that comes to mind, since I survived the reality. Of course, you'd be listening with a cop's ear. Pal, you're making me nervous, stop looking around."

Smiling weakly, Stillman faced Chance. "So, that's all, eh? Nothing to add?"

"Guess not—since I've been boring you. Anyway, the Agency's on notice something unpleasant is about to hit the headlines."

"And you expect us to do something about it?"

"Forget it, Stillman, just go back to sleep," Chance said. "I came in good faith, but all I did was waste time—yours and mine." He stood up. Stillman laid a restraining hand on his arm. "Hey, don't get sore, I've been listening, haven't I? Isn't that what you wanted?"

"Right. A good listener is a rarity these days." He drew back his arm as Stillman looked up unhappily. "What was that name again? I'm not good on Russian names. Sos—?"

"Sosnowski. Pavel Vasilyevich. Major, KGB."

"Ah, you'll write it down for me so I'll have it right? Don't mind, do you?"

"I do—and since you liaise with the D.C. cops who have his body, they'll give you his full name."

"Splendid idea." Stillman rose and backed away, and a sudden sensation of danger flashed through Chance's mind. He heard doors opening behind him but before Chance could react, uniformed men poured out of the barroom and surrounded him, guns drawn.

84

Stillman said smugly, "Speaking of D.C. cops, here they are. Lieutenant, this is your man—Quentin Chance."

They frisked him, took his pistol, handcuffed his wrists behind his back, and shoved him toward the car Stillman had used. The security officer called, "Better think up a better story than the one you gave me, Chance. Only an idiot would believe it."

Before Chance could reply, the lieutenant turned around. "That's enough, Stillman. You done your dirty work, get the hell outta here."

"But—the car, my ride home?"

"You're a snitch and a prick," the lieutenant snapped, "so fuck your way home. Get outta my sight."

"I'll tell the captain about this," Stillman blurted.

"Be my guest—he loves guys like you, Stillman, we all do." Back to Stillman, the lieutenant lowered Chance's head and eased him into the rear seat, got in beside him. A black plainclothes cop sat next to Chance on the far side. The other two got in front and the car pulled away. Chance turned and saw Stillman standing on the sidewalk, watching the receding car.

The lieutenant said, "So much for loyalty and fraternity, eh? Everyone in the CIA like him?"

"I hope not," Chance said, and the lieutenant muttered, "Me, too."

Under other circumstances, Chance thought, he could get to like the lieutenant. The officer had a craggy face, white eyebrows and sideburns, and a crisscross of old stitch scars around his mouth. Parted, the lips revealed two gold teeth. The lieutenant's torso was bulky, shoulders powerful; Chance speculated that he'd played tackle for Fordham or Boston College, though he was too light for the NFL. He asked, "Redskins fan?"

"Hell, yes. This year they go all the way."

Chance nodded agreement. Beyond the lieutenant's profile Chance could see the Capitol and its lighted dome. As they passed the Supreme Court building Chance said, "Time to pay homage to Ernie Miranda."

"Explain."

He gestured at the building. "You haven't read me my rights."

The lieutenant grunted. "Time for that when we get to head-

85

quarters." His eyes regarded Chance with mild curiosity. "You worth all this late-night trouble?"

"No way," said Chance, "but that's not what you'll read."

"They'll blow it up, huh? Damn papers."

Behind them a car speeded up, passed close on the left. So close that metal grated, hooked, clung. The driver swore and tried to disengage, but the overtaking car was slightly ahead, turning, forcing them toward the curb. "God*damn!*" the lieutenant yelled as the car jumped the curb and smashed hard into a lamppost.

The sudden impact slammed Chance forward. Dazed, he heard doors open, looked up, and saw his escorts get out, hands raised. The driver's face was bloody. The radiator steamed.

"You, too," a voice ordered. "Outside." Chance crawled out and was shoved into the other car. There was a man behind the wheel. Outside, three masked men held guns on the four policemen.

When Chance was seated, the gunmen backed into the waiting car, still covering the cops.

As the car raced away Chance figured he'd been better off with the police. For these men had to be the killers of Sosnowski.

FIFTEEN

The car slowed, turned onto East Capitol Street, and continued toward the river. The masked gunmen were utterly silent and Chance had nothing to offer. He was still dazed by crash impact and his spine and neck ached abominably.

He was bitter toward Stillman for betraying him, handing him over to the police, jeering at his story, but of course it was the Agency's way of keeping their institutional skirts from being muddied. CIA could pat itself on the back for delivering a wanted man to justice.

His captors were armed with Colt's latest handgun, the AM 2000. Their small hands made the black pistols seem oversize, adding to the silent menace. The car he was riding in was a black, late-model Chrysler New Yorker. One masked man wore jeans and a dark sweater, the other two charcoal gray single-breasted suits, white shirts, and black ties. Like undertakers, he thought, dressed for the occasion.

I shouldn't have called Stainbeck, he told himself; Jan Abrams would have heard me out and known what to do. Too late now.

The car crossed the bridge to Anacostia and the driver began turning up one street and down another, then doubling back to throw off possible pursuit. Finally, lights out, the Chrysler bumped into a junkyard crowded with rusted cars, and as the driver braked the entrance gate closed.

Chance envisioned himself compressed in a bundle of scrap metal shipped to Japan. Handcuffed, he could do nothing. He was going to die.

He was made to walk to the open doors of a VW minivan. Inside it he sat down on the rough flooring and stretched out his legs. A masked man got in and sat down facing him. Presently the van backed out of the junkyard and for a few minutes drove seemingly at random—until Chance heard the distinctive hollow sound of bridge underplanking beneath the wheels. From that he inferred that he was being taken back into the District of Columbia. To the Soviet embassy?

The smashup and the jolting ride worsened the pain until Chance had to clench his jaws to keep from moaning aloud. He concentrated on the man facing him. Only his eyes were visible in the mask's horizontal slit. Below, there was a dark sweater, gloved hands, dark trousers, and Converse All Stars. Until now, Chance had not spoken. He said, "You mebbe *ninja*-man?"

The eyes focused on him, and through the muffling mask the man spoke. "Who I am hardly concerns you. But, no, I am not *ninja*-man. You have seen too many Japanese-made movies."

"Guess so." Chance again subsided into silence, surprised by the man's precise diction, his unaccented English. Sosnowski's killers had sounded quite different.

The man spoke again. "I imagine you were surprised when we took you from the police."

"I was," Chance agreed, "and it was very smoothly done. How did you locate me?"

"The Metropolitan Police use radios extravagantly—never thinking that others might be listening. No more questions now."

The paving was much smoother than Anacostia's and because the van stopped frequently Chance inferred that the driver was obeying traffic lights. That told him only that the van was moving through populated areas.

Chance said, "You've gone to a lot of trouble to get me, but if you're looking for secret information, I haven't any. I left the Agency years ago."

"Be patient," the man said, "and many questions will be answered."

"Before I'm killed?"

The man said nothing. He stood up, looked through a small window, and said, "Almost there." He braced himself as the van turned into a drive, then slanted down into what Chance decided was an underground parking area. The van turned slowly, backed and braked. The engine stopped, the rear doors opened.

Two young men with black hair and oriental features motioned him out. Their builds were slight and neither was armed. One of them said, "Come with us, please," and escorted him to a steel-shod door. Behind him, Chance heard the van drive away. One man pressed an electronic sequential lock and the door moved aside. They led him down a tiled corridor that reminded Chance of a hotel basement passageway, opened a door, and led Chance into what seemed to be a windowless medical examining room. He decided he was in a hospital.

Behind him one of his escorts steadied his wrists, a key grated, and the handcuffs were removed. Chance stretched his arms. A side door opened and a white-gowned man came in. Like Chance's captors, the man was of slight build. His face was narrow, with oriental features and sallow skin. "Take off all your clothing except your shorts," he ordered.

Painfully, Chance pulled off his jacket and shirt, dropped his trousers, and stepped out of his shoes. The room was cold. He shivered. "Over here." The man gestured at a tilt table under an X-ray machine. As Chance lay down, the man said, "I am a licensed physician, you have nothing to fear."

After two frontal and two side X rays Chance sat on an examining stool while a female assistant—also oriental—took blood samples from his finger and ear and carried the slides to a microscope on the far side of the room. She wore a white button-front covering that showed the hem of a blue pleated skirt, white stockings, and rubber-soled white shoes. Her legs were slightly bowed, her feet pigeon-toed. Under white gauze netting her black hair was cut page-boy style, and she wore thick metal-rimmed bifocals. The woman was as efficient and silent as an automaton.

Chance got into his jacket and waited while the X rays were developed. The doctor clipped them to a light screen and studied them carefully. Turning to Chance, he said, "Those two ribs are cracked and must be immobilized for a while."

The assistant brought a roll of wide tape and held a gauze pad over the rib contusion while the doctor wound tape around Chance's torso. Afterward the doctor asked, "Any kidney pain?"

"No."

"Urine blood?"

Chance shook his head.

"Are you hungry?"

Chance nodded.

"For now you may have liquids. You like chicken soup?"

"If it's good."

The doctor spoke to his assistant in a language Chance assumed was Chinese. She disappeared, and the doctor said, "I will show you to your quarters."

"You mean, my cell."

"Hardly," the doctor said, "but then you are still confused by all that has happened. Tomorrow you will have many questions answered, and it is important that you be rested. After eating, please take this sleeping pill—I assure you it is nothing more than that—and compose yourself."

He led Chance out of the treatment room and along the tiled corridor to a wooden door. Unlocking it, the doctor said, "These are your quarters while you remain with us."

"How long will that be?"

"At least until your ribs are sound." The assistant entered the room with a tray that held a soup bowl and a china spoon. She placed it on a small table and withdrew. Chance went in and found himself in clean surroundings. The windowless walls were hung with oriental ink-brush drawings and colorful paintings. There was a closet, a bathroom, and a hospital-style bed. Chance sat on it and looked up at the doctor, who said, "Please consider yourself a guest here. For reasons you will understand tomorrow, it is important that you not leave—nor try to—without permission. Any reasonable request will be granted. The bell is for your use." He looked at his wristwatch. "Although it is near dawn, I bid you good night."

Chance moved over to the table as the doctor left, locking the door. Chance lifted the spoon and tasted the soup, finding it delicious. The broth contained fine noodles and silvery fibers of shark fin. He ate hungrily, swallowing the last of the soup with his sleeping pill.

Under the pillow he found short oriental-style pajamas and got into them, noticing that the tape around his ribs reduced the pain of moving. He turned off the ceiling light and lay on his back under sheet and blanket.

Closing his eyes, Chance realized that he couldn't remember such complete exhaustion. Somehow he had been plunged into the vortex of a complex operation. He had become a double fugitive, considering the snatch from the police car. Stillman's people would probably believe he had planned it all. And if Stillman believed he had that kind of power, the security officer would have his share of sleepless nights. Terrific!

Whoever my captors are, Chance thought as sleep washed over him, they've fed and treated me, given me a comfortable bed—and a degree of hope. Even though tomorrow everything could change.

SIXTEEN

Chance slept until noon, rang for food, and showered while waiting for it. The bathroom provided shaving equipment, toothbrush, and toothpaste.

His breakfast tray held a plate of egg and noodles, round slices of sweet toast, and a pot of aromatic tea. He ate everything and drank most of the tea. At 1:30 two young oriental males escorted him up a staircase to the second floor, where he was shown into a handsomely decorated office. Thick rugs, wax-rubbed rosewood furniture, antique bronzes, terra-cotta horses and heads, delicate renderings of bamboo and marsh birds. Red velvet drapes concealed two windows.

The man seated behind the desk wore a gray tunic buttoned to the throat. His hair and eyebrows were silvery white, his smooth skin the color of blanched almond, yet, Chance thought, he must be well into his seventies. He waited for the man to acknowledge his presence.

Finally the man said, "Please be seated." A finger movement dismissed Chance's escorts, and Chance chose a cushioned rosewood chair. When they were alone the man asked, "Do you have any idea where we are, Mr. Chance?" His voice was flat, unrhythmic.

Chance looked around. "I've concluded that I'm in a foreign embassy."

"Which one?"

"The Chinese embassy."

The man nodded. "The embassy of the People's Republic of

China. You are an observant man, Mr. Chance, able to draw inferences together and form logical conclusions. Now I will ask if you know or have formed a theory as to why you were brought here?"

"Not yet, not that I haven't tried."

The man nodded. "Then you will not immediately reject the possibility that we share convergent interests."

"I'm open-minded," Chance replied.

"Will you then accept my word that we intend you no harm?"

"Your people could have killed me very easily. Instead I've been well cared for, so I assume my life means something to you."

"It does. May I ask if you are in pain?"

"Very little. Much less than last night."

"There must be many questions in your mind. Some of them I will respond to. Others must be retained behind the veil of secrecy, at least for the present. Now I will exercise a host's prerogative and make some inquiries of you. To begin with, how much do you know?"

"Know—of what?"

"The man Sosnowski—he told you nothing?"

Chance shook his head. "When I entered my apartment he was drugged. I was shot by one of his captors, and when I recovered consciousness Sosnowski was dead. The killers were gone."

"So he never spoke." He looked down at his long, polished fingernails. "Later you were betrayed—as Pavel Sosnowski was betrayed when he reached Washington three nights ago." His gaze settled on Chance. "You did not expect to see the Russian?"

"I'd forgotten he existed," Chance said. "Why did he come?"

The man considered. "I will tell you part of it. Sosnowski was a messenger, a courier. Opposing interests arranged that he be intercepted before he could reach this embassy. A crude effort was undertaken to blame his death on you."

"Was he killed by his own people—the KGB?"

"As of now we are unsure where the order originated. But we know that the details and purpose of his journey were learned by—let us say—a hostile faction in Moscow. Accordingly, there was ample time to arrange his interception. Unfortunately for you,

93

the conspirators selected you to implicate. Fortunately for you, you survived."

"To be suspected of his murder."

"That much of the plot survived with you. But I think they would have mounted a second attempt against you, anything to prevent your appearance at a public trial to establish your innocence."

"When your team snatched me I thought it *was* a second try."

"Understandably." He opened a small drawer and brought out Chance's wallet-checkbook. "An interesting souvenir," he said, handing it back to Chance.

"It didn't convince the man who betrayed me."

"I suggest that you consider your CIA in terms of a small nation. Nations have neither friendships nor loyalties—only enduring interests, it's been said."

"What pisses me off is that no one cared whether I was guilty or innocent."

"After all, Mr. Chance, it seemed entirely possible—circumstantially—that you had indeed killed the Russian, and made good your escape. To avoid complications in this atmosphere of growing Russian-American détente, you were sacrificed." His hands spread. "As simple as that."

The man unfolded the *Washington Post* and held it up to Chance. CIA AGENT SOUGHT IN KILLING OF HUNGARIAN STUDENT the headline read.

"Hungarian?"

"Sosnowski's cover. That was corrected in a later edition, by an anonymous phone call to the editor. The Soviet embassy has not yet confirmed or denied, but it will."

"And try to find me, finish me off."

"Unquestionably."

"I haven't much of a future," Chance said, "have I?"

"Your future is a subject we will discuss tomorrow, Mr. Chance. Between now and then I would appreciate your helping identify the two men who kidnapped and killed the courier, Sosnowski."

Chance nodded. "For me it's awkward not knowing your name."

"For our purposes you may call me Mr. Hsing. If you feel up

to it, perhaps you could begin the identification process this afternoon."

"In return for your protection it's the least I can do," he said, while wondering how long he would live after providing what Hsing wanted.

In a small, well-lighted basement room Chance sat at a table between his two escorts, the templates and transparencies of an Identikit spread out before them. The mustached man's face was the easiest to reproduce, so Chance selected a facial formation and mustache, then added hair, eyes, nose, lips, and chin. Sitting back he said, "The nose was hooked, skin brown."

The Chinese who called himself Sam, said, "Teeth?"

"Too dark to notice."

Sam carefully moved the assembled likeness to the end of the table where a camera was installed, pointing downward. He photographed the likeness and returned with the templates.

The second man—the one who had shot Chance—was harder. "I was looking at his gun," Chance explained, "but he was about the same height and build as the other. Same skin color, beard, same dark hair." He began moving pieces together, trying and discarding as he went. After half an hour he had a second likeness. "It's as good as I can do," he told them.

The Chinese who called himself Lou (Liu? Chance wondered) asked if Chance had formed an opinion as to ethnic background.

"Mediterranean," Chance replied. "Turk, Cypriot, Maltese, Armenian . . . maybe Lebanese."

"Arab?"

"Quite possibly. Yes," he said, suddenly recalling Cairo accents, "I'd say both were Arab."

The Chinese exchanged glances. "That's very helpful, Mr. Chance."

"You think they were based here?"

"I have no idea," Sam said, "but that's where we'll begin. Lou, print those photos and we'll start circulating copies."

That evening Chance dined with Sam and Lou in a small room near the embassy kitchen. The food was exquisite—thinly sliced crisp vegetables, bean sprouts, pork, chicken, shrimp, and steamed buns. As they talked, it came out that Sam was a graduate of Berkeley and Lou had graduated from Michigan State. Lou's family was in Canton, Sam's lived near Hsian. Both had lost relatives during the Great Cultural Revolution. Both young men, Chance assumed, were intelligence officers, as he once had been. As though to confirm his assumption, Sam asked if Chance had ever conducted operations against mainland China.

Chance shook his head. "No."

Lou said, "But you would have if ordered."

"Of course."

"You have no sympathy for the PRC?"

"I haven't thought much about it," Chance replied, then remembered Jan Abrams's words. "China is a fact. Your country has to be taken into account if only because of your gigantic population."

"And our industrial capacity," Sam said proudly.

"Russia fears us," Lou remarked, and fell silent at a glance from his partner.

On that note dinner ended, and Chance went to bed after scanning current copies of *Time, Newsweek* and *Sports Illustrated*—supplied by Sam. It was satisfying to be treated with respect by the Chinese, Chance reflected, after being treated like shit by Stillman and the D.C. cops, his own countrymen.

The next day before lunch he was escorted to the office of Mr. Hsing, who was standing near the desk when Chance entered. Hsing gestured at a folded newspaper and Chance opened it on his desk. The headline read:

CIA AGENT FOILS ARREST
Pistol Killed Russian

Chance refolded the paper. "They're piling it on," he said tightly. "Don't miss tomorrow's episode."

Hsing regarded him thoughtfully. "I have carefully considered your situation and your future. The one desperate, the other promising—if you decide to make it so."

"I'm listening."

"I have a proposal to put to you."

"What is it?"

"That you cooperate in a project of immense importance to my government."

Chance stared at him. "As an agent for Communist China?"

"If you care to put it that way."

Chance sat down.

SEVENTEEN

Near the corner of Ninth and E streets in downtown Washington, Yusuf and Hamid unlocked the front door of their coffee store, reversed the CLOSED sign, and walked inside.

While Yusuf busied himself at the cash register, Hamid headed for the rear storage area and surveyed the piled bags of roasted coffee beans. They came from Colombia, Venezuela, Brazil, Syria, and Mexico. Having three special-blend orders to fill, Hamid drew beans from several bags until a five-gallon can was filled to the brim. He carried the can to the front of the store, began filling the top part of the electric grinder, and pressed the switch.

As his nostrils scented the warm, pleasant odor of fresh-ground coffee, Hamid felt grateful that the KGB hadn't set them up in a fish market. After filling three pound-size bags, Hamid added more beans to the grinder, got out an Egyptian cigarette, and lighted it.

Although the store was located near Washington's Chinatown it enjoyed very little Chinese business, the Chinese preferring tea. So the partners were surprised to find three Chinese their first customers of the morning. Two were men, the third an attractive female in blue jeans and a frilly top. The men walked to the counter while the young woman closed the door and reversed the cardboard sign. Yusuf called, "Hey, don't do that!"

The woman stared at him without expression, and when Yusuf looked down he saw a pistol pointing at his belly.

The other man's pistol covered Hamid.

The partners kept a licensed revolver under the counter to frighten off drunks, derelicts, and stoned teenage blacks, but the weapon was four feet from the cash register and Yusuf discarded the idea of trying to go for it.

"In back." The pistol waved. "Both of you."

Hamid turned off the grinder and, with his arms raised, walked sullenly to the storage room, followed by his partner.

"Turn around," the Chinese ordered, "and put your hands behind you."

Both men felt their wrists being tied with thin cord that bit into flesh. Then their ankles were bound. Pushed from behind, they fell against stacked coffee bags, turned over, and looked up at the two Chinese.

The older of the two, the one wearing rimless glasses, said, "Not to waste time, we know that you killed the Russian agent and shot the American. My question is: Who ordered you, and how did you receive the order?"

After a glance at Yusuf, Hamid shook his head. "You're crazy. We're coffee merchants, not killers."

The door opened and the woman came in, closing the door behind her. From her purse she drew out a leather folder of surgical instruments, selected a shiny lancet, and knelt beside Hamid. Methodically she sliced open his shirt, laying bare his hirsute chest, then drew the lancet blade lightly down his sternum. Horrified, Hamid watched blood ooze from the cut. Angrily, Yusuf said, "You're making a mistake, we know nothing of Russians and Americans."

"Ah, but you do," said the team leader, "and one of you is going to answer my questions." He nodded at the woman who undid Hamid's belt and opened the trouser fly, baring his genitals.

Hamid looked away. Blood pounded in his temples. He felt sick. The lancet moved to his chest, neared his right nipple and rested for a moment. Then the woman's fingers moved deftly, Hamid felt a flash of pain and saw his nipple on the flat side of the lancet. Blood bubbled from the open wound. With a moan he vomited.

Yusuf said, "You wouldn't try this if you knew who you're dealing with."

"I know exactly who you are—well-trained members of the KGB team for special tasks. Who is your controller?"

"You've made a mistake," Yusuf said defiantly. "We're from Palestine, not Russia."

"In my time," said the leader, "I have trained Palestinian terrorists, Africans, Latinos. I know that nationality is nothing. Who is your controller?"

Yusuf bit his lip and said nothing. The leader nodded at the woman, who lifted Hamid's penis in her left hand, extended the foreskin, and cut around it while Hamid bucked and screamed. "Be quiet," the woman said, "or I will cut out your tongue." She laid the foreskin on Hamid's chest. Blood oozed from Hamid's circumcision.

To Yusuf the leader said, "His testicles come next, then yours. You have met with Berlikov?"

Yusuf's eyes were fixed on Hamid's wounds. "I don't know Berlikov."

"Perhaps by a different name, his work name."

Yusuf shook his head. The leader gestured at him and the woman squatted at his side. As with Hamid she opened Yusuf's shirt and trousers, made a shallow cut across his belly. Yusuf screamed in terror and began to sob. The leader said, "Consider how difficult life is for the blind." The scalpel feinted at Yusuf's eyes, twisted back and forth glinting. Suddenly the scalpel entered his nostril and cut upward. Blood surged from the open flap. He felt the woman grip his penis and shrieked.

"Is it worth it?" the leader asked calmly. "Piece by piece you will be taken apart until you reveal all you know." He looked at his wristwatch, sat down on a coffee bag.

"They will kill us," Hamid said faintly.

"Not if you flee them," the leader said. "Besides, who will tell your control that you informed? We merely want to know his name and channel."

As the scalpel neared his penis Yusuf writhed, then blurted, "A phone call summons us."

The scalpel halted.

"Go on."

"We are met at the Jefferson Memorial."

"Who meets you?"

"I don't know."

"His work name." The scalpel moved closer to his penis. Frantic at the threat of being circumcised like a Jew, Yusuf managed, "Calls himself Dayton—Mr. Dayton."

"Very good. Pretense has been abolished." The leader regarded Hamid calmly. "What have you to add?"

Hamid cursed and prayed in Arabic. The woman gripped the end of his tongue and made a shallow, transverse cut. Hamid felt warm, salty blood flowing into the reservoir of his jaw. When she released his tongue he fainted.

The leader turned to Yusuf. "When you contact control, how is it done?"

"By telephone."

"The number?"

"416-7660."

"Confirm."

"Look in the cash register, under the twenty-dollar bills."

The younger Chinese male left and opened the cash register. He lifted three twenties, checked the penciled number, and returned to nod to his leader, who said, "You call, then whom do you ask for?"

"Dayton."

"Dayton is a cutout," the leader said, "a subagent. Who is his principal?"

"He never said."

"Never mentioned Berlikov?"

"Never."

"A disciplined agent," the leader said. "We'll have a talk with him." He got up and looked around, then went to the front part of the store and cleaned out the cash register, leaving the drawer open to suggest robbery.

The woman got up and took a small camera from her purse. She photographed the partners together, then separately, and returned the camera to her purse. Yusuf could hardly believe his good fortune. "You've got your information, release us."

The woman replaced the bloody scalpel in her kit, extracted one with a larger blade, and bent over Hamid. Her arm moved swiftly as the blade slashed through Hamid's windpipe. A second slash opened his carotid. Yusuf screeched and tried to roll away, but she caught him with one arm and quickly cut his throat. While both bodies convulsed in the brief agony of death, she wiped the blade on a coffee sack and returned it to her surgical kit.

At the telephone the leader dialed the contact number. When a man's voice answered, he said, "District Dry Cleaning?"

"Wrong number." The connection broke.

With a slight smile, the leader replaced the telephone and removed his fingerprints. "A man," he said, "whose name and address the reversed phone book will provide."

They left the store then and walked north into Chinatown to caution the owner of the Cheong Lee restaurant, who had recognized the two coffee merchants from photos he had been shown.

EIGHTEEN

From his chair, Chance faced Mr. Hsing, who said, "My proposal surprises you."

"Startles me," Chance said, feeling his throat suddenly dry.

"Consider the quid pro quo. My people extracted you from a situation that threatened your life, and still does, after your own CIA had betrayed you. I suggest that nowhere else could you have found comparable refuge."

Chance agreed with a nod. "About this important mission for your government—will I have to kill anyone?"

"No."

"Act against U.S. interests?"

"No. As I said, it is in behalf of the People's Republic of China. I may honestly describe your role as quasi-diplomatic."

"In this country?"

"In Europe. A desirable location for you until you are cleared of the murder charge."

"However long that takes," Chance mused. Europe sounded good. He looked at Hsing. "False identity?"

"And altered appearance. It is in no one's interest that you be arrested by Interpol and returned here."

"Can you tell me who I will be dealing with?"

"A Soviet official is the most important figure. You will be supported by PRC personnel and by an American in whom we have confidence."

"I'd prefer Americans not be involved."

"He is necessary to your cover."

Chance shrugged. "I'll accept your judgment." He paused. "You understand I don't speak Russian."

"That is known. But you speak German and French."

"How long will the mission take?"

"A week, a month, six months. . . . Depends on circumstances as they evolve—or fail to."

"This Russian is an agent of yours?"

"No." Hsing seated himself behind his desk. "If you accept, Mr. Chance, you will be given full details, but I believe you now know enough on which to form a decision."

"I'll have to think about it."

"Of course. Let us say today and tomorrow. Then I must have your answer."

"That's agreeable," Chance said. "I should be able to reach a decision before then. One final question, Mr. Hsing—if the mission is satisfactorily completed, what options will I have?"

"For one, you will be welcomed into my country. Another is to relocate where you choose, with financial assistance."

Chance got up from the chair. "I appreciate everything you have provided, and I'll carefully consider your proposal." As though I have a choice, he thought, and was walking toward the door when a knock sounded. Hsing instructed, "Please open the door and wait a moment, Mr. Chance. There may be something of interest to you."

Sam walked past Chance and placed an envelope before Hsing, who opened it and studied the contents briefly, then beckoned to Chance. "Please confirm that these are the men you described."

The first photograph showed two bodies lying side by side against a pile of sacks, legs and wrists bound. The next two were close-ups of two faces with staring eyes.

Swallowing, Chance laid down the prints. "They killed Sosnowski," he said.

"Soviet agents," Sam said, "who performed special tasks for the KGB *Rezidentura* in Washington."

"You work fast," Chance said tightly.

"When we have expert assistance," Mr. Hsing said, "such as yours."

Gripped by the knowledge of death, Chance turned and left the room.

NINETEEN

Reading the evening paper in his room, Chance came across a short paragraph ascribing the murders of two D.C. coffee merchants to a morning robbery. That both men had been tortured suggested the killers had been looking for drugs or hidden money. The victims' names were given as Yusuf al-Gizarriah and Hamid Hasouri, both Arab immigrants.

Chance cut out the paragraph and folded it in his wallet, then lay back on his bed and resumed thinking. Hsing's mission sounded both kosher and advantageous, and with Sosnowski's killers dead Chance could think of no way to clear himself. Attorney Jones had done very little to earn his retainer, and Chance reflected that there was probably very little he could do while his client remained a fugitive.

Reluctantly, Chance admired the efficiency with which the embassy's action cell had tracked down the two killers. If he accepted Hsing's mission, he would have to carry it out—or face deadly reprisal if he tried a double cross. But why should I? he wondered. If the job has anything to do with Sosnowski's mission, I want to know about it.

Before dying, the two killers had been tortured, according to the story and the photographs. What questions had been asked them? What information had they supplied? Sam had said nothing about that, nor had Hsing.

Arab killers had destroyed his brother as casually as an insect, so why should the torture of two Arab assassins trouble him? The answer, he told himself, was that it shouldn't. So he would not let it concern him. Even had they confessed to Sosnowski's murder, to framing him for their crime, the KGB would never have permitted them to live. Dead, they could not plea-bargain, and Department 13 had scores of skilled assassins available to replace them. In any case, Chance reasoned, the Arabs hadn't devised the plot; his quarrel lay with those who had. And Hsing wants their identities.

One area in which our interests coincide. And there may be others. For Mr. Hsing was much more than he appeared to be.

From his Asian studies Chance had learned the history of modern China, read about the two-year Long March to Yenan refuge when the Communists under Mao had fled Chiang's armies. He had read about the wartime years when Mao hoarded his resources and let the Nationalists fight the Japanese; then the postwar political victory of Mao, midwifed by the United States; the mainland's Communist paralysis; Mao's intervention in the Korean and Vietnam wars . . .

Chance's mind focused on recall, and memory began releasing a flow of stored details.

Mr. Hsing wasn't old enough to have been a Long March comrade, but his father and mother were in that company. Second child of a Moscow-trained commissar named Hsiao Li-po, Hsing had been born in Yenan. Educated in Moscow, Peking, Rome, and London, the son had risen through Communist party ranks until, with thousands of other educated Chinese, he was swept aside by the Great Cultural Revolution, not beaten to death or shot, but imprisoned. One cellmate was an American Dominican priest, and in sharing their misery, Hsing and Father Dougherty became close friends. Hsing declined conversion to the Christian faith, but he received a different gift—fluent American English.

After the death of Mao and the degradation of the Gang of Four, priest and Chinese patriot were released. Hsing was rehabilitated by the new regime and appointed to the Foreign Ministry. Dougherty returned to America and before dying wrote his China memoir, one of the books Chance had read with interest, though unaware he would meet one of the players.

For the last three years Chance had been periodically aware of Hsing's rise in the Chinese Communist hierarchy. Last year a story from Peking announced the promotion to the post of deputy foreign minister Hsiao Kuan-hua, Hsing's true name. What the dispatch failed to mention was that the post included command of the Central Bureau of Information, Communist China's powerful intelligence agency.

Knowing those facts, Chance had been impressed by Hsiao's clandestine appearance in his Washington embassy, and he inferred that it had to do with the expected arrival of Sosnowski from Moscow.

Why else did Hsiao order my rescue? Chance asked himself, if not to find leads to those who ordered Sosnowski's interception? The Soviet officials responsible are his enemies, and mine.

Hsiao is a disciplined and intelligent man, Chance mused. And his power is such that he is able to honor whatever promises he makes. Moreover, I have no choice. In Europe at least I won't be hunted, as in my own country.

Hsiao offers me time to find redemption, and freedom to develop a future life worth living. The best offer I've had, and the only one.

Before sleep came, he thought of Carla and was thankful that she would never know of his public disgrace.

TWENTY

Alvin Bernbaum lived alone in a walk-up apartment in a disintegrating neighborhood east of Washington's Union Station. He was a physically unattractive man of forty-two with thick lips, protruberant nose, thick spectacles, and long, matted hair. He dressed in an unkempt way, clothing spotted with driblets of food from the cheap restaurants where he ate. Unshaven and scruffy, Alvin Bernbaum looked like a pillager of trash cans and garbage pails, a relic of the protest sixties who had outlived his times, and hopes.

His only friends were associates who worked with him on a weekly tabloid called *Telescope,* an extremist rag that appealed to readers captivated by the conspiracy theory of history. According to *Telescope,* the president and his foreign policy were controlled by Wall Street Jewish bankers. General George Marshall had been part of the international Communist conspiracy, as had President Dwight Eisenhower. President Kennedy had been killed by the CIA. Israel was plotting to control the Middle East and Europe. Germs developed in CIA laboratories were responsible for the AIDS epidemic. . . . *Telescope* offered a weird, irrational mix of Fascist and Communist themes.

The publisher of *Telescope,* a defrocked preacher, embezzler of church funds, and alumnus of Leavenworth, often pointed to Bernbaum when questioned about the anti-Semitism of his publication. Bernbaum is a Jew, he would say. If I were anti-Semitic, would I employ him? And if Alvin was present, he would grin and peer through thick lenses at the challenger.

So there was a symbiotic relationship between Alvin Bernbaum and the disreputable tabloid. Alvin wrote the kind of sensational articles the publisher demanded, and in turn *Telescope* provided Alvin with cover for his true work as a cutout for the KGB.

Sitting at his small, food-stained kitchen table, Alvin pushed aside his chipped dinner plate and picked food from his teeth with a dirty thumbnail. He was watching Dan Rather give it to the Bush administration when his doorbell rang.

With a lingering glance at Rather's stern face, Alvin went to the doorway. "Who's there?"

"Special delivery."

Alvin considered. Occasionally his publisher sent rush night work that way, and less frequently some obsessed reader would volunteer paranoid material in a way guaranteed to get his attention. Alvin freed the the snub chain and looked out.

The hallway was dark, but light from within the apartment revealed three oriental faces. He tried to shut the door, but the nearest man pushed against the door, forcing Alvin backward. "What the hell?" he snapped. "Who are you?"

As the other two Orientals came in, the first man said, "The question is: Who are *you?*"

Better. A mistake. "Alvin Bernbaum," he said indignantly, and saw the woman walk to his telephone. She read off the number aloud. "416-7660."

The first man said, "Your telephone?"

"Of course. It's in my name and this is my apartment. See, you've made a mistake." He cringed when he saw the other man bolt the entrance door. When he looked back he saw the snub nose of a revolver.

"No mistake, Alvin. And you have another name, don't you?"

"Wha—I don't know what you mean."

"I think you do. Because your work name is Dayton." The man's expression was pleasant, but Alvin felt suddenly chilled. Who *were* these people? Vietnamese? "Look," he said, "I was against what the U.S. did in Vietnam, I demonstrated against it, wrote against it."

"That's commendable," said the man, "but it has nothing to do with your work for the KGB."

There it was—although he couldn't believe what he was hearing. Swallowing, he croaked, "FBI? I get to call a lawyer, I don't have to talk to you."

"But you will," the man said coldly, and Alvin felt warm urine crawling down the inside of his thigh. My God, he was pissing his pants! He'd never—

"Yusuf and Hamid are dead," the man said. "They didn't want to talk—but they did. And so we're here."

"Dead?" He couldn't believe it. "When?"

"You should read the morning papers."

Alvin felt his body tremble. The second man went behind him and tied his wrists together. Ankles next, and Alvin was pushed backward into the small room's only chair. "What do you want?" he gasped.

"A name."

The woman took a flat case from her purse and opened it. Alvin could see a row of shiny surgical instruments. His stomach turned over. He managed to say, "What name?"

"Your controller."

"Control—?" He tried to look ignorant of the term.

"The man who ordered you to have those coffee merchants kill Sosnowski and Chance."

Alvin felt the compression of the room. It was becoming smaller and smaller. There was no way out. At the sight of a scalpel in the woman's hand, he screamed.

When his voice died away the man said patiently, "Tell me and you won't have to suffer. You were the cutout, Mr. Dayton—"

"Don't call me that!"

"But I must. It's your name in the world we both inhabit. Yusuf told me before he died."

The woman knelt in front of the chair, unbuckled his belt, and opened his fly. She lifted his shrunken penis and stroked the glans with the flat side of the blade. "Oh, God," Alvin moaned, "don't do it. Please—I'm begging you." His throat and mouth were so dry he could hardly get the words out.

"The name."

Alvin's world—both worlds—were vanishing. Where was the KGB's promised protection? He was abandoned. He began to sob.

Tears rolled through his cheek stubble. Deftly, the woman severed a clump of pubic hair and tossed it at his face.

Alvin croaked, "They'll kill me if I talk."

"We'll kill you if you don't—very slowly. With unimaginable pain."

The woman nicked penis flesh. Alvin saw flowing blood and screamed again. The man behind him cut off the scream with a handkerchief. "Have you decided?"

Desperately, Alvin nodded. The handkerchief fell away and he gasped, "Berlikov."

"Major General Nikolai Petrovich Berlikov, the KGB *rezident?*"

Alvin nodded frantically.

"And you're one of his illegals."

"Yes."

"Why did he order Sosnowski killed?"

"I don't know. I take orders, pass them along. Never ask questions."

"Good agent discipline," the man said, and gestured at the kneeling woman. She got to her feet and put away the scalpel.

From behind, Alvin felt the other man's hand brush his neck as though feeling for an artery. It pressed on a nerve; pain sickened him. The room became dim, then dark.

For a few moments longer the man continued pressing the nerve. Then the woman peeled back Alvin's eyelid to flash a penlight on his pupil. She put the light away and the younger man opened his windbreaker and uncoiled weathered laundry line from around his torso.

Together they dragged Alvin to his bathroom, where they severed his bonds and tied a slide noose around his neck. The two men lifted his body upright while the woman climbed nimbly onto the edge of the bathtub. She drew the rope's end around a heavy water pipe that ran across the flaking ceiling, tightened it with her weight before knotting it. The men moved back, leaving Alvin's body suspended from the pipe. His legs kicked and his hands clawed at the rope until the younger man grasped Alvin's hips and pulled downward. Alvin's tongue protruded, grew purple. His glasses fell off, shattered in the tub. His trousers were stained with even more released urine. A foul smell filled the room as his bowels gave way. The woman gripped his slack hand, felt for a pulse, and shook her head.

Leaving the light on, they left the bathroom. The younger man turned out the kitchen light and switched off the TV just as Dan Rather was signing off.

"Easier than I expected," the team leader said. "Berlikov. I can't say I'm surprised."

Before leaving, they turned off the living room light, reset the spring lock, and closed the door.

"So much for Mr. Dayton," the leader commented. "We'll leave the building one at a time, go in different directions. I'll see you in the morning as usual."

They left at five-minute intervals, and Alvin's body was not discovered until the following day, when his publisher came by to find out why his collaborator had failed to show up for work.

TWENTY-ONE

"Mr. Hsing" tapped a long fingernail on the polished desk top. "I am gratified that you have decided to cooperate in an undertaking of great significance to the world, Mr. Chance. If it is successful, and details ever become known, you will occupy an enviable place in history."

"That sounds tempting," Chance replied, "and I'm ready when you are."

"Good. Before you leave Washington your facial appearance will be altered and you will be equipped with new documentation and another name. All," he added, "to enhance your chances of success," and smiled.

Chance nodded, no longer feeling threatened. "I have a request, sir. I need to contact my attorney and a female friend. The one in connection with the charges against me, and the other to close up my apartments."

"Hsing" thought it over. After a pause he said, "It would be unwise for you to telephone from this embassy, and hazardous for you to make outside calls. I suggest that you write letters instead, and I will have them mailed from, say, Mexico. Is that agreeable?"

"It is."

"Anything further?"

Chance shook his head.

"Very well. Now, in anticipation of your positive response I have brought from Vancouver an eminent cosmetic and reconstructive surgeon who will make certain alterations in your appearance. Your recuperation—a short one, I understand—will begin here and end abroad. You will travel with me under diplomatic immunity, and in Paris we will part company. During the flight there will be ample time to brief you sufficiently. You will have an escort for companionship—you play chess?"

"I have."

"Good. Something to pass time while healing. Your escort will also arrange alias documentation so that when your bandages are removed you can begin work." He glanced at an old-fashioned stainless steel watch, the kind with hands.

"How soon do we leave?"

"Tomorrow. I hope the operation goes well, Mr. Chance."

"So do I."

He found Sam waiting outside the office door, and together they went down to the medical section, where Chance had been examined and treated on arrival. The nurse was there, and when Chance was lying back on the examining chair a door opened and a tall, thin Chinese came in. Without comment he turned Chance's head from left to right, pulled at the skin of his cheeks, and shined a penlight in Chance's nostrils. Then he stepped back. "My name is Shek," he said, "and I will be altering your features somewhat. To the extent possible, I will do so without your feeling pain. Discomfort, yes, but no acute pain. Ten days hence you will be able to walk the streets without being recognized. And you will breathe more freely because I will have reconstructed your damaged septum. A light anesthetic will put you into the equivalent of 'twilight sleep,' but if you feel pain, don't hesitate to say so. There are shaving implements over there; please shave as closely as possible without cutting your flesh."

While Chance shaved he looked closely at his face, realizing that it would never be the same again. A last look at a vanished man. Unavoidably his stomach tightened in a spasm of apprehension.

After drying his face Chance removed his coat and shirt and lay down on the chair, which the nurse had covered with a sterile sheet. A wheeled stand held surgical instruments, and Chance noticed a green oxygen tank and mask positioned nearby. Dr. Shek reappeared in operating gown, surgical gloves, and mask. The nurse inserted a needle in Chance's right arm and connected it to

115

a Y-form tube that carried fluid from two inverted flasks. "Serum and anesthetic," Dr. Shek explained. "First, I am going to remove two narrow triangles of flesh from the corners of your eyes to smooth wrinkles. Next, I take strips from just in front of your ears to tighten your face and mouth." He paused while the nurse swabbed Chance's face with pungent antiseptic. "Finally," he said, "the nose. For that I will insert two metal forms in your nostrils and break the bone against them. If necessary to cut, I will do so from inside, but I may not have to." A finger probed Chance's nose again. "The trauma will produce two cartoon-quality black eyes. As in China, leeches will be applied to hasten the return of normal skin color."

"Leeches?"

"Laboratory-grown and entirely sterile." He paused. "Feel anything?"

"Relaxed."

The doctor's hand moved and he said, "That?"

"Nothing." The surgeon showed him a long needle.

"Close your eyes."

The anesthetic made Chance feel warm and euphoric. He was floating on a soft, billowing cloud. As the light-dome lowered he closed his eyes, felt no pain but only the drawing friction of the first cut. He could hear voices speaking Chinese, hear the clink of instruments. . . . Later he felt mallet blows on his nose, hard and precise, and began breathing through his mouth. So far, no pain. He resumed drifting on his personal cloud.

When he opened his eyes the light-dome was dark, the room lighted only by a small lamp at the nurse's table. He could see a line of gauze running just under his eyelids. Gauze covered his nose, but he could breathe through it, thanks to small, protruding straws.

"Hello," he said, "I'm awake. How did it go?"

"Very well." The nurse got up and came over to him. "How do you feel?"

"Groggy . . . light-headed. Where's the doc?"

"Gone," she said. "You won't see him again."

He wet his lips and the nurse promptly held a glass tube to his mouth. "Water," she said, and he sucked thirstily. "How long did it take?"

She looked at her watch. "Just under three hours. You'll be flying tomorrow, so a good night's rest is important. There's a sleeping pill in your room beside the water carafe. If you feel discomfort or pain, ring for me."

"How do I get to the airport?"

"You will be told in the morning."

Sam came in and helped Chance sit upright. After resting a few moments Chance put his feet on the floor, then Sam and the nurse walked him to his room and eased him down on the bed.

Before leaving, Sam said, "There's paper and envelopes over there when you feel like writing. Or you can do it on the plane."

"Now is better," Chance said. "What time do we leave?"

"Early—are you hungry?"

"Maybe a cup of that chicken soup."

He dozed then, waking when the nurse brought soup and a glass straw. He drank half of it and dozed again. At two o'clock he woke, mind unclouded, and went to the writing table.

Paper and envelopes were blank white. With a ballpoint pen Chance wrote an impersonal letter to Veronica Talbot Boyce, c/o Sally Bevins at the River Road address. In it he asked Rony to seal his Charlottesville apartment to keep his possessions safe. He asked that a year's rent be paid in advance, either by herself or Wilson Jones. He described where he had left his car in the hotel parking garage, suggested she reclaim it for her own use or sell it, if she could. Finally, he thanked her and said he hoped to see her at some future time when the charges were dropped and he could return to the United States.

His letter to Wilson Jones included power of attorney authorizing Jones to pay legitimate bills and maintain his Georgetown apartment unoccupied for the next year. Chance suggested that together he and Rony carry out his wishes.

The final paragraph concerned Carla's future care. The hospital bills were to be sent to the attorney for payment from Chance's bank. Before Chance sealed the envelope he inserted a bullet-pierced check to give Jones the account number.

Not particularly tired, Chance turned on the television set

hoping for a mind-numbing old movie. Instead, the channel showed a female newscaster reviewing yesterday's international, national, and local disasters. The newsbreak included a brief summary of a murder in Suitland–Silver Hill, Maryland. The victim, a government employee, had been shot in his driveway shortly after arriving home. His name was Walter Stillman, and the police were working on the theory that he was the victim of Quentin Chance, who had been snatched from police custody by gunmen after his arrest for the murder of a Soviet citizen, Pavel Sosnowski. Chance was said by the police to be armed and dangerous, and any sightings should be reported promptly to the Metropolitan Police Department. The last was a voice-over while the screen showed Chance's photograph taken from his Agency pass. The next segment concerned the crash of a light plane, stolen by a teenager from a private airport. Chance turned off the set, wondering who had killed Stillman and why.

The police would assume he'd killed Stillman in reprisal for his treachery. Why look for anyone else?

Chance poured a glass of water and swallowed the sleeping pill. As he got between the sheets, he told himself that tomorrow's departure couldn't come too soon.

TWENTY-TWO

In the New York *Rezidentura,* General Berlikov received a personal eyes-only message from his Washington assistant. In the secure code room, Berlikov painstakingly decoded the letter groups, and a premonition of disaster enveloped him.

That Sosnowski was dead he knew from the press. He also knew that the American had escaped, twice. But Chance was being blamed for Sosnowski's murder, as planned, and his violent escape from police custody, probably arranged by CIA comrades, simply confirmed his guilt. What stunned Berlikov was the liquidation of the two Arab agents and their cutout, Dayton, that despicable but dependable Jew. Who could have done it but Chance? No one else had seen the Arabs.

Slowly he tore the message into strips, cross-tore them, and burned the pieces in a metal bowl for that purpose. Almost overnight he had lost a reliable deep-cover agent and two subagents— to a university student long out of the CIA. Unbelievable! Nevertheless, he reflected, their loyalties run deep, unlike ours. Chance knew where to turn for help. He swore aloud.

There were going to be questions coming at him from Moscow—tactful at first, a mere damage assessment without recriminations—but he had seen the investigative juggernaut move inexorably before, and he understood that if the least fault could be attached to his performance, he would be recalled, like others in the business, "for consultations." From which very few returned.

He remembered, asking when younger, about their reassignments only to be met with frowns or blank stares. Within days they became nonpersons, their families rudely evicted from treasured apartments, cars summarily repossessed, children expelled from privileged schools, families banished to the frozen wastes. . . . He shivered.

But General Sobatkin could block any such recrimination if convinced that it was the Arabs, the Arabs alone, who had screwed up. After all, Berlikov thought, I wasn't even *in* Washington when it all occurred. I was here in New York with plenty of witnesses to prove it. He blotted perspiration from his upper lip and decided he would have to see Yevgeni Lubovich and explain as best he could how things had gone sour.

And if Sobatkin—the real initiator of the disaster—proved unsympathetic, then he, Nikolai Berlikov, would produce the incriminating recording and force the old conspirator to set matters right. And in the unlikely event Sobatkin still refused to help him, there were higher places he could go, where the recording would be gratefully received by enemies of Sobatkin and the minister of defense, Marshal Yaroshenko.

He felt somewhat better about his prospects. After all, Sobatkin's scheme had been carried out; Major Sosnowski's mission had been aborted. In the eyes of the public and the law, Chance was guilty, and Chance was on the run, a despised and hunted fugitive. So he would put on a bold face with Sobatkin, refuse to accept criticism for the loss of three agents, however valued they were. Moreover, it was in Sobatkin's interest that those sensitive details not be aired. He decided to visit Sobatkin in Ottawa and tell him as much as needed to stop an investigation before it began. Berlikov printed a short message requesting an urgent interview with General Sobatkin, and gave it to the code clerk to encode and transmit priority.

Berlikov went to his room, packed his suitcase, and had tea and piroshki in the communal dining room, a long, cheerless hall with worn linoleum underfoot and rectangular tables joined to seat twenty or thirty on a side. Several of the tables held artificial flowers so dingy that Berlikov thought the decorative effort a disgrace. At the room's far end a woman in blue work clothing, cap on her head, stolidly mopped the floor. Overall, the place gave off a prison atmosphere, Berlikov reflected, and finished his solitary snack as quickly as he could. Two hours later Ottawa's response came in. Summoned to the code room, Berlikov scanned the clear text. Sobatkin's deputy regretted to inform General Berlikov that his superior was in Moscow and not expected back for two to three weeks. Should Berlikov's message be relayed to Sobatkin in Moscow?

Berlikov gave a sour glance to the code clerk. "Answer in one word," he told the clerk. "No."

Slowly he returned to the guest room that had been made available for his use and sat on the edge of the bed.

Into his mind entered the unwelcome thought that Dayton had identified him to Quentin Chance before dying. After all, Chance had forced Dayton's name from the Arabs, and the American would want to know the identity of Dayton's control. Meaning, he told himself, that Chance now knew who had ordered Sosnowski killed. Would Chance lie in wait to finish him with a well-aimed bullet?

Why not? It would be in keeping with what he knew of the American agent.

Berlikov pounded the bed with his fist. What was he to do now? Nothing, he told himself bitterly, but return to Washington and sweat it out. *Damn Yevgeni Lubovich Sobatkin!*

And damn Quentin Ransome Chance!

TWENTY-THREE

After breakfast Chance was taken to the medical section, where the nurse masked his head and face with gauze, leaving a narrow slit for his eyes. Sam joined him and led Chance to a metal basement door that gave out onto a service area where a private ambulance was waiting. Chance got in and lay down on the gurney. Attendants covered him with a blanket and strapped it across his body. Sam sat nearby, covering the windows with his searching gaze. Chance noticed a shoulder holster under Sam's coat; they were taking no chances.

"Where's Mr. Hsing?" he asked.

"In the ambassador's limousine. We're following it to the airport. When we reach the plane, you'll be carried into it as you are. Don't talk or move. When we're airborne I'll release you." The ambulance began to roll. "How are you feeling?"

"Not bad, skin's a little tight and itchy."

"There's a medical unit on the plane."

"For me?"

"For Mr. Hsing."

The plane, when they reached it, was a Boeing 747 Jumbo Jet, the red star of China on wings and empennage. The airport Chance recognized as Andrews Field, normally used for official visitors from abroad. As the gurney was trundled outside, Chance saw Hsing slowly climbing the steps to the open door. The Chinese official wore a hat, and his coat collar was turned up to screen his face. At the bottom of the mobile staircase the ambassador waved farewells that Hsing ignored. Then Chance's gurney, Sam at his side, was lifted into the center compartment and secured to the deck. The wide door folded back into the fuselage, Sam tightened his seat belt, and the powerful jets flamed and screamed.

Sam said, "We used to fly Tupolevs, but this baby is much more comfortable, longer range, too." He looked at Chance and smiled briefly. "Relations between our countries have improved."

"It took a while." Chance closed his eyes while the aircraft lumbered to the runway.

When the plane was rising over the Atlantic, Sam undid the retaining straps and Chance got up. He moved to a window seat and looked back at the Maryland coastline, trying to pick out shore settlements and beaches he had known. The plane burst into heavy clouds and Chance sat back wondering if he would ever see his homeland again.

Presently a nurse came forward and undid the masking gauze. She spoke in Chinese and Sam interpreted: "Are you in discomfort? Do you want a drink? Food?"

"I'd like a drink—preferably scotch." Sam spoke in Chinese and interpreted the nurse's reply. "Since you're on antibiotics she's not sure alcohol is permitted. She'll consult the doctor."

"Fair enough. Will my letters be mailed?"

"They're in the pouch for Mexico City, where the embassy will mail them." A thin smile moved his lips. "That's a big country for the FBI to search."

"Too bad," Chance said, "but maybe they'll come across another fugitive, so it won't be a total loss."

The nurse returned shaking her head, so Chance requested iced tea. Sam got out a chessboard and put up a table. After an hour Hsing appeared, silent as a shadow, and Sam rose. Hsing took Sam's seat and when they were alone he said, "As you may have inferred, Mr. Chance, I am not a member of our Washington embassy. My post is in Peking where I deal with a variety of matters, including intelligence." He paused. "Does that surprise you?"

"No, Mr. Hsiao," Chance said, "it does not."

Hsiao smiled. "So my pseudonym was insufficient to deceive a perceptive member of the CIA."

"You're a famous man," Chance said, "made so by your own abilities and the memoirs of Father Dougherty, your onetime cellmate."

"Ah, yes, a remarkable man, and for a Western Christian unusually understanding of the Chinese Revolution, despite the sufferings it caused him. Had I learned of his death in time, I would have attended his funeral service, but"—he spread his hands—"at the time it was not feasible. My own survival may be attributable to Father Dougherty; he prevented me from sinking into the passivity with which Orientals customarily regard death. Day after day he urged me to continue hoping, and in the end hope became reality. Because of him my life is richer—indeed, I am alive." He glanced out of a window. "But to the point, Mr. Chance. You should know that I journeyed to Washington for the sole purpose of receiving the now-dead Pavel Sosnowski. He was a courier, an emissary-messenger of a group within the Soviet Council of Ministers that is covertly seeking to lay the groundwork for deeper understanding and permanent peace between my country and the Soviet Union. As with all great initiatives, this one faces hostile opposition in the Kremlin—Peking, as well, to be frank. Like my counterparts within the Soviet Council of Ministers, I am one who foresees great advantages in mutually burying the hatchet and ending the long, unfortunate, and expensive hostility between two great Asian powers."

"So together you can conquer the world."

Hsiao's face twitched with irritation. "I mean that by not having to maintain vast military forces on our common borders, each country would be able to improve the lot of our populations. And postpone if not eradicate the likelihood of a nuclear confrontation." He looked down at the chessboard and moved Sam's knight, then lifted his gaze to Chance. "Unfortunately for both countries, there is a hard-core faction within the Kremlin that not only prefers the status quo but dreams of an ideologically purifying war to restore the Soviet Union's dominant role in the East. Such fanatic Neanderthals are the Conservatives; the faction seeking rapprochement are the Liberals." Coughing, he covered his mouth with a handkerchief and turned away. When the spasm ended, Hsiao continued. "The Conservatives would rewrite history by recapturing their satellites in central Europe, remilitarizing the Warsaw Pact countries, and reinstalling the nuclear and conventional forces withdrawn by treaties the Conservatives consider degrading."

"But that's fantasy," Chance objected.

"Is it? The world thought Hitler's threats to the Rhineland were fantasies, until the blitzkrieg. But disorganized and relatively weak as the Soviet Union finds itself today, the West—by which I mean the NATO countries and the U.S.A.—is equally so. What else but the threat of a militarily strong Soviet Union caused NATO to come into being, maintained it over forty years?"

Chance nodded. "A stand-down on both sides. . . . Even the Berlin Wall is gone."

"But could be rebuilt overnight, as Khruschev did." His head moved slowly, negatively. "Like China, the Soviet Union has been attempting to come into the twentieth century. China's pace has been slow, plodding, and without many apparent successes, but we have avoided the bloody outbreaks that characterize the independence movements of Uzbekistan, Moldavia, and the Ukraine, for example."

Chance eyed him. "What could possibly have been bloodier that the massacre in Tiananmen Square? And the brutal suppressions that followed?"

"I'm not forgetting that, but our Chinese youth was inflamed by the demonstrations in Romania, East Germany, and Hungary that brought down those regimes. The students wanted too much, too fast, and it frightened our aged leadership. I warned the Party's Central Committee not to react violently, but the Maoist faction was adamant. Somewhat to my surprise, General Secretary Zhao Ziyang supported my recommendations, while Foreign Minister Qian Quichen warned also that suppression of the students would cause China to lose what had been gained internationally since Nixon traveled to Peking but the elder leadership scoffed at him."

"And were proven right," Chance remarked heavily. "The West quickly forgot the student slaughter, got back to business as usual."

Hsiao nodded. "And the counsel of Qian and myself began to be deprecated. The major loser, of course, was Zhao Ziyang, who was accused of being prodemocracy, and for that he was dismissed."

"Why was no move made against you and Qian?"

"Because Zhao was a much more important scapegoat. But Qian and myself can be sacrificed whenever the Maoist faction needs more. Ever since the massacre Qian and I have lost influence, and that is one reason your mission is so important to me and to others who would see China become both modern and peaceful." He sighed. "It was the Soviet Union that gave birth to today's China, so it is unsurprising that when the U.S.S.R. coughs, China sneezes."

"Meaning?"

"That like the Soviet hierarchy, China's is divided into opposing factions—Conservatives, let us say, and Liberals. We of the latter persuasion fear that time is running against us and must make every effort to come to an understanding with our Soviet counterparts."

Chance regarded him critically. "Or?"

"Or the Soviet military-industrial complex will ally itself with China's Conservative leadership and launch wars against what remains of the Western alliance, while to the East, Japan, Korea, and the Pacific Basin countries are attacked by a China freed from old fears of the Soviet Union at its back."

The enormity of the concept stunned Chance. Its success seemed hardly possible, but with the West so involved in Middle East convulsions, the timing had never been so propitious. He let out his breath slowly, realizing that the information Hsiao confided was deadly to them both. With an effort, Chance suppressed those disquieting thoughts. "Do you know the Kremlin alignments?"

"To some extent, and from Sosnowski I had hoped to gain confirmation. Although Sosnowski was probably told very little. He was to suggest a site where Liberal representatives could meet in secrecy with members of my government who are of a similar mind. I should tell you, also, that Sosnowski is the fourth emissary intercepted and murdered before reaching a Chinese embassy."

"You knew Sosnowski was en route to Washington?"

"As the Americans do, we have our sources within the Kremlin's walls. Yes, I planned to meet him in Washington. I would have sent a response to Sosnowski's principals expressing general agreement with their proposal and saying my own principals would confer with them at a mutually convenient place and time—in total secrecy.

"That conversation never took place, as you are well aware. I ordered your abduction hoping that before dying Sosnowski might have conveyed part of his information to you. But when I realized that you and he had never spoken, I decided to make what use I could of you."

"Yes," said Chance, "though I don't yet know what you expect of me."

"The officer you know as Sam will provide details during your stay in Paris. In general you will perform as a singleton agent, making covert contact with a credentialed Russian to whom you will convey PRC interest in the Liberal proposal, then transmit his response."

"I see. And where will all this take place?"

"Geneva. At any time, there are scores of international delegations there; representatives come and go, meet at receptions, and otherwise carry out confidential business away from prying eyes, and ears." Gently he touched Chance's bandages. "Are you uncomfortable? The doctor will see you after our talk."

"So from Paris I go to Geneva?"

Hsiao nodded. "I sense that you are too tactful to ask why I chose you for the task, so I will tell you that it is because you were available, you are motivated, and as a former intelligence officer you possess useful trade-craft skills. You are evaluated as highly intelligent, possess an unusually retentive memory, and my assessment is that when you have given your word you strive to keep it. Too, you are Occidental, and those who directed Sosnowski's liquidation will be expecting a reciprocal PRC approach to be made by an Oriental. That further enhances your security and utility."

Chance picked up his glass and swallowed the dregs of his iced tea. "And a final reason, Mr. Hsiao—I'm expendable."

Hsiao inclined his head. "True. If necessary the PRC can always disavow you. But are not those the terms on which you operated abroad for the U.S.A.?"

"Close," Chance agreed wryly, and set aside his empty glass. "Do you know who ordered Sosnowski's execution?"

"We are learning," said Hsiao. "The two Arabs who assaulted you revealed the identity of their cutout. In turn the cutout exposed the identity of his controller: Major General Nikolai Berlikov, the KGB *rezident* in Washington."

"Meaning the entire apparatus of the KGB is engaged in aborting rapprochement."

"That is a logical interpretation. Another is that a part of the Conservative faction is manipulating disgruntled elements within the KGB to destroy the Liberal initiative. However, the true situation is not yet clear. Accordingly, you should remain at distance from members of the KGB."

"How will I identify them?"

"Sam will support you in Geneva. He will also be our private communications channel."

"You mentioned an American agent in Geneva."

"Everyone's agent, actually, useful to many. When the time comes he may be the one to identify the Soviet emissary and bring the two of you together."

"And Sam knows who he is."

"Before reaching Geneva you will be fully briefed."

Chance looked out the window. At forty thousand feet, sun blazed through the portside window. "Does the name Stillman mean anything to you?"

"Should it?"

"He was the CIA contact who turned me over to the police."

"I knew of the episode, though not the betrayer's name. Why do you ask?"

"Because Stillman was shot to death—and I'm being blamed."

Hsiao shook his head. "I was unaware of it until now. Still, it is in General Berlikov's interest that your character continue to be blackened."

"Berlikov, or the KGB?"

"For the present you should assume the entire KGB is hostile. And as a private individual you will not enjoy the normal immunity accorded a diplomatic agent. Meanwhile, my organization will be working to establish the precise situation."

"Suppose something happens to Sam?"

"Remain in place and take no action. A backup will replace

him." Hsiao's face paled, his lips were turning blue. *"Doctor,"* he wheezed, and Chance shouted for the nurse. The doctor came running down the aisle, an assistant carrying a small oxygen tank and mask. With Hsiao seated they pressed the mask over his face and the Chinese began breathing more regularly. Through the plastic mask Chance saw color return. "Asthma," Sam said, "if not something worse. Those years in prison."

After his patient was stabilized the doctor turned his attention to Chance. Forward, there was a small medical salon with a cushioned reclining chair. While Chance's temperature was taken, the doctor checked bandages for signs of bleeding. He found none. There was no infection, and visible stitches were in place. "I predict an uneventful recovery," he said, "even boring."

"Paris never bores me," Chance told him. "It's the Hong Kong of the West."

It was night when they landed at De Gaulle Airport. Rebandaged for anonymity, Chance was transferred to a waiting ambulance and driven with Sam to the western suburb of Passy. The small clinic specialized in plastic surgery, according to a sign he glimpsed while entering, and he was shown to a handsomely decorated room with twin beds.

Sam unpacked a small bag and hung up his clothing. "I'm told the food is at least three-star," he said, "so let's enjoy internment. Put on those pajamas and I'll get rid of your clothes. Tomorrow I'll have a tailor measure you for everything you'll need in Geneva."

In the morning Chance's nose and ribs were x-rayed and found to be healing properly. The torso tape restricted his breathing somewhat, but his reconstructed nostrils compensated, though sensitive to cool air.

As Sam had predicted, the clinic cuisine was excellent and much to Chance's taste. They alternated bouts of chess with TV and symphonies on the radio. Chance read two daily papers and found a short story about himself in *L'Express.* "How does it feel to be an internationally wanted criminal?" asked Sam.

"Not good. Try it sometime."

"No thanks, there's danger enough for me in China."

"And for Hsiao Kuan-hua."

"If what we're doing ever becomes known." He looked curiously at Chance. "You figured him out by yourself."

"I'd read about him."

"I'm glad you're with us on this," Sam told him. "Replacing you would be difficult. I've worked two years for Hsiao and his instincts are incredible—always makes the right moves."

"Speaking of moves, Sam, it's yours. We're playing chess, remember?"

On the fifth day his bandages were carefully removed. A nurse shaved most of his face with great delicacy, then his face was rebandaged, though in the mirror Chance noticed less gauze. On the seventh day the straws and shaping forms were taken from his nostrils, scabs softened and removed. Leeches had drawn out dark blood beneath his eyes, and though Chance could see where their suckers had gripped, the punctures were no larger than mosquito bites. Fading patches of yellow-bronze reminded him of Rony's face after Penn's blows, and he wondered if she'd gotten his letter.

On the ninth day his clothing arrived: three suits, dinner jacket, Harris tweed sport coat, and flannel slacks; raglan topcoat, Burberry raincoat, Locke hat and motoring cap; Peal footwear, Sulka underwear, pajamas, shirts and ties, Solly stockings and garters. . . . Chance gazed at the array. "I've never dressed so lavishly before," he told Sam cheerfully.

"Operational disguise for the continental gentleman. In Geneva you can't mingle in clothing off the rack. And the Soviet contact, when he comes, should consider you a person of consequence."

"What alias documentation will I have?"

"French suit you? That's what I've been considering. Can you think of a name for yourself?"

"How about Duroc? Let's see, Jean-Pierre is easy to remember."

"Paris-born, Sorbonne educated, with a plausible reason for being in Geneva."

Chance smiled. "Taking the waters, gambling at Divonne Casino. I'll enjoy wagering ChiCom money."

"Don't enjoy it too much, I have to account for every franc," warned Sam, alarmed. "I'll start passport preparations except for the photograph. That will be taken when the bandages are off and your features are set in the face you'll have for the rest of your life."

I wonder how long that will be? Chance mused.

Two days after the stitches were removed Chance scanned his face in the mirror and saw a somewhat younger man with a normal, straight nose. Slight bruising still showed on the bridge, but Sam's photographer brushed makeup across it, and Chance was given enough sunlamp exposure to banish his pallor before photographs were taken. After that his rib tape was unwound. Bruise marks from the bullet's impact still showed.

A clinic beautician restyled Chance's hair while a manicurist trimmed and polished his fingernails.

Dressed in new clothing, Chance felt his spirits soar. "Sam, let's go out on the town tonight, have a five-star on the PRC."

"I was going to suggest it myself," Sam replied, "and you saved me the trouble. Tour d'Argent? Maxim's?"

"Surprise me."

"I'll call for a table." He lifted the telephone and replaced it. "We'll leave for Geneva tomorrow, Jean-Pierre Duroc."

"D'accord. Now, who's the American Hsiao told me to deal with?"

"You may possibly remember him from CIA. His name is Paul Valcour."

BOOK TWO

TWENTY-FOUR

Aboard the EE Trans Europe Express—for Geneva, Chance read *Le Matin* in his first-class compartment. Sam occupied a second-class seat in the next car of the high-speed train.

Chance folded the Paris newspaper and set it aside to think about Paul Valcour.

Chance was not eager to meet Paul again. Not that he felt any remorse for having caused Valcour's departure from the Agency, but Chance was now the fugitive charged with capital crimes. They still shared an employer, but one whose identity had changed.

"Everyone's agent... useful to many," Hsiao had described Paul Valcour. Today's loyalty was to Hsiao Kuan-hua. It would be one thing to collaborate with Paul, quite another to trust him. It was not, Chance reflected, that Valcour was an immoral man; he was amoral. He acted as he chose, indifferent to the opinions of, the consequences to, others.

So it was not startling to Chance that Valcour now served those who were or had been his country's foes. They paid—probably well—and Chance imagined that Paul returned good value.

Chance wondered if Hsiao was aware of his past relationship with Valcour. In any case, withdrawal was not an option. He was completely dependent on the head of the Chinese intelligence service for his life, his freedom, and anything resembling a meaningful future. Meanwhile, Hsiao had all the options. After the mission was completed Hsiao could free him, kill him, or force him to continue working as a Chinese agent, perhaps against his own country.

Hearing the dining car summons, Chance left his compartment, locked it, and followed the steward.

After an excellent lunch of grilled lamb chops, endive salad, and a *demi-bouteille* of Bordeaux, Chance returned to his compartment and locked the door, opening it for Swiss Customs and Immigration inspectors, who chalked his luggage and stamped his French passport. Returning it, the officer said, "You are staying long in Geneva, M'sieu Duroc?"

"Perhaps a month."

"I wish you a pleasant stay."

"Thank you." He relocked the door and stretched out on the daybed until the express pulled into Geneva's railroad station, the Gare de Cornavin.

The leased villa lay to the north of Geneva proper, on the slopes of residential Bellevue. Its eastern exposure offered a commanding view of the Lake of Geneva and the distant Alps, but as Chance pointed out to Sam, a lot of airport traffic passed overhead.

"Hey, the hotels are jammed, and places like this—well, you wouldn't believe how scarce they are. Anyway, if the noise gets too bad, there's a deep wine cellar."

Deep enough, Chance reflected, for torture and murder if it came to that, reminding himself that despite surface friendliness, Sam was his watchdog and potentially dangerous.

The villa came with a Swiss chef and a Eurasian maid, who Sam said was Indo-Chinese. After introductions the servants left, and Sam said, "Isn't she gorgeous?"

"Lao-li? Yeah, but I imagine she works for you."

Sam smiled. "Why don't you ask her?"

"Maybe I will. What's the security here?"

"Poor to awful. The hill behind leads up into woods. Down front there's the meadow, the Lausanne road, and the lake. We're approachable from all directions, but I don't expect intruders unless your actions invite them."

"Communications?"

"Emergency transmitter stashed above. Normal messages I'll send through our consulate. My boss told me to stay out of your way and I plan to."

"Suppose I tried a getaway?"

"I'd kill you," Sam said flatly, "but you won't. Where could you go?"

"The Sovs?"

He shook his head. "They'd squeeze you—then kill you. You know that—why are we playing games?"

The master bedroom was high-ceilinged and filled with late Victorian furniture, heavy drapes across barred windows. Framed oils on the walls depicted Swiss mountains and valleys, placid, bucolic scenes. There was a wide fireplace set with wood logs. As Chance began unpacking, he heard a knock at his door. *"Entrez."*

It was Lao-li. "May I bring you anything, m'sieu?" she asked in excellent French.

"Not at the moment, thanks."

"Then let me do that for you."

Chance stepped aside and watched her remove his clothing, hang up the outerwear, and place his underwear in a tall, old-fashioned chest of drawers after fluffing it out. Her skin, he saw, was the color of burnished ivory, her diminutive figure perfectly proportioned. Legs nicely tapered, small nose, and wide-set eyes. She was what they called around Hong Kong an ivory figurine.

Sam came in as Lao-li was leaving. "You're having dinner away from here tonight."

"Who with?"

"Valcour. His car will be here at seven. Black tie."

"Giving me maybe two hours. I think I should have a car, Sam."

"Check the garage. You like Mercedes?"

"I have one—had one."

"Want me to get a chauffeur's outfit, gray whipcord and cap?"

"Are you kidding? Sure. The Russian and I may have things to discuss. And I talk better when I can concentrate. Besides," he added, "you can keep tabs on me for Hsiao."

"Makes sense, M'sieu Duroc."

"Does Valcour know my true name?"

"No." Sam took an automatic pistol from his pocket and placed it on the bureau. "With Valcour you won't need this, but you might want to keep it close to your bed."

Chance picked up a new nine-millimeter Walther PPK, full

magazine. "Too bad I didn't have this when I walked in on Sosnowski and the Arabs."

Sam shrugged. "They died hard. What will be, will be."

"Old Chinese maxim?"

"Old Hitchcock film." He paused at the doorway. "Can Lao-li do anything for you?"

"Bottle of Black Label, ice, and spring water."

"I'll tell Lao-li."

Chance placed the pistol under his pillow and undressed to shower.

The tiled bathroom was a large, old-fashioned affair with a serpentine rack of hot-water pipes where towels hung to warm. Chance opened the shower door and stepped into a cloud of steam. He was groping for a towel when he felt one placed in his hand. *"Ici,"* Lao-li said, and helped drape the towel around his body.

The drink tray was on the porcelain ledge. The girl said, "Shall I mix for you? How do you like it?"

"Just a splash of water." He took the crystal glass from her and sipped. "Do you work for my companion—Sam?"

"Did you ask him?"

"He said I should ask you."

She looked away. "Does it make a difference?"

"Not to me."

"Then I would rather not say." She moved behind him and he felt her fingers kneading his shoulder muscles, unknotting them, relaxing the triceps, and working magic with her fingertips along his spine. "You like that?" she asked.

"Of course."

"It is much easier when you are lying down."

"I'd fall asleep," he said, "and I have to shave and dress."

Her fingers stopped working. "Black tie? I will lay out everything for you."

After shaving, and before he got into his starched white shirt, Lao-li gently rubbed his back with cologne that had a faint scent of jasmine. She set black studs and cuff links in his shirt, helped him into it, and neatly tied his black silk tie. She buffed his patent-leather shoes on her apron, peaked a handkerchief for his breast pocket, and stepped back. "You are a handsome man, M'sieu Duroc."

Feeling sudden empathy with her, Chance took her hand. "And you are a lovely young woman." Her eyes looked down.

Chance said, "Do you often have to pretend to be a servant?"

"What do you mean? I *am* a servant—here to serve you, sir."

He smiled. "As you prefer," he said, and went down to the drive where Valcour's pearl gray Daimler was waiting.

TWENTY-FIVE

The chauffeur was a burly man with the battered face of a pugilist, but he drove skillfully through off-highway areas unfamiliar to Chance, who noted landmarks for future use.

After heading south toward the city the car turned west to pass the wooded Bois de Vengeron and followed autoroute One to the turnoff at Chemin de Valerie. Half a mile and the chauffeur turned north onto Chemin de la Fontaine, a paved road that rose gradually among mansions and grand residences, until a turnoff ended at a wide grilled gate. From the gatehouse a uniformed guard peered into the limousine and the gate slid aside.

At the crest of the drive stood a Doric mansion of beige stone with fluted columns that faced the Lake of Geneva. To the left was a four-car garage, doors closed. A man sat on a sheltered perch from which most of the sloping grounds were visible. Two sturdy Alsatians rested in front of him, chain leashes in his hand.

Ready for action, Chance thought. When the limousine stopped at the front steps, he got out.

The doorway opened and Paul Valcour appeared. He wore a tailored, shawl-collar dinner jacket, silver-embroidered opera slippers, and a gates-ajar collar. His handsome face was tanned, and his silvery hair looked professionally waved and set. He came down the steps and, smiling, extended his right hand. Then his eyes narrowed. "M'sieu Duroc—forgive me, but I have the sensation we've met before." His gaze searched Chance's face. "Have we?"

"In a former life," Chance said. "Hello, Paul. I'm Quinn."

Valcour stared at him, recovered composure, and said, "Good

God! I never thought I'd see you again—never expected to. . . ."
He waved off his chauffeur. "I heard you were—let's talk inside."
He led the way, pausing at the entrance long enough to say,
"Welcome to my abode." Then he walked down a polished marble
entrance hall and opened a carved walnut door. "The library,
Quinn. Drink?"

"Whatever you're having."

"Campari and soda." He closed the door behind them and
stared at Chance. "This is incredible! I didn't know who Duroc
was, but I certainly didn't expect you. Changed flags, Quinn?"

"For this job." As Valcour moved to the ornate cellarette,
Chance glanced around. Two walls held shelves of books, many
with ornate bindings. There was a French Renaissance desk with
a gilded telephone, behind it a computer terminal. Light sparkled
from twin crystal chandeliers, illuminating two medieval tapestries
on the third wall. The setting was both opulent and tasteful,
compatible with Chance's memory of his onetime boss.

"You . . . look different, Quinn, but not greatly so. Took me a
moment before I—" He swallowed, seemed more at ease. "But
then I saw you often, sometimes every day for months." He poured
Campari into two glasses, squirted soda from a mesh-covered
siphon, and handed a glass to Chance. "We should toast to something."

"Not the past."

He gave Chance a relaxed smile. "Then the future—a long,
safe, and profitable future." He sipped. "Under other circumstances I might think you'd come back to haunt me, return me to
Washington for judgment."

"You're forgotten," Chance told him, and sipped the bittersweet
aperitif. "Written off."

"Possibly I should resent that—but then you've taken my place
as Most Wanted, haven't you?"

Chance nodded. "I didn't kill the Russian."

"I didn't kill Nzdwali."

"Then why refuse a polygraph?"

"Because it was demeaning."

"There *was* the missing gold."

"So there was." Valcour shrugged. "Let's talk of pleasanter

things, shall we? By the way, there'll be two others at dinner—my personal secretary, Maurice, and my sister, Toni—you remember her?"

"Of course. A lovely young woman."

"Better known as Princess Azira, recently divorced from Prince Mohammed al-Hazawi." He drank again. "I assume you want your operational alias protected, so I'll introduce you as Duroc, say we were Paris acquaintances." He paused. "How are you papered?"

"French."

Valcour moved his head slowly. "Incredible you should show up here, Quinn. Did you know I'd be working this end?"

"I learned yesterday. But I'd heard you were in Geneva from Penn Boyce's wife." He sat down in a red-leather chair while Valcour lounged against its matching sofa. "I've done well by being useful to different interests," his host said, "and I want to do even better in the future. I know very little about this . . . enterprise—doubtless you know much more than I—but from the way things are being assembled, I assume it's something very big."

"Global. You're to put me together with a particular Soviet official. Who?"

Valcour shook his head. "I haven't been told. Anyway, I doubt he'll be traveling under his true name."

"Then he's not in Geneva."

"If he is, he hasn't contacted me." He drained his glass. "I thought you might have a time frame."

"Anywhere from a week to several months."

"God, I hate these slow-developing deals! Dividend?"

Chance held out his glass. Filling it, Valcour said, "I don't collect the rest of my fee until I've made the connection. You?"

Chance smiled. "I get expenses—and protection."

"I see. Well, you're reasonably safe in Geneva. The hockey nose was your giveaway feature. Tell me, are the Sovs after you?"

"I'm avoiding them all—except the guy I'm expecting."

Valcour nodded. "Imagine you representing the Red Chinese. You'll tell me how it came about?"

A knock on the door. It opened and in walked—glided, Chance thought later—a figure in close-cut evening garb, wavy hair so blond it glinted in the lighting; straight features, deep blue eyes, and creamily tanned skin. Glancing at Chance, the man said, "Oh. Excuse me, Paul, I didn't know—" He smiled amiably at Chance. Valcour said, "My secretary, Maurice. M'sieu Duroc."

Maurice extended one smooth, manicured hand. *"Enchanté."*

Chance bowed slightly. Turning to Valcour, his secretary said, "An urgent call from Vienna—shall I say you're occupied?"

"I'll take it in the office." He left and Maurice followed, glancing back at Chance. "See you at dinner."

Chance smiled.

Well, this was a new side to his old leader. Maurice was a gorgeous blend of Miss and Mr. America with an androgyne's ambivalent charm. Doubtless he was useful to Valcour in numerous ways.

While awaiting Valcour's return Chance scanned the library bookcase. Volumes in French, English, German, and Italian, titles imprinted in gold leaf on calfskin bindings of blue, brown, and red. There was a large TV screen and speakers for a concealed stereo receiver. By the Daiwa computer terminal, a rack of videocassettes. Home movies?

Valcour returned alone. "Sorry about that," he said, "but Maurice can be pushy." He swallowed more Campari. "As you saw."

"How old is he?"

"Thirty at least, though he admits to only twenty-six. I'm not ashamed and I'm not apologizing."

"You never have."

"Perhaps you'd go through life more smoothly if you took things as they are."

"I'll remember the advice," Chance told him dryly. "When do I see Toni?"

"Antoinette is at her toilette." He rolled the words exaggeratedly. "As always. The desert sand and sun ruined her hair, skin, and complexion, she says. Though she spent little time in the kingdom. Usually she was in Paris, London, or the Costa Smeralda."

"Children?"

He shrugged. "Prince Mohammed—she said—is impotent, but who knows? Or cares? The divorce left her a considerable fortune, and I remain on good terms with the prince."

"For business reasons."

He looked sharply at Chance. "I'm a businessman, Quinn. Sentiment doesn't enter in."

Not even Maurice? Chance wondered. When a dinner bell chimed in the corridor, Valcour set down his glass and took Chance's arm companionably. "Shall we go in?"

The dining room table was set for four. The single chandelier's soft light was reflected by gold-washed cutlery, bone white, gold-rimmed dishes, and crystal wineglasses. Valcour sat at the head, Maurice to his left, Chance on his right. The fourth place, Antoinette's, was empty. The three men sipped a dry chardonnay while they waited. And waited. Finally the host snapped, "Enough. We'll begin."

At that moment Princess Azira pirouetted in, a gauzy sari swirling from outstretched arms. The translucent silk in pink and violet pastels revealed more of her figure than it concealed. Underneath she was wearing loosely tapered leggings of gold lamé, jeweled Persian slippers on her feet.

Her dark hair was drawn back from her forehead and circled by a gold band, from which hung a large teardrop pearl centered on her forehead. Her thick eyebrows were accented with maquillage and her eyelids dark with kohl, her lips painted bright red.

But none of the heavy makeup could disguise an extraordinarily beautiful, snub-nosed face with high cheekbones and small, impudent chin. The overall effect was at once innocent and erotic. She was, Chance thought, no more than twenty-five.

"Gentlemen," she said in French as a servant held her chair, "you may now begin."

"Our guest," said her brother with restraint, "is Jean-Pierre Duroc, from Paris." Chance rose and bowed. Valcour continued, "And as for royal permission to begin, you're no longer princess of a dustbin kingdom, so can it, Toni."

Blithely ignoring the rebuke, she turned to Chance. "Do you come often to Geneva?"

"Not often." He thought he detected an odd glitter in her eyes, and the pupils were contracted. Amphetamines? Coke? Her hands moved nervously, her voice was brittle.

Valcour said, "Monsieur Duroc speaks excellent English, Toni. *And* he is happily married."

Toni glanced coldly at her brother. "How nice," she remarked. "As you may know, my former husband was a pig."

"Toni!"

"Well, it's true, Paul. Just because I don't talk about it doesn't mean it's not so." She smiled winningly at Chance. "Does it?"

"I suppose not." He lifted his spoon and tasted the consommé. "Are you staying with us, M'sieu Duroc?"

Her brother said, "Our guest has a villa of his own, in Bellevue."

"Why, that's close by," she said silkily. "Maybe I'll come visit."

"You will be welcome," Chance said politely.

"You mustn't impose on him, Toni," Valcour cautioned. "Jean-Pierre is a very busy man."

"Oh? You sell oil and weapons?"

"Nothing so dramatic. I like the ambience of Geneva, and it's close to Divonne."

She squealed, "How exciting—you must take me gambling—I miss Monaco so."

"Delighted." Chance laid down his spoon.

Toni said, "Geneva is *so* dull, don't you think? I mean, ten o'clock, lights out, that sort of thing. Unless one follows the diplomatic party circuit, it's a crushing bore." She gazed at Maurice. "And there's a total absence of presentable escorts, isn't there, Maurice?"

"So I hear," he said blandly. "Is that why you never go out?"

Her cheeks flushed. "You know damn well I'm particular. Besides, I'm supposed to lay low till the divorce is final." She looked at her brother. "This *is* my home, isn't it, Paul, still?"

"As long as my patience holds out."

To Chance she said loudly, "Isn't that charitable? My brother pimped for al-Hazawi, and now in the ashes of that stirring front-page romance he grows impatient with me."

"You did rather well out of it," Valcour remarked tightly. "Eight million from that little shit."

"May I tell him you said that?"

Valcour glared at her. "Toni, since you're not comfortable with us . . ."

145

"I should leave, that it?" Turning, she handed her soup plate to a servant. "Wine," she demanded.

Valcour said, "You may have had enough."

"Not after the dry sands of Samarkand. I fled with an unquenchable thirst. It may take the rest of my life to rinse out the taste of my marriage."

For a few moments the room was silent. Finally, Chance cleared his throat. "I'm not terribly familiar with the Mideast, but I've lived in Cairo."

"An appalling city," Toni pronounced. "Dusty monuments and dirty Arabs. And that cemetery—the City of the Dead—gives me creeps to think of it."

"Still, the Nile has its charms," Chance suggested.

Her lips set. "You French should never have backed down and surrendered Suez to the gippos." She turned to her brother. "Right, Paul?"

He shrugged. "World opinion—very persuasive at times. And of course the Soviets were poised to strike. . . ." He dabbed a napkin at his lips. "The West has made many gross errors—don't you think, Jean-Pierre?"

Chance said, "What I think is unimportant."

"Oh, come now," Toni coaxed, "you French are experts on defeat and decay." She turned to Maurice. "And decadence."

Maurice's eyes narrowed. "Shall we leave me out of this, dear?"

"Why should we? You're part of this household—an indispensable part. Why, Paul couldn't live without you. Isn't that so, brother?"

Valcour's face had whitened. Ignoring her, he spoke to the butler and presently servants removed the first course. Toni seemed tense, a panther preparing to spring, and Chance wondered how much further the baiting would go. Her exotic makeup magnified the bitterness of her expression. She drew resentment from a deep, inexhaustible well, he thought, and he pitied her.

Toni waved aside the partridge and wild rice, the blanched *asperges,* drinking sullenly through the men's desultory conversation. Valcour edged back his chair and rose. To Chance he said, "My sister can be as difficult as a refractory child. I apologize for her behavior."

From her chair Toni looked up, eyes blazing. "Don't insult me, you disgusting old queen!"

"Toni," Maurice said urbanely, "Paul is *not* that old."

But Valcour was advancing on his sister. He was a strong man who had been a parachutist and karate fighter, and his sister cowered, trying to escape his reaching hand. But his fingers closed around the back of her neck. She yelped, then her head dropped forward. Stepping back, Valcour turned to Maurice. "Take her to her room, and if you find any of those damn pills, get rid of them."

"With pleasure." Maurice lifted her as though she were a straw mannequin and carried Princess Azira al-Hazawi from the dining room. The ex-princess, Chance corrected, and followed Valcour to the library.

There Valcour warmed brandy glasses over an alcohol flame. "My profound apologies, Quinn. Please ignore that unpleasant scene."

"Of course." He took the brandied glass and cupped it in his palm.

"Prince Mohammed led a very fast life, too fast for Antoinette, and she couldn't keep up with him. Too, her husband indulged some—ah, unusual tastes that Toni found offensive. I thought—hoped—that here she could recover from it all, but it seems less and less likely."

"She's still young," Chance pointed out, "and quite lovely. In time the past will be forgotten."

He sighed. "That's my hope, of course, but I'm damn sick of her demonic scenes. As long as she's here I try to be a steadying influence, hard as it is. But if she lived alone, I'm afraid she'd destroy herself." He sipped and sat in a chair near the desk. Looking up, he said, "Speaking of the past, you think I bombed Nzdwali's plane, don't you? And stole the bullion."

"It's long ago," Chance said, "and it doesn't matter what I think."

"Still, because of our old friendship it matters to me." Valcour sipped again, as though to gain strength. "The circumstances were damning, I admit. But the fact is that my African friend was assassinated by secret agents of his own government." His lips twisted. "Now you know what it is to face charges you have no way of disproving."

"And the gold?"

"Ah, yes, the gold. His aides took it."

"Then how do you explain this villa, your wealth?"

"To no one but you, Quinn, would I explain." His head rested back on the chair, his gaze focused on the ceiling. "When I realized the truth would never be believed, when I was ordered to submit to polygraph, I knew I was finished at the Agency. I left America and came here, almost penniless but possessing something of value—knowledge of Nzdwali's assassination. I used that— through intermediaries—to persuade the ruler of that African wasteland that it was in his consuming interest to pay me for my silence." His gaze lowered to Chance. "I used those proceeds to make a number of investments that turned out exceedingly well."

"I would have thought it easier to kill you than pay you."

"I operated against him, Quinn, as I would have had he been an Agency target. He couldn't locate me. In the end he paid."

"But you live openly. . . ."

"And he is dead, assassinated by trusted aides as Nzdwali was. One of those innumerable palace coups, you know. If Nzdwali hadn't died in the bombing, he would have been killed after he gained power." He shrugged. "What does it matter, really? Colored shapes on the map of a huge continent. Borders shift like the sands, names and colors change, and the poor damn blacks suffer on in the misery they've always known." He drained his glass. "Doubtless you find me cynical—you're more the humanist than I ever was—but we must live our own lives after all. Treat fortune and misfortune with equanimity, deal with both as best we can. You and I were blessed—if that's the word—with excellent minds. If I've used my brain and experience to gain a congenial way of living, should I be criticized?"

"Not if you've told the truth," he replied, wondering how much of Valcour's monologue *was* truthful.

"I have—because I respect your personal honesty." He hesitated. "Your character." He laughed shortly. "How long since I've used or heard *that* word."

"Well," said Chance, "I appreciate the compliment. Now, is Maurice aware of our arrangements?"

"No. I'm fond of the dear lad, but I'd never trust him with knowledge that could be used against me should his affections falter."

"Nor would I," said Chance.

"Of course, with you and me it's different. We're professionals. We understand how covert deals are made, arrangements laid on. Even without knowing details I've concluded that you and I will be making world history." His face was transfigured, Chance thought, but he said nothing as Valcour continued: "To be at the conjunction of historic crossroads—to play a role in creating dé-tente between two giant adversaries. . . . Quinn, do you realize how significant it can be for us both?" His cheeks were flushed and he leaned forward. "If I'm right, it reduces that Camp David agree-ment to a political flyspeck. Sadat, Begin, Carter—pygmies on an overpowering stage. And, Quinn . . . there's plenty for both of us—if we play things right."

Chance regarded his old colleague and said quietly, "Don't crowd me, Paul."

"Crowd—? Quinn, I just want you to grasp the potential." Valcour pulled back, suddenly aware that his enthusiasm was not shared. "Just don't crowd me, that's all," Chance said. "Now, when the Soviet representative arrives, how will you know him?"

Valcour blotted perspiration from his face. "He knows my name and the signal. . . . Contact will be made discreetly. I'll be attending the normal diplomatic entertainments; the Soviets, you'll recall, like making contact in a crowd."

"So until you're contacted, I wait."

"Enjoy freedom and good living. Take Toni to Divonne if you care to, escort her to balls and entertainments. She'll be good cover for you. Hell, even the KGB understands romance."

Chance smiled thinly, not welcoming the prospect.

"You'll be doing me a favor, too," Valcour admitted.

"I can't pull her off drugs," Chance said bluntly. "She has to do that on her own."

Her brother nodded. "She's not deeply addicted yet. But inevi-tably she'll turn to coke and other things. Everything is available in Geneva for a price, and there's nothing my sister can't afford."

Chance set aside his glass. "I'm dead tired. Time for me to—"

"I'll have Albert take you back. And, Quinn, I'm glad it turned out to be you. We're working together again, like old times."

"Tell Toni good night for me. I'll call her soon."

Riding back to the villa, Chance could hardly keep his eyes open, but his mind was busy with Paul Valcour.

Had Paul told the truth? Conversely, what did it matter? For he realized now that his old leader was obsessed with power. Whatever stood between Paul and his objective was going to be brushed aside—or crushed.

Time and wealth had not mellowed Paul Valcour but hardened him into a cunning adversary. That was a factor, Chance thought, he would be prudent not to forget.

Sam opened the front door. "How did it go?"

"I'll tell you in the morning." He walked toward the staircase.

"Any problems?"

"Terminal jet lag."

Chance undressed, got into bed, felt the automatic under his pillow. Moonlight slanted through parted blinds. Wearily Chance turned over.

Later, when the moon had set, he was wakened by a body beside him, flesh both warm and cool. Delicate fingers stroked him, aroused his penis. . . . He was aware of velvety lips and female moistness. When she mounted him he saw the almond face of Lao-li and touched her small conical breasts in drowsy wonder. Moaning, she impaled herself more deeply, bucked and writhed and urged him on to climax. Then with a sigh she lay forward, cradling his head with her hands, nuzzling his lips in afterglow.

He slept—and when he woke he was alone, and he wondered if it had been a dream. But a subtle scent of jasmine lingered.

TWENTY-SIX

Defense Minister Yaroshenko's private office was hidden away in the old arsenal tower at the northernmost point of the walled Kremlin. From one window he could look down on the Memorial to Russia's Unknown Soldiers, and see the long, narrow arsenal enclosure, where for centuries czars' soldiers and palace guards fell out on parade. In the western distance lay the smoothly rolling Lenin Hills. From another window Marshal Yaroshenko could glimpse the nearby Saint Nicholas Tower, Ivan the Great's clock tower, and the entire inner expanse of the Kremlin, plus a bend of the Moscow River as it flowed beyond the turreted and crenelated wall.

According to tradition the office had once been living quarters of the devil-monk Rasputin, accounting for its stark, ascetic furnishings so in contrast to other sumptuous Kremlin rooms. The bedroom, though, where Rasputin was said to have seduced countless royal and near-royal damsels, was large and comfortable. There the defense minister rested and slept during times of crisis. Desk telephones were part of the Kremlin's secure communications system, the Vertushka. From any one of them he could speak with his chief subordinates and, if necessary, with the premier himself.

He puffed at an old and battered pipe, stem clenched between his stained, uneven teeth. The pipe had belonged to General Andrei Vlasov, and Yaroshenko had acquired it when the renegade officer was shot for collaborating with the Wehrmacht during the Great Patriotic War. In those days, the defense minister reflected, there were traitors everywhere; even today the poison of treachery flowed through the Kremlin like a hidden stream, silent, unseen. Stalin would have known how to root out treason.

He turned from the window and faced Lieutenant General Sobatkin, who stood rigidly before him. "At ease, Yevgeni Lubovich," he said in his rough, not unfriendly way. "You are ready to return to Ottawa, are you not?"

"Assuming those are your orders, Comrade Minister."

Yaroshenko fingered his pipe and studied the face of his subordinate. "It appears," he said, "that there is further work to be done, additional information necessary." He sat behind his desk and motioned Sobatkin to a chair. "A week's physical and electronic surveillance of Minister Kirilenko has produced nothing that would in any way confirm what was extracted from the late Major Sosnowski." He removed the pipe and gazed at the scarred bowl. "In your mind, there is no question that Sosnowski named Kirilenko as his principal?"

"None whatever," Sobatkin replied. "Berlikov was present for the full interrogation, as was Chavadze of the GRU."

"Then what am I to conclude?"

Sobatkin swallowed. "That Sosnowski lied, to conceal the identity of his true sponsor."

"Unfortunately," Yaroshenko said, musingly, "Sosnowski cannot be recalled for further questioning." His eyes narrowed. "Leaving whom? The two 'wet' agents are dead, as is their intermediary, liquidated by the American. Are those the facts?"

"That is what we surmise, Comrade Minister," he agreed, uncomfortably.

"So our ignorance is mutual."

Sobatkin said nothing. He wanted only to be on the plane for Canada, back on his own hunting grounds. But his superior continued, "So of all the principals only the American remains alive and able to talk."

"If he lives."

"And he has shown a remarkable capacity to survive. No one thought the tethered goat would suddenly become a stalking tiger."

"No, Comrade Minister."

"Yevgeni Lubovich, I put it to you that there has been a failure of operational intelligence in correctly estimating the situation. I put it to you further that there has been a failure in the execution of your orders to the Washington *Rezidentiy.*"

"Undoubtedly, Comrade Minister."

Yaroshenko picked up a message form and shook it at Sobatkin. "What can you tell me about this? What does it mean?"

Sobatkin recognized the text and felt even more uncomfortable. "General Berlikov sent it to Ottawa on the assumption that I was there. My deputy, following standard procedure, relayed the message here." He wet dry lips.

"Berlikov seeks a conference with you. How are you going to respond?"

Sobatkin swallowed. "In whatever way the comrade minister desires."

Yaroshenko's fist crashed on his desk, shaking it. *"Gavno!"* he yelled. "Don't give me bureaucratic shit! Again I ask: How will you respond?"

Sobatkin's mind had been working. Forced to decide, he said, "On my way to Ottawa I will stop in Washington and meet him."

"Good! Excellent! Let us hope that Berlikov has developed information that can be used. I want the American found, do you understand? Found and interrogated."

Sobatkin said, "We have been given to understand that Chance was kidnapped by CIA hooligans. Thus the likelihood is that the American is sequestered somewhere."

"Which should not be too difficult to ascertain, eh? If our access to CIA information is as good as it is said to be."

"Quite so, Comrade Minister."

"Have you formed an opinion as to why Berlikov wants this meeting?"

"I can only speculate that he wishes to impart information to me in private."

Yaroshenko got up and went over to the window, hands clasped behind his back. "You should be aware that the Liberals will probably dispatch a fifth emissary to the Chinese—if that has not been done already. And I have received information that a reciprocal approach may be made by the Chinese."

"Here—in Moscow?"

He knocked dottle from his pipe, bit down on the stem again. "Given the efficiency of our domestic security, that would be foolhardy. My expectation is that their reach will be in the direction of some international meeting site. Does one come to mind?"

Hastily Sobatkin considered. "Stockholm?" he suggested.

"Unlikely," the defense minister said with a touch of scorn. "Anyone not looking like a blond Swede is instantly noticed. Where else?"

Sobatkin sucked in a deep breath. "Switzerland," he ventured.

Yaroshenko's lips pursed as he stroked them with two fingers. "Bern? Zurich?"

"I would think not, Comrade Minister. Those locales are frequented by bankers, businessmen." Almost in desperation he said, "Were I arranging such a meeting, I would select Geneva."

"Yes," said the minister, turning back to Sobatkin, "it's a meeting place for all nationalities." He nodded thoughtfully. "Alert our people there. Tell them only what is necessary to gain their full cooperation."

"I understand, Comrade Minister."

Marshal Yaroshenko approached Sobatkin and gripped his shoulders. "Geneva first, eh? Then Berlikov in Washington."

"I understand, Comrade Minister," he repeated, more anxious than ever to go.

"Our foreign minister travels there in a day or so for more of those interminable showcase negotiations with the Americans. As a matter of convenience I suggest you arrange to fly to Geneva with his delegation."

"I will do so, Comrade Minister."

"Lose no time. *Dosvidanaya.*"

Sobatkin executed an about-face and strode from the presence of the defense minister. Going down the spiral staircase, he paused to wipe his face. He felt limp from the confrontation but vastly relieved that he had not been personally criticized. Automatically he returned the salutes of staircase guards and emerged into a passageway that ran the length of the arsenal.

As he walked, Sobatkin felt tension leaving him and he began looking forward to a brief but pleasant sojourn in Geneva. Then

Washington. Kolya Berlikov had to comprehend the seriousness of the situation and give it his full attention.

He was going to have to tighten the screws on Berlikov until fear produced what orders had been unable to.

Quentin Chance had to be found.

TWENTY-SEVEN

Antoinette "Toni" Valcour, lately Princess Azira al-Hazawi, didn't wait for Chance's call. Exercising royal prerogative, she drove over to his villa the following afternoon.

Toni was wearing a faded denim shirt with rolled-up sleeves, knitted racing gloves, and stone-washed jeans. Through wrap-around sunglasses she looked at Chance over the padded doorsill of her pink Lamborghini roadster, waved, and called, "Hi."

"Hi, yourself." He laid aside the cloth he had been using to polish the Mercedes's rearview mirrors and walked over to her. She gunned the engine and it gave off the throaty growl of a hundred lions. "Like it?"

"Love it." He stroked the waxed acrylic finish appreciatively.

"Just took delivery. Let's try it out."

He got into the other seat and buckled waist and shoulder straps. Toni said softly, "I was pretty crazy last night, wasn't I?"

"Compared to what?"

She pouted. "That's not fair, Jean-Pierre—actually I've behaved much worse, but I came here by way of making a sort of apology and your smart-ass attitude isn't helping."

"You don't owe me an apology, Toni. I'm just passing through."

"Are you?" She revved the engine again. "Last night I was sober long enough to form a somewhat different impression of you. Want to know what it is?"

"I suppose you'll tell me anyway."

"Well, you're quite different from Paul's usual visitors—fat German bankers, hissing Japanese, faggoty Brits, and lecherous

156

Latins." She glanced at him. "So since you're obviously not gay either, I figure you were someone from his colorful past—the CIA."

Chance smiled. "Why would you reach that conclusion?"

"For one thing, you didn't ask questions, just listened. For another, your American English is simply too good for a Parisian."

"Quite a jump," he said, "but it happens I studied several years in Philadelphia."

"Where?"

"Wharton Finance."

"Shit! I really thought I had you figured out. And you really are married?"

He nodded. "But why would anyone from the CIA come calling on your brother?"

She adjusted her wrist straps. "To tell him all's forgiven and he can come home."

"You've lost me," Chance said. "Let's drive."

She floored the accelerator, tires sprayed gravel, and the pink roadster shot down the drive.

Gaining autoroute One at lakeside, Toni turned north, accelerating, shifting, watching the RPMs until the speedometer registered 150 kph. Breeze tore at Chance's face and he shielded his eyes until Toni leaned across him and opened the glove compartment. Her breasts grazed his thigh as she fumbled for a package. Straightening, she watched Chance open it and pull out a pair of Lamborghini wraparound shades that matched hers. "Thanks."

"Came with the car."

He could see the road ahead now. In overdrive she streaked into the outskirts of Lausanne, slowed, and pulled up in front of an attractive-looking restaurant with garden tables. "Tea time," she said, unbuckling.

Walking beside her, Chance said, "You drive well, Toni."

"It's a great car, anyone could. I like the performance. I'll keep it." Gesturing at a tile-surfaced table under a striped side awning, she walked to it. Chance followed and drew back a chair. Flower beds had been tilled, he noticed, but it was early yet for blooms. Around them gnarled old oaks showed the light green of barely formed buds. In summer, he thought, the place would become a true lovers' rendezvous. Before seating himself Chance reached over and took off her glasses, looked at her eyes, and replaced the dark shades. As he sat across from her she said, "What was that for?"

"Pupil check," he said. "Last night you were on speed."

"Was I ever. Whoo-ee, what a buzz. Going to denounce me?"

"People on speed tend to drive more aggressively than I like."

"And if I hadn't passed the pupil exam?"

"I'd hitchhike back."

They ordered pâté sandwiches and wine spritzers, enjoying the breeze through the trees, and Chance saw that without the Scheherazade makeup her face was truly lovely. Subtle eyeliner and a touch of iridescent lipstick that brought out the fullness of her lips.

"Now that you're single again, what are you going to do with your life?" he asked.

"Any suggestions?"

"What wealthy women usually do—charity work, subscription balls, ballet, opera. . . ."

"Until I find Mr. Right?"

Chance shrugged. "You have your choice, Toni."

"Because of my money, you mean?"

"Because you're clever and beautiful."

"Well, thank *you*, m'sieu. Thought you'd never say it." She drew her nails across the back of his hand, lightly, provocatively. "You're damn attractive yourself, Jean-Pierre—but then there's that wife pining away back in Paris. Otherwise I'd make a pass at you, or shouldn't I?"

"My wife is an invalid," he said tightly. "It would hardly be sporting."

"Well, well, a man of high morals." Her hand withdrew. "My brother should keep your bust in his study."

"Don't be snotty," he said, remembering that he had been physically unfaithful to Carla last night. Not that it had been his idea. And when Lao-li brought his breakfast to the patio she had neither said nor done anything to remind him of what had taken place between them. Could women sense that he was famished for love?

Toni said, "I'm sorry, Jean-Pierre. Sometimes I'm so bitchy I hardly know myself. Believe it or not, I was a nice girl—once."

"I believe it—and I'm a stuffy older man."

She smiled thinly. "As Maurice said of Paul last night, you're not *that* old." She downed the rest of her spritzer.

"Well," he said, "unless I'm disqualified, how about going with me to the casino tonight?"

"Divonne? I'd love it."

"Pick you up at seven."

Her gaze held him. "I feel I'm going to be very lucky tonight."

On the drive back to Geneva, Toni kept at 100 kph, tooling easily and confidently around the curves. Behind them from time to time Chance glimpsed a gray Peugeot sedan that seemed to be straining to keep up with them, and by the time they reached his villa Chance was sure they had been followed.

Toni, immersed in the enjoyment of her new car, hadn't noticed. But then, Chance reflected, she hadn't been trained to do so.

The villa's Mercedes was a sedate, older-model black sedan. It lacked the power of Toni's roadster but made up for it in comfort. Toni, strapless in a sheath dress of silver lamé, wore a gauzy shawl. She sat quietly beside Chance during the twenty-minute drive across the French border to Divonne's main casino, where he turned over the car to an attendant. Before they entered the casino she adjusted his black bow tie and said, "I'm starved, Jean-Pierre. How about you?"

"I can eat almost anything."

"No lamb or mutton for me—that's all Arabs eat."

Large chandeliers illuminated the gaming tables and the bar that occupied one end of the room. They ordered champagne cocktails and carried them across thick, sound-deadening carpeting to the nearest roulette wheel. Toni won and Chance lost the first spin, not really minding, for Sam had bankrolled him with five thousand Swiss francs play money. The crowd at the gaming tables was small; Chance knew the main action wouldn't begin until after dinner. He bought more chips and bet on black consistently until all his chips were gone. Toni, however, had increased her winnings, and as she cashed her chips at the cage she said, "I told you

I felt lucky tonight, Jean-Pierre. Better let me place your bets after dinner."

"Gladly." He escorted her to the dining room. Its wide entrance enabled diners to view the gaming crowd from their candlelit tables. Chance noted with approval the starched white napery, gleaming silver, and sparkling glasses. At each table there was a spray of roses, and when Chance had seated Toni he gave her a rosebud for her hair. "Thank you, sir," she said and gestured at the large, leather-bound menu. "Surely we're not expected to read the whole thing?"

Chance turned to the maître d'hôtel and asked him to order for them. So they dined on cold vichyssoise, Iceland salmon, *pommes de terre rissolée,* salad, and a tart lemon sherbet. Their wine was a light Neuchâtel Riesling, then café espresso, with demi-snifters of Hine cognac that they carried to the gaming room. During their hour-long dining the number of players had tripled. The buzz of conversation, the calls of croupiers, the whir and click of wheels and chips stimulated Chance as he sipped cognac and admired the elegance of the polished wood-and-brass tables.

Together they played baccarat, chemin de fer, birdcage, and blackjack, winning more than they lost. The sporting crowd had thickened, and Chance saw that most of the men were in dinner attire like him, but there was a scattering of street-dressed males, many of whose faces were taut with the desire to win. Toni was betting their stake alternately on red and black, odd and even numbers, and Chance saw their chip pile steadily grow. She was drawing in another stack when a man edged through the crowd beside her and spoke into her ear. Toni faced him, said, "No," brusquely, and continued bringing in her winnings. The man grasped her wrist. Annoyed, she shook her arm, but the man smiled wolfishly and tightened his grip. Chance left the table and moved swiftly to the man's other side. Quietly he said, *"Mon ami,* I have a message for you."

Turning his head, the man said, "And what is that?"

"Your life is in danger."

The man grunted, "So? From what?"

"From me. Let her go."

160

"Stay out of it," the man snapped. "It's not your concern." His face was pockmarked and his teeth were tobacco-stained.

Chance drove his right arm upward so the heel of his hand slammed against the man's chin. The man's head snapped backward and he was out cold. Chance caught the sagging body and lowered it to the floor, hearing gasps around him. "Croupier," he said, "this man needs assistance."

His gambler's face showing no expression whatever, the croupier said, "Certainly, m'sieu," and pressed an unseen button.

Beside Chance, Toni said, "My, that was fast, Jean-Pierre. Do you do it often?"

"As necessary," he said. "Are you all right?" He looked at her reddened wrist.

"Fine. But he was determined that I leave with him."

Two dinner-jacketed attendants appeared and lifted the man by shoulders and feet, and carried him off through the parted crowd. Chance turned back to where play had resumed. "Anyone you know?" he asked.

"Not really—just a lackey of my husband's—my *ex*-husband." She finished stacking her chips. "It seems Mohammed wants me back, the bastard."

"And you?"

"Death would almost be preferable." She moved her thigh against his. "Thank you for ending an unpleasant scene so efficiently. Do you hire out on weekends?"

Chance smiled. "Depends on the client."

"Well, it's obvious I need protection. Imagine—coming after me in a crowd like this. Mohammed thinks he can get away with anything, and he usually does." Chance decided not to tell her about the Peugeot, but to mention it to Paul.

The wheel spun, the ivory ball clicked, the croupier made crisp monotone calls, raked and pushed chips here and there, until, their stake steadily shrinking, Toni said unsteadily, "Let's take a break, shall we? I'm not betting well."

"Champagne's the cure," Chance said and walked her to a table in the lounge. They touched tulips of iced Veuve Cliquot and Toni said, "To tomorrow?"

"To all the tomorrows," he said, and they sipped.

161

After a while she said, "Paul saw that I was schooled in a protective environment, so when I met Mohammed I was unbelievably naive. He can be delightful when he wants to be—after all, he went to Le Rosey and Cambridge—and with me he was all Prince Charming," she said bitterly. "But the other side of him is brutish, animal, and that part he concealed until we were married. As his third wife I followed an Egyptian and a Parisian, both of whom he dismissed when he tired of them."

"Making him a three-time loser."

She shrugged. "Which he apparently doesn't want to be. The royal custom, I quickly found out, is to treat females as community property, and I was always being grabbed at by Mohammed's brothers and half brothers, even the king himself. When I didn't submit, Mohammed beat me up, yelling I was disgracing him with his family." Her face set. "Can you imagine that? *Me* disgracing *him?* He liked groups, too, and when I refused, that got me more beatings. Life on the royal track was pretty shitty if you get my meaning." She drained her glass and Chance refilled it and his own.

Her lips formed a thin smile. "He liked being whipped—and believe me, I was glad to lay on the lash—it was the only time I enjoyed kinky sex. Unfortunately, it didn't happen often enough, so I gathered my jewels, and the next time our plane landed in Paris I made straight for the first gendarme I saw and asked for protection. The French didn't like it—they have old colonial ties to Mohammed's house—but I was allowed to stay, found a tough attorney, and filed for divorce. To shut me up Mohammed agreed, and my brother gave me shelter." Her gaze lifted to Chance. "Temporary, of course."

He said nothing.

"If you don't know Paul well, Jean-Pierre, never trust him where his own interests are concerned. He's done business for the al-Hazawi clan, and for all I know he'd sell me back to them." She paused. "Charming, isn't it?"

"It's—unusual, but I have the feeling you're quite capable of taking care of yourself. And everyone's entitled to a mistake now and then."

"Mine was mountain-size." She drank deeply.

"Still, you were compensated, Toni."

162

"Yes," she said slowly, "there is the money, but I still feel shamed."

"You'll get over it." He glanced around at the well-dressed crowd. "Feel up to more wagering?"

"Why not? It's only money."

They returned to the roulette table where Toni's determination and skill tripled their winnings. At midnight they enjoyed a buffet supper from a sumptuous spread served by three mushroom-hatted chefs, more champagne, until at one o'clock Chance stifled a yawn. "I'd better be getting you back to Paul's domain or risk his displeasure."

She smiled. "I doubt that counts much with you. Besides, I'm not only of age, I'm a divorcée, so my brother's no longer responsible for whatever remains of my reputation." As they left the table she said, "For me this has been a wonderful evening, Jean-Pierre. It's therapeutic to be out and around with people again. And especially with you."

"My pleasure," he said truthfully and walked with her to the cage where she dumped their considerable winnings in the cashier's tray. The cashier exchanged chips for francs that Toni divided, and Chance gained seven thousand francs above Sam's stake of five.

As they left the casino, Toni said, "I wonder if you'd care to go with me to a reception tomorrow night? The Mexicans are entertaining various delegations to some sort of treaty conference."

"The Mexicans?"

"They're always trying to get on the world stage by intervening in things that don't concern them, disarmament in particular. It's at the Hilton, so the food should be good. Interested?"

"Delighted," he said. "Will Paul be there?"

"Probably, but on his own business. I plan to avoid him."

The attendant brought up Chance's Mercedes and they got in. Toni sat close to Chance, and as they drove toward the highway he checked the rearview mirror and saw a gray Peugeot sedan pulling out of the parking area behind them.

"Buckle up, Toni," he said as he hit the accelerator. The powerful engine kicked into overdrive and Chance turned onto the divided highway with screeching tires, wishing he'd brought the Walther along. Toni turned and glanced back. "Faster," she said anxiously, "they're gaining."

TWENTY-EIGHT

As he sped toward the Swiss border Chance saw the Peugeot closing faster than he'd thought possible. "Keep your head down," he ordered, "the crazy bastards may shoot."

Obediently she lowered her head so that her cheek rested on his thigh. "I suppose," she murmured in a muffled voice, "if Mohammed can't have me back, he'd prefer me dead."

"Why?"

"Pride—and paranoia."

The Peugeot was only a few yards behind. Abruptly, Chance swung into the left lane and braked hard, and the Peugeot sped past, missing the side of the Mercedes by inches. Chance floored the accelerator and when his car's nose was even with the smaller car's rear wheels, he turned into it. Sparks showered as he bore relentlessly into the Peugeot, shoving its rear end toward the shoulder, making it fishtail across the highway. He braked and saw the Peugeot slam into the dividing embankment, climb partway up and turn over, rolling back to the highway, where it landed on its side.

Resuming speed, Chance glanced at the rearview mirror and saw the disabled car's headlights still on, and no fire. Just before he took a curve he saw a man scramble from the upper door. "God, that was exciting!" Toni gasped. Her fingers dug into his arm. "You didn't care if you killed them."

"No time to determine their intentions, Toni, so I assumed the worst." He glanced at her. "Bother you?"

"Heavens, no." She began fluffing out her hair. "You're adding a new dimension to my life, Jean-Pierre. I've only read about this kind of stuff."

"That same car followed us from Lausanne," he told her.

They stopped briefly at the frontier for passport checks, after which Chance rounded the airport and drove directly to Valcour's manse. As he opened her door Toni said, "After that, I need a drink—will you join me?"

They found Paul Valcour in his library, wearing half-lenses and working at the Daiwa computer. Toni kissed his cheek and told him what had happened while Valcour filled and warmed brandy snifters. Handing one to Chance, he said, "What do you make of it, Jean-Pierre?"

"She ought to have a bodyguard or two when she's away from here."

"I think you're right—though you might have been the target." He gazed meaningfully at Chance over the snifter rim. "Any chance?"

"None. Just a domestic dispute."

"And a very nasty one," Toni added. "Thanks to Jean-Pierre I'm not on a plane bound for God knows where."

"Well, we're sincerely grateful to you," Valcour said, "and I'll look for an opportunity to express my gratitude."

"Toni's companionship is reward enough, Paul." He drank and wondered what business deal Valcour was working on so late at night. New York banks and stock exchanges were closed, but in Peking it was midday, morning in Moscow. Paul's computer could receive and transmit information almost instantly via satellite or land line connections.

Chance finished his cognac. "If you'll excuse me. . . ."

Toni kissed his cheek lightly. "Thank you again."

"Thank you for my winnings."

Valcour went with him to the door and down the steps to the Mercedes. Chance saw that the wraparound bumper had protected the front end, although the right fender was bent inward and stripped of paint. Valcour touched a bare patch. "I'll have Albert take care of this in the morning. The car should be ready by midday. Mohammed will try again, you know."

"Get her a bodyguard," Chance said, and got behind the wheel.

166

"Any signs of the Russian?"

"Not yet. He may be arranging things so his leaving Moscow won't arouse suspicion."

Chance nodded. "I learned patience a long time ago, Paul. Good night."

Back at his villa, he found Sam asleep on a sofa. Chance went quietly up the staircase to his room. In the bed, he found Lao-li, breathing softly and rhythmically. He got under the covers without waking her, kept to his side of the bed, and quickly fell asleep.

In the morning, after Valcour's driver had taken the Mercedes off to a body shop, Sam said, "I don't think you ought to get involved in Princess Azira's problems. Things could have turned out differently last night and we'd have lost our investment in you."

"Valcour's getting his sister a bodyguard."

"Good. We have bigger things to worry about."

"Even so, Toni gives me mobility, a reason for being here and there."

"Cover is okay. When you get horny, remember Lao-li is your therapist."

Chance grunted. "This morning I told her I'd tell her if I wanted her again. I'm still married, Sam."

"Okay, okay, whatever you say. To Lao-li it's just a job."

"She's a good worker," Chance commented dryly.

In the library Sam took files from a heavy built-in safe and went over a list of active local Soviets. In addition to consular personnel, KGB and GRU types were part of every international organization based in Geneva. Chance said, "At least a hundred, yes?"

"One twenty-one identified intelligence agents as of yesterday's count. Probably a dozen more under deep cover—sleepers and covert support agents."

After Sam left for the consulate to check on messages from Hsiao, Chance studied file faces and names. Agent histories were in Chinese, but it was visual identification he wanted. Four KGB faces were familiar from previous posts where Chance had operated against Soviet *rezidenturas,* but their names were different per KGB procedures. A blown or persona non grata agent was withdrawn and repapered for a different foreign post. CIA was quick to identify the agent to the local service, but usually the foreign ministry was either indifferent or so firmly in bed with the Soviets that the effort was wasted. Only in Britain and the U.S. had there been significant expulsions of Soviet intelligence personnel.

Why is a Soviet agent like your lap? the old Agency jest had gone. Because when you stand up it creeps around behind and turns up under a different name. Ha-ha, thought Chance, except it isn't funny.

During lunch on the patio Chance scanned the *Journal de Genève* and came across a short paragraph describing a one-car accident on route 5 near the French border. A Peugeot sedan had swerved into the highway divider and turned over. The driver escaped with bruises, but a passenger was hospitalized with concussion and broken bones. Police charged the driver with careless manipulation of his vehicle but declined to give out the names of those involved.

This time I was lucky, Chance thought. If Pockmark was the driver, he knows what I look like. He decided to buy a shoulder holster.

Presently Albert drove up in the Mercedes, expertly repaired. M'sieu Valcour had taken care of the bill, Albert said curtly, and he drove off in Paul's Daimler.

While Chance was taking a sunbath Sam returned and said there had been no communication from Hsiao Kuan-hua. "However," he said, "we have information that a power struggle inside the Politburo is just beginning to surface."

"That's pretty routine," Chance remarked.

"Unless it relates to our project. I wish it would finish up one way or another. I'm getting restless. Besides, I have leave due and I want to visit my family."

"Where?"

"Hsian. My father is a construction engineer and my mother teaches school."

"I thought you might be married."

"In time," he said. "Two more years abroad and I get a desk job in Peking for four years."

His words sent a pang through Chance, reminding him of Carla and their hopes of children. Chance turned over and let the sun bake his back. Sam, he thought, was able to plan six years ahead, while he couldn't be sure of the next six hours. If the project was an abort, would Hsiao cancel his obligation and allow him to travel where he chose? Or would the wily old man decide Chance knew too much and have him killed?

Even if he were released, what would he do with his life? Of one thing he was sure—it would be a long time, if ever, before he could return to his homeland and pick up the threads of his life. It was far easier to live abroad under an alias than in the U.S. If he became involved in a traffic accident, his prints would be run through the computer and his true identity revealed. So his only course was to do Hsiao's bidding, and hope for the best.

In chauffeur's uniform, Sam drove him to Valcour's place that evening, and when Toni appeared she was accompanied by her brother. "I'll be along a little later," Paul said. "Toni, have a good time." She was wearing an ankle-length gown of patterned taffeta, a platinum-set solitaire on her right ring finger, and a diamond necklace that shimmered under the car's ceiling light.

When they entered the Hilton ballroom they went through the receiving line, meeting the Mexican consul general, the Mexican ambassador and foreign minister, and their wives. The first two diplomats addressed Toni as "Princess," and the foreign minister smiled tolerantly. Of proletarian background and devoted to an extreme leftist ideology, the foreign minister declined to acknowledge a privileged aristocracy.

Leaving the line, they found themselves among three or four hundred guests, a few of whom were Toni's acquaintances. The decorations and buffet tables featuring ice sculptures of patriotic Mexican symbols were lavish, and Chance whispered, "For a country with a staggering and unpayable foreign debt, Mexico does pretty well."

"The poorest countries often put on the most extravagant displays. Must have something to do with inferiority complexes."

"Conspicuous consumption," Chance nodded, "calculated to impress lenders that Mexico's a reliable borrower of international funds." He looked around at the crowd. "Assuming World Bank

169

people are here, they'll be hearing from Mexico in the next few days."

They chatted with groups from the International Labor Organization, World Health Organization, International Red Cross, GATT, the European Economic Community, and World Court. There were diplomats from Western Europe, Latin America, and Scandinavia, and Chance noticed a group of men so poorly dressed as to be immediately identifiable as SovBloc creeps.

He steered Toni away from them, and she avoided OPEC ministers and other Arabs. When the U.S. secretary of state came in with his Soviet counterpart, many of the guests applauded. Both officials had security guards in train as well as members of their negotiating teams. From twenty feet away Chance spotted the president's national security adviser in naval uniform; beside him stood a bald man in a dark suit, wearing a black band around one arm.

Chance felt his mouth go dry.

Jan Abrams. Would he recognize Quinn Chance? Would he give him away to his security men? Chance realized he was staring at Jan. With an effort he forced his gaze away, saw Jan's glasses glint under the blaze of the chandelier, and knew that Jan Abrams was staring back.

TWENTY-NINE

After reaching Geneva with the foreign minister's party, General Sobatkin summoned the KGB *rezident* from the Bern embassy and gave him private instructions to prevent a possible approach by agents of the People's Republic of China. Without explaining the connection, Sobatkin left photographs of Quentin Chance with the *rezident,* identifying him as a deadly enemy of the Soviet Union to be captured and held for interrogation by Sobatkin.

Then he flew on to Washington. Now in the embassy's sound-proof chamber he faced an apprehensive Nikolai Berlikov.

"So," said Sobatkin, "you wanted to see me. Well, Kolya, here I am."

Berlikov drew in a deep breath, for this was the confrontation he had been dreading. "I appreciate your taking time to come here, Yevgeni Lubovich," he began. "And because of what happened in the wake of Sosnowski's execution, I felt it extremely important that you understand just where the responsibility lies."

"For the deaths of three *shpiks?* They were your agents, were they not? You transmitted their instructions—where else does the responsibility lie but on your shoulders?" He took out a package of Marlboros and lighted one. After exhaling he said, "To that, add the escape of Quentin Chance and we have a pot of putrid turnips clogging our nostrils."

Berlikov tried to keep his voice steady. "Permit me to remind you, Yevgeni Lubovich, with all deference, that the *shpiks* were in place here before I arrived. I did not recruit them or train them or vouch for their abilities. That the two Arabs failed to kill the

American is hardly my fault. That the American tracked and tortured them to reveal their cutout's name is not my fault either." He breathed deeply again. "How could one anticipate Chance's rescue by a special faction within CIA when CIA itself delivered Chance into the hands of the police?"

Sobatkin's lidded eyes regarded him as a hawk focuses on a sitting marmot. "All very well," he said with a shrug of indifference, "but the facts of your rank, your pay, and your privileges demonstrate clearly that you are responsible for the actions of your subordinates. Is it not true that had you been successful, you would have been commended?" He exhaled across the narrow table. "Since the days of Cheka and Okhrana, we have followed a chain of command that establishes obligations and responsibilities. You and I are part of that chain, Kolya, like it or not, and for your information I have recently come from an unpleasant meeting with Marshal Yaroshenko. Fortunately for you, I defended you and told the marshal that you would most certainly get off your ass and apprehend Chance in the very near future." He flicked ash from his cigarette. "Was I correct in that assumption, Nikolai Petrovich?"

"Of course," Berlikov said hoarsely. "Absolutely."

"Well, we will see, will we not? And to possibly lighten your burden, our comrades in Switzerland will be on the lookout for Chance should he surface in Europe."

Berlikov sighed in relief. "Between there and here I have no doubt that Chance will be found."

"He had better be," Sobatkin said menacingly, "for I need hardly detail the consequences to you of failure. Nor will I accept black marks from Marshal Yaroshenko because I vouched for you. Once, yes. A second time, no."

"I understand," Berlikov said quickly. "The American cannot hide forever. He is, after all, sought by the FBI and by Interpol as well."

"Into whose hands he must not fall, eh?"

Berlikov quickly reckoned the disparity between whatever efforts he could make and those thousands of law enforcement officers also seeking Chance, and despaired. To change the focus he said, "May I ask whether an official investigation has been launched with regard to the deaths of the three *shpiks?*"

"I thought that might concern you," Sobatkin replied, "so to relieve your mind I can tell you that there is at present no investigation under way. Nevertheless that could change in the event of further difficulties." He stubbed out his cigarette. "By that I refer to Marshal Yaroshenko's displeasure should his wishes fail to be carried out. In that case I would be unable to head off an investigation, you understand."

"That would indeed be unfortunate," said Berlikov, "since a thorough investigation would necessarily reveal not only your role but that of Marshal Yaroshenko."

Sobatkin considered the implication. "Perhaps. In any case, it would be best for all concerned that no investigation take place. From time to time," he went on, "each of us must consider where his best interests lie. In the present case I have done so, and I expect you have done so as well." Meaning, thought Berlikov, that the old bastard would dump me like a turd, deny giving me orders, and become one of my prosecutors.

Briefly he considered informing his superior of the recording, then decided that this was not the moment. He would use the recording to protect himself only in extremis, as a desperate last resort. Meanwhile, he would have to deploy all his resources against the American, play for time, and hope for a break.

Sobatkin stood up and straightened his jacket. "I authorize you to utilize Chavadze and his GRU assets to assist you in whatever way you deem advisable. And I will so inform him before I leave."

"Thank you, Yevgeni Lubovich. I have no doubt that Petya will willingly assist."

He followed Sobatkin out of the air-conditioned chamber, they gave each other a soldierly parting, and Berlikov returned to his office. Pulling off his uniform jacket, he tossed it at a chair and missed, watched it slide to the floor. An omen? he wondered, and sat down behind his desk. Sobatkin was like a raven bringing bad luck, even death, wherever he alighted. He felt trapped and helpless. The American was gone, vanished, and Berlikov wondered what exactly Sobatkin expected. The reality was that the odds lay heavily against his ever locating Quentin Chance. Failure would bring reprisals from Sobatkin and Marshal Yaroshenko, and he had no doubt that he would end up either a *zek* in the frozen north or staring at a firing squad.

He looked at his doorway and again wondered whether he should warn Sobatkin of the trump card he held. Sobatkin was only a few yards away. . . . Perhaps the American would be caught by Interpol or the FBI; at least that would end pursuit and his responsibility for it. But would that satisfy Sobatkin and Yaroshenko? He doubted it.

The wire recording was taped behind a bookcase in his home. He must make a copy and tell Irina how to employ it in case of his sudden disappearance. With that leverage she might be able to save his life and career and the lives of herself and the children.

Or—and this possibility sprang into his mind with shocking force—he might claim asylum from the FBI. Would that be his *sudba*—his fate?

Berlikov wiped heavy perspiration from his face and forehead, and ordered his secretary to bring him a glass of sugared tea. Lieutenant General Yevgeni Lubovich Sobatkin, he told himself, had become his most threatening enemy.

THIRTY

"Excuse me," said Chance to Toni, and he walked directly to Jan Abrams. In German he said, "You seem to look at me as though you recognized me."

"Yes, that's so," Jan replied in German. "There is a great similarity to another person, a friend, especially the voice." He paused. "I was hoping to convey some information to him. Sad information," he added. "I wanted to tell him that his wife died peacefully ten days ago." Absently, he fingered his mourning band. "Shortly after my own wife passed away."

Chance stared at him, feeling tears gather in his eyes. Looking away he said hoarsely, "I'm sorry about your wife and the wife of your friend. Perhaps you will encounter him in your travels."

"Perhaps," Abrams said. "Unfortunately, my friend is in grave difficulties even though they may be no fault of his own. I would like to see him, talk with him about his problems, but under the circumstances I fear it is impossible. So it is in life—one makes one's own way as best one can."

Chance dabbed the moisture from his eyes. "I'm sure your friend would value an opportunity to talk with you and receive your counsel. But as you say, his situation may prevent his doing so. Evidence can be faked, an innocent man implicated in heinous crimes—we know these things happen in today's world, do we not?"

"Not only the world of today," Jan Abrams said, "the world of yesterday—my world. A time when the accident of birth or religion was enough to send men, women, and children to the gas chambers. But then"—he paused and looked around at the national security adviser, who was baffled by the German conversation—"we are here on a mission of peace, looking toward the time when such catastrophic cruelties may never again occur. Ah—my name is Abrams, Jan Abrams. Is it permitted to know yours?"

"Duroc. Jean-Pierre Duroc."

They shook hands, and Abrams continued in German, "You live in Geneva, Herr Duroc?"

"Temporarily," Chance said. "Like yourself, I am here on a mission of peace."

"Interesting. May I know in what capacity?"

"Well, I'm only a private citizen—French—but I've been retained by the government of China as a representative in a highly secret matter. Groundwork for a rapprochement with the Soviet Union—you won't betray the confidence, I trust?"

"Certainly not," Abrams said, "although I find the information of considerable value—and not to be entrusted to normal diplomatic channels."

Chance shook his head. "Elements on both sides oppose it, thus the extreme caution."

"I would have thought so. Well, I won't ask indiscreet questions of you, and in any case my mind is filled with my friend's tragedy. Had I encountered him, I would have told him that his late wife was buried near the hospital where she died. I was at the services, as were his lawyer and a friend named Veronica. It was a beautiful, clear day, Herr Duroc—he would want to know that as well."

"Without question," Chance said, his voice thickening. "Doubtless he would have been there had circumstances permitted."

"But perhaps it was just as well—there were strangers there who sought my friend. In any case, his wife rests with mine in eternal peace."

Chance could not speak. Abrams took his arm and whispered, "Good luck," as he moved away.

For a few moments Chance stood dumbly, mind blank with sorrow. Then he forced himself back to the present, turned, and walked to Toni, who was talking animatedly with an elderly gentleman, whom she introduced to Chance as a member of the Swiss

Parliament. They chatted until he excused himself. Toni said, "Were you talking with an old friend?"

"I recognized him from Philadelphia," Chance lied. "A professor of economics at Penn. He didn't know me, of course, but he was glad to find a former pupil in this crowd of strangers." He looked around but could no longer see Jan Abrams. "He's an adviser or consultant to the American delegation. We talked briefly about the coming negotiations with Russia."

He wondered if he had said too much, but he wanted to explain his absence and too little was as dangerous as too much. For despite her hedonistic glitter, the former Princess Azira had a sharp and perceptive mind. Like her brother, Chance thought.

They headed for the nearest buffet table, but Chance had no appetite. He wanted to be by himself so that he could come to terms with his grief. While Toni ate, he toyed abstractedly with his food and drank three glasses of champagne, hoping it would dull his inner pain.

When Toni finished, he said he was feeling unwell and asked if she minded leaving now—or she could stay and the car would return for her.

"We'll leave together," she said firmly. "Paul's over there talking with those unattractive Russians, and I don't want to be drawn into *that!* Besides, we'll have other times together," she said softly, "won't we, Jean-Pierre?"

"Of course," he said.

Alone in his bedroom, Chance filled a glass with whiskey, then another. Sobbing brokenly, he lay down on the bed while kaleidoscopic memories of Carla flashed through his mind. Finally, the colors faded into a screen of motionless gray, and his mind dissolved into drunken sleep.

When Lao-li woke him the room was flooded with sunlight. "You have a visitor," she said, and brought his dressing robe. Chance splashed cold water on his face, combed his hair, and went unsteadily downstairs.

Paul Valcour, in riding costume, was waiting for him by the

entrance. "Toni said you weren't feeling well last night—hope you're better now."

His head throbbed abominably, but he said, "I'm okay. What's on your mind?"

"I picked up a piece of interesting information last night, Quinn, but you weren't around to share it. Apparently the Soviet delegation is expecting the arrival of the Kremlin's number two man—Yegor Ligachev—but it's being kept quite secret."

"So?"

"It occurs to me that the deputy premier may be the man we're waiting for."

Chance's head ached. The news of Carla's death had drained him. He shrugged indifferently.

Valcour said, "You were seen with our old colleague, Jan Abrams. What were you talking about?

"Fuck off," Chance said, and went back up the stairs to bed.

THIRTY-ONE

Before retiring in his suite at the Hotel du Rhône, Jan Abrams ordered a carafe of warm milk and a plate of sugar cookies. Except for salad and a glass of tomato juice at the Mexican reception, he had eaten nothing, avoiding the buffet's rich, cholesterol-laden offerings. Besides, since conversing with "Herr Duroc" he had been preoccupied with two problems, one moral, the other procedural.

Jan went over to the window and stood for a while, looking out across the lake, seeing the high, flowering Jet-d'Eau illuminated from below. On the lake itself were a few boat lights, barges, perhaps a few fishermen plumbing the dark, snow-fed depths. Lights rimmed the far shore, dotted the foothills beyond. The lake was ringed with mansions and palaces of the famous and/or wealthy. Keats, Byron, Shelley and Mary; Eisenhower; the grossly fat old Aga Khan whose weight was balanced in diamonds; scores more whose names Jan did not particularly want to recall.

He had been in Geneva many times, always appreciating the physical beauty of the setting—the quaint Old Town, the lake's dark waters, and the awesome snowcapped mountains ranged protectively beyond . . . but toward the country itself and its people Jan felt an old hostility. Jews who fled from the Holocaust could enter only if they were wealthy; Swiss factories manufactured munitions for Allies and Nazis alike, whoever could pay. There seemed to be no moral standard higher than trade and commerce. Swiss buildings, banks, and services were available to every nation great and small, and Geneva itself had become the locus of notori-

179

ous Western diplomatic failures that Jan did not care to think about. Summits uncountable, OPEC meetings . . . Geneva was a huge whorehouse where rooms were rented indiscriminately by the hour.

To be neutral, he thought, was not as praiseworthy as the Swiss claimed. For how could one equate Evil with Good on any value scale? You had to take a stand and live or die by your choice. Still, he was here, playing a minor role in yet another meeting between a Russia that knew exactly what it wanted, and an America that could hardly define its interests and always downplayed them in a spirit of compromise.

Like all American presidents, Jan reflected, the current White House occupant had never lived abroad, spoke no foreign language, and had only slight understanding of foreign affairs. He wanted peace, wanted to be seen signing yet another agreement with the Soviet Union, whose history and goals the president was far from understanding. Thus Jan Abrams felt that his own work was mostly useless. It was bad form to question the intentions of the Soviet Union, much easier to be a team player and not "irritate" the U.S.S.R. Just as, in 1938, France and England shrank from challenging Herr Hitler. Appeasement then, appeasement now, appeasement forever.

Sitting on the bed, Jan sipped the warm, fresh milk and munched a sugar cookie. For a while he gazed at Sarah's photograph on the night table, where he could view it during restless nights, and wished she were there to advise him.

Always through the years she had been his conscience, his good angel, counseling him to patience when his inclination was to be impulsive. "Act only after you think," was her guidance, "never before." And inevitably in the long run Sarah had been right. He had been anticipating her death for so long that when the call came it was as though the screen had gone blank at the end of a long movie. He had burst into tears, of course, but they had said their true good-byes weeks earlier. He was left with an unfillable emptiness that clung to him as closely and darkly as his shadow.

Jan added more milk to his glass and sipped again. Even that was a reminder of Sarah, who customarily brought him a late-night snack in his study. It was bad to sleep on an empty stomach, she always said, and it was true that without milk and cookies he often slept poorly.

Bringing his thoughts back to the present, he summed up his moral problem: Quinn Chance was a known fugitive, charged with the murder of a Soviet citizen. The press had not revealed that Pavel Sosnowski was a major in the KGB, but Abrams had computer-queried the Agency and received printout confirmation. The press speculated that Chance might also have slain Walter Stillman but there was no direct evidence linking Chance to Stillman's shooting, in fact no evidence of any kind, and the murder remained a mystery. Abrams believed Chance. Chance was an intellectual, not a killer, a man who had left the Agency to live quietly among books. So forget the Stillman matter.

As for Sosnowski, it was true—as the press said—that there had been a brawl between Chance and Sosnowski in Cairo years ago, but would that old, brief encounter be reason for murder? Not that disposing of KGB officers was necessarily a bad idea—they were storm troopers and SS criminals in different uniforms—but if Chance had nursed a grudge against Sosnowski, he surely wouldn't have acted on it in his own apartment.

As an experienced intelligence reports officer, Jan Abrams was willing to attach due weight to circumstantial evidence, just as the legal system did. But he had always lectured novice officers that such facts were the basis for further investigation, not the decision itself; they had to be vetted out, confirmed independently—or discarded altogether.

Jan selected another cookie and nibbled at its rim. He had taken three oaths in his life: One when he was granted U.S. citizenship just after the war; one when he was sworn in to what became the Central Intelligence Agency; the latest when he became a White House aide and counselor to the national security adviser. He had always honored them.

Their encounter had taken place on neutral ground, where FBI agents in the delegation had no power of arrest. And since I could not then, or now, positively identify Jean-Pierre Duroc as Quinn Chance, I had no responsibility to raise an alarm, embarrassing our Mexican hosts and my delegation as well. So by keeping my thoughts to myself I did the right thing. He studied Sarah's photograph, and said aloud, "Did I not, my dear?"

But he admitted that he had been engaging in sophistry to ease his conscience. A Talmudic argument had been made, whereas in reality he knew perfectly well that Duroc and Chance were the same man. With that acknowledgment Abrams ate another cookie and considered the weighty information received from Quinn Chance. If the historically inevitable alliance between Russia and Communist China eased tension and permitted both countries to devote more resources to the welfare of their separate populations, then well and good. But if rapprochement foreshadowed massive joint military action, it represented a threat of awesome dimensions, a menace the West could not ignore. And the United States would be forced to take preemptive action to prevent that evil alliance from being formed.

You won't betray the confidence, I trust? the man had said, and Abrams remembered replying, *Certainly not.* So his word had been given.

He thought back to reporting discipline and format. How would an informant such as Duroc routinely be evaluated? As an unknown, untested source of unidentified nationality volunteering speculation in the guise of information. Under that heading no report would ever be written, much less circulated at policy levels, where it might be of galvanizing interest if verifiable. So the identity and motivation of the source was fundamental. But I have no responsibility for law enforcement in the United States, Abrams reminded himself, much less in Switzerland. I'm not a cop or an investigator. I'm not even in the business of intelligence-gathering; I'm an analyst of information acquired by others. What I will do is remember what the source told me and be alert for confirming indications, if they ever come. The world was asleep when Stalin and Hitler signed their pact; we can't afford to be asleep again.

The last of his cookies was gone. He finished his milk knowing that more remained in the carafe should he require it later in the night.

"Have I done right?" he asked. He picked up the photograph of Sarah and pressed his lips to hers. Then he undressed, pulled on shapeless pajamas large for even his large frame, turned off the light, and got into bed.

Before sleep came he wished that things would enable Quinn Chance to return to America and visit his wife's grave in peace and safety.

THIRTY-TWO

Late the next day Sam returned from the Chinese consulate for a stroll in the spacious terraced garden with Chance. The air was cool and misty, reminding Chance of London this time of year. Alpine peaks were hidden by gray clouds. At the garden's center, breeze swayed spray from a stone naiad fountain wetting earth furrows from which flowers had yet to emerge. In conversational tones Sam said, "That suggestion of Valcour's about Yegor Ligachev doesn't jibe with the facts. He's always been known as a hard-liner, an irredentist as regards China, an ideological conservative. Hsiao doesn't believe Ligachev will come here—*if* he comes—bearing any welcome gifts for my country."

"Still, a hard-line reputation would be useful cover if Ligachev wants to establish better relations with China."

"He'd be playing a very dangerous game."

"There's danger everywhere," Chance observed. "Look what happened to me."

Sam nodded. "Until recently Deputy Premier Ligachev was believed to be the premier's strong right arm, his enforcer, but he's spoken publicly against some of the premier's proposed economic reforms. If Ligachev is sent to Geneva, Hsiao believes it will be to get him out of the Kremlin while the premier shuffles some of his ministers. It's happened before. In short, we don't believe Ligachev in any way represents the Liberals who want to deal with us. And if he does represent the Liberals, I'm not sure we'd be sufficiently confident of his future to talk seriously with him."

"Well, it was only Paul's supposition."

"It's true Valcour spends a lot of time with the Soviets, but I don't think he can supply much more than travel information."

They were strolling down a gravel path toward the high stone wall at the foot of the garden. Chance asked, "Does Hsiao trust Valcour?"

"Within limits. Valcour has always been much closer to the Soviets than to us. If he thought it to his advantage, I don't doubt he would betray everyone involved." He glanced at Chance. "That's Valcour's history. Do *you* trust him?"

"I trust him to do what he's paid for. What counts with Paul is the bottom line, nothing else."

"So far he hasn't given you away."

"In a showdown I don't doubt that he would—and he knows the KGB would like to finish me off."

"What about his sister's feelings for you?"

"Whatever they are, they wouldn't matter to Paul. He regards Toni as a rebuke to the way he raised her and married her off."

"How do you feel about her?"

"She's a lost child, Sam; I feel sorry for her."

Their conversation was interrupted by the throaty roar of Toni's pink Lamborghini mounting the drive. She braked near the garage, spraying gravel against the door, got out, and walked toward Chance. "I'm in a spending mood," she said as Sam drifted away. "Let's go and unload my winnings, okay?"

"Where's your bodyguard?"

"Obviously my car won't hold both of you. Besides"—she took his arm"—I have confidence in you, Jean-Pierre."

"I'll put on a clean shirt," he said, and went up to his bedroom, where he changed into town clothes and strapped on a nylon shoulder holster. Inserting the Walther automatic, Chance pulled on a tweed jacket and joined her in the roadster.

She drove rapidly into Geneva, parked near the broad place des Alpes, and they strolled along the rue's shop-lined walk. Here in the heart of Geneva's shopping center, prices were not calculated to attract buyers on limited budgets, and discount was a dirty word. Frontage on the rue des Alpes was scarce, high-priced, and coveted. Accordingly, stores that sold gems, antiques, optical specialties and objets d'art were narrow and separated only by common walls. Unlike Fifth and Worth avenues, Geneva's pricey shops lacked eye-catching decor. In fact, Chance reflected, most of them looked downright stodgy from the street. Inside, though, merchandise was displayed and lighted with attractive precision. Toni tried on rings, bracelets, and necklaces in two stores. Chance had been feeling morose and depressed over Carla's death, but Toni's insouciant chatter brought him out of it, and he began enjoying the expedition. At a third store, Jovin's, she held up an emerald pendant. "What do you think?"

"It's beautiful."

"Well, if you like it, I'll take it."

"I'm not much of a gemstone judge," he said, "but if you like it, then you should have it."

"No, I want you to decide." She laid the glittering stone in his palm. Chance studied the brilliant green facets and nodded. "Buy it." While the salesman was wrapping the necklace in black velvet, she said, "I want to wear it for you, Jean-Pierre, so let's find opportunities."

He slipped the small package into his pocket, and they walked slowly down to the cobbled quai des Bergues where the Rhône flowed into the Lake of Geneva—or Léman, as the Swiss called it. She held his hand. "I don't know how long you'll be here, but I want you to have a souvenir of Geneva so you'll remember me. What would you like?"

"Oh, a necktie would be fine," he told her, and she guided him to a men's clothing store, where he selected a dark blue silk tie dotted with red-and-white rondelles. From there they walked to a sidewalk café facing the Rousseau monument, ordered coffee and small pastries—it was teatime—and watched the passing crowd.

One of the passersby was Jan Abrams. They nodded at each other and Jan shambled on without speaking. Toni commented, "Your former professor looks like a nice old man."

"He is."

"If you'd asked him to join us, he could have satisfied some of my curiosity about you."

"He remembered my face, not my name. He's taught thousands in his time. And what's this curiosity?"

She shrugged. "You never seem to have much to occupy your

186

time, Jean-Pierre; it's as though you were waiting for something to happen."

"I'm passive by nature," he said, "but I want to improve on that. Dinner tonight?"

"Love it. There's a three-star restaurant near the Vandoeuvres Golf Club"—she gestured across the lake"—or we can dine at the Richemond or the Hilton."

He looked away. Beyond the gunmetal lake the foothills were purpling in early twilight. The moment seemed suspended in time, and he rebuked himself. What right did he have to be in one of the world's most beautiful settings, in the company of an attractive young woman, while Carla . . .

"Which do you prefer?" Toni asked, looking at him quizzically.

"Oh." His mind whirled back to their discussion. "Hotels," he said dismissively. "Let's try your three-star place tonight."

La Belle Equipe turned out to be in a small Germanic castle that retained much atmosphere of ancient times. Guests parked in a lot surrounded by groves of beech and pine, and crossed a small drawbridge over a watered moat. Domestic and oriental ducks and geese paddled the lighted water as they probably had in medieval times.

An evening-frocked headwaiter bowed to Toni, addressing her as "Princess," and showed them to a deep banquet table guarded by two standing suits of medieval armor. The decor was armorial: halberds, pikes, swords, and battle banners set against the stuccoed walls. At the far end of the main room was a walk-in fireplace burning five-foot logs. In addition to warming the room, the fire was grilling fowl and roasts, chops and sausages, whose combined scent made Chance's mouth water.

Over frosted glasses of vodka martinis they remarked on the restaurant's pleasing atmosphere. "It's far enough away from downtown to avoid the tourist trade," Toni pointed out. "People have reasons for coming here that don't include mention in a travel guide."

He was staring at the distant flames, not really aware of what she was saying. Her fingers snapped under his nose and he blinked.

"Hey," she said, "come out of it. You looked hypnotized—or am I that boring?"

"Not at all—and forgive me. I was remembering my mother's home and a fireplace much like that." He sipped his drink to cover embarrassment. "Haven't been there in a long time. I suppose being alone so much causes me to think back to my childhood."

"Happier times?"

"Much happier."

Her hand curled over his. "I'll miss you when you're gone," she said quietly, "even though you don't take much notice of me. Is it because I'm just the kid sister? Or because you saw me make a particularly bad scene? If that's it, I haven't taken speed since that night. I want to make a good impression on you."

"You have, Toni," he said honestly, "and you're much more than Paul's younger sister. You've seen more of life than most women at any age." He breathed deeply. "I've got a lot on my mind, can't seem to shake free."

"Money worries?"

"I think we share the same uncertainty—what to do with the rest of our lives." He ordered refills from the hovering waiter, remembered sharing drinks with Rony the night her husband interrupted them. His past claimed his thoughts.

Toni interrupted his gloomy reverie. "After you leave, Jean-Pierre, I think I will, too. I have to hide out somewhere until Mohammed marries again or forgets me."

"Any place in mind?"

"Oh, Buenos Aires, perhaps, or Rio. Cities where Mohammed isn't likely to look for me."

"Buenos Aires is laid out pretty much like Paris," he said. "The people are congenial and hospitable and very much like ourselves. I assume you ride, and that's an entrée to desirable circles."

"Then I'll look it over. Any other thoughts?"

"Cuernavaca is fairly cosmopolitan. Get a beach house or condo in Cancún or Ixtapa when you need freedom to do whatever you want."

"Meaning—?"

"Everyone needs to get away from routine, a change of scene."

"Would you visit me?"

"I'd like that," he said frankly. "It'd give me something to look forward to."

They ordered a cocktail of small, succulent river crayfish, mountain trout with almonds in a white sauce, and broccoli *au hollandaise,* and took coffee and cognac in comfortable leather chairs ranged near the glowing fire.

As Chance gazed into the embers, he was aware of the empathy that had grown between them. He'd probably miss Toni more than she would miss him. For the present she was a semirefugee at loose ends, but her adult life had been lived on a broad, spotlit stage among the world's beautiful people, and he felt she would return to it once she'd recovered her emotional bearings.

Most of the diners had left when Chance paid the bill and led Toni back across the drawbridge. A nearly full moon reflected from the moat's still waters, night wind whispered through the trees, and Chance was thinking how intimately enjoyable the evening had been as they neared his car.

Then from the shadowed grove two men stepped out, weapons in their hands.

THIRTY-THREE

Moonlight showed the partly bandaged face of the shorter man, whose wrist was also bandaged. He would have driven the crashed Peugeot, Chance thought irrelevantly; he scanned his partner. Taller and thinner, the man wore a mustache and full beard. His hair was wild as a bushman's; his eyes glinted yellowly as a cat's. Pointing his handgun at Chance, he said in French, "Get away from her."

But Toni—clinging closely ever since the men appeared— blurted, "No!"

"Do as he says," Chance told her loudly. "Everything will be all right." And whispered, *"Pretend to faint."*

With that, she rolled her eyes and crumpled to the graveled drive. Yellow Eyes stared at her in surprise, took a step toward Toni, halted, and gestured with his pistol. "Turn around," he ordered Chance.

"Don't hurt her," Chance said. "Take her if that's what you want, but don't hurt her." He was turning as he spoke, and when his back was to them, he moved fast. His right hand whipped out the Walther; he dropped into combat crouch, spun around, and fired at Yellow Eyes. Then dropped the man's bandaged partner. He got up and kicked their guns away.

Toni was sitting up wide-eyed. Before she could speak Chance ordered her into the car. Dazedly, she walked toward it as Chance stood over Yellow Eyes, who was clutching his belly and moaning in pain and fear. His partner was finished, a bullet puncture in his throat. The dead man's pockmarked face was that of the man who'd hassled them at the casino. Chance picked up his two ejected nine-millimeter shells and holstered the Walther. Just then footsteps came pounding across the drawbridge and Chance saw the headwaiter sprinting toward him, swallowtails horizontal behind his moving body. His gaze took in Chance beside the fallen men and he panted, *"What happened?"*

"I'm not sure," Chance told him. "One's still alive. I think. Very strange."

"You saw it *happen?*"

"Not really," Chance replied, and he gestured at his car. "We were getting in, heard shots; Princess Azira fainted. I'd better get her home—you'll call an ambulance?"

"Of—of course—but there may be questions."

"Why don't you spare the princess annoyance?" He took a sheaf of francs from his pocket and handed them to the headwaiter. "We appreciate it." He glanced at the fallen men—Yellow Eyes was barely stirring—and said, "Look like immigrant workers, don't they? Arabs probably. Crazy." He shook his head and got into the Mercedes beside Toni, who was still trembling. "Oh, God," she breathed, "you killed one."

Starting the engine, he nodded. "It may be two any moment." Steering past the headwaiter, Chance patted her arm. "Those two won't bother us again."

"I guess *not,*" she said heavily, and slumped against him. "I wonder what you'd do if someone got you *really* angry?"

"It hasn't happened."

"When it does I don't want to be around." Her shivering had ended. "Every day you become more mysterious, Jean-Pierre." She began brushing gravel from her arms and dress. "Were you with the *paras?*"

He shook his head. "A year ago I took an executive protection course near Paris."

"Oh, because of all those terrorist kidnappings." She nodded understandingly. "You're obviously a quick study. Paul won't believe what happened."

"Don't tell him—or *anyone,* Toni. Otherwise, you'll be answering tiresome questions from the police and the press, and I don't think you'd enjoy it."

191

"I wouldn't." She kissed his cheek. "It's as though you're making a career of protecting me. I'm very grateful." For a time she was silent. Then she said huskily, "You risked your life for me. No one's ever done that before."

"Had to save myself, too, remember? Now, try to put it out of your mind. You weren't hurt, neither was I. Think of it as a bizarre end to a pleasant evening, nothing more."

As he spoke, Chance realized that he no longer had obligations to care for anyone. It was as though Carla's death had freed him to risk his own; and that very indifference could be the edge against dangerous enemies and hostile odds.

"Do you think Mohammed will stop now?" she asked.

"I can't say, don't know him. Three of his Mamelukes are out of action, but he probably has plenty of replacements."

"I'm afraid he has. Desperate men to do anything for hash and a few francs." She shivered. "I never thought Geneva would become so frightening."

"But you mustn't let it affect you. Between Paul and your bodyguard I think you're pretty safe."

"Paul—?"

"Well, he mentioned combat in the Korean War—or was it Vietnam?"

"Korea. But as far as I know, he hasn't touched a gun in years. Anyway, you're my first line of defense."

"I was thinking about after I'm gone."

He was driving past the Parc des Eaux-Vives and the yacht basin at the lower end of the lake. Translucent mist clung to the water. The yachts, sails furled, looked ghostly in the pale moonlight. He continued on and at the National Monument turned right to cross the lake end by the Mont Blanc bridge, then right again to follow the lake's western shore. The sky was nearly cloudless, an aura of peace seemed to envelop the city, and Chance reflected on its contrast to the violence of only a few minutes past. He had no remorse. Challenged, he reacted, and was glad he had.

As they neared Paul's manse Toni said, "I'm chilled and shaking, Jean-Pierre, and I badly need a drink. How about you?"

"I'd welcome a nightcap," he said, and after pausing at the gate for the guard's inspection, he drove up to the entrance.

Only a hall light burned. Toni opened Paul's library-office and went to the cellarette. "Cognac?"

He nodded, took out his pistol, set the safety, and holstered it again.

As she brought his glass she said, "I'm glad you carry a gun, but why do you?"

"As you said, Geneva's become a dangerous place."

"For me, I meant."

"Well, it's better to have a weapon and not need it than the reverse."

Her glass touched his, giving off a slight crystal chime. They drank together in the room's near darkness and he saw her eyes studying his face. Quietly she said, "I've never been in love before, didn't want to be, but I've fallen in love with you." Her face lifted and her lips pressed his. Chance felt her velvety tongue thread between his lips, then she murmured, "How can I seduce you?"

"Sure you want to?"

"I've never been more sure of anything." Her free hand trailed downward, touched his swelling penis. "You want me, too."

"I do," he said thickly, "but until now I haven't let myself think about it." He put down his glass and took her in his arms. Her loins pressed his as their tongues played together. As his hands molded her firm young breasts, her eyes seemed to glisten. Chance pulled up her dress and drew down her panties, feeling their female moisture. Her fingers undid his belt and freed his hardening penis. "I can't wait," she whispered. "Here, the rug."

Chance lowered her and she undid her top while he shed trousers and shorts. Kneeling between her legs, he kissed her nipples, her mouth, and entered her warm vagina. He wanted her desperately, but as they thrust together he wondered if this was a sudden irrational transfer of his feelings for Carla. He stopped moving, but she cried "Don't stop. God, I need you. Fuck me. *Fuck me hard!*"

His mouth on hers, he plunged into the whirlpool, finally drawing her with him to a shuddering climax. Her sex continued contracting around his, milking his semen until he was drained and exhausted. Then as he tried to ease his weight from her body she said, "Don't—I want to feel your body on mine, all of you." Her

193

hands laced behind his neck and pulled his mouth to hers in a long, gentle kiss. His fingers touched her hair, toyed with the dark strands, and she murmured, "You don't have to love me. Just let me love you as long as I can."

What could he say? he wondered. Finally he rolled aside. Toni sat up and handed him his glass. On one elbow he sipped cognac and found it restorative. *"Chérie,"* he said, using his first word of endearment, "you may be confusing gratitude with love."

"No—oh, no. I know the difference now, believe me."

"I'm at least ten years older than you."

"So? You're with me and that's all that matters."

When their glasses were empty they made love again, slowly, deliberately, savoring every moment, drawing the ultimate in pleasure from their joined bodies until they could do no more. Then she rose, stripped off her clothing, and stood naked before him. "I've wanted to show myself to you, darling, have you see me as I truly am." Turning, she raised her arms above her head, and he was awed.

"Is that perverse of me?" she asked in a little-girl voice.

"No, not at all. Natural . . . and delightful."

She knelt before him and cupped her breasts. "Everything I am is yours. Please don't deny me. . . . Now that I've found you I can't bear to think of losing you."

"You won't," he said, "ever," and wondered if he was lying. And as his emotions steadied, he knew that parting from her would be one of the hardest things he had ever done in his life.

Suddenly the ceiling light went on. From the doorway Maurice was looking at them, a startled expression on his face. Without trying to shield her body, Toni said, "Well, well, Maurice. Yes, we've been fucking—be sure to tattle to your lover. Now get out, you dismal ponce!"

The light went out, Maurice disappeared, and Chance relaxed. "Will he tell Paul?"

"Who cares?" She began gathering up her clothing, and Chance got dressed. "What a wonderful, incredible night," she murmured. "And this is just the beginning. Can I sleep over at your place?"

He thought briefly of Lao-li, dismissed her. "Whenever you want."

"Every night, as long as you'll have me."

She was still naked when they kissed good night, and as Chance drove away he realized that he wanted the Russian to stay in Moscow, not come to Geneva and close out his mission. He wanted, needed, more time with Toni. . . . How long would they have? The next day Toni drove over with two Hermès suitcases and in effect moved in.

THIRTY-FOUR

As Lao-li silently helped Toni unpack in the other room, Sam said disapprovingly, "I don't think it's a good idea, but I can't tell you not to."

"Sure you can," Chance said, "and we'll find other lodgings."

Sam shrugged. Chance told him there would be two at dinner from now on, and to let the chef know.

"You're complicating things," Sam pointed out. "Have you told her anything?"

"Nothing. And we agreed Toni enhances my cover."

He shrugged and went away.

She enhances my life as well, Chance told himself, restoring me to the living. I don't think Carla would object.

Late in the afternoon they drove to Valcour's manse, around the south side to the stables. Chance counted six stalls, each faced with gingerbread woodwork and painted to resemble the entrance to a mountain hut. Toni explained that of Paul's four Thoroughbreds one had gone lame and one was in foal. "So I'll ride Paul's chestnut and you'll have mine." But while the groom was saddling their mounts Paul appeared. To Toni he said, "Who gave you permission to take my horse?"

"I'm going riding. Do you expect Jean-Pierre to jog beside me? And you haven't ridden in weeks."

"I guess it's all right," he said grumpily. "Just be back before dark so the groom can get some sleep."

"Never fear, brother," she said coolly, "and since it's a problem, I'll buy a horse for Jean-Pierre tomorrow." Boot in stirrup, she swung lithely into the English saddle.

"That isn't necessary," Valcour said, scowling. "I spoke before I thought. Jean-Pierre can ride whenever he likes."

Toni laughed shortly. "What you're upset about is that I'm sleeping with Jean-Pierre."

Valcour's face colored and Chance saw him swallow. "I'll admit I hadn't anticipated that, Toni, but if it's therapeutic, so be it."

Without a word she turned the chestnut mare and ambled away. Chance lifted into the saddle and began adjusting his stirrup leathers. Valcour came over and murmured, "We need to talk, Quinn. Our man may already be here."

"See you when we get back." He dug blunt spurs into his horse's ribs and followed Toni down the trail.

They rode through fields and purpling meadows into the foothills skirting the border with France, and when they pulled up at a narrow stream to let their horses drink, Toni said, "I don't know why I let Paul bug me so—but he does, and it's mutual."

"Sibling rivalry," he smiled. "And I guess you resent the fatherly eye. Anyway, this is too fine an excursion to be marred by a grudge."

"You're right, of course—you're always right, damn you, and it *is* a lovely ride." Leaning over, she kissed his cheek. "I'm not used to discipline, you'll have to break my undesirable traits." She stroked her horse's mane. "As this one was tamed."

"Without breaking her spirit."

"You can if you want to, *chéri*, because I feel so different today—fulfilled, reborn . . . you know what I'm trying to say?"

"I feel that last night a new life began for me, Toni," he said, and wondered if his feelings were more than infatuation with a young and fascinating female. Or was he just quenching long-stayed desire at the first available fountain? "But I can't read the future."

"Then we must let it take care of itself, *non?* And live for now, today—as long as it lasts."

"It's the only way," he agreed, and reined back his horse's head.

They rode back through soft twilight, dismounting to hold hands while their horses grazed, then strolled wordlessly, reins in hand, for a time before remounting and riding the rest of the way. At the stables Toni stroked and gentled her mare before yielding to the waiting groom. Chance loosened his saddle cinches and led the gelding to the water trough, where the groom took over.

When Toni went up to change out of her riding habit, Paul Valcour motioned Chance into his library and closed the door. "For my sister's sake," he said, "I'm glad she found someone like you, Quinn, and I say that sincerely; I know you won't abuse her or create false expectations. But that's not what I want to talk about."

"You mentioned the expected Soviet."

He nodded. "As you know, my Russian contacts are good. They trust me, as far as they trust any not their own. Early this morning an unscheduled Aeroflot plane came in at Genève-Cointrin. There were only two passengers, and both came through Immigration with ordinary passports. No Swiss reception committee, and no Soviets to meet them, either."

"So?"

"A special Soviet flight laid on for only two passengers means one or both rank very high, high enough to warrant official reception. Yet they got into an ordinary airport limousine and headed for a downtown hotel."

"Which one?"

"My contact didn't say. There are probably a hundred Soviet nationals in Geneva's hotels and I don't have the travelers' names. If our man is one of the two, he knows how to contact me."

"What's the recognition phrase?"

Valcour smiled. "He says, 'Geneva is beautiful, but I dislike mountains.' I say, 'You might prefer Holland and its windmills.' "

"And then?"

"I set up your meeting. Here, if you agree."

Chance glanced around the library. "I assume you've bugged it."

"I'll disconnect beforehand." He crossed his heart. "Promise." And smiled the old, winning smile Chance remembered. Only, Chance mused, how much was a Valcour promise worth?

"So we go on waiting, right?"

Valcour nodded. "I thought you ought to know—in case you and Toni were thinking of going off for a while."

Toni's footsteps sounded on the stairs. Valcour opened the

library door and Chance went out. Toni looked freshly scrubbed and glowing. She wore a white silk blouse and a green skirt that matched her emerald pendant. "Bye, Paul. Don't wait up for me."

"No," he said diffidently. "Enjoy yourselves, young people." And closed the door.

The chef had prepared an oriental meal—thin strips of teriyaki beef with crisp bean sprouts and vegetables, steamed *jaodzes* and plum confiture. Impassive, Lao-li served them skillfully and filled their glasses with tingling-cold Chablis. As far as Chance could tell, the young woman did not resent being abandoned for the *nai-nai;* if she did, she was too well trained to let it show.

Toni occupied the chatelaine's seat at the head of the table and Chance sat on her right. With chopsticks they fed each other tidbits until Toni said, "I'm having this fantasy we were married this afternoon in a big cathedral and now we're in our own castle for as long as we want to be. No one to disturb us."

"I'll share that fantasy," Chance agreed with a grin, quite enjoying the unexpected domesticity.

"It's romantic—and all I can think of is our marriage bed. And I hustled some of Paul's champagne...." She munched an almond. "Mind going to bed with a thief?"

"I'd make love to you if you robbed banks for a living."

Her chopsticks deposited a water chestnut slice in his mouth. "Suppose I were a secret robber of jewelry stores?"

"Anything goes."

Her expression grew serious. "Will you ever tell me about yourself, more than the little I know?"

"In time," he promised. "Let's say I'm reluctant to disillusion you."

"You couldn't. Whatever you are, whatever you've been, I want to be with you, *chéri*, always." Her hand reached over to clasp his. "Let me keep telling myself that if your circumstances were— different—you'd want to marry me. It's not too far-out, is it?"

"It's very close to the truth," he said, and kissed her hand.

Chance got glasses and a bottle of Moët & Chandon from the refrigerator and followed Toni up the staircase to the big bedroom, where Lao-li had turned down the covers and plumped the pillows. Chance locked the door and twisted out the champagne cork. At the *pop* Toni laughed happily and insisted on drinking from the foaming bottle. Then he filled their glasses, and they drank with linked arms as lovers do.

Slowly, he slid off her shoulder straps and her dress dropped into a pool at her feet. He unhooked her cup bra and kissed each nipple in turn. She shivered and pressed his head against her breasts. He peeled off her panties and knelt to kiss and savor the perfume of her motte until her thighs trembled. "My turn," she said huskily, and drew off his shirt and trousers, knelt to take his swelling organ in her mouth. In ecstasy he clutched her head until he could bear it no longer, raised her to the bed, and thrust into her. Moaning, she raked his back with her nails, bringing on his climax much sooner than he wanted.

After more champagne they made love again, then curled together spoon-fashion to rest and drowse until passion stirred once more.

He woke in darkness to pounding on his door. Sam shouted, "Trouble at Valcour's. Shooting. His driver wants the princess."

Chance bolted off the bed.

THIRTY-FIVE

"*No,*" Toni said in a high, brittle voice. "I'll go—you stay here."

"*Merde,*" Chance snapped, pulling on his trousers. "I'm going, you stay."

"Damn you, he's my brother, not yours." She was already sliding into her dress. "I want you here—safe—when I return."

Chance stepped into shoes, no socks, fought his way into his shirt. "We'll go together." He called out to Sam, "Police know yet?"

"Valcour's phone line is cut."

"Wait ten minutes and call them. How bad is the scene?"

"Bad—the chauffeur found bodies, tried phoning, and drove here."

"Jesus!" Chance said half aloud, and tucked in his shirt. Grasping Toni's hand, he drew her to the door and unlocked it. Sam's pale face stared at him. They hurried down the staircase and outside where Albert stood beside the Daimler. His ugly face was red; tears flooded his cheeks. Chance snapped, "Can you drive?"

"Yes, yes, sir."

Chance shoved Toni into the rear seat and followed, slamming the heavy door shut. Albert got behind the wheel and the Daimler accelerated down the drive. Chance kissed Toni's cheek. "Maybe it's not as bad as it sounds."

"He's *dead,*" she moaned, rocking back and forth. "I know they killed him—all those slimy deals. . . ." She mopped at her cheeks as Chance put his arm around her shoulders and held her close, suffering because she was.

Albert reached the gatehouse in seven minutes, braked long enough for Chance to see the guard slumped over his table—dead. They reached the plateau fronting the mansion before spotting the dog handler and his two Alsatians lying on the grass border, sprawled grotesquely in death. The sight started Toni sobbing; she burst from the car and ran up the steps. To Albert, Chance said, "Got a gun?"

Wordlessly, he handed over a Webley revolver. Chance opened the cylinder to see if it was loaded, snapped it back, and ran after Toni, catching her on the staircase. "Stay behind me," he ordered, and climbed to the second floor.

Gun in hand, hammer cocked, he went to the lighted doorway, gasped at what he saw. Naked, Paul Valcour lay under a blood-drenched sheet.

Chance turned quickly and locked the door, ignoring Toni's cries and pounding. He went quickly to Valcour, pressed hard into the carotid, and felt a faint pulse. Jerking back the sheet he saw two chest wounds, a third in the belly. Chance followed a crimson chain into the bathroom. There, slumped against the tub, was the naked body of Maurice, head thrown back, eyes staring dully at the light, mouth open as though trying to speak. . . . Chance pressed his carotid artery and shook his head. No pulse. Much of his blood pooled under the dead man's thighs; red fingers ran downward to the sloping drain. Chance took a deep breath and, Webley still in hand, opened the door for Toni. She tried to burst in, but he held her shoulders. "Your brother's still alive," he said levelly. "Just barely."

She stared beyond him at Paul's bloodstained body and screamed. "Nothing we can do," he told her. "Help is on the way." He stood aside and she rushed to the bedside, covering her brother's face with kisses, moaning and sobbing, crying he mustn't die, until Chance drew her away so that he could pull a warming blanket over Valcour's motionless body. "He'll need transfusions. "What's your blood type?"

"I—I don't know."

"There may not be time to type it—will you give blood?"

Staring down at the still figure she said, "Of course."

A siren pierced the night, then, coming closer, was joined by a police car's harsh Klaxon. Chance drew her to him. "He has a chance," he promised her. "He's tough, you know that."

He tried to quiet her trembling, but she was close to hysteria. "Why, *why?*" she said in a ragged, high-pitched voice. "He never hurt anyone. It was never anything but money."

The siren was screamingly close. Chance drew her into the corridor. Outside, the ambulance sprayed gravel as it braked, the siren whined off. Running footsteps up the stairs. As three medics reached him Chance pointed to the bedroom. "One still alive, one dead."

Two white coats went quickly in. The third asked, "Who are you?"

"Friend of the family. This lady is sister to the man in the bed. His name is Paul Valcour."

Plasma arrived, and an IV started before the litter came. Carefully they carried Valcour down the stairs and out to the waiting ambulance. As it growled away, the police arrived. Like a stone figure, Albert stood in the drive, staring helplessly. Chance went to urge him to talk to the police. "Tell them everything. We'll be at the hospital."

He turned to Toni, thinking she should have something to do. "You drive the Daimler," he told her. "Follow the ambulance."

"I—I'm too unsteady." She held up trembling hands.

"I can't drive the damn thing," he lied. "You'll have to get us there." He opened the passenger side, and got in. Hesitantly, Toni got behind the wheel, and after a deep breath she wiped her wet face and engaged gears. Smoothly, the limousine pulled away. The effort steadied her, and by the time they parked at the Hôpital Cantonal Chance saw her emotions were under control. The hospital was a gray-faced four-story building, some of whose upper windows were barred. A forbidding-appearing place, Chance thought, but he kept his reaction from Toni, who said, "Without you I'd have come apart completely," and as they hurried into the hospital she added, "And if I hadn't been safe at your house, I'd have been killed, too." He couldn't disagree.

They had barely reached the area outside the OR when Toni was asked to give blood. She kissed Chance and said, "At least I'm doing something to save him," and went off with the technician.

Because Toni wanted to stay near her brother, Chance drove alone to Paul's mansion. There Albert vouched for Chance to police investigators who then allowed him to enter. Their caution and apparent efficiency impressed Chance; he took Albert aside and learned what the retainer had already told the police: He had been sleeping in his quarters above the garage when he heard the guard dogs barking, the voice of their handler. Muffled gunfire, then silence. Through the window he had seen two men hurrying into the mansion. He began dressing and, before he finished, saw the men come out and walk down the drive. They disappeared from view, an unseen car started, and Albert heard it drive away. He went into the house and found M. Valcour and M. Maurice. Touching nothing, he tried to phone for help, but the line was dead.

"What about the groom? The bodyguard?" Chance asked.

"The groom sleeps in a room off the stables and heard nothing. Monsieur Valcour released the bodyguard in the afternoon, as the princess had moved out." He wiped at his eyes with a cabbage-size fist. "The other servants live in town."

"You didn't see the two men's faces?"

"Too far away. They wore dark clothing, that is all I can say." He gulped air. "I told the police everything, as you said I should." He wet bulbous lips. "And Monsieur Valcour . . . ?"

"They're operating on him now." He patted the chauffeur's shoulder. "You're a loyal man, Albert, and you've done the right things. All we can do now is hope."

He left him in the hallway and went up to the master bedroom. As he had anticipated, the bedroom was exquisitely feminine: dusty rose walls, gauzy pink curtains, subdued lighting, a pair of white-and-pink antiqued vanity tables enhanced by flouncy pink material; quilted pink silk coverlet bloodstained at one edge, and lace-fringed pillows.

Police floodlights seared the interior as two photographers covered every square meter of the scene before moving into the bathroom where Maurice's body still lay. Chance glanced back, noticing a jar of Vaseline on the floor by Valcour's side of the queen-size bed. To a middle-aged police inspector he said, "Any brass recovered?"

"No, m'sieu. Evidently revolvers were used, with silencers, if the chauffeur reported accurately." He eyed Chance. "What do you make of this affair?"

"Robbery?"

"Monsieur Valcour's safe is intact. His and his friend's billfolds are plump with currency." He shrugged. "A vendetta among homosexuals?"

"Perhaps, though Monsieur Valcour did not seem to be promiscuous. The relationship with Maurice seemed a stable one."

"But one can not rule out some jealousy from their pasts."

"As good a theory as any." Chance preferred the investigation not veer off into international intrigue. With Paul out of action it was going to be difficult enough for the expected Soviet contact, if not impossible. Sam could relay the changed situation to Hsiao in Peking. Hsiao would make the operational decision.

Leaving the sordid scene, Chance found a door leading to the third floor. He went up the jagged staircase and found himself in a storage room piled with surplus furniture, bric-a-brac, and luggage. A single cobwebbed, dusty window overlooked the rear garden and stables. Chance saw a black coaxial cable hanging from the window ledge and pried open the window. Balancing himself, he looked out and upward, saw a satellite dish fixed on the roof. He assumed it was for television reception, until he saw that the cable ended a few feet from the window. He lowered it and looked around.

Most of the luggage was coated with dust. But one suitcase, a cheap old fiber-sided piece, was cleaner than the others. Curious, Chance laid it on its side and undid worn canvas straps. Inside, a compact radio transceiver was set neatly into Styrofoam blocks. One held a squirt device that could compress normal-length transmission into two or three seconds, avoiding direction-finding locating by hostiles. There was a nickel-cadmium rechargeable battery pack, miniature earphones, and a small Morse key. The unit was an agent set some ten years old, of CIA manufacture.

The power ruby lighted when he pressed the ON toggle, and the absence of dust indicated occasional use. But to whom had Paul Valcour been transmitting via satellite? From what source did he receive? The frequency dial was set in the TRANSMIT mode.

What was Paul's old commo call sign? Pollux? That was it, and headquarters was Castor. The heavenly twins.

To satisfy curiosity Chance tapped a clear language message into the squirt transmitter:

TO CASTOR: POLLUX IN EXTREMIS FOLLOWING SHOOTING IN HOME. THREE OTHERS KILLED. ASSASSINS UNIDENTIFIED. END MSG.

He screwed the satellite coax into the transmitter and activated the squirt for six consecutive transmissions. After that he switched to RECEIVE mode and waited to determine whether the frequency was being guarded.

Ten minutes later the small digital display lighted.

IDENTIFY SENDER. NO PLAIN TEXT. CASTOR. END MSG.

Chance deactivated the set, detached the cable, and packed the set back up as it had been.

His curiosity had been satisfied; Valcour had a radio link with CIA. Why? he wondered as he left the storage room. Was Paul a double or even a triple? Where did his loyalty lie?

Paul's relationship with headquarters disturbed Chance. Did CIA now know where he was, his role in the Sino-Soviet intrigue? If so, should he pack and run or wait things out? Had a hostile service decoded Pollux-Castor exchanges and decided to liquidate the Geneva end?

Maurice's blanketed body was being carried out on a litter, and Chance followed it down the staircase.

His gaze caught the library door and he remembered Valcour's mention of the special Aeroflot flight. Valcour had thought the two unidentified Soviet arrivals high-level officials, but what if they were "wets," *mokriye dela* thugs from Department 13, dispatched for the sole purpose of neutralizing Paul Valcour? Two men had left the plane, two men shot up Paul's home.

He saw a policeman using a cellular phone. When the call was over, Chance dialed his villa and heard Sam answer. "Remember what I told you about that Aeroflot arrival yesterday morning?" he asked.

"Think there might be a connection?"

"It might be useful to get someone to the airport, check if the plane's still there."

"Will do."

Outside, the dog handler's body was being removed. As Chance walked toward the Daimler, Albert joined him. "I would like to go to the hospital. M. Valcour has been a very good employer."

With Albert at the wheel, Chance sat back in the soft upholstery and reflected. Homosexual vengeance was unlikely. The existence of the transmitter opened other possibilities, especially regarding Paul's role as matchmaker between two great powers. During the flight to Paris, Hsiao had revealed that a number of Soviet emissaries had been killed before making contact, which required foreknowledge on the part of Conservative Soviet officials. If Paul's role had become known, what better way to thwart a Soviet-PRC meeting than by eliminating the intermediary?

Chance suspected that selecting and briefing Paul's replacement would be slow and painstaking. Would Hsiao keep Chance in Geneva until alternate arrangements could be made? Or would he figure that "Jean-Pierre Duroc" had been blown along with Valcour and was now a risk?

Still, it was worth pointing out to Sam and Hsiao that the killers could have eliminated Chance as easily as they had swept through Valcour's grounds and mansion. Bottom line: Chance had not been targeted. But I still head Berlikov's hit list, he reminded himself.

At the Hôpital Cantonal, Chance led Albert to the OR waiting room just as Toni was being wheeled out. Her face was pale; an inverted bottle fed plasma into her veins, replacing the loss of transfused blood. Holding her hand as he followed the gurney down the hall, he asked, "Any news?"

She licked dry lips. "Paul is very close to death," she said tightly. "Bullet wounds in liver, spleen, and a corner of one lung. He's critical from loss of blood, and shock. One doctor said Paul would be dead from shock if he hadn't been warmly covered." She smiled wanly. To Albert she said, "Thank you for coming. If my brother lives, it will be because of your prompt action."

"I can give blood, too, Princess. Gladly."

"Thank you, but while they were transfusing me directly they took his blood type and found they have more than enough on hand."

The orderly steered her gurney into a bare white-painted recovery room, positioned it beside some chairs, and said, "When you feel strong enough to walk, Princess, you can leave."

Chance bent over and kissed her dry lips. A nurse brought in a cool sucrose solution. "For energy," the nurse explained, and waited until the glass was empty.

Chance went to the window and pulled aside the blind. The Old City was graying in early dawn; buildings screened the lake, but he could make out the tall spires of Saint-Pierre Cathedral. The end of a momentous night, he reflected. He and Toni had dined *en famille* for the first time; they had made love as extravagantly as newlyweds; and Paul's home had been invaded in a murderous attack. Moreover, he had discovered Paul's covert connection to their former organization, a discovery whose implications would become clear only if Paul survived.

Toni said, "I'm feeling better now—what time is it?"

He looked at Albert, who examined his wristwatch. "Almost six, Princess," he replied, and asked Chance, "Is there further danger, sir?"

"I think it's safe to go back to the residence." He pressed Toni's hand. "Are you sure?" she asked anxiously.

"Paul was their target. Not you, or me."

"But they killed two others, and Maurice."

He shrugged. "They were in the way. The killers didn't want to be identified."

She sat up and drew her legs over the gurney edge. "Do you have any idea who they were?"

"No," he lied. "They came, did what they were supposed to do, and fled." Leaving Toni in Albert's hands, he walked back to the OR, where two policemen were obviously on guard. To one he suggested, "Might be a good idea to let it be believed Monsieur Valcour died in the assault."

"For what reason, m'sieu? I understand that he is as good as dead already."

"Should he live, the killers might try again, in this hospital," Chance pointed out.

"Ah." He nodded approvingly. "That would be a calamity indeed. But let me ask, why do you believe Monsieur Valcour to have been the principal target?"

"I don't believe that his companion, the gate guard, or the dog handler were targets, do you?"

"When you put it that way. . . ." He stroked his graying mustache. "Logical. So in the unlikely event that Monsieur Valcour lives, we will let it be thought otherwise."

A young surgeon came out of the OR stripping off mask and bloody gloves, and Chance followed him into the recovery room. To Toni the surgeon said wearily, "Mademoiselle, we have repaired your brother's grave wounds as best we were able. His vital signs are stable, but the best I can say is that he is alive. The rest depends on his constitution."

Toni smiled—and promptly broke into tears. When she could speak she said, "May I go to him?"

The surgeon shook his head. "He is still under anesthesia, mademoiselle." He looked at his watch. "Until evening Monsieur Valcour will be monitored in critical care. Call then, and the physician in charge may permit a brief visit."

"Thank you, thank you, Doctor," she said fervently.

"We are here to serve," he said modestly, and left the room. To Albert, Chance said, "We'll go back to my place. And when your staff arrives, have them begin putting everything as it was before."

"Certainly, m'sieu."

"And be aware of strangers," Chance cautioned.

Back at the villa, Chance settled Toni in the bedroom they had so abruptly left.

"You need rest," he told her, "and I need a drink." Downstairs he gulped half a glass of Black Label. Strolling around the first floor, he agreed with Sam's evaluation that villa physical security was nonexistent. No alarm system or barred windows. Assault could take place with even less difficulty than at Paul's.

As he headed back upstairs he heard the Mercedes pull up, and presently Sam came in. He beckoned Chance to join him on the patio. "A big Tupolev was taking off just when I got there. I checked Cointrin flight control and learned the pilot hadn't bothered to get formal clearance. The controller said that doesn't often happen in Swiss airspace—even by the Russians."

"Somebody wanted to get the hell out of town."

Sam nodded. "Seems that way. Is Valcour dead?"

"Barely alive. We'll know more tonight."

He eyed Chance. "I'm going to change and get to the consulate, send off the bad news." Sam's gaze lifted upward. "How's she taking it?"

"In control again. Resting after giving blood."

"Lucky she was here."

"She knows that, and so do I. Sam, I've been thinking about that D.C. *rezident*, Berlikov. Could your people pick him up and sweat him?"

"Probably, but Hsiao would have to have a good reason."

"Try this: Berlikov set the Arabs on Sosnowski and me. Someone gave him those orders, and I'm pretty sure they came from very high up. If he'll identify his principal, we'll know more about the Kremlin factions, and that could help Hsiao make a fresh assessment." He paused. "Otherwise, we'll be sitting around swatting flies and watching grass grow."

Sam grinned. "I'll pass it along."

Back upstairs Chance found Toni asleep. He locked the door and got into bed beside her, making sure the Walther was where it belonged—under his pillow. Her exhaustion was more psychological than physical. Stress exhaustion. Whatever happened to Valcour, she was going to need sleeping pills and tranquilizers, and Sam ought to be able to get a supply.

His preference was to keep her sedated for the next twenty-four hours. By then Valcour would either be in a private room able to see her or on an embalming table. Someone—family, a former lover—would probably claim Maurice's body, which was no concern of theirs. He had to stabilize his own situation. Unless he could continue to be at least potentially useful to the ChiComs, they'd put him down the tube. Snatching Berlikov should buy some time.

Toni's face was relaxed after hours of strain. Even tousled hair enhanced her beauty.

He wanted to be around her as long as he possibly could. They were compatible and companionable, and they respected each other. Even though she doesn't know thing one about me, he mused, and wondered if the time would ever come when he would be free to tell her the elaborate, complicated truth.

If the Soviets found out they'd failed, Chance feared they would try reaching Valcour through his sister. The danger from Mohammed's ragheads was trivial compared to what experienced Soviet "wets" could do. They would be safer if Paul died.

His hand reached out to touch her arm, and his eyes closed.

THIRTY-SIX

Toward midday Chance left Toni sleeping and drove to Geneva's central railroad station, the Gare de Cornavin. In the old, cavernous stone-floored interior, with its worn wooden benches and brass-railed ticket counters, Chance used a pay phone to contact the UN press office, and learned that Jan Abrams was staying at the Hotel du Rhône, a few blocks away. From the hotel's lobby phone he called Jan's room, but there was no answer.

On hotel stationery Chance wrote that he needed to talk with Abrams ASAP and suggested that they use pay phones to establish a rendezvous. He printed the number of the station phone he had used and said he would guard it on the hour until seven. He signed the initials JPD, sealed the note in a hotel envelope, and left it in Jan's room-key box.

From there he drove to Paul's villa and found that the servants had cleaned the bedroom and bathroom. Albert had engaged a friend as temporary gate guard, and told Chance that M. Valcour's vital signs were stable and no infection had developed.

Bullet wound infection developed not from the red-hot bullet itself, but from bits of fabric driven into the wound. Since Valcour had been naked, Chance figured Paul's chances were better than average, unless internal damage was too severe. The lung wound, of course, made his body susceptible to pneumonia, but the physicians would be alert to it.

In Paul's medicine chest he found Doriden sleeping pills and Valium tranquilizers and pocketed them for Toni. Chance considered confiscating the transmitter pending Paul's explanation.

212

Somewhere Paul had hidden code materials, probably onetime pads, but Chance had no reason to search for them unless he should need a crypto-system. He hadn't used pads in a decade, but like Morse code, the technique would return.

Onetime pads, Chance recalled, had been devised by the Germans eighty years ago and remained the one unbreakable system that even the Walker-Whitworth code betrayals could not compromise. The trade-off was that manual encryption took a lot of time.

Back at the villa, he found Toni eating egg-drop soup on the patio. They kissed and he took a chair beside her. "How are you feeling?"

"A little frayed, but I expected that. The hospital says Paul is holding his own."

"Albert told me. You may be able to see him tonight."

"I hope so, but I'm trying to restrain optimism. Did you see a morning paper?"

"Nothing in it. Too early." He accepted a cup of tea from Lao-li and thanked her. Toni said, "A radio report said Paul had been killed during a robbery. Why?"

"Probably so the assassins will think they accomplished their job. Otherwise, they might try again at the hospital, or move against you."

She shivered. "I hadn't considered that. Of course, I don't know anything about why those men shot Paul. But I do know robbery wasn't the reason."

"Let the police puzzle it out," he advised. "What's important is protecting you and your brother."

"While he's recovering I think you and I should leave Geneva for a while."

"I can't," he said bluntly, "but I'd be glad to join you in a safer place—like Buenos Aires."

She finished her soup and dabbed her lips with a napkin. "I don't want to go anywhere without you," she said firmly, and looked into his eyes. "You know more about this than you're saying, don't you? Does it have to do with Paul's having been in CIA?"

Chance stirred his tea. "I don't know that he was," he lied, "and

213

even if so, why should old enemies wait so long? Paul's lived here openly for years."

"Then something developed recently, perhaps when you arrived." Her eyes searched his face.

After a moment's pause he said, "Paul and I have a business arrangement, or rather, the hope of one. With him off the scene, I need to be on hand."

She looked away. "Poor Maurice. Much as he gave me the creeps, he worked hard for Paul. He'll be hard to replace." Her gaze found Chance again. "Did he know your and Paul's business?"

"Paul said not, and I wanted it that way. Maurice was killed because he could have identified the killers. But they're gone now, back to wherever they came from."

"Sure of that?"

"The police are."

She stood, and they strolled down through the garden holding hands. "Finding you, loving you, made me feel my life had come together again. I was working things out, finding a serenity I hadn't felt for years. Then. . . ." She waved one hand dejectedly. "It's as though I'm back in the center of a maelstrom without knowing how I got there, or why." She stopped and faced him. "Have you ever felt that way, Jean-Pierre?"

"I have, but things always worked out."

"I haven't your experience—in anything."

"I'll be doing all I can to make things work out for both of us." He kissed her for a long time, her body yielding against his.

Then she said, "All factors considered I want to stay here with you. Paul's house is—"

"I want you here."

At the villa he gave her a tranquilizer and said he'd be back later to go with her to the hospital.

"Can I go with you now?"

"Business, *chérie,* and the hospital may phone you."

At three he waited beside the station phone, but it didn't ring. He went to a nearby sidewalk café for coffee, brandy, and a sweet bun. He bought a paper and read a sketchy account of the slayings. Paul was described as an American investment banker known for discreet dealings with an international clientele. Maurice de

Rochepin had been his executive secretary, and the names of the dead guard and dog handler were listed. The search for their assassins was focusing on clients who might have been dissatisfied with Valcour's handling of their funds. End of story.

And just right, thought Chance, except that the Russian envoy was now cut off from contact.

As he folded the paper he wondered what he would do if he were the Russian. Contact Paul's sister, he told himself. It would risk little and might be productive. Why not?

He walked back to the gare and took up position beside the coin phone. He unfolded his paper to the financial section, smothered a yawn, and began to read.

The telephone rang.

THIRTY-SEVEN

"*Ja?*" he said. "Who is this?"

"The man you asked to call." Jan Abrams's voice. "I hoped we would be in touch again. Where shall we meet?"

"Tour boats leave the *débarcadère* every half hour. I thought we might take a short cruise together." He looked at his watch. "Four-thirty suit you?"

"It does." Abrams hung up.

After leaving the Gare, Chance walked down the rue des Alpes where he and Toni had shopped only yesterday afternoon. At the rococo Brunswick Monument he turned left and went two blocks along the quai du Mont-Blanc until he reached the excursion boat dockage. He sat on a bench and watched one of the large open boats gliding slowly around the lighthouse at the end of the long jetty from which rose the three-hundred-foot-high fountain that symbolizes Geneva as the Eiffel Tower is the emblem of Paris. As the boat neared, Chance got in the ticket line and, when he was pocketing change, saw Jan Abrams shuffling along the quai past the American Church, bald pate shiny in the afternoon sun.

After returning passengers debarked, Chance took a seat at the boat's stern—only seven others were boarding, Jan among them. The crewman cast off, and Jan looked around and selected a chair near Chance, who said, "I've done this before, but I always enjoy it."

"I enjoy the lake's peacefulness," Jan replied, and moved closer. None of the passengers was within fifteen feet, and the breeze carried their voices astern. Chance said, "The information I gave you the other night—did you make any use of it? Pass it along?"

"No, I agreed to keep the confidence. Do you have more to add?"

"In a negative way." The guide began to describe shore points over the boat's loudspeaker as the boat doubled around at the lake's end and began proceeding slowly along the eastern shore, where the Shelleys had lived. "You remember Paul Valcour, of course?"

"Certainly, not in a favorable way. He was killed last night along with members of his household."

"Yesterday when you passed me, I was with his sister, Antoinette. While his place was under attack she was with me."

Abrams nodded thoughtfully. "A fortunate young woman, in several ways. Why do you think Paul was killed?"

"Because of the reason I'm here—to bring the Soviets and ChiComs together. Paul was the intermediary."

"The *shatkin*," Abrams smiled. "To you, the marriage broker. So now what will happen?"

"I don't know. We have a sort of gridlock, a stalemate. If the Chinese have no further use for me, I assume they'll silence me, and I'm not ready to die working for world peace."

Abrams shrugged.

"I thought you might have some ideas, Jan. I don't."

"That's unusual, Quinn."

Hearing his name, Chance eyed Abrams before saying, "Valcour heard Yegor Ligachev is coming to Geneva."

"We have similar information," Abrams acknowledged, "and we assume it's to sign whatever agreement we reach with the Soviets." He sighed. "Our president feels that any agreement—however flawed—is better than no agreement at all. I disagree, but then I'm not a policymaker."

"Valcour thought Ligachev might be the secret emissary."

"Oh? The deputy premier is certainly in a position to lend the effort credibility. But we see him as a man still rooted in the Lenin-Stalin dream of world conquest. If he's changed his spots, we have no hard intelligence to suggest it." He leaned forward. "What's on your mind?"

"Perhaps there's some discreet way you could determine if any Soviet arrivals are looking for Valcour or his replacement."

"Conceivably, but the odds are very long against my hearing anything like that. Especially since Valcour is known to be dead." He eyed Chance.

"I think the killers—two of them—came in yesterday morning on an unscheduled Aeroflot flight. The same aircraft took off this morning before dawn, ignoring clearance formalities."

"Sounds like a vest pocket op," Abrams mused, "using *spetznial-niy*. Why don't you just walk away?"

"For one thing, I'm curious to see how things turn out. And in return for safe haven I agreed to stay with it until the mission is over. Break my word and Hsiao Kuan-hua will have me liquidated."

"Hsiao? I didn't realize you were dealing so high up."

"He's my principal. A couple of his watchers are installed at my villa. And Toni's there for safekeeping. I'm boxed in, Jan, don't know what move to make."

"Would you consider U.S. protection—if I could arrange it?"

"Not if it means facing prosecution for crimes I didn't commit." He looked up along the lakeshore, where mansion gardens and lawns sloped down to meet the lake's chill waters. Ornate piers sheltered pleasure craft from gentle swells. Someone's version of paradise. "I think you better know how everything began, Jan, and why I owe Hsiao."

"I've always been a good listener." He leaned back against the railing. "How much is off the record?"

"You know what it is to be persecuted. I trust your judgment."

The excursion boat had turned and begun its down-lake leg before Chance finished talking. Except for two clarifying questions, Abrams remained attentively silent while Chance repeated, word for word, his conversation with Hsiao during the flight from Washington. Now Abrams turned to the breeze and for a while was lost in thought. Finally he said, "Startling information, greatly disturbing. But why would Hsiao entrust it to you?"

"To motivate me for his purposes . . . and because he can kill me when I'm no longer useful. Will you pass along what I've told you?"

218

Abrams grimaced. "I'd need to source it," he said, "and there are so very few people I can trust with anything, Quinn, let alone such extremely sensitive information. Justice people would be all over me trying to get at you. The Agency? Well, you've learned the institutional attitude—you're an embarrassment. State? An anachronistic organization of timeservers who avoid waves as though they were corrosive acid. Yet the Soviet initiative—wherever it comes from—is too significant and urgent to ignore. And you're the one who knows most about it."

Through his loudspeaker the guide was proudly pointing out magnificent international buildings on shore: the Palais des Nations, conservatories, museums, villas of the world-famous, graceful botanical gardens. . . . Chance asked, "So?"

Abrams faced him. "Valcour may know more than he's told you, Quinn. When he can talk, question him. And it might prod him to know you discovered his transmitter and found the link is active. I'll confess I was astounded. Were it to become known, his private business would be destroyed. It's a lever you can use."

"If he lives." He looked away from Jan's intent face. "You—your delegation—gets the daily secret intelligence summary, ComInt?"

"Yes, we eavesdrop on their diplomatic traffic, always have."

"How about their Daleth transmissions?"

"KGB operational traffic? If it's available here, I haven't seen it, but the Agency officer may get it for his own use."

"Could you monitor those intercepts?"

"Maybe, if I could come up with a persuasive reason. Wait a minute, I've got one: General Yevgeni Sobatkin came in with the foreign minister's group, stayed a couple of days without mixing at all, and flew to Washington." He looked at Chance. "Know who Sobatkin is? No? Well, he's pegged as the overall ops controller for the western hemisphere, a sort of super-*rezident* based in Ottawa, representing the Tsentralnoye Byuro Politicheskoy Informatsii—Central Bureau for Political Information—a secret arm of the Central Committee. I could review Daleth intercepts for his travel and contacts, using the excuse that Sobatkin may be involved with the negotiations."

"But he isn't."

"Let's say he's not a declared member of the Soviet team. So he was here for intelligence reasons, maybe preparing the ground for the envoy's arrival, or arranging to abort it."

"And went on to Washington."

Abrams nodded. "Probably to relay Moscow orders to GRU or KGB *rezidents*. Question is, which Kremlin faction is Sobatkin working for?"

"Daleth might give the answer." The boat slowed as it approached the *débarcadère*. "Sobatkin comes to Geneva, leaves, and two *spetznaz* thugs try to kill Valcour and everyone around him. Sobatkin could have learned Paul's role and ordered him liquidated."

"If that's true, then Sobatkin works for the Conservative faction that's fighting rapprochement." Abrams removed his spectacles and polished light spray from them. Glasses in place, he said, "As an intellectual exercise it's fascinating. As a strategic intelligence question it's challenging—but we have no facts to support either conclusion. Again, Valcour may have a significant piece of the puzzle, Quinn. I hope he lives long enough to yield whatever he knows."

As the prow bumped the pier, Chance added, "I suggested the ChiComs pick up General Berlikov in Washington and question him."

Abrams smiled briefly. "Keep me posted."

"If they tell me anything, you'll know." He helped the older man onto the landing stage and they walked toward the quai. "I think we need a way to communicate securely. Any further written messages could be intercepted, and your room phone is probably monitored."

"Open-code phone's the answer. We'll call Moscow Washington, the bad guys inside traders. The envoy will be the platinum dealer. . . . Let's see: Sobatkin can be the secretary of commerce— what else?"

Chance glanced around. "An emergency meeting—here—will be indicated by Mont Blanc. ChiComs—African delegates."

Abrams nodded. "Valcour, the stockbroker? No, too close. Call him the Persian rug dealer."

"Good. Where I'm staying the phone number is 14-71-46. Valcour's in the directory."

"How's his sister taking it?"

"She's worried, frightened, and baffled, but tough—like Paul."

"The two of you make a handsome couple." Jan smiled and walked away.

It was midafternoon when Chance picked up Toni and drove her to the hospital. Outside the CCR they found the surgeon, who said, "Your brother is holding his own, gaining a bit of strength, mademoiselle."

"Would you say he's stabilized?" Chance asked.

"That may be putting it too strongly. He's on IV feeding, and I ordered another half-liter of whole blood a while ago. I hope we won't have to operate again."

"May I see him?" Toni asked.

The surgeon partly opened the door and let them look in.

An oxygen mask was clamped to Paul's pale face. Tubes ran in and out of his body. Electrode wires fed into a bank of cathode monitors. Toni whimpered, clutched Chance, and began to sob.

"Easy," he said, "Paul's alive; the worst may be over."

The surgeon nodded. "Quite so. Having survived surgical trauma and anesthesia, Monsieur Valcour has a chance. One lung is collapsed to permit healing, but his heart is strong." He lowered his voice. "As the police requested I am allowing it to be believed that your brother died. However, for his protection I feel he should be moved elsewhere when that becomes possible."

Chance said, "You have a place in mind?"

"My brother operates a small private clinic off the Lausanne Road." He gave Chance a card. "You might care to inspect the facilities."

"Thank you," Toni said, "we'll do that."

After a last glimpse of her brother she closed the door and walked silently away. When she was out of earshot Chance spoke to the surgeon. "When can I talk to him?"

"If he survives the night, perhaps tomorrow, late in the day. Call me."

Chance joined Toni and at her request drove her to Valcour's place. She entered the empty mansion hesitantly, then gathered strength and went from room to room, leaving Paul's bedroom until last. Stepping just inside, she said, "It's all so normal now. But I'll never forget. . . ." Her voice trailed off.

"Albert had Maurice's belongings packed and moved to the garage—for whoever comes to claim them."

"We'll pay for his funeral, of course, and any salary due him. Would you take care of that, dear?"

"Glad to. And it's good that you think of others." He kissed her and led her outside.

Outside, the moon was just breaching the horizon. Through the mist gathering across the lake small lights twinkled. A fairyland, Chance thought, violated by conspiracies, menace, and murder. He would never again be able to think of Geneva as a tranquil, civilized city.

When they got back to his villa Toni went upstairs—to change for cocktails, she said, but Chance sensed she wanted time alone to grieve. Much as she offended and antagonized her brother in public, Toni undeniably deeply loved the brother who had filled her parents' place.

He was in the library putting together vodka martinis when Sam came to him and said quietly, "I've received word from Hsiao."

Chance added ice to the shaker, twirled it, and partly filled a glass. He drank it down and looked directly at Sam. "The suspense is killing me."

"Expecting bad news?"

"It'd be par for the course."

Sam took a folded sheet from his pocket. "First, is Valcour alive?"

"So far."

"Talked to anyone?"

"Maybe tomorrow."

Sam nodded. "My—our—instructions are to stay put. The operation is still on. After forty years' alienation, a few more weeks or months waiting for Soviet reconciliation are insignificant. Hsiao thinks an alternate approach may be made to Valcour's sister, so you should prepare her for that, keeping it in a business context. Can you do that?"

Immensely relieved, Chance nodded but said, "That endangers Toni."

"She'd be dead now if she hadn't been sleeping with you. So I've decided to have Lao-li guard Toni whenever she leaves here without you."

"*Lao-li?*"

"She's an educated woman, knows kung fu, and is an expert pistol shot."

"And I thought she was just a great piece of ass."

Sam's face tightened. "More importantly, Lao-li will protect the princess with her life." He refolded the paper. "Soviets are arriving daily to fill out their negotiating team. This is the best possible time for an envoy to come."

Chance tilted the shaker and refilled his glass. "Suppose Valcour had been eliminated?"

"I was prepared to do the same to you," Sam replied bluntly, "but Hsiao was ordered to make this work." He tapped the folded paper. "Our investment in you, setting all this up, is too great to abandon—now. You fail, he fails, and you will share the consequences."

Hearing footsteps on the staircase, Sam tucked away his notes and smiled obsequiously as Toni entered the room.

"I'm feeling much better," she said, and looked it in a beige-and-brown paisley cocktail dress. A saddle-leather belt accented the curve of her hips. "Now, what have you two been talking about?"

"Girls." Chance kissed her cheek and handed over a vodka martini.

THIRTY-EIGHT

Wearing a Knott's Berry Farm T-shirt, Major General Nikolai Petrovich Berlikov stretched comfortably in his easy chair before the family TV set. Although he had scraped dinner dishes with Irina and helped her load their dishwasher, she was still fussing in the kitchen. She was a good wife, he reflected as a fast-food commercial occupied the TV screen, and an excellent cook. What could be more satisfying than pot roast, boiled potatoes, and tartly pickled beets? The children were in bed, thank heaven, and peace reigned in his household.

"Hurry up," he called, "or you'll miss *Nightline.*"

"I'm just setting the breakfast table. Who's Koppel's guest?"

"Oh, some public official, a senator, I think."

"What's he done?" she called back. "The senator?"

"Taken too much election money, something like that."

"Imagine," she chuckled, "such a thing on Moscow television. These *Amerikanits* are crazy—but I adore Ted Koppel."

So she did, Berlikov reflected, and every other American television personality. Having no embassy employment because of her husband's senior position, Irina divided her time between their two children and the TV set. When she left their duplex it was to shop with the Sovietskaya Kolonia group; an embassy bus took them to the Giant supermarket in Friendship Heights near the District line.

Wiping hands on her apron before untying it, Irina came in and sat beside her husband, rapt. As Ted Koppel said, "Good evening," she sighed. "What a head of hair, Kolya. Just as perfect as a wig."

"Maybe it *is* a wig," he said irritably. "These TV talkers are masters of disguise. And—"

"*Shhhhh!* I want to hear everything he says."

After describing his guest's background, Koppel began questioning him. Berlikov looked at his wristwatch; he would have to leave shortly, so it was just as well this program wasn't particularly interesting. Still, it was good for Irina's English and kept her from moping around the way so many SK wives did. Maintaining Party morale in the midst of capitalist luxury was an ongoing problem for the SK leader, and Berlikov was glad it wasn't part of his duties.

Duty. He looked at his wristwatch again. Almost time. Ever since Dayton's demise, he had had to fill in, servicing agent dead drops—*duboks*—and making scheduled payments. The bookkeeping alone was enough to drive a man mad, and there was the added danger of FBI detection. He didn't know the outlying area as Dayton had and not infrequently got lost. If stopped by the FBI, he'd have no recourse but to produce his diplomatic carnet and demand that his ambassador be notified. Such an encounter would of course peel away his nearly transparent cover like an onion skin, he thought bitterly. When would Moscow send Dayton's replacement? Or was he expected to recruit one on his own, a lengthy, laborious process both distasteful and dangerous?

Stretching, Berlikov got up and belched softly. "Have to go now."

Without taking her eyes from the tube, Irina asked, "How long, Kolya?"

"Two hours, three. Don't wait up."

"I worry when you're away at night."

He kissed her tilted cheek and thought, So do I.

From the closet he took a wool jacket, and from a shoe box three packages of currency wrapped in brown envelopes. One for "Betty," the agent who worked at the U.S. Bureau of Standards; one for "Yoder," a low-level Pentagon typist who had access to copying machines; and the the thickest package for "Claire," who held a midlevel job in the National Reconnaissance Office, the NRO, which dealt with satellite intelligence and photoimagery. "Claire" was perhaps his best source, and though his demands for more money were becoming persistent, his take was steadily improving. Even so, Moscow Center had not approved the increase, and Berlikov was not prepared to deal with the agent's complaints—that was for a *shpik* like Dayton to manage, not a major general in the KGB.

He got three empty Coors beer cans from under the sink and put them with the currency in a paper shopping bag. Then he left by the rear door and went into the garage. He unscrewed the diplomatic license plates from his Ford and replaced them with Maryland plates taken from a junk car purchased for that purpose alone.

As he backed out of the drive, Berlikov saw that his duplex neighbor's lights were out. Kondratsev was the SK leader and kept close tabs on everyone's comings and goings. Mikhail was a fanatical Party man hated by everyone in the SK, including Kolya Berlikov, who had warned Irina never to borrow as little as a cup of salt from his sour-faced wife.

Before turning into the street, Berlikov looked around for surveillance cars and saw none. Of course FBI watchers could be positioned in any—or all—of the neighboring houses, ready to radio ahead for mobile surveillance. But so far Berlikov hadn't experienced any government tails.

Leaving Jennifer Lane, Berlikov proceeded north on Wisconsin Avenue to the intersection with Western Avenue. He turned right and drove past handsome old homes to Chevy Chase Circle. To check surveillance he went three times around the circle before going two blocks north on Connecticut. To shake or confuse possible pursuers he turned onto Irving Street, and where it ended at Cedar Parkway he turned north again, then east on Lenox and finally back to Connecticut Avenue. Through it all he had watched the rearview mirror, and now he settled back and drove within the speed limit as far as Bethesda. There, in an all-night parking garage, he left his Ford and rode the Metrorail to Shady Grove. Three blocks from the Metrorail exit he unlocked a parked Plymouth and drove into the Maryland countryside.

The first drop site was at the end of an unpaved lovers' lane off Route 28 near Seneca Creek State Park. The remote lovers' lane was deserted and Berlikov, using his penlight, found the old fallen tree without difficulty. He covered the currency package with a curved section of bark and placed a Coors beer can on its end less than a yard away. He looked around the area for its mate and found it on its side by the bole of a maple tree, partly pinched, indicating that it was loaded. Berlikov picked it up and shook out two rolls of Minox film, which he pocketed.

Suppressing nervousness, he headed toward Gaithersburg. Reaching a creek, he pulled off the road and walked down under the bridge. He hid the payment package in an old rubber boot and placed another Coors can nearby. Further under the bridge pediment he came across a pinched can on its side, extracted a roll of film, and tossed the can into the creek.

Heading back toward Rockville, and towards home, Berlikov found a grove of hickory trees and parked on the road's shoulder, lights off. He crossed a strip of meadow and searched the nearest trees until he found one carved with a double heart. Behind it lay another pinched beer can. Unloading the three rolls of Minox film, he replaced it with his third can. He set the currency package under three fist-size stones, stood up, and turned to go.

Light blinded him. *"Don't move,"* a voice snapped, and Berlikov felt his muscles dissolve.

From behind a man blindfolded him while another patted him down for weapons and removed the Minox cassettes from his pockets.

"Hold out your hands, palms up," the voice instructed, and Berlikov complied, feeling the cassettes placed on his palms. Through the blindfold he could see a camera flash, then two more. The cassettes were removed and he was turned and shoved deeper into the grove.

As he stumbled along he wondered why they hadn't examined his documents. In a strained voice he said, "I'm a diplomatic official of the Soviet embassy."

"We know that," the voice responded. "Why else do you think we are here?"

Berlikov felt himself pushed against a tree trunk, and his hands were tied behind him. He thought he heard the soft hum of a tape recorder. There were at least three men, maybe four.

"We could torture you, kill you, or both," the man told him, "and that's for you to decide."

Berlikov felt close to vomiting. Had Quentin Chance finally tracked him down? But the voice had an uninflected, singsong cadence that didn't sound like American speech. Swallowing, he bleated, "You have to read me my rights."

"Rights? You have none, Nikolai Petrovich."

Weakly, he asked, "What do you want?"

"First, consider your situation. You have been photographed with the take from three agent drops. If that photograph were sent to your embassy, you would be sent back to Moscow immediately. And how you would be treated there I don't need to tell you." After a pause the voice said, "Do I?"

"No," Berlikov croaked.

"And there is your family to consider—Irina and your *precious* children, Andrei and Katya. You know what would happen to them."

"What do you want?" he whispered.

"Information, General. Supply it and your films will be returned and you will be allowed to go home as though this . . . interruption never occurred."

Berlikov swallowed. "What kind of information?" A chill seized him, but not because of the cool night air.

"Think back to the reception you gave Major Pavel Sosnowski, a fellow officer of the KGB."

So that was it. Only why were friends of Sosnowski speaking English? He said, "Sosnowski—you mean the poor fellow murdered by the American?"

The voice harshened. "I mean the Sosnowski your Arab agents shot. Don't trifle with me, General. I don't propose to waste time on you. You arranged his reception and killing."

Berlikov hung his head. What did he have to gain by denial? "I admit it," he said huskily.

"That's a beginning. Now, that was an unusual action, General. You had been told when Sosnowski would arrive, even his flight. Correct?"

"It's true." His heart pounded frighteningly.

"And you implicated the American in his murder. Correct?"

"Correct." Blood pulsed painfully in his head.

"Your idea, General?"

Berlikov's lips felt parched. With difficulty he swallowed, shook his head.

"Speak," the voice ordered.

Berlikov said, "Not my idea."

"Then this is the question on which your life depends: Who ordered you?"

Even though his eyes were blindfolded, he closed them as though to shield himself from reality. Everything was coming apart. Desperately his brain searched for a way out. Found none.

"A superior officer," he said, and leaned slackly against the tree's rough bark.

"Of course—obviously you don't accept orders from subordinates. *Which* officer, Nikolai Petrovich?"

He tried moistening his dry lips, tried breathing deeply to still the terror growing inside. Finally he yielded. "Lieutenant General Sobatkin," he gasped.

"Full name—speak up!"

"Yevgeni Lubovich Sobatkin."

"Position?"

"In Ottawa he represents the Bureau for Special Political Information."

"And his authority?"

"It extends over North and Central America."

"Who is his principal?"

"The minister of defence, Marshal Yaroshenko."

"So, to be clear about it, Sobatkin ordered you to liquidate Sosnowski in such a way that the American would be blamed?"

"Yes."

"And his orders came from Marshal Yaroshenko."

"That is what he told me."

"So you had a conversation with Sobatkin, at which time the plan was laid out."

"It took place in the embassy, in the secret chamber."

"You and Sobatkin were alone?"

"General Pyotr Andreyvich Chavadze was present."

"And what part did Chavadze play?"

"None. I gave the orders."

"To Dayton, I believe."

"Yes." They knew everything, *everything*. How could it be?

"Sobatkin told you why Sosnowski had to be liquidated."

"He said Sosnowski was to be prevented from making contact with the Chinese embassy."

"And what reason was given you?"

Berlikov told them everything then, the two Kremlin factions, one wanting rapprochement, the other domination . . . and when he finished he slumped weakly against the tree.

But it was not over. Not yet.

The voice said, "You interrogated Sosnowski for two days before killing him. Who did he say sent him to Washington?"

"He named Kirilenko, minister of education."

"Did you believe him?"

"I had no reason to disbelieve him. Sobatkin later said he lied."

"So if Kirilenko was not behind it, who was?"

"I have no idea—I don't know anything about Kremlin disputes and quarrels."

"Only what Sobatkin tells you, eh?"

Berlikov said nothing. The taste of beets was sour in his throat and mouth. He knew that he was close to tears.

"Have you forgotten to tell me anything? Have you lied?"

"No. I've told you everything I know."

"If you haven't, expect another visit, General. One more painful and permanently damaging." A hand squeezed his scrotum and Berlikov yelped. The pain diminished and he pleaded, "You'll let me go now?"

"Take your films and go. I don't want your routine to seem disturbed. If you are wise, you will say nothing of this episode to your wife, anyone in your embassy, or General Sobatkin. If you do, we will know, and your punishment will be worse than anything you can imagine. Do you understand?"

"I understand. But I've been gone longer than usual. How can I explain it?"

"Say you had a flat tire; use your imagination."

Berlikov heard the soft tread of feet over leaves. They were beginning to go. Hands freed him from the tree. "A final question, General: What does Valcour mean to you?"

Valcour? He searched his memory. Was it a perfume? A maker

of men's clothing? A foreign automobile? The name of a town or village? He shrugged vacantly. "Nothing," he said.

"You're sure Sobatkin never used the word?"

"Not to me, never. I swear I never heard the word." He was afraid to ask its meaning.

"Then forget it, put it out of your mind. Now, count to five hundred—slowly—and return to your car." The cassettes were inserted in his pocket. For a while no sound broke the night stillness. Then from a distance a voice called, "Keep counting," and in a mocking tone, *"dosvidanaya,* Comrade General."

Berlikov sank to a sitting position, too weak to stand.

He counted to forty and heard a car engine start. He pulled off his blindfold and gazed around. The grove that had seemed so peaceful, so secure, was hateful now, violated by his captors, contaminated by his own betrayals. He felt raped.

One twenty, one twenty-one . . . Doggedly he kept counting, grateful that he had not been harmed, determined to follow their orders as he had followed Sobatkin's—blindly.

An owl hooted in the grove, making Berlikov start. Four hundred.

How had they followed him when he thought everything was clear? Then he thought: That damned Dayton must have told them about the drops, the servicing schedule. . . . Who else knew?

He was vulnerable now, he knew; they had photographs and the recording. Either could destroy him. At least they hadn't confiscated his microfilms; so they weren't FBI.

Whose agents were they? Hooligans from the CIA? The ones who rescued Quentin Chance?

Four seventy-nine, four eighty. His legs were stiff from inaction. He flexed his knees, felt prickles as circulation eased.

He would have to pretend that nothing had happened, try to live and work normally despite the terror. He feared his captors as he feared Sobatkin. The difference was that he had satisfied his interrogators, but he could never satisfy Lieutenant General Sobatkin. Five hundred. Unsteadily he got to his feet, blinked at his watch dial. Nearly two. He shivered.

Sobatkin was insane to think that Chance could be located in America. Sobatkin was old, probably growing senile. Any more shit from him, Berlikov thought as he began walking over plowed furrows toward the road, and I'll let him hear a replay of those insane orders he forced on me. Fuck him, he thought as courage returned and he saw his car ahead, undisturbed. It's his fault I'm in this mess. I'd like to see him hanging by his thumbs in the lowest cell of the Lubyanka.

He opened his car door and got in. Before he turned on the ignition General Berlikov leaned back and drew in three deep breaths. Steadier now, grateful for escape, and loathing Sobatkin from the bottom of his soul, he started the engine and drove slowly back toward the safety of his home.

BOOK THREE

BOOK THREE

THIRTY-NINE

Four nights after the shooting, Paul Valcour was transferred by ambulance to the Clinique Mirabeau in the foothills some five miles north of Geneva. Valcour's recovery had been steady, but he remained in critical condition. He was installed in a second-floor room, where guards hired by Albert protected him round the clock. The clinic, Chance learned, catered to jet-setters of both sexes who required a discreet abortion, face-lift, or tush-tuck. Not infrequently an internationally famous music or film star would undergo alcohol or drug withdrawal away from public notice. So the clinic was accustomed to patients who required privacy and paid heavily for it.

Unlike the stark exterior of the cantonal clinic, the Mirabeau resembled a small, handsomely designed hotel of forty rooms or so. Its three-floor façade of varicolored firebrick crawled with vines whose leaves were not yet showing. There were window boxes and perimeter flower beds; around back, a high brick wall topped with barbed and razor wire. To Chance it looked as secure as a prison, with the distinction that its inmates paid for the privilege of con-finement.

Toni was permitted to visit her brother alone for brief periods. On his sixth day of convalescence Toni told Chance that Paul wanted to see him. "I want to see him, too," Chance told her.

"Paul's already told the police he can't add anything; he was asleep when he was shot."

"There may be something he prefers the police not know."

"He's grateful for what you did that night, all you've done to protect us."

"That's what friends are for." He smiled, and drove to the clinic that afternoon.

When Chance entered the room, Paul raised one hand weakly and murmured, "Thank you for everything." His words were distorted by the oxygen mask.

"Anyone would have done it." Chance drew up a chair at bedside. "Circumstances indicate you were hit by a *spetznialniy* team on a round-trip from Moscow. That special Aeroflot plane you told me about took off a couple of hours after the attack."

"God!"

"For safety you have to be kept out of sight, Paul. What's the fallback plan?"

After a few moments Valcour murmured, "No one anticipated I would be *hors de combat.*"

"That's not an answer. For once in your life, tell me the whole goddamned truth. How were you brought into it?"

"By computer."

"Computer?"

"I was accessed and a meeting arranged. It's not hard to contact me that way, I'm on the financial circuit."

"So you met someone—who?"

"Brush contact in the airport. He paid half my fee and I never saw him again."

"Can you contact him?"

"I don't know how."

Chance got up and went over to the barred window. Below in the walled yard he saw patients playing shuffleboard and Ping-Pong; others strolled along a leafless, serpentine hedge. A man and woman were playing cards on a bench. Two white-jacketed attendants leaned against the wall, smoking as they watched their charges. Looking back, he asked, "How much did you tell the Agency?"

"The Agency? Why would I—?"

"Careful, Paul. I found that old TR-51 set, sent out a signal, and got a reply. Did you ever really break with the Agency?"

Valcour swallowed. "I wanted out, wanted to make some money. Brigand was an opportunity to leave and develop credible cover."

"What have you been reporting?"

"Arab oil deals, Soviet sub rosa investing . . . commercial intelligence."

"Did you give me away?"

"No, I swear I didn't." His lips twisted in pain. "The Agency knows nothing of our operation."

"Someone does," Chance said, "or you wouldn't have been shot." He went back to the chair. "What did Maurice know?"

"Maurice," he murmured and his eyes filled with tears. "Maurice knew nothing from me. Not a word, Quinn. Believe me."

"Could he have recovered info from the computer?"

Valcour was silent for a while before saying, "It's possible. I didn't erase the memory bank for several days. But Maurice would never have betrayed me. He would have asked me what the message meant, no more."

Dead end, Chance thought. "Paul, I've helped you stay alive. I need you to return the favor. If the Soviet envoy can't find someone to talk to, the op's finished—and so am I. Knowing you I'm damn sure you set up an alternate contact. Whose name did you give? Maurice? Toni?"

"Toni," he admitted, "but I never briefed her. There was no need unless I had to be away from Geneva." His gaze fixed on Chance. "Shall I brief her now?"

"Yes, damn it," snapped Chance. "For all I know, the envoy's already attempted contact and returned to Moscow."

After a few moments Valcour said, "You've done wonders for my sister, Quinn, and I'm grateful. . . . How do you feel about Toni?"

"I'm living an hour, a day at a time, Paul. I can't make plans."

"You haven't thought about what you'll do after this op is over?"

"I've thought survival. After that, find a hole and crawl in."

"Toni told me she loves you. She could help you, Quinn."

He shrugged. "She's disoriented by all that's happened."

The door opened and the attending physician came in. A green OR cap covered his hair, a green mask hung under his chin. To Chance the doctor looked to be in his late thirties. His smooth skin was slightly olive and he wore a narrow black mustache. After scanning the monitors he spoke nervously to Chance. "The patient must rest now, m'sieu."

Chance got up and moved the chair away. "Get well," he told Valcour and left the clinic.

At the villa Sam asked, "Learn anything?"

"Toni's Valcour's alternate contact, but she doesn't know it—yet."

"Well, that's something," Sam remarked. "I'm more optimistic now."

"Where's Toni?"

"Out shopping, with Lao-li." He looked at his watch. "They'll be back soon. I've arranged to have calls to the Valcour mansion transferred here. Also, there's been a development you should know about. General Berlikov named a General Sobatkin as the man who ordered him to intercept Sosnowski. Berlikov declared the plan originated with the Soviet defense minister, Yaroshenko. With that information Hsiao can possibly determine the Kremlin lineup—friendlies and hostiles."

Chance remembered Jan Abrams's mention of Sobatkin but said nothing.

Sam continued. "Interestingly, Sobatkin passed through here just before the attack on Valcour."

"That sort of nails it down," Chance observed. "Where does Sobatkin hang out?"

"Ottawa. Chief of North American ops."

Chance smiled. "So you leaned on Berlikov."

"And Hsiao appreciates your suggestion. You could have a good career with us."

"Thanks, but I want to get back to books and classrooms."

"Think it over."

In late afternoon, while Toni was visiting her brother, Chance arranged a meeting with Abrams at the *débarcadère*, the lakeside dock used by tourist launches and private craft, and passed on Sam's information. After a low whistle Jan said, "Meaning the Soviet military establishment is conspiring against rapport with China." He looked at Chance. "That's valuable enough to report,

Quinn, but I have no way of sourcing it. If I say I picked it up at a social gathering, it becomes gossip rating no more than D-4 evaluation. You understand the problem."

Chance nodded. "It now looks as though Sobatkin probably issued orders for the attack on Valcour, but the question is: How did Sobatkin know Paul was the contact point? Anything in the Daleth intercepts?"

Abrams shook his head. "The few I was able to read concerned other ops. But there's a good deal of KGB-type radio traffic we can't decipher. NSA thinks it's probably dummy traffic to keep our people occupied, but it could be a special double cipher used by Sobatkin. We just don't know." He removed his glasses and slowly polished the lenses. "How much will Valcour tell his sister?"

"Only that she's to expect a special business contact, and the recognition phrases. I wish Paul had made other arrangements."

"You're fond of her, aren't you?"

"Sure, but it's like a cruise ship romance—great till the boat docks. No future, Jan."

"Don't be too sure of that," Abrams advised, "and negative thinking never helps. Besides, situations can change abruptly, so never foreclose the future."

He looked out over the water for a while. Gulls squawked, lighted on pilings, flapped away. "I'm being realistic," he said quietly, "and what began as a simple contact operation has gotten complicated beyond belief. If I can get out alive, I'll consider myself lucky."

"The way I see things," Abrams mused, "is that all of us who seek peace are lucky you have a part in it."

Turning slowly around, Chance scanned the quai du Mont Blanc and said quietly, "Don't look, Jan, but there's a pair of Soviet scumbags pretending not to watch us."

"Oh? How can you tell?"

"My Chinese buddy showed me photos of local help. Have you been tailed before in Geneva?"

"Probably; I haven't paid attention. I guess I should."

"We'll change the rendezvous site, make it the newsstand in the gare. And be careful in general. I'm afraid I've put you in danger."

Abrams shrugged. "Don't worry about that, Quinn. I haven't a lot left to live for."

"You're wrong, but I won't request a meet unless one's essential." He patted his friend's arm. "Wait here and see if they follow me. If they don't, phone your delegation and have a couple of burrheads pick you up."

"I'll do as you say. And, Quinn . . . it does me good to talk with you."

"Me, too," he said, and walked away, concerned about Jan.

One *topolshchik* followed him while the other sat on a bench and watched Abrams. Chance boarded the first passing tram and rode into Old Town as far as the Florissant stop. He got off and walked unconcernedly into a department store, took an escalator to the second floor, ducked into a lavatory, and waited five minutes before coming out. He left the store by a rear door, walked to the Tranchées station, and rode a Brown Line tram back to the Chante-Poulet stop, two blocks from where he had left his car. Before unlocking the door he made sure the tail was not in sight— probably still wandering around the department store—then he drove back to the villa and found Toni waiting for him.

She had made a shaker of martinis and pointed to it. From her expression he realized that she was several glasses ahead. He went to kiss her, but she turned her cheek. "I'm upset by what Paul told me."

"Taking it out on me?" He strained liquor into his glass. "Why?"

"Why not? Neither one of you is telling me the truth, at least not all of it."

He settled in a chair and looked up at her. "You'd better tell me what he said."

"It's what he *didn't* say, Jean-Pierre. He told me a tale about a big international deal you two are waiting to consummate. An unknown messenger is supposed to come here and begin negotiations. It's all so secret there are even confidential phrases to exchange." She laughed shortly and drained her glass. "The whole thing sounds preposterous. He's *hors de combat,* so little sister is to take his place." She splashed a refill into her glass, spilling some on the carpet. "It's dangerous, and I don't like it worth a damn.

240

Furthermore, I'm sure you've been lying to me. You screw me and bullshit me, and who the hell do you think you are?"

"My business is with your brother," Chance replied evenly. "It's a confidential matter I had no right to discuss with you, or anyone. Are you going to do as he asks, or are you going to turn back into the snotty brat I met that first night?"

"Damn you!" she cried, and her arm slashed downward to slap his face, but he caught her wrist and shot to his feet. "Don't play the arrogant little bitch with me," he snapped. "I saved your life once, maybe twice." Roughly he freed her arm.

"You hurt me," she whimpered, and began licking her reddened wrist.

"You provoked it, Toni. The question is whether you'll fill in for Paul until he's able to circulate again."

Her arm dropped to her side. "It's really important, then."

"Unbelievably important."

"And you want me—"

"I want you to follow Paul's instructions. After contact is made you're out of it. You can go away, do whatever you like." He drained his glass, shook his head when she held hers out. "You've had enough," he said, "and it's bedtime."

"Bedtime? But it's only . . ." Her lips closed when she grasped his meaning.

He scooped her body up and she went rigid. Her fists pounded his face and head. He slapped her cheek and she screamed, but her body went limp. Suddenly her mouth pressed his and she bit his lips as he carried her up the stairs. He opened the bedroom door and kicked it shut behind them. "Brute," she said throatily. "I've never been forced before."

He dumped her on the bed, drew off his jacket. "Take off your clothes," he ordered.

"Make me." Her eyes glittered lustfully.

With one hand he ripped her blouse to her belly. She struggled to get away, but he tore off her skirt. She cowered while he stripped, and then he pulled off her panties. Naked, he kneed her thighs apart. She moaned in passion and raked his back with her nails as he entered her wet vagina. Eyes starry, she thrust back frenziedly, tongue lancing his mouth, urging him not to stop.

Finally she climaxed, arched her back, and collapsed. He finished in a wild rush of emotions and lay atop her while their breathing slowed. After a while she murmured, "God, that was terrific. It's never been so good."

"You told me you needed discipline."

"Promise you'll be brutal from time to time."

"Whenever you get out of line." He rolled aside, staring at the ceiling. "You'll do as Paul asked?"

"Always intended to." She yawned, covered her mouth with her hand. "Suddenly I'm famished."

"Me, too."

"We can dine on each other—or go out to eat."

"We'll go out—first."

"We still have a bottle of champagne."

"It won't last the night."

He raised his hand to her lips, and she kissed it. "I love you and I don't care who you are or how sinister your business is. I'll do whatever you say."

"Turn on the shower and scrub my back."

She sat up and swung her legs off the bed. "Anything else, master?"

"We'll see what develops."

The next day after lunch the contact call came through.

FORTY

He was in the library with Toni when Lao-li handed her the receiver. As Toni listened her gaze darted to Chance. Nodding, she said carefully, "Then you might prefer Holland and its windmills."

The words hit Chance with electric force. Mouth suddenly dry, he took the phone. "I'm M'sieu Valcour's associate. What can I do for you?"

Startlingly, the voice was female. In excellent English she said, "I believe we have business to discuss. I have very little time and would appreciate an early meeting."

"At your convenience."

"Good. Suppose I come to the Valcour residence. The files are there?"

"They are."

"Then we can get down to business without losing time. Is an hour agreeable?"

"I'll be there." The line went dead and he replaced the receiver. Face taut, Toni said, "That's it, then."

Unless it's a setup, he thought. Chance nodded.

"Is there anything I can do? You'll tell me?"

"It's up to me now. Tell Paul; it might relieve his mind."

"I'm sure it will." She turned to Lao-li, who lingered in the doorway. "We'll go to the clinic," she said. "Bring your little gun." Kissing Chance, she said, "I hope everything goes well, *chéri*."

"I do, too." Watching the two women leave, he thought that if Lao-li could shoot as well as she could screw, Toni was safe.

Sam had gone to the Chinese consulate, so for a while the villa would be empty. Chance went upstairs, and while he was strapping on his holster he realized that he might soon be able to leave Geneva and start another life somewhere. He pulled on a jacket, locked all doors, and got into the Mercedes.

Twelve minutes later he braked to let the gate guard look in and gave instructions to admit a female visitor arriving shortly. Behind the mansion Albert was polishing Paul's Daimler. The driver tipped his hat and walked over. "Is there news of Monsieur Valcour's condition?"

"Improving daily," Chance told him. "We're confident he'll recover. Meanwhile a woman is coming here within the hour. I'll see her alone; keep anyone else outside."

"I understand, m'sieu." He touched his visor respectfully. "You expect trouble?"

"No, and I don't want any. Is the groom around?"

Albert nodded toward the stables. "He has no pistol."

"A pitchfork can be useful."

"As you say, m'sieu." His battered face showed traces of a smile. He walked off toward the stables.

Chance entered the mansion. He went to the library-office and opened the cellarette. There was ice and assorted liquors. Two frosted bottles of Chablis, one of Cordon Rouge. He set champagne glasses to chill and partly opened window blinds for light. Then he pulled out his pistol and chambered a shell, leaving the safety off. He replaced the Walther in its holster.

Everything ready, he told himself, except for one thing: Who the hell is she? What are her credentials? The last Russians had come in with guns blazing. What could he expect from this one?

He sat down in a leather chair and stared at the bookshelves. Perhaps an hour from now he would be freed of his obligation to Hsiao; in turn, the Chinese master spy would have no further use for Quentin Chance. Prudence told him to act promptly. But where could he go? And what about Toni?

He wanted her with him, but her life would be at risk.

Get settled first, he reasoned, then send for her. Argentina was a huge country; he could go into the Andes, hide where so many

Germans had. Eventually they could move into Buenos Aires, find safe haven there or in Montevideo or Rio.

He heard gravel crunching. Parting a window blind, he looked out, saw a Fiat taxi pulling up. A woman got out, paid the driver, and the taxi turned down the drive.

The woman wore a gray tailored suit with a white blouse and a large black bow. A purse depended from one shoulder. For a moment she stood gazing at the mansion's facade, and then she started up the steps. Chance left the window and went into the hall to meet her. The bell rang and he opened the door.

She was younger than he had assumed from the severity of her dress—late thirties. Her complexion was pale and her dark eyes were deep-set. Her titian hair was fashionably waved, her only adornment a necklace of seed pearls. Thrusting out her hand, she said, "I am Natalya Yegorova. Who are you?"

"Jean-Pierre Duroc. Please come in."

She hesitated. "I expected an American."

"I'm American," he said, "like Valcour."

Entering slowly, she looked around the corridor. "Are we alone?"

"Two servants are elsewhere in the house. Outside, two men are guarding us." He lifted the purse strap from her shoulder. "Mind?"

She shrugged, and he opened the purse. It contained feminine articles, Swiss francs—and a small 7.65-millimeter automatic. "I'm in a strange country," she said.

He drew out the magazine and replaced pistol and magazine in her purse. "You've come a long way, Miss Yegorova. Some refreshment?"

"Vodka, please, on ice." She followed him into the library.

He poured two drinks, she took her glass and sipped delicately. *"Na zdorovye,"* she said, and Chance echoed the toast.

"How much time do we have?" he asked.

"Perhaps an hour. Yesterday I arrived with delegation personnel, and there is a communal dinner this evening, before the negotiations begin tomorrow." She glanced around the room. "This is where Paul Valcour was shot?"

"Upstairs. Three dead, he barely survived. He's hidden away, recovering." He sat down facing Natalya Yegorova. She was not the first Russian woman he had met, but she was by far the most attractive. Full breasts, narrow waist, ample hips, lips that were sensuous without being de trop. She moved in a controlled, confident way, probably fully aware of her impact on men, he told himself, and he felt the beginning of an erection.

Swallowing, he said, "From what we've been able to gather, the hit was made by two *spetznialniy* who came here for that purpose and left by the special Aeroflot flight that brought them."

She listened, her tongue moistened her lips, and she said, "That explains some things. I am the fifth emissary to attempt contact with the Chinese, so I am interested in details of what has taken place." She sipped again. Chance felt a strong urge to push away the glass and kiss her lips.

"Collateral information acquired by the Chinese indicates that Lieutenant General Yevgeni Lubovich Sobatkin has been directing operations against your friends." He had to look away from her before he was mesmerized. My God, what a woman! he thought. "Additional information has it that Sobatkin carries out orders from Marshal Yaroshenko."

"The old warlord," she said musingly, the tip of her tongue tracing the rim of the glass. "It's entirely logical." Her gaze found his eyes. Hers were unbelievably dark and deep. "So the Chinese learned all this." She leaned forward. "How do you like working for the Chinese?"

"It's a short tour," he said, "and they've treated me fairly." He cleared his throat. "I've been instructed to say that the government of the People's Republic of China welcomes the initiative of the Union of Soviet Socialist Republics and will send appropriate emissaries to confer with Soviet representatives at a mutually convenient site."

She smiled. "On behalf of the Soviet Union I acknowledge the fraternal response of the People's Republic of China. And I am authorized to arrange a time and place for the meeting. Do you have a suggestion?"

"Not at this time," he said. "Perhaps you do."

She laughed lightly. "We sound like two fencing diplomats, Jean-Pierre. Let's put formality aside and talk plain language." She extended her empty glass, and Chance made another pair of drinks. He was about to resume his chair when she gestured at the sofa. "Sit here and we won't have to talk so loudly."

He sat next to her and felt the warmth of her thigh against his. "Your English is flawless," he said. "You didn't learn it in Russia."

"I have a degree from Boston University. Also, I was a vice-consul in Toronto, and since then I have been with the Foreign Ministry." She drank deeply.

"Is Yegorova your work name, or——?"

"My husband was Mikhail Yegorov, an air force officer."

"Was?"

"Killed in Afghanistan," she said quietly. "Four years ago. That is one reason I risk so much to bring about peace with our Chinese neighbors."

"I admire you." He meant it. "Now, where shall the meeting take place?"

"My principals suggest Denmark," she replied slowly. "Both countries have embassies there and Copenhagen is cosmopolitan, filled with foreign visitors and tourists. Also, for us it is easy to get to Denmark from Helsinki." She paused. "Relatively easy, for it is never simple to leave the Soviet Union."

He nodded. "I'd like to offer an alternate site to the Chinese. Is Brussels a possibility?"

"It is. Do you have a date in mind?"

He said, "There's been so much delay. Suppose we recommend two weeks from today? I believe the Chinese would like to meet as soon as possible."

"Three weeks from today," she countered. "Things move slowly in Moscow. When do you think you can confirm arrangements?"

"Very soon, I think. How long will you be in Geneva?"

"Perhaps ten days. The delegation plans on concluding negotiations by then—one way or another."

She drank the rest of her vodka and drew off her gray coat. Her face was flushed, Chance saw. He folded her coat over the back of a chair, got up, and opened the champagne. "I think a toast is in order," he said. "A minor celebration."

She loosened her flouncy bow and unbuttoned the blouse collar. "Warm, isn't it?" she said. "Is Geneva always like this?"

His throat was thick. "It's a short spring," he said, and handed her the filled glass. Rims touched, and as they sipped together he felt that he had never been so powerfully attracted to any woman. She looked at him and her expression was both innocent and expectant. *"Na zdorovye,"* she murmured.

As though magnetized, Chance's hand touched her chin, one finger drew across her lips, and her tongue touched it before it was entirely gone. "I have a little time," she said huskily, and one hand drew his against her breast. He pressed his lips to hers. Her mouth opened and accepted his questing tongue. He unbuttoned her blouse and freed her breasts. Natalya wriggled out of her skirt, pulled up her slip, and opened her loins to his rigid penis. Her pubic hair was dense, a forest penetrated without resistance. The tightness of her vagina, the smallness of her nipples told him that she had never borne children. She lay back on the sofa and clutched him to her undulating body. He felt engulfed by her femaleness. Bodies wet with perspiration, they thrust together until she cried out, moved rapidly against him and spent moments before he did.

Chance felt utterly drained. Dazedly, he kissed her breasts, took her nipples between his lips. Natalya stroked his head and murmured, "That was marvelous—it's been so long for me. . . ."

He found himself wondering if she had screwed her way upward in the Foreign Ministry, despised himself for the thought, and said, "Will I see you again?"

"Once more—as planned. Then . . ." She left the thought unfinished. "We do well together, don't we?"

He nodded and she laughed lightly. "An entente cordiale our masters never dreamed of."

"Nor I," he said. "Will you go back to Moscow?"

"Yes—and you?"

"I don't know. But I'll never forget you, Natalya." He sat up and her head bent over while she cleansed him in her mouth. They kissed then, and he rose unsteadily to freshen their forgotten champagne. Drinking together, they touched each other's bodies, experienced the feel of their skins in a new and different intimacy. After a while he said, "From my Chinese principal I learned that there is a hard-line faction in Peking just as there is in Moscow.

248

The Kremlin faction may already have established contact with the Chinese. Do you know anything of this?"

"Not in detail, but it is more than a possibility. I would speculate that Marshal Yaroshenko is a tool of the Kremlin Conservatives, the leaders who would roll back the few liberalizing gains our premier has achieved, end *glasnost* and *perestroika;* return to the cold war posture and rearm." She eyed him. "Who is your principal?"

"Hsiao Kuan-hua."

Her eyes narrowed. "Head of Chinese Intelligence, Kryuchkov's opposite number. What else did he tell you?"

"That the Kremlin hard-liners want to join efforts with China to divide the world between them. Hsiao suggested that with Western Europe largely disarmed and my country deeply involved in Mideast problems, the situation is propitious for a double strike."

Natalya shuddered. "Horrible. But its very boldness gives it plausibility." She looked away. "I suspect Yegor Ligachev would support such a scheme—even though I am protected by him." She touched his arm. "Jean-Pierre, I am grateful for what you've told me, but I have no power to do more than act as a messenger."

"Perhaps Marshal Yaroshenko could be discredited," he suggested.

"How?"

"Thrugh his instrument, Sobatkin."

She nodded slowly. "Only, how to compromise General Sobatkin?"

"I hoped you'd have some ideas."

Natalya shook her head. "This is too new, too sudden. I'll have to think about it." She looked at her wristwatch. "Oh, I must go. I don't want to . . . you understand?"

"I do," he said, and reluctantly watched her dress. "How will I contact you?"

"It's safer if I call you, ask for you by name."

"Can you come here tomorrow?"

She shook her head. "Like everyone, I'm watched."

"I'll drive you to the city," he offered, and began putting on his clothing.

"Only as far as a taxi stand. No, have your driver take me."

"Whatever is safer for you. We'll work things out," he promised.

She drained the last of her champagne, kissed his lips, and walked to the door. Chance unlocked it, and while Natalya was freshening in the entrance powder room he went out and gave Albert instructions.

Natalya joined him, looking almost as prim as when she first arrived. Chance opened the Daimler door, they held each other's hands for a moment, and she said, *"Dosvidanaya* doesn't mean forever."

He watched the Daimler roll smoothly down the drive and went back into the mansion. He put away their glasses and looked around the spacious room. Something momentous had occurred within these walls, he told himself with a feeling of awe. In addition to one of the most passionate encounters in his life, two great powers, antagonists for forty years, were drawing together in the first cautious moves toward understanding and eventual peace.

He was eager to see Natalya again, but he realized that the next phase brought increased danger to them both; they would have to be extraordinarily discreet. Much as he wanted her, he would not have her risk everything to be with him.

Two hours ago he had not even been aware that Natalya existed. An hour later he had begun to respond to her incredible allure. Now it was time to relay the Soviet response.

FORTY-ONE

Sam was at the villa when Chance returned. "Have you been visiting Valcour again?" he asked. "Don't you—?"

"Get off my back, Sam. I was meeting the Soviet contact."

Sam gaped. "You mean it? What happened? What did he say?"

"*She* said her side wants a Copenhagen meet three weeks from today. Can your people make it?"

"A *woman?*"

"A well-educated Soviet officer."

"Name?"

"Calls herself Yelena," he lied, not wanting Chinese surveilling her. "Brussels is okay if your people prefer. But the Soviets can make Cope more easily."

Sam sucked in a deep breath. "Exciting. Did she name the Soviet representatives?"

"That comes later. If the chef's back, I talk better with coffee."

"Right." Sam hurried to the kitchen, returning to the library with cup and saucer. They sat down, and after Chance sipped coffee to cut his vodka high he said, "Hsiao should okay place and date, and supply the names of your delegation and the contact arrangements." He finished his coffee.

Sam asked, "When's your next meeting?"

"After Hsiao replies. I thought her side ought to know their enemies, so I told her about Sobatkin and Yaroshenko."

"Berlikov?"

"No need to name him."

"Right, just checking. What's Yelena look like?"

251

"She's a Soviet woman, what can I say? Solid build, severe dress, Slavic face...." The hell with Sam. Now that things were moving, his role was crucial; henceforth, Sam was going to have to take whatever he dished out. And like it.

"Operating alone?"

"Far as I can tell. Look, Sam, she has a strict schedule. We covered details and she had to leave. Like everyone in Soviet delegations, she's watched, checked on, you know that. Better get going."

"Okay, okay. Hsiao is going to be *very* pleased." He went off to the consulate.

Chance went up to the bedroom and changed clothing. Paul must feel better about things now, he thought; he'd get the rest of his pay.

He felt relieved that Valcour and Toni had no further responsibility. From now on, everything would be accomplished by himself and Natalya. No need for anyone else. After that, he'd move along, find a place to go underground, safe from feds, Sovs, *and* Chinese. Tired, he lay on the bed and closed his eyes, slept until Toni wakened him for dinner.

Over consommé she said, "So everything went well?"

"Instant meeting of the minds. Give Paul credit for setting it up so perfectly."

"And your business deal, it's going through?"

"I expect it to," he told her. "I'll know more in a few days. She has to report back to her principals." He sipped the warming broth.

"I'm glad," she said softly. "But after everything's arranged you'll leave Geneva—won't you?"

"When Paul can handle things."

She laid aside her spoon. "I don't want you to leave. If you do, I want to go with you."

He took her hand. "I'm not an entirely free agent," he said quietly. "You've understood that all along. I'll have to make arrangements, Toni. Personal changes in my life."

"And how long will that take?"

"A month or so, maybe more. And while I'm doing that, why don't you check out B.A. and Mexico?"

"Unless that's a subtle way of getting rid of me."

"It's not. As soon as possible we'll be together."

"Promise?"

"Promise."

Lao-li began pouring their wine.

After dinner Chance drove to the Clinique Mirabeau and waited outside Paul's guarded room while the sheets were changed and a full flask of IV sucrose replaced the empty. Valcour looked better, more color in his face and lips. "So it's done, eh? How did it go?" he asked.

"We reached an understanding."

"Meaning what, Quinn?"

"Meaning your part is over, Paul. The op's in my hands now."

Valcour frowned. "The need-to-know dictum. Well, I'd do the same. But can you give me any hints?"

"Let's say the beginning went well. The outcome depends on the people involved."

Valcour sighed. "So where will you go?"

"Undecided. Toni wants to go with me."

"I'm not surprised. How do you feel about it?"

"You know my situation—hunted by the FBI, Interpol, the KGB—perhaps the Chinese. I can't expose your sister to that kind of danger."

"I wouldn't want her to be. This—illness of mine has brought us together. Thanks to you, she's a new woman."

"Until I can establish myself securely, there's no future for us. By then she may develop other . . . interests."

"How do you propose to handle it?"

"You could help by counseling patience."

"Toni, patient?" Valcour shook his head slowly on the pillow.

"If she loves me, she'll wait for me. If not"—he shrugged—"it's been memorable."

Valcour reached for the oxygen mask, placed it over his face, and breathed several times. Then he laid the mask aside. "It was good for Toni that you came, Quinn—good for both of us. I love my sister very deeply—always have. We share certain faults, which perhaps makes for closer understanding."

"Take care of her," Chance said, and left the room.

All next day Chance waited for Natalya's call, and when night came he let Toni persuade him to go with her to a Canadian reception at the Palais des Nations. Yegor Ligachev was expected, he heard, but was said to be closeted with the American secretary of state and might come later.

At the buffet table Chance noticed Jan Abrams noshing nearby and casually edged over to him. In German he said, "Contact made, the two sides will be meeting."

Smiling, Jan took his hand and shook it. "How nice to see you again. When?"

"Maybe a month." He speared a Swedish meatball.

"Where?"

"Scandinavia."

With tongs Abrams added a croissant to his plate. "Care to be more specific?"

"No."

"Then you'll be leaving soon?"

"I expect to." Turning, he felt Jan's hand restraining him. "Don't forget me," Jan said in a low voice. "I'll help you any way I can."

"Thank you, Herr Professor," Chance said, and moved away. Moments later Toni said, "It's nice there's someone here you know."

"I know you; the others don't matter."

She kissed the side of his face. "That's the nicest thing you've said since you ravaged me. You *can* be charming when you want to."

There was a stir beside the entrance, and the Soviet foreign minister's party came in, about twenty in all. Half, he estimated, would be legitimate working diplomats, half KGB security thugs. He forked an oyster into his mouth and felt Toni elbow his side. "This *is* the new face of communism," she murmured. "Look at that stunning Russian."

Chance looked up from his plate and saw Natalya Yegorova standing near the foreign minister. She was talking animatedly with the Canadian ambassador, and she was wearing an iridescent silk evening gown, whose low cleavage accented her breasts. The simple seed pearl necklace was replaced by one of gleaming diamonds—or zircons, Chance thought. The foreign minister drew her away from the ambassador and presented her to the president of Switzerland, who lifted her hand to his lips. The foreign minister seemed to be treating her like a personal possession. Chance felt a pang of jealousy. *Why hadn't she called him?*

"Are you *that* smitten?" Toni pouted. "I thought you hated all Russians."

"There are exceptions," he said and steered her into a side room where a small orchestra, mostly strings, was playing dance music. They danced several numbers, then took champagne to the balcony. The grounds were lighted, and illuminated fountains sprayed glittering droplets into the air. "I'll miss you," he said, thinking, and I'll miss Natalya.

"Wherever you go I'll come to you—however long it takes."

"I'll count on it."

Before leaving the palais he glimpsed Natalya again and realized she had seen him, too, though her expression didn't change. As they worked their way through the crowd—Ligachev had just arrived—Chance noticed a group of OPEC Arabs applauding the deputy premier. "Pigs!" Toni snarled. "Let's get out of here."

He drove back to the villa wondering if there was a connection between yesterday's contact and Ligachev's presence in Geneva. Could he be Natalya's principal? In the Russian labyrinth anything was possible.

In the morning they went riding over trails they had explored before. Afterwards, while Toni went up to shower and change, Sam came out of his room and beckoned Chance aside. Excitedly he reported, "We have full approval for the meeting. Here's the list of those who will attend." He handed over a sheet of paper with three hand-printed names: Shek Po, Chen Ling—and Hsiao Kuan-hua.

"The big man himself," Chance remarked. "Who are the others?"

"Central Committee members. Pass this to Yelena."

"Yelena?" Momentarily he'd forgotten the fabricated name. He placed the paper in his billfold, and joined Toni in the shower.

That afternoon Chance answered the phone. It was Natalya Yegorova.

255

FORTY-TWO

The sound of her voice made his heart race. "I must see you," she said. "Same place? One hour?"

"I'll be there." He replaced the telephone as Toni came into the room. "Business again?"

"Another conference."

"Then I'll visit Paul. See you later, darling."

A few minutes later he heard her Lamborghini roar out of the drive and felt guilty as a husband bent on adultery. Still, he had made no binding commitment to Toni, he told himself, and Natalya would soon be a memory.

He drove to the mansion. Once there, he got out glasses, ice, and vodka, and chilled a bottle of champagne. Preparing a lovers' rendezvous was a long-forgotten ritual and he found it exciting.

As before, Natalya arrived by taxi and came directly in. When he closed the door she said, "This place—it's facade reminds me of the Kirov in Leningrad. Valcour must be a very successful capitalist."

"He is," he said, and drew her to him. Through the thin summer dress her body molded against his. They kissed lingeringly until she said, "No purse inspection today?"

"Is it necessary?"

She opened her purse and took out a black-and-white photograph, showed it to him. It was the one copied from his CIA badge. "This American," she said, "is being sought by the local *Rezidentura*. Except for his nose and eye areas he resembles you. The photograph is being circulated among our delegation, apparently on General Sobatkin's orders." She tucked away the photograph. "The man's name is said to be Quentin Chance, once of the CIA. Of course, if Sobatkin is his enemy, then Chance is our friend."

"I am," he said, "and deserve your help."

"I thought you might feel that way. Now, last night I saw you with a very attractive young woman."

"Valcour's sister, the former Princess Azira, who thought you were stunning." He led her into the library and locked the door. "You are."

"Thank you. It's not often I'm able to don capitalist finery."

"But you like it." He poured their vodka drinks.

"Adore it. What woman wouldn't?"

She looked fresh and rested, he thought as she sipped from her glass. After a moment she said, "The Soviet principals agree to the time and place of the meeting. I have their names for you." She opened her purse and took out a piece of paper with Cyrillic writing. "I'd better transliterate," she said, and began printing the names in English. "Two are cabinet ministers: Yuri Fedotov, technology; and Boris Grachev, agriculture. The third is Mikhail Kapitsa, our foremost expert on China." She handed him the paper. "You understand the grave risks they run by going to Denmark. Nothing must go wrong."

He opened his billfold and took out the Chinese names. "These men will be there for the meeting."

He glanced at her list. "I thought Ligachev might be here."

"Yegor? He's a fence straddler. He'll go with the prevailing side." She began unbuttoning her dress. "I know him."

"That well?"

She hesitated. "I've been his mistress." She took his hand. "I'm not promiscuous, not at all. But Yegor wanted me, and as a widow I had no one to protect me. Then I arranged to have his wife find out, and she broke it off." Natalya smiled, "Wasn't that clever?"

"Brilliant." He finished undressing her. The perfume of her warm body invaded his nostrils, arousing him as she pressed his face between her breasts.

They made love quickly, sipped champagne and embraced languorously, stretching side by side the length of the sofa. Stroking and touching each other's bodies, kissing and caressing until

Natalya said she had to go. He held her for a final kiss. "Will you come again?"

"There'll be more details to exchange. Yes."

As he walked her to the Daimler he asked, "Is there any chance you might want to stay in the West? Ever?"

"Someday perhaps, after my work is done." She kissed his fingertips. "Thank you for the invitation. Our paths have crossed, Quinn Chance. My Russian mysticism tells me they will cross again."

Reluctantly, he watched her drive away.

His mind filled with confused emotions, Chance drove back to the villa, gave the Soviet names to Sam, and confirmed penultimate arrangements. He was tired of the whole thing, and when Natalya left he wanted out.

Every passing day lessened his value to Hsiao Kuan-hua. Moreover, the circulation of his photograph among Geneva's Soviet citizens warned that his enemies were closing in. His escape must be planned with precision and care.

Toward six when Sam returned, Chance said, "It's getting warm. I want that swimming pool repaired so Toni and I can use it."

"What's the matter with it?"

Chance walked through the patio and gestured at the pool. "Tiling's cracked and the circulating system doesn't work. As England was once described, the pool's a fen of stagnant waters."

"Sounds like a lot of money to put out for short-term use."

Chance's eyes narrowed. "Short-term? I'm here as long as Hsiao wants me around." Before Sam could reply, Chance continued, "Furthermore, Toni deserves a reward for her services."

"Well, what did you have in mind?"

"Something worth fifty thousand francs."

"*Fifty*—you got to be kidding!"

Chance eyed him coldly. "Am I dealing with an official of the People's Republic of China or some Chop Suey Charlie? You're in the big time, Sam—act it."

Sam thought it over. With a pained expression, he said, "Okay, fifty it is. I'll get it from the consulate tomorrow."

Chance patted him on the back. "Thinking big makes a man grow."

For Toni fifty-thousand francs were pocket change. For Chance it was a getaway stake. He didn't plan to stick around long enough to enjoy the renovated pool.

FORTY-THREE

Over the next three days, hearing nothing from Natalya Yegorova, Chance became increasingly preoccupied and irritable.

Sam said, "Whassa mat'—figure Ninotchka's gone over the hill?"

"Don't bug me, boy—how the hell do I know? Maybe the whole plan's collapsed. Or maybe there are problems Moscowside, but everything points to the meeting, right?"

Sam nodded.

"Then lay it to bureaucratic delays. Those Ivans have got to move carefully; their lives are on the line."

"That matter to you?"

"It does. I've been in this too long to see it fall apart."

"Well, it's getting on your nerves. You need to relax, take it easy."

"You do the same."

He took Toni to La Belle Equipe that night, and the headwaiter greeted them suavely, never indicating he had seen them before. They had drinks in a lounge away from the fireplace, and after a while Chance realized that the mellow atmosphere was easing his mind. Cocktails helped restore his usual good humor, and he became attentive to Toni, enjoying her conversation.

Over poached salmon she said, "Ever since these negotiations began I've noticed a change in you. I was afraid I was losing you even before you went away. But now you're turning back into your old self, the person I fell in love with."

"Shouldn't let business matters affect me, and from now on I won't. I apologize."

She clasped his hand firmly. "We have so much to live for, look forward to."

"And Paul seems out of danger."

"Yes, the drains come out next week and he can begin a soft diet. You've been a good friend, Jean-Pierre, and I hope Paul appreciates how much you've done for him—and me."

"I think he does. If not, it hardly matters." He let the sommelier refill his wineglass.

She glanced around. "I can't help remembering the last time we were here, the parking lot. Expect any more trouble from Mohammed?"

"He's had time to act—let's hope he's found distractions."

"Then I won't need Lao-li with me wherever I go?"

"I wouldn't dispense with her services yet. You don't get along with her?"

"Oh, she's not very . . . conversational. I think she secretly disapproves of me. She's lovely, though, isn't she? So fragile and unassuming."

Chance sipped wine and nodded. If Lao-li had let something slip, he wasn't going to confirm it.

"Have you decided about the French Ball tomorrow night? It's at the Aga Khan's old chateau."

"If you want to go we'll go."

"The subscription was five thousand dollars a couple—why waste it?"

"Especially if the fish and chips are good."

She smiled tolerantly. "Not to mention the caviar and champagne."

"Life's basic necessities." He kissed her hand. "What different worlds we've known, *chérie.*"

"Not so different, I think. But in the future I'm willing to compromise."

After dinner they crossed the drawbridge and Chance loosened the Walther in its holster. He scanned the parking lot's perimeter, detected no danger, but kept his hand on the pistol while Toni got

261

into the Mercedes. Driving back to the villa, he saw no following cars, but as he steered toward the garage area his headlights flashed across a long black limousine and he glimpsed diplomatic license plates.

Gripping his arm, Toni said, "What on earth? Who—?"

He had decided to back around and run for it when he saw a face appear above the rear doorsill. Natalya called, "Jean-Pierre—please come here."

He said, "I think it's all right."

He left the engine running and said, "Stay here," but he heard Toni following. Reaching the limousine, he looked in and saw a man sitting in the far corner holding a gun on Natalya. "I'm sorry," she said simply.

The gun moved to cover Chance. The man holding it said, "Get in—the lady, too."

"*Run!*" Chance snapped, but behind Toni a man appeared and pressed a gun to her spine.

The door opened and helplessly Chance got in beside Natalya while Toni was shoved into a jump seat facing them. The other man occupied another jump seat and closed the door, and the limousine accelerated down the drive.

Natalya's face was paler than he had ever seen it. "What could I do?" she whispered.

The gunman beside her took away Chance's Walther. Chance said, "Let the princess go, she has nothing to do with this."

"She will have an opportunity to establish that," the man said. "All of you have questions to answer, many questions."

Tremulously Toni said, "I—I don't understand. What is this all about? Who are you?"

Chance remembered the gunmen's faces from Sam's KGB files. Boris Klipsov's skull was shaven, while Nikolai Surikov had brush-cut hair and a dark close-cut beard. To reassure Toni and give Natalya a lead, he said, "Must be the competition I told you about, *chérie*. I was afraid they'd try to strong-arm their way into my business."

Natalya's lips mouthed: I said nothing.

Surikov said, "You will tell us everything you know."

"Of course. No business deal, no amount of money, is worth

one's life. I'll sign over all papers to whoever you say—just get it over with. The ladies are frightened and that's not necessary."

Klipsov said, "You're talking rubbish," but there was a harmonic of uncertainty in his voice.

Chance laughed shortly. To Toni he said, "And you thought my precautions were foolish. Obviously I wasn't careful enough."

Contritely, Toni said, "I'm sorry I doubted you and Paul."

"Well," Chance said resignedly, "the best-laid plans, eh? Still, it's only money." The route, he saw, was taking them down around the Palais des Nations. The driver turned south on avenue Motta, passed the Varambé stadium and made a hard right onto the rue du Vidollet. Two blocks and the limousine turned into a high-walled estate.

The building was a turreted château and Chance was relieved to see it unlighted. He guessed that the gunmen would hold them while the driver went for a senior interrogator. That would lower the odds somewhat, although he was unarmed against two KGB thugs and handicapped by two women whose lives he couldn't risk in a wild gamble for his own freedom. Toni stared past him unseeingly. Natalya's expression gave away nothing.

The limousine stopped and Klipsov told them to get out. He led them toward the house, Surikov behind them, and while Klipsov unlocked the side door the limousine turned around and drove away.

That gives us maybe half an hour, Chance figured, and he followed the ladies into a sparsely furnished ground-level room, probably the servants' dining room when the place was occupied. Now there was dust everywhere, and the place smelled of mildew and disuse.

Standing in front of the women, Chance spoke to the gunmen. "How much are you being paid? I'll pay more."

"A million francs, just for letting us go," Toni offered.

Klipsov said angrily, "We're not mercenaries—ask *her.*"

His pistol pointed at Natalya, who shrugged. "I don't know what they are. It's all a mystery to me."

"Is it?" Klipsov strode to her and shoved his pistol against her throat. "You'll talk, you'll tell everything about the negotiations."

"Not if you shoot me," she said calmly, and slowly pushed aside the pistol muzzle. "Think what you could do with a million francs—or more."

Klipsov looked at his comrade and smirked. In that instant Natalya's knee slammed hard into his crotch and her left arm deflected his pistol as a shot exploded above her head. His left hand grabbed for his damaged crotch, and as his torso jackknifed forward, her hand chopped down on his neck. Surikov yelled, and before he could move Chance dived at him headfirst, butting the Russian's thorax and knocking him backward. Panting, they fought for the pistol, then Toni got into the fray. Repeatedly she kicked Surikov's head with her pointed shoes, drawing yells of pain from his mouth, blood from his punctured face. Surikov tried to fend off her kicks, letting Chance grip and twist his pistol wrist with both hands. Toni stamped on Surikov's face and kicked the back of his head brutally hard. Surikov's grip relaxed and Chance pried the pistol free, then turned to Klipsov.

He was on his back, Natalya atop him, raking his eyes and face with her nails while Klipsov held on to his pistol, trying to bring it against Natalya's body. Chance vaulted over Surikov and slammed his pistol against Klipsov's head. The Russian groaned and his head fell back. Natalya pulled the pistol from his hand and stood up.

Impulsively, Toni hugged her. "Thank you, thank you!" she cried. "You were wonderful!"

"You *were,*" Chance agreed, "you both were. Let's get out of here before others come."

"I can't let them live—you know that," Natalya said, brushing dust from her dress.

Toni gasped, "Just kill them?"

"My dear, you don't know what is at stake. Believe me, they would have killed us all."

Chance said, "She's right," and retrieved his Walther from Klipsov's pocket. The man's face was bleeding profusely from Natalya's attack.

"Take her outside," Natalya said, and cocked the pistol. Chance put his arm around Toni's waist and guided her out of the door into the shadows of the shrubbery. One pistol shot sounded, then another. Toni began whimpering and clung to Chance.

Presently Natalya came out. "We have to wait for the others, dispose of them, otherwise our lives will be worthless." She touched Toni's arm. "I know you're unaccustomed to violence, but this is self-preservation."

Toni said, "I—I don't understand anything. How do you know Jean-Pierre?"

"Let him explain," she suggested with a brief smile.

Toni faced Chance, who said, "Natalya represents the foreign group Paul and I are dealing with. And she's right, we have to finish this off, tonight."

Natalya said softly, "You've shown a great deal of courage, Princess, and I admire you for that. Now I suggest you conceal yourself over beyond the garage, and Jean-Pierre and I will do what is necessary."

Chance saw movement at the end of the hedge and pointed his pistol at the man who emerged in the moonlight. *"Sam!"*

The Chinese walked toward them, followed by Lao-li. Both were carrying machine pistols. Sam said, "I saw them taking you and decided to follow." He looked around. "Where's the enemy?"

"Inside," Chance said, "and dead. Thanks to Ninotchka."

"My compliments," Sam said to Natalya. "The car is outside the gate."

Natalya said, "More are coming."

"In that case," Sam offered, "Lao-li and I will wait and clean things up." Lao-li nodded and fingered her machine pistol. "We have the firepower and the advantage of surprise."

As Toni gaped, Natalya said, "Jean-Pierre, let's do as our friend suggests. It's late and I have to send out a warning as soon as possible."

Sam handed Chance the Mercedes keys. "How will you get back?" Chance asked.

"Don't worry about us."

Followed by Natalya and Toni, Chance walked down the drive and found the Mercedes pulled off the road. He unlocked the doors and the women got into the rear seat, Chance behind the wheel.

The dash clock showed 11:14. He retraced the route past the

265

Palais des Nations, where Natalya leaned forward and asked, "Do you have a radio transmitter?"

"Valcour has."

"Take me to it."

Toni said, "Paul has a radio? He never told me."

Natalya said, "Wasn't he in the CIA?"

"Yes, but I thought that was all behind him."

Natalya sighed. "I wonder if it ever is."

At Valcour's, Chance drove into a garage stall and locked it behind them. In the library he poured three glasses of vodka, tossed his off, and urged Toni to drink hers. Natalya took a refill and carried it upstairs, waiting while Chance gave Toni a mild tranquilizer and said he'd be with her soon. Obediently, she began getting into bed. Then Chance led Natalya up to the attic, turned on the light, and opened the transceiver case.

"I've seen this model before," she said. "An old one, but I can use it."

Chance made the satellite connection and as Natalya linked the squirt unit she explained, "I have to warn my principals there's been a compromise at this end." Sitting down, she took off one shoe, twisted the heel and removed a postage stamp–sized pad from a cavity. Alternate pages were printed in red and black, their small squares filled like a crossword puzzle with Cyrillic letters. She got a pencil from her bag and began working on the onetime pad while Chance sipped from her drink. She set a transmitting frequency and activated the unit to send out a call sign repetitively, then stopped and set a receiving frequency.

"You didn't learn this at Boston U.," Chance said.

"And your name isn't Jean-Pierre Duroc."

The key began clattering and she smiled in satisfaction. "I'll be here awhile," she said, "so why not get some sleep?"

"If there's nothing I can do—"

"We'll sort things out in the morning."

He left her drink and went down the stairs. Toni was half-asleep when he got into bed beside her. Groggily, she said, "I have so many questions. . . . Will I ever know the truth?"

"Soon," he said soothingly. "You're safe now, go to sleep."

266

He lay back, pushed away his own unanswered questions, and let sleep surge over him.

Sometime before dawn he was wakened by the mattress yielding to another body. Opening his eyes, he saw Natalya lying down beside him. Pressing against Chance, she whispered, "I've been ordered back to Moscow where my people can protect me."

"How soon?"

"Tomorrow." Her face turned to the window curtains graying in the first light of dawn. "Today."

"How will you get away?"

"Ligachev will arrange it—he owes me."

"Will I ever see you again?"

"I hope so. Until the leak is closed, the meeting is postponed. And you must leave Geneva."

"I plan to," he said, and kissed her, knowing it was for the last time.

When Chance woke, sunlight filled the room. Toni and Natalya were sleeping side by side, their faces calm, untroubled, and he knew that he was going to miss them both. He dressed without waking them and drove to the villa expecting to find the limousine, but it was not there.

He found Sam sleeping beside Lao-li. Quietly, he woke Sam, who got out of bed and met him in the hall. "How did it go?"

Yawning, Sam said, "Three of them came in the limo. As they walked to the house, we opened fire. They never knew what hit them."

"And—?"

"Stuffed all five into the limo. It went over a cliff on the Lausanne Road." He stifled a yawn. "Big explosion. We took a bus partway back, walked the rest of the way. Look, can we talk later? I'm dead tired."

"You'd better tell Hsiao what happened. Ninotchka radioed her people to warn them, and she's leaving today. The meeting's postponed until they can stop the leaks."

His eyes widened. "I was afraid of that. I'll have to report and wait on orders."

"I'm going to get some sleep."

267

Chance went up to his bedroom, shaved and showered, and changed clothing. When he heard Sam drive away he began to pack a bag.

Time to set his own plans in motion.

He placed his holstered Walther between folded clothing, added shirts and toiletries, and closed the bag. As he lifted it from the bed, his door opened and Lao-li stood there. "Leaving us?" she asked. There was a machine pistol in her hand.

FORTY-FOUR

Nikolai Berlikov sat alone at his kitchen table and stared at an unopened envelope in his hand. Postmarked Buffalo, New York, three days earlier, the envelope was addressed in longhand to George L. Gordon at a post office box near the National Zoo. "Gordon" was Berlikov, and the box was a clandestine letter drop.

Bursts of audience laughter assaulted Berlikov's ears; Irina was watching a popular sitcom that featured the antics of three middle-aged bourgeois ladies, whose suggestive banter would never be permitted on Moscow television. And rightly so. Irina enjoyed the program as a fill-in before *Nightline* and her beloved Ted Koppel.

Berlikov did not enjoy the prospect of his next task. With a kitchen knife he carefully slit the envelope. Typed double-space, the English-language letter addressed him as "Cousin George" and described a visit to Niagara Falls that the whole family had enjoyed, particularly little Mary. "Regards from everyone," the text ended, and was signed, "Your cousin, Gregory."

Berlikov checked the typed date—the third of the month. The numeral three indicated the steganographic system employed by the originator and told Berlikov which reagent would bring out the secret text *en clair*. He went over to the spice cabinet and examined its contents. The cumin seed label bore a small 3, and Berlikov brought it to the table. He measured out a quarter teaspoon of the powdered contents and dropped it in a glass. He filled the glass halfway with distilled water and stirred until the powder dissolved and the solution was entirely clear.

As Irina chuckled, oblivious, he went to the bathroom and took

269

several cotton-tipped swabs from the medicine cabinet. He dipped one "wand" in the developing solution and wet the area around the date. As he watched, a pink-blue numeral appeared—another 3, confirming the reagent indicator.

He went quietly into Andrushka's room and removed the blotter from the boy's writing table. He spread the blotter pad across the kitchen table and flattened the letter against it. Next he used the wand to stripe the letter diagonally, testing to determine whether the letter had been intercepted by Canadian or American security agents, but no black or purple discolorations appeared. The message was pristine.

Wetting the wand again, he carefully stroked solution across the face of the letter and saw printed interlineations begin to form. He continued until the entire surface had been moistened. When the full Cyrillic text appeared, Berlikov blotted the excess and covered the paper with a pane of window glass to keep it from curling as it dried.

Then he read the Russian text:

THIS IS TO ADVISE YOU THAT YOU WILL SHORTLY RECEIVE OVERT ORDERS TO RETURN HOME. THE CENTER WISHES TO ACKNOWLEDGE ITS GRATITUDE AND APPRECIATION FOR YOUR ACCOMPLISHMENTS IN OBTAINING EXCEEDINGLY VALUABLE INTELLIGENCE FROM CLAIRE AND BETTY RPT CLAIRE AND BETTY. YOU ARE TO BE AWARDED A HIGH DECORATION FOR YOUR PERFORMANCE AND YOUR WIFE AND CHILDREN ARE TO BE PRESENT AT THE CEREMONY. TO THAT I ADD MY PERSONAL CONGRATULATIONS AND ASSURANCES OF MY HIGHEST PROFESSIONAL ESTEEM. ESSENTIAL YOU MENTION THIS MESSAGE TO NO ONE BECAUSE OF ITS PRIVATE AND CONFIDENTIAL NATURE. GREGORY.

"Gregory" was Lieutenant General Yevgeni Lubovich Sobatkin.

Berlikov stared at the letter and barked, *"Gavno!"* For days, weeks even, he had been dreading recall orders, knowing they would represent nothing less than a death sentence. Yet the disingenuous old fox, Sobatkin, had thought to disarm him with this flattering message.

He snatched up a vodka bottle, filled a tumbler, and drank half in a long swallow. Well, it was in the fire now, and Sobatkin was out of reach. Or was he?

Sitting at the table, he stared at the message while volleys of studio laughter ricocheted around the living room. What would Irina think of the situation? How would she react? How could he save his family—and himself?

He drained the tumbler, shook himself, and began to think.

He saw his life and future unreeling like a film of another dismal, tragic Russian drama wherein good people were overwhelmed by circumstances and forces they could neither understand nor control. They resisted as best they could but in the end faced their fate with stolidity and resignation worthy of the Russian ethos. Not me, he blurted half-aloud and pounded the table, making the glass jump.

Forcing himself to calm down, Berlikov began examining his situation as objectively as he could. One, he was supposed to take the fall for Sobatkin. Two, he, Kolya, faced extreme reprisals in his homeland. Three, it was within his power to use the tape to incriminate Sobatkin, destroy him and perhaps Marshal Yaroshenko. Four, he had knowledge of a secret plan inspired by a faction of powerful Kremlin ministers to effect a military standdown with China. Five, to survive and protect his family he had only a few hours in which to act. Six, he must tell Irina as much as necessary to convince her of their peril. And seven, all four of them had to move with speed and discretion.

His mental outline completed, Berlikov reexamined it and found no flaw. One final factor remained.

He went to his library desk and opened the lower left drawer, which was filled with newspaper clippings about Sosnowski's murder and the pursuit of Quentin Chance. He rummaged through them until he found a name he was looking for, checked the telephone directory for address and telephone number, and scrawled them across the clipping. He pocketed the clipping and returned to the kitchen.

The plain-text message lay below the flattening glass, words etched in venom. He went to the doorway and watched Irina smiling contentedly at the television set as a graphic teaser announced the imminent beginning of *Nightline*. For a moment he hesitated, knowing that his next words would shatter her world—their world—forever. With a sigh he went to her side, bent over, and kissed her forehead. As she looked up in surprise, tears uncontrollably filled his eyes. "Kolya," she remonstrated, "it's my favorite—" and broke off seeing his grave face. She put aside her knitting and stood up. He embraced her desperately, blurting, "I have to talk with you," and led her into the kitchen.

He pointed out the message from Sobatkin and poured himself another glass of vodka as she sat down and hesitantly began to read.

In less than an hour they packed their essentials in a few bags—one with children's toys—and stealthily loaded the trunk of Berlikov's Ford sedan, terrified lest Mikhail Kondratsev or his venomous wife, their SK neighbors, notice. But the adjoining house was dark.

With Irina trembling in the rear seat, Berlikov went back inside, bundled up their children, and brought out Katya, then Andrushka, delivering them to their mother's tearful care. He returned a final time, took prepared bundles of agent-payment currency from the closet shoe box, and stuffed them into a briefcase. To it he added the original and duplicate recordings of Sobatkin's criminal orders and pocketed a nine-millimeter Steyr semiautomatic pistol. Not Kondratsev, not anyone, was going to obstruct him now.

Berlikov turned off all house lights, blanked the TV screen a final time, and locked the rear door, leaving keys under the mat.

Working in the darkness of the garage, he quickly replaced diplomatic license plates with Maryland tags and fitted the DPL plates into his briefcase. Then he backed out of the garage, closed the doors to avoid Kondratsev's morning scrutiny, and with headlights still off swung onto Jennifer Lane.

Through midnight darkness he drove east to Nebraska Avenue and took Military Road across Rock Creek Park, then Missouri Avenue past Fort Totten; beyond the District line to Chillum, where he pulled into a small motel whose blinking neon sign read: VACANCY.

As he signed the registration card he showed the clerk the forged Maryland driver's license and paid in advance with a hundred-dollar bill. Their bags in the room and children asleep in a double bed, Berlikov kissed his wife. "The worst is over. You're safe and I'll be back before dawn."

She glanced at the sleeping children. "This is hard," she said quietly, "hard for me and the children. Especially hard for you, Kolya, but as always I trust your judgment." She hesitated. "But what if you don't come back, dear?"

He gave her the duplicate recording. "This is your passport to freedom. Use it as I instructed you. But I'll be back before dawn, don't worry."

He kissed her again, quieted her sobbing, grabbed the briefcase, and left.

Outside, he walked to a corner telephone booth, got out the newspaper clipping, deposited a quarter, and punched the number he had scrawled, hardly daring to breathe as the phone rang, rang, and rang. Finally, a man's voice grumpily answered, "Yes? Who is it?"

"You are lawyer Wilson Jones?"

"Yes, but it's . . . my God, man, two o'clock. Call me at my office in the morning."

"This cannot wait, lawyer Jones. Quentin Chance is your client, yes?"

"Yes," the lawyer conceded. "So?"

"I have information of great value to him, sir. I will drive to your building at once. Say nothing to anyone." He broke the connection and leaned weakly against the glass door.

After a few moments Berlikov left the booth and got into his Ford. Referring to a street map, he took Route 50 south to Rhode Island Avenue, following it to Scott Circle, where he picked up Massachusetts Avenue; he drove carefully up Embassy Row and beyond the Naval Observatory, where the vice president's residence was located, then to the apartment building where lawyer Wilson Jones lived. Parking in the oval drive, Berlikov locked his car and carried his briefcase to the entrance where he rang Jones's sixth-floor call button. The door lock buzzed to let Berlikov in.

As he rode the elevator to Jones's floor, Berlikov realized his throat and lips were dry, his palms wet. He forced himself to breathe deeply, licked his lips, and got off. Standing in an open doorway was a short man in a striped bathrobe. Steadying his voice Berlikov strode to him. "Lawyer Jones?"

"That's me. Come in." He closed the door behind them. "Quentin Chance sent you?"

"I didn't say that." He went into Jones's lighted office and placed his briefcase on the desk. He laid before the lawyer his diplomatic carnet. "I am Major General Nikolai Berlikov of Soviet Intelligence, and I am willing to help your client clear himself—if certain conditions can be met."

Jones settled down in his desk chair and got out a legal-length yellow pad. "I'm listening."

FORTY-FIVE

Lao-li took a few steps into the room. "Leaving us?" she repeated. "Without telling Sam?"

Chance saw her finger resting on the trigger guard. She could cut him in half before he could rush her, and the bag was too heavy to throw. "I don't know what you mean. I thought Sam understood I was going to Zurich with Toni."

"I don't think so." She shook her head. "He ordered me to make sure you were here when he returned from the consulate."

Chance shrugged, put down the bag. "In that case, I'll wait for him." He looked at his watch. "Shouldn't be long."

"No."

"Mind if I have a drink?"

She shrugged and followed him downstairs to the butler's pantry, where he poured Black Label over ice. Sipping the drink gave him time to think; he hadn't expected the delay. Casually he strolled into the living room and turned on the TV. The air was warm, and outside he could hear masons chipping at the empty pool. In a few days it would be ready for use.

Last night Lao-li had helped Sam kill three Soviet officers, and she was a kung fu expert besides. She might fuck like an angel, he thought, but her nerves were those of an automaton, and she would shoot him dispassionately for the greater glory of the PRC.

"It's all over with, isn't it?" Lao-li said. "Last night finished it." She glanced at her weapon.

"Oh, I don't know. Those weren't mainstream Ivans we polished off, just part of the renegade faction that's been hostile all along. It just might make things easier for the people approaching your country."

"Where is Ninotchka, as Sam calls her?"

"Yelena? Making her report, I guess. She's under Ligachev's protection, by the way."

"You didn't tell that to Sam."

"I didn't learn it until last night."

"I think she's a Soviet intelligence officer."

"Well, she's shown skills she didn't learn at her mother's knee."

She stared at him stonily. "Also, I think you prefer the Soviet side to ours."

"Suddenly you're a psychiatrist? What happened to the humble, self-effacing servant girl who treated me to a one-night stand? I got rid of two Soviet officers last night. What does that tell you?"

Small spots of color appeared on her cheeks. "You don't have to be unpleasant."

"When you're acting like a prosecutor, threatening me with a gun? Am I supposed to like it?"

"I'm only following orders," she said evenly. "You know that. I can't help it if you're late for your date with La Princesse."

Chance needed a diversion. *"Fuck it!"* he snarled, and slammed his glass against the wall. "After all I've risked for you bastards!"

But she never glanced at the shattered glass.

Shit, he thought, and tensed his muscles to lunge.

The telephone rang, and he strode toward it.

"No!" Lao-li snapped, "I'll answer it," and moved to cut him off.

"Got a problem?" Chance sneered, and snatched up the receiver. "Duroc here," he said. "Who's this?"

She was less than a yard away when he heard Jan Abrams's voice. "Sam?" he said loudly, trying to sound pleased, "will you tell Suzy Wong that you okayed my trip? Here"—he held out the receiver and as she began reaching for it, he slammed the receiver against the side of her head. Lao-li gasped and fell back, hitting the floor hard. Chance grabbed up the machine pistol and held it on her motionless form while he spoke. "Sorry about the interruption. Give me ten minutes and call back." He replaced the receiver and saw that she was stirring.

He hit the back of her head with the pistol butt, and her body

276

went limp. Goddamn her, he thought, and dragged her by one arm to the staircase. There he hoisted her light body across his shoulders and, with the machine pistol in one hand, climbed up to his bedroom. He gagged her with pillowcase strips, pulled off her clothing, shoes, and stockings, and bound her hands behind her naked body with cord torn from the window curtains. He tied her ankles together and carried her into the bathroom.

He sat her on the floor, leaning against the toilet, and turned on the shower. While steam was building inside the shower enclosure he got four sleeping capsules from the cabinet and emptied them into half a glass of water, stirring until the solution was the color of clear lemonade.

When he looked down at her, her eyes were open, staring at steam gathering across the ceiling. "Listen, cunt," he snarled, "two things can happen to you. I'll dump you in the steam and watch flesh peel from your body. Or you'll drink this—*all* of it—and have a refreshing sleep. Which is it? Boiling water or a cool drink?"

Her head bobbed at the glass in his hand.

He knelt and loosened the gag. "Every goddamned drop," he told her, "and no gagging. Try that and you're boiled alive."

He held the glass to her lips. She swallowed, grimaced at the sour taste, and kept on swallowing. Chance tilted the glass for the last drops and closed her mouth, watching the movement of her gullet. When he was satisfied the solution was all the way down, he replaced the gag and turned off the shower.

He left her there and closed the bathroom door; he picked up the machine pistol and listened. The house was still, so was the drive. Sam was transmitting a lengthy message to Hsiao, standing by for a reply.

The bedroom extension rang. Chance answered, heard Jan's voice again, and said, "Had a spot of difficulty for a few moments, but it's resolved now. Anyway, I want you to know that the Washington inside traders managed to compromise the platinum dealer and so the meeting's off. Postponed sine die."

"Yes, I understand. When will I see you again?"

"Can't say. I have business in . . . Zurich."

"Was the secretary of commerce involved?"

"Pretty definitely. Take care of yourself."

"You, too." The line went dead, and Chance hoped Jan remembered the open code they'd arranged at their last meeting. At least he remembered Sobatkin was the "secretary of commerce."

Now he had to get away before Sam returned—probably with orders to liquidate him. Certainly not with a bonus and a Red Star medal. Chinese Red.

He opened the bathroom door and looked at Lao-li. She had fallen sideways, eyes closed. He opened her eyelids and saw constricted pupils. Her pulse was slow, breathing shallow. Her body was pink from the shower's considerable heat.

He undid her bonds and hid them in a dresser drawer, then pulled back bed covers and slid her body between the sheets. There was a bruise on her temple from the receiver blow, and the back of her head was moist with blood.

Me or you, baby, he thought, and drew the covers over her still form. Then, bag in one hand, machine pistol in the other, he went quietly down the staircase and out to the Mercedes.

He shoved the machine pistol under the front seat and drove to the airport, where he left the Mercedes in the long-term parking lot. Checking for watchers, he carried his suitcase around the front of the airport and boarded a luxury express bus to Lyons, 153 kilometers inside France. At the nearby border control point Customs and Immigration stamped his French passport, welcomed him to La Patrie, and ignored his travel bag. For the first time in the hours since he and Toni were taken, he felt he could relax. As he stretched back in the comfortable seat, he breathed deeply, slowing his pulse, and closed his eyes. The bus's rhythmic motion, the low hum of its engine lulled him, and in a little while he slept.

Two hours later Chance got off at the Lyons bus terminal and taxied to the gare, where he bought a compartment on the next train to Vienna.

Remnants of his mother's family still lived near Salzburg—Uncle Klaus, Cousins Ruprecht and Sofia. He bought four bottles of Hine cognac, thinking they might warm his welcome after the years of silence since his mother's death.

He bought two Geneva papers, two from Paris, and one from Vienna. His train was called, and a porter carried his bag to his compartment. Chance locked the door and got out his wallet. It contained the fifty thousand francs he'd conned out of Sam, plus eight thousand of his casino winnings.

Before the train pulled out of the station he slid his holstered Walther under the daybed mattress and hoisted his closed suitcase to the overhead rack. Then he pulled off his coat, loosened his tie, and lay back on the daybed, pillow comfortably under his head.

As the train gained speed he wondered if Natalya, too, had managed to get away, with her former lover's laissez-passer. Or had she only said that to ease his mind about her future? And what of Toni? What would she think? Well, he'd warned her he would have to leave, and last night's bloody episode would help her understand.

He remembered his last sight of them, peacefully sleeping in the large bed. The lovely princess and the extraordinarily beautiful KGB officer. What a pair, he thought, the epitome of every man's fantasy. Well, he'd always have that to remember.

In the Geneva paper he read of a fatal crash off the Lausanne Road in which five Soviet officials had been killed in their limousine. No further details at press time. How would Lieutenant General Sobatkin like *that?*

So far, he mused, the Soviets had lost a lot of assets—assholes—in this deadly counteroperation. Eight he knew of, nine if you counted the hapless Sosnowski.

There was no way he could ever get at Sobatkin, but if he could somehow get back to Washington, he'd have a crack at Berlikov. In Washington, Soviet officials didn't lead secure, protected lives as in Moscow. They just thought they did.

The train entered a tunnel and Chance pulled down the window blind. The train would stop briefly at Bern and Munich, then switch to electric engines for the pull through the Arlberg and finally into Vienna's Westbahnhof. He looked forward to *kaffee mit schlag* with his breakfast, a turn around the Ringstrasse to see the new sights and clear his head.

Then down to business again. Surviving.

FORTY-SIX

Wilson Jones held up a hand. "You'd better stop right there, General. You need a lawyer, but I can't represent you; it would be a conflict of interest."

"Explain."

"Well, it may develop that your interests and those of my client, Quentin Chance, diverge."

"But how can that be?" protested Berlikov. "I will testify that he did not kill Sosnowski. That is greatly to his interest."

"That's true," Jones conceded. "And in return for that testimony you want what? Immunity from prosecution?"

"Otherwise, why should I . . . defect?" He hated the word, loathed thinking of himself as a defector, that most miserable of breeds.

"From what you've told me, your life is threatened by your own people. That makes you a refugee, not a defector."

Berlikov liked that word better. He opened his briefcase again and took out the packet of currency originally intended for Agent Betty. "How much to hire you, sir?"

"Got a thousand?"

Berlikov counted out ten one-hundred-dollar bills while Jones signed a hand receipt. "Tentatively I'll represent you in your dealings with the U.S. government," he said, "but if it appears that your interests differ from those of Quentin Chance, I'll return this retainer and find you another lawyer. You understand?"

"I understand. Please—we have little time."

"How far away are your wife and children?"

"Less than an hour's drive, and I must be with them before dawn. Otherwise certain things will take place that I prefer not to, for the present."

"Then I'll have to make phone calls, get government officials here for a preliminary interview. While they're on their way I'll draw up a preliminary agreement to get you that immunity." He reached for the telephone, drew back. *"You* didn't kill Sosnowski, did you?"

"No, I just—"

"Don't tell me more. There isn't time for it." He checked a small Rolodex file and called the home of an assistant attorney general in the Department of Justice, with whom he had clerked for a federal district judge.

After ten rings he heard his friend answer. "Wilson Jones, Tommy. Yeah, I know it's late, but I have an urgent situation that demands your immediate involvement. Now, wake up and listen. I have with me a high-ranking official of a foreign country with which our relations are extremely complicated. He wants to come over and he has a fascinating story to tell. In addition, he's very big in the spook business. Now, in a couple of hours his colleagues will be hunting him down, him and his family, so I want you here as fast as damn possible. Bring a couple of Bureau guys, and if you can wake someone at the spook factory, get them here on the double, too. . . . What? Of course I'm representing his interests. Yes, I'll have coffee ready. Make it fast, Tommy. Damn fast."

He eyed his new client and studied his face searchingly. He saw a gray-faced man with short-cut salt-and-pepper hair, an exhausted man who looked fifty-five or sixty years old with vacant, deep-set eyes. And as Wilson Jones studied the face it dissolved into another face, then another, the changes quick as a slide show. Tensely he stared, seeing the faces of men he had prosecuted, men he had defended, big men once, larger than life on their own turf, now played out, humbled, pleading with their eyes. A long fall into nothingness. . . . And as the faces faded, merged into Berlikov's, the lawyer felt a surge of sympathy for this man who had commanded power and respect in the Soviet world but from now on would be a nullity, a shadow figure in a different world. Then, focusing his thoughts, Wilson Jones abruptly reminded himself that the Soviet

281

son of a bitch was responsible for Quinn Chance's plight. He fitted paper into his electronic typewriter and asked, "Do you know where Chance is?"

Berlikov shook his head.

"Is he even alive, for God's sake?"

"I don't know. The KGB hasn't found him, nor has the FBI nor Interpol."

"I know that!" he exploded. "But it would be damn helpful if you could undo some of your damage while he's still alive. A posthumous apology won't help Quinn Chance."

Berlikov hung his head. His eyes were heavy. He dozed in the chair while the typewriter clicked back and forth across the paper. That done, Wilson Jones plugged in a large percolator, got out coffee, sugar, cream, and mugs. He looked at his watch. Four A.M. damn it. Why had the bastard waited so long to jump?

When coffee was ready, Jones fed a cup to Berlikov, drank a cold glass of half-and-half, swallowed a tablespoon of Maalox, and returned to his client. "How soon will your absence be noticed?"

"About eight-thirty. My neighbor is the SK leader."

"*Shit!* Listen, when these men get here I'll do the preliminary talking. When I tell you to talk, start talking, not until then."

Berlikov nodded. He was thinking of Irina and their children huddled in the bare motel room. He hoped they were sleeping, but he was afraid Irina would be too frightened. He himself was less frightened than at any time since reaching his decision. Lawyer Jones seemed to be able to act quickly and know American procedures. That an official of the Department of Justice was now involved encouraged Berlikov. Trying to deal with ordinary FBI or CIA agents would be as frustrating and unproductive as trying to negotiate with a couple of illiterate privates from the KGB.

The buzzer rang. Wilson Jones said, "Stay calm," and left the office. Berlikov heard him speak over the security intercom before returning. "There's a bathroom over there. Take a pee, wash your face, and comb your hair. Stay there until I call you out."

While Berlikov was following instructions, he heard the men arrive. One man said, "Well, where is he?"

"C'mon in, have a cup of coffee. Sit down, gentlemen. As we say in Acapulco, '*Está en su casa.*'"

Berlikov heard spoons clinking in coffee mugs, then, Jones's clear, steady voice. "Gentlemen, we're part of an amazing episode, but before I present the individual to you, please understand that although he will be able to respond to a few preliminary questions, he must leave immediately to protect his family—temporarily hidden from Soviet search and reprisal."

"*Soviet?*" someone barked.

"That's right. This officer, who has in his own way chosen freedom, is the head of a Soviet spy network whose details he is willing to reveal if his conditions are met."

"What conditions?" A deeper voice. Unfriendly.

"Hold your fire. Up front I'm going to concede that this officer was substantially involved in a conspiracy that caused the murder of a Russian I'm sure you'll all remember, the late Pavel Sosnowski."

"Shit, Wilson, that's pinned on your client, Quentin Chance, who happens to be a fugitive from justice."

"Wrongfully so—as my client is prepared to testify."

"In return for what? What's the bottom line?"

"In return for truthfully testifying and revealing the names of the perpetrators, as well as the Soviet officials who ordered Sosnowski's execution, my client requires and deserves immunity from prosecution. Tommy, here's an agreement for your signature. While you're looking it over, is there anyone here from the CIA?"

"Liaison office said someone might be along—if they could locate someone."

"Fuck 'em," another voice drawled, "those mothers are never around when you need 'em, always snoopin' around when you don't. Anyway, this is FBI business by law. Maybe we'll let the spooks have a crack at him when we're finished interrogating. And that could take a long time." He chuckled unpleasantly. "Damn long time."

"Wilson, I can't sign this until I know what kind of cat we're dealing with," the unfriendly voice objected.

"How would you go for a major general in the KGB?"

"The Washington *rezident?*"

"The fucking *rezident.* The big enchilada."

"No kidding?"

"You have my word, Tommy, and if I'm in any way untruthful you can have me up before the bar—but that won't happen. All right, you've signed, you two gentlemen please witness, and add the date and hour.

"Thank you. Now here's his diplomatic carnet by way of authentication. Also his diplomatic license tags."

"Berlikov! Holy shit."

"Exactly. Now, we have the immediate problem of protecting Madame Berlikov and their two children. The general needs to return to them before dawn and I suggest that FBI agents accompany him and take them all to a safe house. Okay, Tommy?"

"Sounds good. One of you guys phone the Washington field office and have a car come here. No explanation, my orders."

"Right, Mr. Levitt."

"I'll go, too," Wilson Jones said, "to make sure my four clients are properly received. Now, before I bring in General Berlikov, I'd like to remind you of an incident that's been going through my mind ever since my client arrived here. As you may remember, in 1945 a Soviet code clerk with a bunch of Russian codes wandered the frozen streets of Ottawa trying to request asylum. Canadian officialdom turned him away all night long, not wanting to offend Uncle Joe Stalin. Well, it wasn't until Soviet thugs began breaking down his door to kidnap the clerk and his family that neighbors called the Royal Canadian Mounted Police. They arrived in time, shooed away the thugs, and began listening to Igor Gouzenko's story. His revelations, gentlemen, resulted in the roundup of the Canadian Atom Spy Ring, the eventual arrest of Klaus Fuchs, with great benefit to the West, and a general eye-opening to the realities of Soviet espionage. Had you gentlemen not responded, I was prepared to call a couple of friends at the *Post* and *Times* and protect the Berlikovs myself until our government took proper action. You responded, and I'm glad that force majeure was not required. Gentlemen, I present Major General Nikolai Berlikov, late of the Soviet embassy."

Berlikov opened the bathroom door and walked into the office. Wilson Jones said, "General, these men are Assistant Attorney General Thomas Levitt, and Special Agents Hanrahan and Rourke of the FBI. They will see to the safety of yourself and your family.

284

Tommy, I believe you have some pro forma questions to pose to the general."

Berlikov looked at their faces. Levitt was tall, lean, and around Jones's age. The FBI agents nodded neutrally. Rourke was red-haired and freckled; Hanrahan had close-cropped brown hair and mustache; under a blue blazer he wore a red FBI Academy T-shirt. Both agents, Berlikov thought, were somewhat younger than himself. Levitt rose beside the standing agents. "Please state your name, sir."

"Nikolai Petrovich Berlikov. Major general in the Soviet KGB."

"Is your life threatened, General?"

"It is. And the lives of my wife and children."

"You have approached us requesting asylum of your own free will?"

"I have."

"And you will cooperate unreservedly with United States authorities, disclosing everything you know about Soviet espionage activities here and any other place?"

"I will."

"Then," said Levitt, "I welcome you to the United States in the status of political refugee and hereby place you and your family under the protection of my government. Now, let's go get your family."

"Just a minute," Jones interposed. "As is customary in these cases, my client expects protection, new identities, financial support, and relocation to a venue of his choice."

"The whole nine yards," Levitt said. "Let's move."

On the ride down in the crowded elevator Jones said, "Tommy, I want those indictments against Quentin Chance quashed as soon as you can find a judge."

"That may take a while, Wilson. If we go public with what the general says about the actual perpetrators, the Sovs will know we have him and they'll start beating down the doors at State for a chance to pressure him into changing his mind. And they could arrest or expel some of our people from Moscow."

"Fuck the Department of State," Agent Hanrahan said to no one in particular, "and the horses they ride."

Levitt added, "However much I may subscribe to that unofficial

285

view, Wilson, I don't feel I can move on those charges without further advisement. Heard from Chance?"

"Not since that letter from Mexico, copy to you."

"Hell, you don't even know he's alive."

"Unfortunately. But wherever he is, I'll tell you this, he has to be on the run."

"Well, he's damn good at it, I'll say that. Mud all over the Bureau's face."

Berlikov heard Agent Rourke grunt. Then the door opened and he was convoyed out to a black Ford sedan. Agent Hanrahan got in first, then Berlikov and Wilson Jones. Agent Rourke drove and a second car followed with Assistant Attorney General Levitt and a detail of special agents. Berlikov told Rourke where the motel was located, Rourke relayed it cryptically to the following car, then turned on rooftop flashers and sped over deserted streets, reaching the motel just before dawn.

Berlikov hurried down the hall, opened the door, and found Irina and the children sitting together on one bed. Katya was playing with her Garfield toy while Andrushka was listening to his mother reading about Peter Rabbit. Startled, she looked up, the children froze, and Berlikov gathered the three of them in his arms. "We're safe, we're safe!" he cried, and he began to weep uncontrollably.

The desk clerk appeared in the doorway. "What the hell's going on here?"

"Bug off, buddy," Rourke snapped, and turned him around and shoved him down the hall. When Rourke came back the Berlikovs were sobbing and embracing. What we need here, he thought, is a gallon of borscht and a couple dozen blini. He went back along the hall, hit the Coke machine with a slug. While the field office guys carried out the Berlikov luggage, Rourke leaned against the machine and sucked on a bottle of real, honest-to-God, made-in-America Coca-Cola.

Lucky fuckers, he thought as he watched the family Berlikov escorted down the hallway, but the son of a bitch better produce or he's gone like a snowflake on the lid of hell.

FORTY-SEVEN

In the morning Chance checked his bag in a bahnhof locker and taxied to the Sacher for a hearty breakfast in the hotel's Victorian-style dining room. He noticed a good many British around him, for the famous hotel had been a British officers' billet during Vienna's postwar Four-Power Occupation. The Americans had used the Bristol, and the Sovs had nearly destroyed the old Majestic Hotel with vodka-inspired vandalism. But all that was past now, part of history the gemütlich Viennese had chewed on and spit out as indigestible.

The bomb- and artillery-damaged buildings had been demolished or rebuilt, and the Staatsoper stood resplendent, gilt on its baroque facade gleaming in the morning sun.

As the old waiter refilled his coffee cup, Chance said in German, "I'm a journalist, *vater,* and I need a small amount of information to help me with a story I'm working on."

"What kind of information, sir?"

"It's generally understood that refugees arriving here from Russia, Hungary, and Czechoslovakia often need *special* documentation in order to move on."

"*Ja,* that is so." He nodded vigorously.

Chance laid a fifty-schilling note beside his coffee cup. "I should like to know how those documents are obtained—understand I'm in favor of the free movement of peoples, and I would never betray a source."

"*Ach,* then you must talk with an expert in such things."

"Perhaps you know such a person . . . or could ask around?"

287

The waiter's plump hand momentarily covered the bank note, and when he removed it the bank note was gone. "Customarily," the waiter said in a low voice, "residents of the same ethnic origin aid their transient countrymen."

"Being French, I'm not eligible for such aid."

He scratched his chin. "True, but you speak a very fine German."

"When I was much younger I attended the hochschule in the Fünften Bezirk."

"*So? Ach,* the old place is gone, replaced by a fine apartment building. So many things change, *nein?*"

"And many things remain the same." Chance produced a twin of the vanished bank note. It, too, promptly disappeared. "As I am on my way to Steyr," he continued, "I have little time. Perhaps you could give me a lead—say within the next hour. I would be glad to reimburse you for your trouble."

The waiter nodded. "An hour then. Ask for Heinz Lüdtke."

"*Danke schön.*"

"*Bitte schön.*"

Chance paid his bill and departed.

Shops were opening. On Karntnerstrasse he bought a Tyrolean hiking outfit: rough gray lederhosen, knee-length wool socks, hob-nailed ankle boots, sheath knife, heavy shirt, and a velour hat decorated with a wisp of *gampsbard.* He returned to his locker and added his purchases to it, then consulted bahnhof schedules for trains to Salzburg. They left approximately every two hours, he found, and he wanted to reach Uncle Klaus's home by nightfall, to avoid showing his passport at a hotel.

The KGB was witting of his nom de guerre, as were the Chinese who had supplied his documentation. And even if the Chinese presence in Austria was limited (and he was uncertain of that), the Soviets regarded Vienna as practically a suburb of Moscow.

He found Lüdtke setting tables for midday diners. The elderly waiter came over and said softly, "With some difficulty I obtained a name and an address." He shrugged apologetically. "Perhaps it will not meet your needs, but it is as good as I could do."

Chance placed two hundred schillings in his hand.

"Follow the Graben," Lüdtke said in confidential tones, "and at

Hilferstrasse 73 there is an artistic printing shop, whose proprietor is said to be sympathetic to the problems of refugees. His name is Nozack."

"I'm much obliged to you," Chance said. "Long life to you, *vater.*"

"*Danke schön.*"

"*Auf Wiedersehen.*"

Twenty minutes later Chance was talking with proprietor Horst Nozack, a man of sixty or so with sparse gray hair and a thin face. Thick silver-rimmed spectacles perched across the high bridge of his thin nose. He listened unblinkingly as Chance said, "Like certain of your customers, Herr Nozack, I am embarrassed by the lack of papers adequate to the requirements of frontier inspectors."

"And what, young gentleman, leads you to believe that I can in any way help resolve this problem?" One finger adjusted the temple of his spectacles.

"An acquaintance I chanced upon at the Hotel Sacher."

Nozack grimaced. "With what documentation did you reach Vienna?"

Chance handed him the French passport and followed Nozack into his office at the rear of the printing-engraving shop. The cluttered space had unfinished wood shelves sagging under the weight of stacked paper and ink supplies. The desk was a disordered litter of bills, invoices, bottled chemicals, engraving tools, an elderly telephone and an out-of-date calendar. Door closed, Nozack sat down, set a jeweler's loupe in his left eye, and turned a powerful lamp on the passport page by page.

Turning off the light he squinted at Chance. "This passport should give you no difficulties whatever. It even bears authentic exit and entry stamps. Tell me precisely what your problem is."

"The name," said Chance, "is troublesome."

"Ah, you are perhaps wanted by the police?"

"No, but certain business competitors try to keep track of my travels. How much?"

"For the name change only, one thousand schillings."

"When will it be ready?"

Nozack rubbed the point of his chin. "Fortunately I have few distractions this morning. Let us say noon. Five hundred now, *bitte.*"

Chance turned over the money. "Let us alter the name to Paul Charles Picquet." He printed it on a piece of notepaper.

"Until noon," Nozack said. Chance left him counting the down payment.

On the way back to the bahnhof, Chance stopped at a luggage store on the Heldenplatz and bought a medium-size A-frame backpack. Made of aluminum and covered with dark green nylon, the backpack was both light and typical of the region where he was headed. In a compartment within the *Herren* lavatory, Chance changed from rumpled city clothing into mountain apparel. He transferred suitcase contents into the backpack and placed the holstered Walther in an outer utility pocket closed by Velcro fasteners.

Abandoning his travel bag, he left the lavatory and had a late-morning cheese and sweet roll snack at the station's *kaffee* bar. Then, shouldering his backpack and adjusting the straps for comfort, Chance left the bahnhof and walked toward Horst Nozack's establishment, breaking in his new walking shoes along the way.

The air was cool, sun bright, and Chance felt reasonably optimistic. After the sedentary life he had been leading, it was going to be good to be back in the Hohe Tauern Mountains and the foothills of the Salzburg Alps. He remembered fishing with his father in the clear waters of the Salzach River, swimming near shore with Roger when they were kids. He was lost in reverie when he turned into Hilferstrasse and down the shady side of the street, across from Nozack's shop.

The forger's place of business was located toward the far end of the block, and as Chance neared it he saw parked, and slightly protruding into the intersection, the unmistakable snout of a Vienna *polizei* vehicle. Slowing stride, he walked past 73 and glanced casually at the open doorway. Horst Nozack was talking with two plainclothesmen. The sight chilled Chance, but he continued his walk and crossed, like a law-abiding citizen, at the intersection.

The uniformed driver at the wheel of the police car paid no attention to the mountaineer. Chance passed the car and turned into a service alley that ran the length of the block behind Horst Nozack's shop. The rear door was locked, but Chance worked his knife blade into the weathered jointure between door and frame, and forced the spring bolt aside. Carefully, he opened the door a crack and saw that it gave into the closed office where he had done business with Nozack.

It was possible the police were giving Nozack a routine shake-down; equally possible the forger had reported a French customer with whom he had no political, ethnic, or compassionate ties. A trade for tacit tolerance.

Whatever the case, Chance needed his passport and saw it lying on Nozack's desk. He eased into the closed office and picked up the passport. His photograph and description hadn't been changed, but the bearer was now identified as Paul Charles Picquet.

He heard the policemen bid Nozack good-bye, and their de-parting footsteps. The police car's engine started and Nozack opened the office door. Startled, he blinked at Chance, who gave him a hard stare. "What did the cops want?"

Nozack licked thin lips. "Last week my shop was broken into, some frames and paintings taken. The policemen came by to tell me they have a man in custody." He shook his head. "A boy who once worked here as an apprentice." He squinted at Chance. "You thought . . . ?"

"Never mind." Nozack's explanation was too plausible to have been concocted on the spur of the moment. He tapped the pass-port. "You do good work. Many thanks." He left as he had come, quickened his stride and reached the Westbahnhof in time to board the departing train for Salzburg.

As the train moved out of the yards, Chance felt an unexpected thrill of anticipation. Often as he had taken the train in his boy-hood, he had never gone alone, always accompanied by mother, father, Schwester Herta, and Roger who loved trains . . . and grew to love airplanes.

So this was his first time alone on the smoothly accelerating express. He remembered the holiday spirit that had imbued those adolescent trips, but this one was different. He was running for his life.

BOOK FOUR

FORTY-EIGHT

Jan Abrams stood at the clinic bedside of Paul Valcour looking down at his former colleague's pale face. "How are you feeling?"

"Better, Jan, much better. Still weak."

"It was a narrow thing, wasn't it?" Jan commented.

Valcour smiled thinly. "Much too close for comfort. I'm told I survived because of prompt action by . . . a friend."

"Quinn Chance."

"Ah, you recognized him. He told you?"

"Quinn was never one to boast of his accomplishments."

"You mean in contrast to myself?"

"I meant it as an observation on the character of a man I admire. Do you know how I can get in touch with him?"

"No. And my sister, Antoinette, is grieving. Do you know why he left so suddenly?"

"Your operation came apart," Abrams said bluntly. "Chance predicted the Chinese would liquidate him, so he got away. Safely, I hope."

Valcour's eyes narrowed. "How much do you know about the op?"

"Not enough to report; besides, there's nothing left to report. An in-depth Counter Intelligence review might reveal where betrayal occurred, but counterintelligence was never my forte." The room smelled of disinfectant, reminding him of Sarah's. "Nor yours, if I remember correctly."

"Your memory was always accurate."

"But not as prodigious as Quinn's."

"Will he remember my sister, send for her?"

"I don't know—his situation is difficult, unresolved. But there's been a development I wanted him to know about that might ease his mind." He looked toward the curtained window. "I was trying to phone him when . . . there was an interruption."

"At least he got away," Valcour said. "The villa is empty, his Chinese associates decamped." His head moved on the pillow. "Too bad about the operation. Quinn and I, we would have been making history."

"You may have," Abrams said enigmatically, "but that's not what I came to discuss."

"Nor my plight, eh? I hoped you might possibly have come to express sympathy—as one old colleague to another."

Abrams gazed at him. "To me, Paul, you're a renegade, a mercenary who used the Agency for his own purposes. We have nothing in common except Quinn Chance. I'll be leaving Geneva soon, but you'll be here. If you can get a message to him, tell him he's no longer being blamed for the murder of Walter Stillman."

"Stillman? Oh, the Security fellow."

"For once the police made a thorough investigation. It seems Stillman had a longtime affair with his secretary, kept it going with promises of marriage, that sort of thing."

"Not uncommon in the Agency."

"She was questioned routinely, came apart, and confessed. They'd had a confrontation and she realized Stillman wouldn't marry her. So she picked her time and shot her lover, assuming Chance would be blamed because Stillman had betrayed him—as Stillman had betrayed her." He sighed. "But that was never more than a minor obstacle to Quinn's returning. . . . In any case, I wanted him to know."

"If he should make contact, I'll tell him."

"He's gone through so much—Carla, her death . . . hunted for crimes he didn't commit. It's terribly wrong. Is he likely to contact your sister?"

"She expects—hopes—so."

"What does she know about Quinn?"

"From me, nothing, not even his name—especially not that. But from his Russian liaison contact, the woman, I don't know what Toni may have learned."

"Did the liaison know his true name?"

"Perhaps. From what Toni told me, she was probably KGB, and the KGB has been looking for Quinn worldwide." He paused as though to recover strength. "The woman saved their lives, all three of them. Toni was grateful, admired the woman. Who knows what confidantes disclose?"

"Too much," Abrams said dryly. "Always too much." He looked at his watch. "Good-bye, Paul." Abrams turned and left the room.

As the delegation car drove him back into Geneva, Abrams reflected that he would have preferred confiding in Antoinette Valcour, and his visit to her brother was principally to determine whether that was feasible. Now he doubted it.

Still, there might come a time when everything would be cleared up, all secrets made known. Quinn Chance was too valuable a man to let vanish unremembered.

FORTY-NINE

As the train pulled into Salzburg's bahnhof, Chance could make out the steep Alpine foothills that marked the city: Kapuzinerberg to the east and Mönchsberg beyond the river. Evening lights twinkled through twilight, and Chance felt a profound sense of homecoming to this city of venerable baroque beauty.

Indistinguishable among dozens of travelers, he shouldered his A-frame and left the train. The central bus station was only a few blocks away, so he walked along the chestnut-lined Elisabethkai, glimpsing the deep-flowing Salzach that divided the ancient Celt-founded city. As never before, Chance appreciated the settled, secure atmosphere of Salzburg. Here people were pleasant without prying; they valued privacy and usually extended that privilege to tourists and other strangers. In Salzburg he was not going to be mugged or hassled; it was a city of kultur, music, food, and wine. How fortunate its citizens were, he reflected as he strolled on.

Not for an hour and a half was a rural bus leaving for Waldober-am-See, where his mother had been born, and where he hoped to find living relatives. So he ate wurst, potatoes, spinach, and *schwarzbrot* in a small, clean restaurant, drank a stein of dark beer, and set off over cobbled streets to settle the heavy meal and refresh his memories of the picturesque city.

He crossed the square in front of the seventeenth-century cathedral where *Everyman* was performed during Salzburg's annual Mozart Festival. The cathedral itself, modeled after Saint Peter's in Rome, was a traditional object of tourist photos.

Then on to Mozartplatz and the ornate monument memorialing

Salzburg's most famous son, along with the alchemist and physician, Paracelsus, whose quest for immortality had ended in Salzburg.

And the massive old Hohensalzburg fortress crowning the peak of a hill and silently, ominously, dominating the peaceful setting below. Chance remembered visiting the citadel with his family, and how frightened he and Roger had been at the sight of its cells, racks, and implements of medieval torture.

The bus, a modern, German-built diesel, left on time and headed into the outlying hills, stopping now and then to pick up or unload passengers.

Much of the route was over poorly lighted roads, but moonlight revealed sturdy farmhouses and barns, stone fences, cattle, goats and horses, hayricks and watering troughs. His mother's line, the Herz family, had been landowners and breeders, living comfortably for generations from land rents and harvest sharing. Then, in the aftermath of the First World War, the family had begun to sell its holdings to former tenant farmers with whom it remained on friendly terms. Cousin Ruprecht, son of Uncle Klaus, was the last of the Herz line, as far as Chance knew, unless Ruprecht had produced a male heir, as he himself had not.

After an hour's travel, the bus stopped in the center of Waldober and Chance got off, watching its taillights recede before reshouldering his backpack. In his youth the old town had comprised perhaps five thousand residents; now, from the look of things— new shops, cafés, and restaurants—the population had at least doubled. The changes were inevitable, he supposed, though to him distasteful.

He began hiking up a well-worn road, wound up and around gentle hills until he could see the lake, whose name was coupled with the town's. Four miles long and perhaps a mile wide, the *see* was fed by springs, rain, and snowmelt from the nearby Alps. The lake was a source of irrigation, drinking water, and clean, sweet whitefish, and its tree-lined shores were enjoyed by campers, boaters, and swimmers who would never in their lives see a larger body of water.

Chance came wearily around the final bend, seeing the big

schloss—as children called it in their exaggerated way—imposing against the skyline, and the smaller barns and outbuildings. Thick-roofed, erected of stone and oak, the old three-story house had withstood centuries of storm and avalanche, battles, pillage, and fire, and to Chance its lighted windows represented the haven he so desperately needed.

The stone path to the porticoed entrance was defined by a rail fence useful in winter when snowdrifts obliterated footpaths. He breathed deeply, leaning against the door frame, and pulled the cord of a heavy bronze bell. It clanged loudly in the stillness.

Soft footsteps nearing. The door opened and a light-haired young woman looked out. *"Grüss Gott,"* she said. "You want the pastor?"

"Grüss Gott. The pastor?"

"Pastor Herz, my father."

He lowered his backpack, let it hang from one hand. "You're Sofia, then," he said, and took off his Tyrolean hat. "I'm Quinn, your American cousin."

Her chestnut hair was drawn back in a tight bun; her cheek-bones were angular, her nose straight; she had freckled face and forearms, deep brown eyes, and a determined mouth and chin.

With a little cry she came forward and hugged him tightly. "Welcome, welcome, Quinn, I'm so glad you're here! All of us have been so worried. Here, let me help with your backpack." She insisted on taking part of the burden and led him up the broad wooden stairs down whose long, smooth banister Chance used to slide.

"So you didn't know your uncle became a pastor, did you? Lutheran." She smiled. "In Salzburg Province, where everyone is Catholic, as you remember. Quinn, you look so fine, so strong . . . but tired. You'll have Ruprecht's room; he lives nearby with his wife and child. Have you been traveling long?"

"Forever, it seems." He dragged himself onto the carpeted land-ing and left his rucksack to follow Sofia into the big book-lined room where a gray-haired man sat behind a scarred writing table, reading from a thick book.

"Father," she called, "it's Quinn."

"Quinn?" Startled, he looked up and rose to greet him. They

met halfway, and the powerfully built older man hugged Chance in a bearish embrace whose strength he remembered from childhood. "Ah, Quinn, my boy, my boy, so like Erika." He stood back gripping Chance's arms, then wiped a wet cheek. "Thank God you're here! Sofia, bring wine for your cousin, for all of us." He drew Quinn to a smoke-stained wall hung with old photographs and family portraits. "It's been so long, Nephew, you must get to know your family again. Tomorrow we'll talk, eh?"

Below an unruly shock of gray-brown hair the pastor's square-set face resembled a block of weathered granite. His thick arms and massive shoulders made him seem far more the hardworking farmer he had been than the man of the cloth he had become. But the corners of his eyes still crinkled when he smiled and his gaze was as kindly as Chance remembered.

While they were sitting, Sofia brought glasses and a decanter of amber wine; when she had filled them, the Herzes toasted his arrival. Then Uncle Klaus said soberly, "After we learned of your . . . trouble, we hoped you would come to us—hoped and feared. And prayed God would guide your steps aright."

Chance sipped the sweet wine. "Feared? Have police bothered you?"

"Not yet, Quinn," Sofia said, "but only a week ago—wasn't it, father?—a reporter came here asking for you. A journalist from America."

"We'll hide you, of course," his uncle said, "help you through this time of trouble."

At the word *reporter* Chance's mouth went dry. "I can't endanger you," he said, "I have no right to interfere in your lives."

Sofia had gone to a card tray. Sifting through cards she said, "Here it is—the journalist's name," and handed it to Chance.

Reluctantly, he took it, read the engraved words in astonishment: VERONICA TALBOT BOYCE. Finishing his wine, he said, "I know her, she's a friend."

"She was disappointed that we knew nothing of you, but she left a letter," Pastor Klaus Herz told him. "Sofia, please bring it."

Sofia parted two books and brought out a sealed envelope. On it was written QUINN.

Sofia said, "She told us what happened to you, said Carla had died. We're terribly sorry, Cousin. She wanted to help in any way she could."

"Of course," her father continued, "we thought it might be a trick to gain our confidence, but in truth we knew nothing of your whereabouts. So she left the letter for you and went away."

"Back to America?"

"I suppose so." Sofia refilled Chance's glass. "Have you eaten, Quinn? Are you hungry after your journey?"

"I ate in Salzburg," he said, "but there was always hot soup in your kitchen kettle."

"And still is," Sofia smiled. "Bread, too, baked this morning by the cook."

When she went to the kitchen, Uncle Klaus said, "Nephew, I don't believe you guilty of any crimes, so I won't ask. In this house of God everyone is welcome. Let God judge, not man."

Before Chance ate at the kitchen table, Klaus said grace, blessing the food, the house, and its occupants. And as Chance scented the savory mix of thick beef stock and vegetables, he could hardly wait to eat, feeling famished as a child after a long day's playing in the fields. He daubed chunks of farm-churned butter on slabs of rich brown bread and soaked up the nourishing soup, while his relatives watched with pleasure.

Coffee then, flavored with the caraway bite of schnapps, and as they sat together around the old, scarred table Chance said, "I don't want to endanger any of you by telling you anything beyond the fact that I was framed and forced to flee. For a time I was helped by people until they turned against me; now I'm on the road again." He looked at the shiny old pots, pans, and kettles hanging on the kitchen walls, the carefully arranged spoons, knives, and cleavers—symbolic of their owners' ordered lives, their untroubled dignity—and he was glad that through his mother he shared their blood.

Klaus said, "I've been thinking whether to bring over your cousin Ruprecht."

"Why not? I've looked forward to seeing him."

"Ah, he hasn't changed, but that wife of his"—the pastor shook his head—"a Czech. Pretty, and a good wife to Ruprecht, but suspicious and given to loose talk."

"It's true," Sofia affirmed, "and my brother tells her everything. The journalist had hardly left before Mikela was telling the entire town."

Klaus poured more coffee. "How long can you stay with us? As far as we're concerned, you're welcome to make a new life here, where your mother and I were raised, our fathers and their fathers, too."

"That time may come," Chance said, "but for now I want to rest a few days, make plans to move on where I'll be safe. I have a passport that I can't use much longer."

Klaus said, "Ruprecht and you might pass for one another—and he has a good Austrian passport from last year when he and Mikela visited Norway. What do you think, Sofia?"

"Perhaps," she said, "if my brother could refrain from telling his wife. But there's no hurry, is there? We can think about that—and other things—tomorrow."

The pastor nodded. "Sofia is engaged, Quinn. Her young man is an engineer at the Kaprun Dam, his family roots are in Styria, and he's intelligent and God-fearing."

"And we love each other," Sofia said with a trace of shyness. Quinn kissed his cousin. "I hope you'll be as happy as Carla and I were."

"Harald comes on Sundays when he's free," she said, "I'd like the two of you to meet."

"If my identity wouldn't burden him."

"My fiancé is discreet and not the least political," she said proudly. "But it's up to you and father."

"We'll discuss that, too," the pastor said, and ran a large-boned hand through his shock of hair. "Now I have a sermon to prepare, so if my daughter will make my nephew comfortable for the night, we'll meet for breakfast." The two men hugged each other again, and Sofia led Chance to the beamed third-floor room with its big feather bed that Ruprecht had shared with him and Roger on their childhood visits.

Chance hung his rucksack on a wall peg and pulled off his clothing. He lay back on the enveloping eiderdown, too tired to read Rony's letter, reflecting only that if Rony had been able to trace his Austrian family, so could his enemies.

FIFTY

The Berlikov family's custodians—the FBI—moved them by night in a guarded caravan to a large, comfortable house in a remote area of the huge Fort Belvoir military reservation in northern Virginia. There was a fenced-in playground for the children and a sparkling pool. To Irina's undisguised pleasure, a basement recreation room contained a large television set. Guards shopped for her at the base commissary, and nurses and physicians were available on demand.

With half of Kolya's salary always having been withheld in escrow rubles, Irina had never been able to afford the variety of frozen foods and TV dinners now stocking her large freezer. A Russian-speaking female FBI agent accompanied her to the commissary store so Irina could select clothing for herself, Katya, and Andrushka, and toys. The children's demands were inexhaustible, but as her husband said, "We're guests and dependents of the U.S. government, and this capitalist paradise can easily afford to be generous. In exchange I'm giving information that would cost them millions—if they could even get it. Believe me, dear, we deserve everything we're getting."

The FBI tacitly agreed. Within hours of Berlikov's unannounced defection, surveillance on Betty, Yoder, and Claire was in place. And Berlikov identified nine other agents in a network that extended from Bath, Maine, to the nuclear submarine base near Savannah, Georgia.

Assistant Attorney General Levitt overruled the FBI and permitted CIA to have *one* officer present at formal debriefings to which the protected code word *Sachem* was assigned. Mark Ramey, who represented the Directorate of Intelligence, chafed at restrictions imposed on him. His debriefing notes were impounded in a Bureau safe after each session; no tape recordings were permitted, and he was allowed to take from the safe house only what Sachem material he could carry in his head. Complaining to the deputy director in his large sixth-floor office, Ramey said, "Those Bureau guys treat me as if I were the enemy."

"They got it wrong," his chief replied. *"They're* the enemy, but they don't realize it—yet. Calm down and wait until they've squeezed all this domestic shit from Berlikov; it's their bag and we can't use it anyway. But when the general shifts to foreign intrigue, we jump in. After that, for the Bureau Berlikov becomes a sweet memory, like your first fuck on a hot Sunday afternoon. Got it?"

"Got it," Ramey said. "I'll follow through." He stood, turned to leave, and stopped. "Chief, there's one potential trouble spot you ought to know about. Berlikov claims that one night while he was servicing drops he was grabbed and tortured until he confessed about Sosnowski and Quentin Chance. On tape."

"So?"

"Berlikov is obsessed with the idea some of our people did it."

"So what's the problem?"

"The Bureau guys look at me and smirk."

"Meaning . . . ?"

"Maybe some Bureau mavericks did it. . . ." He shrugged. "I dunno . . . I suppose it's possible."

"Mmmm."

Ramey looked at his chief for a lead, got nothing, and decided to continue. "To add to the confusion, Berlikov thinks the same bunch snatched Chance from the Metro cops."

The Deputy Director Central Intelligence frowned while he considered. Finally he said, "Let's assume some Bureau enthusiasts went after Berlikov directly, a hip pocket op, no funding, no records. . . . If that pushed the general to defect, it was a good night's work; in the long run we benefit and so does the USG." His hands spread, palms up. "What's bad about that, Mark? I don't see the problem." Peripherially he could see the greening lawn of

Langley headquarters, the budding trees, the muddy Potomac beyond.

Ramey cleared his throat. "Berlikov suggests our people were involved."

The DDCI grunted, reached for a cigarette, and fondled it before replacing it. "I didn't hear that," he said ominously, "because I don't want the inspector general getting his snout in and creating another CIA uproar. And you—you forget you heard it." Swiveling slowly around in his large executive chair, he looked at the blue CIA flag on its gilt standard and thought the job wasn't worth the aggravation: no real power and ninety percent of the responsibility.

"So," Ramey asked nervously, "what do I tell Berlikov?"

"Tell him it was the PLO," the deputy director snapped. "Now, get down to Belvoir and keep listening."

In Levitt's Justice Department office Wilson Jones was handed a blue-bound folder printed: TOP SECRET/SENSITIVE/SACHEM/LIMDIS/NOFORN. A diagonal red stripe was taped to the cover, and a lined distribution sheet was stapled on the back.

"What is this?" Jones asked Tommy Levitt.

"Sign and find out."

Jones examined the distribution list. Levitt's signature was first, the second was that of the director of Central Intelligence, and a National Security Council signature followed. Jones prepared to sign. "What's the purpose of this lending library card?" he asked.

"Any leaks, we know who to go after."

Jones signed and turned aside the cover sheet. "Why am I accorded this dubious privilege, Tommy?"

"Because the material came from your client, Berlikov. It's the transcript in English of a conversation he recorded without the knowledge of his superior officer. It pretty much clears your absent client, Quentin Chance. That's why you're getting a look at it."

"I gather it's not admissible as exculpatory evidence."

"Considering the manner in which the material was obtained, no. And because it involves very high level Soviets, it's being back-burnered for possible future use."

"Who made that decision?"

"Either the president or his national security adviser." He shrugged. "You can't use the stuff, neither can I."

"Leaving Quinn Chance out on a limb." He adjusted his bifocals.

"Was it JFK who said 'Life is unfair'? Or Jimmuh Carter?"

FIFTY-ONE

By daylight, Chance saw that Cousin Sofia's smoothly oval face, firm chin, chestnut hair and deep brown eyes were greatly reminiscent of his mother's photograph in her twenties. During breakfast in the kitchen he mentioned it and Klaus Herz nodded. "Often thought so myself. My sister Erika was a lovely young woman."

"And she was lovely until the day she died." Chance cut into a thick slice of snow-cured ham. With bowls of cottage-fried potatoes, cheese, toasted bread, and currant jam, the table held enough food for a dozen. "I can't remember how long it's been since I slept as well."

"Just remember," Sofia said, "this is your home as long as you care to stay."

The cook refilled their cups with strong black coffee and brought in a plate of hot sweet buns. Klaus patted his stomach. "I think we ought to resolve your onward travel, Nephew, so you can enjoy your stay without that particular concern. Sofia, you might consider taking Mikela into town for lunch or shopping, so Ruprecht won't be interrupted."

"Shall I telephone her, Father?"

"Just go, spur of the moment, and when that's settled tell your brother I want to see him here."

After Sofia left the table, her father said to Chance, "I gather your problems came out of your intelligence work."

"Apparently," Chance admitted.

"I have no love for the Russians," Pastor Herz said, "having seen how they ravaged poor Vienna. And but for the American Army,

Salzburg and Waldober would have suffered equal horrors and atrocities, so I am not one of those churchmen who regards the U.S.S.R. with equanimity. Evil is evil in whatever form and must be identified and denounced. Which is why," he continued, "in addition to our bond of blood, I am more than eager to do all I can to protect you from the Russians."

"Mikela, as a Czech refugee, should detest the Russians, too."

"She does, but she gossips unthinkingly, never considering the harm a loose tongue can do." He sighed. "Human frailty," he said, and frowned at the sound of a vehicle arriving outside.

From the window Klaus said, "The best-laid plans, eh? Here's Mikela now."

The engine cut off and presently Chance heard footsteps on the stairs. Then into the room came a petite, dark-haired young woman wearing a flowered dirndl. Her cheekbones had the Slavic slant, and her nose was small and pert. She embraced Klaus and turned to Chance. Klaus said, "This is our cousin, Roger, from America."

She came to him and offered him her hand. "Welcome," she said cordially. "I have not known any Americans."

"He's here on a hiking trip," Klaus said, "and to renew family acquaintance."

Thinking it best to let his uncle make explanations, Chance asked, "Will you have coffee?"

"No, thank you." Her dark eyes searched his face. "I was going to town and thought Sofia might like to come with me."

"I'm sure she'll be happy to," Klaus said. "Is your husband at home?"

She nodded. "Doing accounts, and I know better than to be around when he's so absorbed."

Sofia came in and the sisters-in-law embraced. They left together and Klaus went to the telephone. When Chance heard him phoning Ruprecht, he left the table and went up to his bedroom. There he opened Rony's letter.

I hope in time this will reach you because your lawyer and I received your letters from Mexico City and have carried out your instructions. I wish there was more we could do. Wilson continues in frequent

309

touch with the Department of Justice but holds out little hope for your vindication absent some dramatic turn of events. I'm sorry to have to say this, but telling you otherwise would be a disservice to you. I just hope that somehow the situation will clarify and you will be able to return to Washington and the university. Meanwhile, Penn took early retirement, having been offered a position with American Express in Monaco and persuaded me to join him there for at least a try at reconciliation. Whatever I may have fantasized about you and me is now best left unsaid. Carla died peacefully, and Jan and I saw to her funeral arrangements. She was a wonderful person, and I often envied the happiness the two of you shared. Wherever you are, I think of your safety and hope that someday we'll talk again. With every good wish,

Rony.

A friend worth having, he thought soberly. He tore her letter in strips and flushed it down the toilet. The fact that Rony had come to Waldober-am-See from Monte Carlo made it less likely she had been trailed by his enemies. Still, the Chinese were aware of her name and Washington address.

He heard his uncle calling and went down to find Cousin Ruprecht grinning happily. He wore a bristly beard and his hair was as thick as his father's, but his features were unchanged. They shook hands warmly and Ruprecht said, "I was beginning to fear I'd never see you again." He handed Chance an Austrian passport. "I can say this was lost and get another without difficulty."

Chance opened the passport to his cousin's photograph and saw that it showed Ruprecht with beard and unruly hair. "Thank you," he said gratefully. "I can always say I shaved off my beard."

"Exactly. Now, we'll let Mikela keep thinking you're Roger— no harm in that—and much as I love my little wife, I agree that she talks too much. Now, how shall we celebrate your coming?"

"Mikela said you were doing accounts."

"They can wait. Speak, Cousin."

Chance looked at his uncle. "I'd like to visit some of the places we went as boys. The tree house up on the hill, fish the lake. . . ."

"Then we'll do it," Ruprecht said heartily, and went to the kitchen for coffee.

Klaus said, "Now that you have a passport, where will you go?"

310

"Argentina."

"So far? Well, you know best. If you're short of funds . . ."

"I have enough, thanks."

"There's never enough, Quinn. At least let us buy your ticket. Call it a birthday present from your family."

"Thank you, Uncle."

So Chance spent most of the day with his cousin, hiking the sweet-smelling fields, climbing the mountain foothills, talking about their contrasting lives, and reminiscing about pleasures they had shared as boys together. The memories recalled Roger vividly and there was so much of Roger in Cousin Ruprecht that Chance was affected by an intense feeling of kinship—as though Ruprecht was a surrogate brother.

And as an ending to a day of nostalgia, the two cousins went down into the cool, earth-floored storm cellar below the main house. Heavily timbered to withstand the crushing weight of avalanches, the room stored boxes of vegetables and barrels of fruit, for there had been no avalanche in years. Chance remembered hiding there with Roger, munching pilfered apples while worried adults searched for them above.

That night they dined in rural splendor at the huge table Chance remembered so well. Candles on the table, gleaming silver, and after saying a fervent grace, Pastor Herz carved the roasted lamb. Mikela had bought a new dress in town, one that showed her slim waist to advantage and kept Chance, who sat next to her, aware of its décolletage. She was a foxy little piece, and Chance wondered if it troubled her husband. There was a good deal of local wine, and when it was gone Ruprecht and Mikela went back to the farm, and Chance dozed off in his chair.

In the morning Klaus brought tackle to Chance for his fishing excursion with Ruprecht, then went off to visit a sick parishioner. Chance was digging worms from a compost pile beside the stable when Ruprecht's pickup drove up. He filled the bait can and walked halfway to the pickup before realizing that it was Mikela at the wheel.

"Grüss Gott," he said in formal salutation, "Where's my fishing partner?"

311

"Ruprecht begs off, Cousin, he has a thick head this morning and the accounts to do. So I volunteered."

"You like fishing?" He placed rods on the flatbed and got in beside her. Chance was disappointed but tried not to show it.

"Everything but baiting the hook." Her eyes were bright. She was wearing jeans and a loose white sweater.

She drove a couple of miles to a secluded cove beside the lake, surrounded by huge conifers. After parking in shade she took a lunch basket from the flatbed, managing to brush against Chance as he got out the rods and bait, and spread a blanket in the sun. Mikela wriggled out of her jeans and pulled off her sweater, revealing a scanty pink bikini. "Hey," he said, "I thought this was a fishing trip."

"I'm much too pale. I'll fish in a while." She lay down on the blanket and stretched luxuriously.

Chance had expected to be out in a boat where the water was deeper and the fish larger. But he went out on a rim of rocks and dutifully began casting. To his surprise his third cast brought a two-pound lake trout to the hook. Tossing it onto grass he called, "Better join me while they're biting."

"I'm too comfortable," she called back. "You can have my share." Her shoulder straps were down. He looked away and rebaited his hook. His next catch was one of the lake's famed whitefish, about a pound-and-a-half. Clearly, the area hadn't been fished out, because the next hour produced three more trout and two whitefish. Then as the sun rose high, shadows disappeared and the fish stopped biting.

Mikela opened the picnic basket and produced a bottle of red wine and a corkscrew. Thirsty, he drank deeply after Mikela, then set about gutting his catch and rinsing the fish.

She brought the bottle to Chance and squatted down beside him. "You're the first American I've ever known, but your German is perfect and your mother came from here, so I guess you're not a typical American." She drank and passed him the bottle.

"We're not all cowboys," he told her. "I was lucky to have spent so much time in Austria and Switzerland."

"Still, life here in the country can be . . . boring. Prague was an exciting city despite certain drawbacks. I'd like Ruprecht to move

312

to Salzburg, but he's bound to the land, like all the Herzes, I guess."

"It's a life I envy," he said truthfully. "I could be contented here."

"Could you?" She drank again. "You seem like a man who's accustomed to travel, living in the world's biggest cities. You must find us very . . . provincial." Her face was pink from sun and wine. "You're so much like Ruprecht, and so unlike him in other ways."

Chance strung a line through the fishes' gills and trailed them in the water. "I'm hot," Mikela said, "and need to cool off." She ran into the water, and when it was hip-high she dived and began swimming strongly toward the rocks' curving end. Reaching it, she waved at him then started back. She swam well, and her sleekly muscled body moved through the water like a dolphin. Then she reached shore and ran shivering to him. "The blanket," she said, teeth chattering, and when he'd draped it around her she wiggled out of her wet bikini.

He gave her the wine bottle and after drinking she said, "That's better, *much* better, Cousin." She sat in the sun and fluffed her hair to dry. He sat beside her in the warm sun, and suddenly she turned her face and kissed his lips. Then she lay back on the blanket and drew him down beside her. "I want to make love," she said throatily. "No one will ever know."

"I'd know," Chance reproached her, "and I can't betray my cousin."

"Ruprecht? He's always too tired for sex. I need a man, a strong man like you." She reached for his crotch, but he held her hand. "Mikela," he said, "you're beautiful and desirable, but you're my cousin's wife. Let's be friends." He kissed her forehead gently.

"You *are* a bastard," she snapped angrily. "Are you also queer?"

"Let's say I am," he said, pulling her to her feet.

As she stood in the sunlight, naked as a young goddess, he momentarily regretted his scruples. Then he brought over her jeans and sweater, and while he spread the blanket in the shade, she sulkily pulled on her clothing.

Almost without speaking they shared roast chicken, bread, and spring onions, and finished the wine. He thanked her for the repast, suggested they put the episode behind them, and collected their things in the flatbed.

313

Grumpily, Mikela drove back to the farmhouse and waited behind the wheel while he took out rods and catch. Then he walked around to her side and gripped her wrist. "I'm flattered you found me attractive," he said, "and I could wish things were different. But they're not, so don't make trouble." When he released her wrist, she jammed the gearshift and drove away.

Chance turned his fish over to the plump, elderly cook who greeted them with exclamations of pleasure, and then he went up to his room to shower off fish smell and perspiration. As warm water cascaded over his body, Chance realized that he ought to move on. That night, after a fine fish dinner, Chance reluctantly asked Ruprecht to buy him a flight ticket from Salzburg to Buenos Aires.

FIFTY-TWO

From the Clinique Mirabeau, Paul Valcour was taken by ambulance to his mansion. Toni had had a hospital bed installed in his office, the doctor promised regular visits, and she felt free to leave.

Albert was loading the Daimler with her luggage when she came to her brother's bedside and told him her decision. With a grimace, Valcour asked, "Why, Toni, why? Haven't you been happy here?"

"You've done your best, Paul, but too many frightening things have happened in Geneva. To me, to you. . . ." She looked away. "I don't feel safe any longer; I'm going away."

"To follow Jean-Pierre?" he asked thinly.

"Perhaps. And that isn't even his name."

"Who told you differently?"

"The Russian woman showed me a photograph the KGB was using to locate him. And she said that since Quinn's enemies knew his name, there was no reason I shouldn't."

"I suppose so," Valcour sighed. "When the house burns down, everything's revealed."

"Do you know where he's gone?"

"It's a big world, Toni. Quinn could be anywhere. Please reconsider."

"I've thought about it for days, thought of little else." She bent over and kissed him. "You've been a pretty good brother, Paul, but I have to wonder how good a friend you've been to Quinn."

Albert drove her to the airport, where she boarded a flight to Mexico City. Seated in the first class compartment, Toni accepted champagne from the steward and sipped as the windows whitened in clouds that hung over the Alps.

She was profoundly aware of how dramatically her life had changed since she had met Quinn Chance. She had never met a man remotely like him, and now that she knew more about him from Natalya Yegorova, she admired and loved him so deeply that thinking of him was agony. She let the steward refill her glass and glanced at the engraved menu card, told the steward she would order later.

Before Natalya flew out of Geneva that final day—the day Chance left—she told Toni something of her own, seldom happy, life; the secret work in the KGB that she loathed and that Chance had suggested she leave for the West. "You should," Toni responded, "and I'll help any way I can." In retrospect Toni realized she should have revealed her relationship with Chance, but because of Talya's haste the opportunity passed. Anyway, she would probably never see Natalya Yegorova again, which was probably just as well, for the woman was undeniably attractive and cloaked in an aura of sexuality to which Toni did not want Quinn exposed. Reluctantly Toni acknowledged that she had been drawn to Talya, felt stirrings that, had they been stimulated, could have led to seduction.

At Madame Dupleis's boarding school in Montreux, Toni recalled, her music teacher, Romaine Lavalle, had introduced her to tribadic pleasures when she was fifteen. And during the hateful marriage to Prince Mohammed she often remembered Romaine with longing. Now that she thought of it, there were certain things about Talya that reminded her of Romaine: Talya's soft voice and gentle touch, the natural way she displayed her lovely, mature body. Was there something there? Toni wondered, or had she merely felt what she wanted to feel? Perhaps it had something to do with her admiration of Talya for boldly saving their lives. Or had she sensed a certain undercurrent in the Russian? Whatever the reason, it was exciting to think of, and who could say; the day might come when they would meet again. . . .

But now, she reminded herself, her quest was for Quinn Chance and a life they would have together. In Cuernavaca she would look for a suitable home. Then Cancún, following the route Chance had suggested. She would stay there long enough to look for Chance, then visit Rio, hire detectives, and exhaust all possibilities before going to Argentina.

The plane landed in Paris to refuel and take on additional passengers. Airborne again, Toni ordered from the elaborate menu, and as she ate she realized how accustomed she had become to dining with Chance. He had come to fill a void in her life whose existence she had been unaware of. Now, without him, she was desperately lonely.

On the other side of the aisle, and one row behind Toni, an oriental gentleman—a commercial traveler, she had supposed when she noticed him—removed his shoes and fitted his feet into airline-supplied slippers. With a blanket across his lap and a pillow under his head, he watched Toni until he was satisfied that she slept. Her handbag was on the seat beside her, and the oriental gentleman waited until the cabin lights were dimmed before he took her bag into the lavatory and went through it.

FIFTY-THREE

Jan Abrams and Wilson Jones had last seen each other at Carla Chance's funeral. Jones, visitor's pass clipped to his lapel, sat in Abrams's high-ceilinged office on the second floor of the grim-looking Old Executive Office Building next to the White House. Jones said, "I appreciate your seeing me on such short notice—especially since you must have a good deal of catch-up work after Geneva."

Abrams nodded. "You're Quinn's lawyer and Quinn is my friend. How can I help you?"

Jones sat forward. "We may be able to help each other, and benefit my client. First, I must establish that this conversation is entirely confidential."

"It is."

"Then I'll tell you that I've come by some astonishing information from a recent Soviet defector, who happens also to be my client."

"You refer to General Berlikov?"

Jones nodded. "Your knowing his identity helps me put things in focus. Berlikov is being debriefed at a secure location by the FBI, and I'm allowed to see my client from time to time. So far he's cooperating fully and being well treated in accordance with signed agreements; no complaints there. Now, one of the few barter items Berlikov brought with him was a taped conversation with a superior officer named General Sobatkin."

"Lieutenant General Yevgeni Lubovich Sobatkin. Yes, I'm generally familiar with his position and responsibilities."

"Are you familiar with the classified code word *Sachem?*"

"Afraid not."

"It covers Berlikov's defection and all the related intelligence. Sachem is top secret, sensitive, all that. I've read the English translation of the conversation with Sobatkin and it completely clears Quentin Chance of any wrongdoing. Sobatkin ordered Sosnowski's murder and Berlikov had it carried out." He took a deep breath. "One of the concessions made by Justice was a grant of immunity to Berlikov under which he can't be tried or punished for his role in the murder conspiracy. Berlikov, however, is willing to testify to the facts and clear Quinn Chance."

"Sounds good," Abrams said. "What's the problem?"

"The problem," Jones said heavily, "is that Justice and the FBI are suppressing exculpatory material."

"Why?"

"I know very little about clandestine operations, but I gather that the material is being held for eventual use against Sobatkin and possibly against Soviet Defense Minister Yaroshenko. In short, Quinn will remain a fugitive for the foreseeable future unless that transcript can be broken out and used."

Abrams leaned back in his chair and looked up at the high white ceiling. "I see the problem," he said after a while. "Quinn sacrificed."

"With no time limit. You understand international geopolitical machinations, I don't. But I did apprentice at Justice twenty-odd years ago. And once something is filed away, it can easily be forgotten. Meanwhile, Quinn Chance is out there somewhere, running, hiding, and I'm damned if I want it to go on. For all I know, Chance is dead by now."

Quietly Abrams said, "In Geneva he was very much alive."

"You saw him?" Jones gripped the arms of his chair, leaned forward.

"Several times—and that's a secret I'm entrusting to you. His appearance was somewhat altered and he was using another name. But he was alive and well."

"Thank God!"

"Without ladening you with details, Mr. Jones, I have to tell you

319

that Quinn is sought not only by the KGB but the Chinese intelligence service as well."

"Damn! Is he still in Geneva? Can I talk to him?"

"No. The Chinese involved him in something that came apart. With Chance dead they could plausibly deny involvement in the operation."

"And you don't know where he went."

"No. But I know that after Quinn left, the Chinese vanished, too."

"That adds a different and rather frightening dimension," Jones commented.

"And complicating," said Abrams.

Jones reflected for a few moments. "Do you speak Russian?"

"No, but one of my sons is a professor of Russian studies at George Washington. From time to time he's done translating for me. What do you have in mind?"

"Just thinking hypothetically, as lawyers do. If Berlikov had made a duplicate recording, in the right hands it could clear Chance." He looked away and seemed to be thinking aloud. "I don't work for Justice, the FBI, or the CIA. I work for Quentin Chance and my professional responsibility is to him, although I consider myself a loyal citizen."

"I'm sure you are, know you are. So we have, in effect, a Gordian knot situation—can't be untied, has to be cut."

"Exactly. And there might be a quiet way to do it."

"Like yourself, I have no law-enforcement responsibilities, but I like to see justice done," Abrams said. "If something occurs to me, would your counsel be available?"

"Certainly." From his pocket Jones removed a small object and placed it under a sheet of paper at the edge of Abrams's desk. Abrams seemed not to notice.

"Well, then," said Jones as he got up, "you've relieved my mind. I hope we'll stay in touch. Thank you for seeing me."

"My pleasure," Abrams said. They shook hands and walked to the door. He watched the lawyer go down the corridor floored with alternate squares of white and black marble to the broad staircase, closed the door, and returned to his desk.

He lifted the sheet of paper and saw a microcassette recording.

Picking it up, Abrams reflected that Wilson Jones was not a particularly subtle lawyer; he just understood how to get things done. He placed the cassette in an envelope, sealed it, and placed it in his breast pocket. He was dining with his son that evening.

As he settled behind his desk to study a memorandum, Abrams reflected that much as he would like to see Berlikov punished, it often happened that you had to trade something in order to get something of greater value.

And he wondered where Quinn Chance was.

FIFTY-FOUR

It was still dark in Chance's bedroom when Sofia wakened him. "Time to go."

He sat up groggily, blinked, and looked around. "You don't have to drive me all the way to Salzburg. I can take the bus from town."

"I'll feel better taking you. There's coffee and bread in the kitchen. I'll be waiting."

He looked at his watch: five o'clock. Farm days began early.

He had his ticket and Ruprecht's passport. Last night he had said good-bye to Uncle Klaus.

Dressed, he repacked his backpack and carried it down to the kitchen. "My plane doesn't leave for hours," he pointed out. "Why the early departure?"

Sofia was standing by the window looking out over the road. "Frankly, I don't trust my sister-in-law. Yesterday Mikela was asking all sorts of questions about you, in a nasty way. So it's just as well she thinks your name is Roger." Sofia turned to him. "Did something happen between the two of you?"

Chance sipped coffee and began buttering a slab of bread. "Nothing worth mentioning. While I was fishing, Mikela took a sunbath." He dripped farm honey onto his bread. "Why should anything have happened?"

"Because she can be vicious, Quinn. There's an unpleasant side to her that Ruprecht chooses to ignore."

"Well, she has no reason to act badly as far as I'm concerned." Just a third-degree case of hot pants, he thought.

Sofia looked out of the window again and came over to the table. "In town she's said to be flirtatious."

"She's very attractive. And men sometimes assume the wrong things because a woman is . . . open with them."

"That's true. But we expected you to stay much longer, then suddenly you had this urge to go."

"Wandering spirit," he said curtly, and finished his coffee. The angry barking of a dog rang out. From the window Sofia called, "Someone coming. Take your backpack and go down to the storm cellar—I'll tell you when it's safe to come out."

"What could happen?" he said, but he shouldered his backpack, went down the rear staircase, and stooped low to enter the storm cellar, closing the door behind him and setting the old wooden bar across it from inside.

By then he could hear a car engine nearing. It stopped, but the dog continued barking. From the other side of his door Sofia said, "It's Hunsacker, the policeman. Keep quiet."

Chance heard her opening the outside door. *"Morgen,"* she called. "What brings you by so early, Herr Hunsacker? We've had not even a sickle stolen of late."

"Grüss Gott, Fräulein Sofia. Humble pardon, but I must ask some questions." His footsteps clumped inside. "Is Pastor Herz awake?"

"No, thank heaven, for he worked much too late on Sunday's sermon and I'll not wake him for anything. Coffee?"

"Thank you, I will. Most folk in town are still sleeping." Quinn heard the squeak of a kitchen chair as the policeman settled himself at the table. "Ah, that's fine coffee . . . but here on the farm. . . ."

"Yes, our lives are ruled by our animals. But you said you have questions?"

"Unfortunately so—and I must say I'm embarrassed to have to ask them—but duty requires it."

"Please go on. You have me completely mystified. There, more sugar? Cream?"

"You're too kind, Fräulein. Well, to the point, then. Information was given to the effect that a refugee of some sort—illegal alien, fugitive—has been staying here."

"What a fascinating concoction," Sofia exclaimed. "Here—in the home of Pastor Herz? Is it alleged that my father is aiding some criminal? Surely the charge is all too reminiscent of the old days,

Herr Hunsacker, when gray-coated *kriminalpolizei* frightened everyone so during the war, when neighbor denounced neighbor and people disappeared in the dark of night." Her tone became bantering. "Here, handcuff my wrists and I'll go quietly—just don't waken my father."

"Fräulein, please, you know I could never do anything to frighten you. But here in my notebook it says that this person is an actual member of your family, a man from America named Roger. Is such a man in your home?"

"Herr Hunsacker, I swear that no person named—Roger, did you say?—is anywhere on Herz property. One moment, though—I had a cousin named Roger, but—wait please, and I'll look for information."

Chance heard her heels clatter on the floor above and wondered what she was up to. Presently her steps returned to the kitchen and Sofia said, "Here it is—an old article from the *Wiener Tageblatt*. See for yourself: My cousin Roger was murdered by Arab hijackers, terrorists. That's his body lying there after they threw it from his plane."

After a few moments Hunsacker said, "Fräulein—my humble apologies. I had no thought to revive grievous memories—forgive me."

"Of course, Herr Hunsacker, you are only carrying out your duties. Is there anything else?"

"There is, Fräulein. I would take it as a personal favor if you would not feel obliged to mention this . . . episode to Pastor Herz."

"Well, if he heard you arrive and asks me, I can't tell a lie."

"No, no, nor do I expect you to. But if he should *not* inquire?"

"Then the matter is between us, I promise."

"Thank you, Fräulein, and for your good coffee. I feel more badly about this than you can imagine." His heavy footsteps trudged toward the door. *"Wiedersehen."*

Chance heard the door close behind the policeman. In a few moments a car engine started, and as the sound faded away Sofia rapped on the cellar door. "It's safe now."

As Chance emerged blinking, she said, "You heard?"

"I heard."

324

"Only one person thought your name was Roger. That little bitch!"

"Well," he said reflectively, "you were right, Cousin."

"That my brother should be married to such a creature," she said angrily.

"Nothing's to be gained by telling Ruprecht," he pointed out, "so let's forget it. And you were magnificent."

"I was furious," she said, "and from Hunsacker my little sister-in-law will get a tongue-lashing she won't forget. Well, Cousin, it's time we were on our way. Just stay down out of sight as we go through the village, in case Hunsacker isn't in the barracks as he should be."

Dawn greeted them with pink-gray skies as they drove to Salzburg. Chance said, "I'll miss all this, you, the family, Ruprecht. You've been wonderful to me."

"You'll come back, Quinn? Promise?"

"I promise," he said, "though it can't be soon."

At the airport entrance Sofia drew over to the side of the road and asked, "What if that journalist comes again?"

He took pencil and paper from the glove compartment and wrote four names: Veronica Talbot Boyce, Wilson Jones, Antoinette Valcour, and Jan Abrams. "With all of these you may be frank, but with no one else. And you must talk to them in person, never by telephone."

"I'll remember." She tucked the paper into her handbag. "You were so tired when you came here; you look much better now. Still, it's a long flight. Will you be able to write?"

"I'll try," he said. "Give my love to your father and brother."

"And Mikela?" she said mischievously.

"The back o' me hand." He grinned. "I hope you and Harald will be very happy."

"And you must find happiness, too. May God go with you."

"And with you."

Chance went into the quiet airport, thinking how crowded it would be all during the summer Mozart Festival. He gave ticket and passport to an incurious clerk and checked his backpack.

After stamping the ticket and issuing a boarding pass, the clerk said, "You change in Vienna—one hour's delay." He looked at his watch. "Your flight will be called in an hour and fifteen minutes."

"Thank you." In the coffee shop he was the only customer, and he ordered mixed grill with eggs and potatoes. While he was breakfasting, morning papers from Salzburg and Vienna arrived and he bought them to read until boarding time.

Settled in a rear window seat, Chance reminded himself that from now on his name was Ruprecht Alois Herz and his destination San Carlos de Bariloche in the Argentine Andes. Purpose of trip? To visit Swiss-Austrian relatives he had not seen in many years.

The plane's jets screamed, and the aircraft soared steeply into the Alpine sun.

FIFTY-FIVE

In his private Kremlin office Marshal Yaroshenko pounded his desk. "An unmitigated disaster," he roared. "Five more men lost in Geneva, and Berlikov vanished. How do you explain it, Yevgeni Lubovich?"

Standing stiffly at attention before the minister of defense, General Sobatkin stared straight ahead. "The opposition was stronger than estimated, Comrade Minister."

"Obviously," he sneered. "Stronger and more intelligent. What have you to say to that?"

"Comrade Minister, I request that I be relieved from duties I was unable to perform."

"Oh, you'll be relieved, never worry. You must have frightened Berlikov into defecting; otherwise, why would he betray our Motherland? Bad management, Yevgeni Lubovich, very bad. On the face of it I judge that you need a refresher course in dealing with troops. Starting at the bottom, say, as guard-sergeant in one of the severe-regime camps—Magadan, for example, or Stalinogorsk or Kargopol. What is your opinion?"

Sobatkin swallowed. In all likelihood, that was where he would end up, but with death staring him in the face he thought he might as well defend himself.

"Comrade Minister, while I certainly deserve a dressing-down, I don't believe that I deserve such a *strogach*. Although it is quite true that bunglers lost their lives in Geneva and Nikolai Berlikov disappeared, the transcendent fact is that the Liberals have been foiled and defeated. There will be no rapprochement between the

327

Motherland and our Chinese enemies. Surely, there is satisfaction in that achievement—which was, after all, the goal of our undertaking."

"Nevertheless, Chance was in Geneva and slipped through your fingers again."

"One man. . . ." Sobatkin shrugged. "What does he know? What damage can he do? Compared to what was accomplished, Comrade Minister, he is nothing."

"The point," said Yaroshenko, "is that we don't know how much he *does* know—and what he can tell the world. I can't risk being compromised by a man you say knows nothing. And, of course, there is Berlikov to consider. That traitor knows everything."

"But can prove nothing."

Yaroshenko scratched the point of his chin. "Where is Berlikov?"

"The assumption is that he is in the hands of the Americans."

"Being interrogated, evaluated, telling everything. Already I understand he has compromised a large number of productive assets in America. Do you deny it?"

"No, Comrade Minister, the traitor Berlikov is destroying years of hard work in America."

"And that is only the beginning. Berlikov knows far too much of our work in Western Europe, our sabotage capabilities, our agents of influence. . . ."

"Warnings have been sent out, Comrade Minister. Damage will be contained. Once Berlikov and his family are located, punitive action can be taken."

Yaroshenko shook his head. "Exemplary punishment, eh? After the door is shut on an empty barn. I have to admire your optimistic spirit, Yevgeni Lubovich. You find a bright jewel in every cesspool. Incredible!"

Sobatkin paused a few moments before saying, "I have never found anything to be gained by negative thinking. Had our leader, Iosif Vissarionovich, succumbed to despair in the worst days of the Great Patriotic War, the siege of Stalingrad would never have been lifted."

Yaroshenko studied his subordinate's rigid face. "You are clever to invoke the example of Stalin. What you say of his fortitude is quite true and it is a national disgrace that our Council of Ministers is not imbued with his noble spirit." He shook his head. "Weaklings everywhere. The fires of war are essential to purge a nation's soul, Yevgeni Lubovich, remember that."

"That has always been my belief, Comrade Minister. Let weaklings drown in the healing flood of patriotic sacrifice."

Yaroshenko opened a desk drawer and removed an envelope. He slid the contents onto the desk top and shoved two color photographs toward Sobatkin. "The renegade Berlikov," he said, "caught in the act. Note the fear on his face, the film rolls in his dirty hands. Then this"—he pushed a small tape cassette at Sobatkin—"the traitor's confession. Naming you, Yevgeni Lubovich . . . and *me.*" His voice took on a menacing edge. "Have you any idea how this came into my hands? No? Then I will tell you it was mailed to me—here—in Moscow. What do you think of the provocation? Who is responsible?"

Sobatkin licked dry lips. "Just before leaving Ottawa I received a similar package, Comrade Minister. I brought it with me to show you."

"You did, did you? Then you must have formed an idea of the perpetrator. Quentin Chance?"

"That name occurred to me immediately," Sobatkin said, "but Chance was in Geneva."

"What is the alternative? The Americans—the FBI?"

"Perhaps," Sobatkin said, "but Berlikov had not yet defected."

"Sure of that?"

"Unless Berlikov has been a longtime FBI agent-in-place. If so, then he cooperated in this charade. The other possibility is that the Chinese are responsible."

"And the Chinese retain the original photographs and confession."

"Most probably, Comrade Minister."

"That was also my conclusion." He grimaced. "It is my belief that this material was sent as an impudent warning. Berlikov must be discredited, of course."

"Yes, Comrade Minister, the embassy is making the usual charges of embezzlement and demanding return of the criminal."

"With what result?"

"Thus far the Department of State denies any knowledge of the defector."

"You believe that?"

Sobatkin said, "I believe the Department of State may be ignorant of FBI and CIA machinations; there is a history of ill feeling between those organs. They distrust one another."

"With reason, eh? Well, Berlikov is hidden away by the Americans, but his fate is sealed. The Chinese have this material so compromising to us, which can be discredited along with Berlikov." He got up from his desk and went to a window. Gray clouds hung low over Kremlin towers; he could barely make out the river. There was thick mist over the parade ground below. Midafternoon, he thought, and the sun had yet to break through. With his back to Sobatkin, the defense minister growled, "Leaving Chance the one credible witness to everything. What do you propose to do about him, Yevgeni Lubovich?"

"Chance must be found and executed."

"With no mistakes this time." He turned to Sobatkin. "And who better fitted for that task than yourself?"

"*Me?*"

"Listen closely. I am giving you one final opportunity to redeem yourself, Yevgeni Lubovich. You are relieved of your Ottawa post—indeed, your replacement is on the way there now—freeing you to make a final effort to destroy our enemy. You know his character, his habits, and no one has a greater stake in his destruction than yourself. In short, comrade, it is you or he. If you fail, don't bother to return and report. We will find you. Understand?"

"I understand," he said hoarsely.

"If you want *spetznialniy* to assist you, I will assign them."

"No, Comrade Minister." He breathed deeply. "I have in mind an agent who is peculiarly suited to the task. Through him I am confident of success."

"It's your neck," Yaroshenko said harshly. "Leave Berlikov to me and the KGB. *You* are responsible for Quentin Chance. Dismissed!"

FIFTY-SIX

From Vienna, Chance's plane flew to Madrid for refueling before the long transatlantic flight to Recife on the bulge of Brazil. It stopped at São Paulo and Rio before terminating at Ezeiza international Airport in Buenos Aires.

Argentine *aduana* and *inmigración* inspectors gave Chance no difficulties, and although he spoke good Spanish, having served in Buenos Aires, he responded to questions in a mix of French and German compatible with his Alpine garb.

Argentina's principal airport looked grubbier and more disorganized than ever. Perhaps, he thought, public employees had been on one of their frequent strikes for higher pay. But Chance was glad to be there and felt reasonably confident that he had made the long journey undetected. Still, it was premature to lower his guard, for he had many miles to go.

He checked on flights to Bariloche, a thousand miles to the southwest, and bought a ticket on the flight departing midafternoon. Then he went to the lavatory and changed into street clothing from his backpack, which he repacked and stored in an public locker.

Noticing the airport's international telephone office, Chance weighed the risks of calling Toni and decided that even if Valcour's phone was tapped, eavesdroppers could not identify where the call originated. He wondered what she was doing, what plans she'd made, and wanted to reassure her that he was alive and well. And the sound of her voice would reassure him, too. The servant who answered at the mansion said that the princess had left Ge-

neva, and Chance broke the connection, feeling flat and dissatisfied. Well, there were things he had to do. He taxied to the center
of Buenos Aires, crossed the Plaza de Armas and entered *La
Nación*'s flatiron-shaped building. The advertising office was on the
street floor. There was a long wooden counter for composing ads,
and behind it heavy wire screening. He wrote a personal in French:

> Toni: Contact J.P. at
> Box P-451, *La Nación,*
> Buenos Aires

and passed it to the clerk via a recess in the counter. The ad was
to begin in a week and run for a month of sequential insertions in
La Nación, Rio's *O Globo,* and Cancún's *El Sol.* He told the clerk he
would telephone from time to time, paid, and walked three blocks
through busy streets to a large, well-stocked *armería* on Rivadavia.
La Porteña had been in business since 1857, and once Chance was
inside, the sight of well-stocked gun cabinets, the mixed scent of
tanned leather and gun lubricants stimulated a feeling of déjà vu
that cheered him. Here, at least, nothing had changed.

After browsing the length of the store, Chance bought a collaps-
ible fly rod and an assortment of flies, an Argentine-made 7.65-
millimeter Mauser rifle with a Zeiss 8-power scope and wooden
carrying case; two boxes of 150-grain rifle ammunition, and a box
of 9-millimeter cartridges for his Walther pistol. He selected a
quilted anorak and a pair of lined gloves, remembering that south
of the equator the seasons were reversed, and the Argentine autumn was beginning. Where he was going in the Andes, it would
be a lot colder than in sunny Buenos Aires.

The fire in La Cabaña restaurant warmed him as he ate a thick
churrasco grilled *a la parilla* and drank a half bottle of Valpolicella.
He remembered taking Carla there on one of their first dates and
how charmed she had been by the old restaurant's smoky atmosphere, the cowhides on the timbered walls, and the prosperous-
looking *bonarense* clientele. Now he was alone, a transient looking
for a place to hide, wondering whether what remained of his life
span would be measured in hours, days, or weeks.

At the airport he bought a bottle of locally bottled Old Smuggler scotch and checked his baggage through to San Carlos de Bariloche. Boarding the aircraft, he remembered his flight with Carla aboard an old lumbering Aerolineas DC-6, a flight that had taken five hours. This time his aircraft was a jet, flight time two hours.

He dozed over the flat, endless pampas, waking as the plane gained altitude to climb the eastern foothills of the cordillera. The plane swept low over fifty-mile-long Lake Nahuel Huapí for the benefit of first-time visitors and turned east to settle down on Bariloche's windswept landing strip, only slightly delayed by head winds.

Four other passengers left the plane with Chance, the others staying aboard for the final two-hundred-mile leg over the Andes's spine to Puerto Montt on the Pacific. Protected by his hooded anorak, Chance made his way to the small, one-story airport building, collected his baggage, and took a taxi to the Hotel Ansonia on the lakefront.

The mountainous setting reminded Chance of the Pacific Northwest, the Canadian Rockies, and almost any Alpine lake village in Switzerland or Austria. Thick pine forests covered steep slopes that led up from the lake to the high snow-covered razor-backed ridges of the Andes. There being few guests this time of year, Chance had his choice of hotel accommodations and selected a comfortable room with a fireplace that overlooked the lake.

Dinner was grilled lake trout, salad, and a cold bottle of Chilean Riesling. He slept ten hours and in the morning walked through the thin, cold air to the tourism office by the five-story stone tower that marked Bariloche's civic center.

A large catamaran was docked at the village pier while its twin was across the lake, sightseers looking out from behind the catamaran's windows. The vessels resembled cross-channel Hovercraft ferries, he thought, though without aisles for trucks and cars. Once you got to Bariloche, he reflected, there was nowhere else to go.

While buying fishing and hunting permits, Chance scanned bulletin boards for rental bungalows and chalets. He wanted a remote retreat, but not so far from Bariloche that getting supplies would be difficult. With help from the clerk he arranged to see four of the offerings through rental agents.

333

The rustic cabin Chance chose was of solid log-and-stone construction, the kind of chalet an affluent Swiss family might build near a favorite ski resort. Well insulated, the cabin was furnished with bedding, butane oven and range, cutlery, and a powerful shortwave receiver. Beside the rough stone fireplace half a cord of seasoned wood was piled, another two or three cords stacked outside. The cabin was set on a wooded hillside toward Cerro Otto, inland from the lake, but with an overview of Bariloche, eleven kilometers away. Chance rode back to town with the agent, paid two months rental in advance, and bought meats, vegetables, bread, canned goods, and liquor at the main market before taking possession of his new abode.

He started a fire, found the chimney drawing well, and went outside to sight-in his rifle before dark. The heft of the Mauser gave him a feeling of security; with it he could protect himself and his sanctuary.

He paced off 150 yards from the cabin porch and tacked a paper target to the trunk of an old pine tree. Retracing his steps, he set his rifle on a rustic table and, after ten rounds and four scope adjustments, was able to group the next six bullets within a three-inch circle. He noted prevailing wind, then went into his cabin and barred the door. While dinner cooked in the oven, Chance cleaned and oiled the Mauser, filled its magazine, and stood it on the floor beside his bed.

As he ate he listened to a music program from Paris, and when that ended he switched to news in French from Geneva. The OPEC ministers were holding an emergency meeting to curtail oil production and raise the world price of petroleum. Soviet-American nuclear reduction negotiations had ended without final agreement being reached but could resume sometime over the summer. That meant that Jan Abrams was back in Washington, doing whatever he did for the national security adviser. Two members of the British royal family were visiting Switzerland and would be coming to Geneva for a two-day stay during which time they would be feted by members of the international community.

Paul Valcour would probably be there, Chance thought, even if Albert had to push his wheelchair through the throng.

He found a Rome station broadcasting *Così fan tutte* and listened to the opera while he washed up. Feeling drowsy, he banked the fire and turned on the radiant heater set into the bedroom wall. While his bedroom warmed, Chance checked cabin windows to make sure they were locked, then propped a log under the handle of the back door. He did not think he was in danger that night, but he wanted to organize defensively, establish a security routine that would become automatic in days and nights ahead.

Before he fell asleep he listened to wind scraping pine boughs outside the cabin, and he decided to take rod and flies to a mountain stream that tumbled down the hillside and filled a shaded pool where brown trout were likely to be found. There were worse places to take refuge, he told himself, though loneliness would be his unavoidable companion. Perhaps Toni would notice his ad in her travels and manage to get in touch with him. If not, after a few months, when he felt it safe, he would go looking for her.

At least cousin-by-marriage Mikela wasn't around to tempt and betray him, the sly little fox. He thought of Natalya Yegorova, too, and wondered if she was safe in her homeland. She had blazed through his life like a comet whose brilliance burned in his memory. Perhaps he would see her again somewhere, someday. If he lived. His fingers probed under his pillow, felt the cold reassuring steel of his pistol.

During the night he was wakened by howling near his cabin. Sleepily, he thought it was a wolf, then realized it was a dog. He turned on the outside lights and saw a brown-and-black Alsatian baying at the moon. The dog's coat was burred and its flanks were so thin he could almost count its ribs.

From the refrigerator he took a steak and tossed it near the dog, who bolted it down in three gulps. Then, wagging its skinny tail, it walked over to Chance. There was a frayed collar around its neck, and he figured the famished animal had been abandoned when its owners left Bariloche after the summer season. Chance let the dog in, poured a bowl of water, and led it to the warm hearth.

If no one else wanted the Alsatian, he did. He saw the dog settle down on a rug before the embers and knelt to stroke its head. The dog's tail thumped happily. "Your name is Wolf," Chance said

335

aloud, "and I'm glad you came by. I need you as much as you need me, and tomorrow we'll get to know each other."

In a better frame of mind, Chance went back to bed. He had a companion now.

BOOK FIVE

FIFTY-SEVEN

In addition to other duties, Jan Abrams served as NSC representative on a National Foreign Intelligence Board panel that met periodically to coordinate National Intelligence Estimates prepared by the Central Intelligence Agency. At Langley headquarters a large, airy, well-lighted room on the seventh floor was used for the panel's deliberations. Representatives grouped around the long boat-shaped mahogany table came from State, Defense, DIA, NSA, and (by sufferance) the FBI. The top secret NIE under discussion was titled *The Future of Sino-Soviet Relations,* and Abrams had given his draft copy considerable thought since receiving it four days earlier. It was a significant paper, Abrams had reflected, since it could be the basis for a change in U.S. policy.

Mark Ramey had been entrusted by the deputy director for intelligence with honchoing the estimate through the coordination process. He sat at one end of the conference table bright-eyed, clean-shaven, wearing a gray flannel suit across the vest of which hung his Amherst Phi Beta Kappa key. Abrams, who had studied at Uppsala, Cambridge, Fribourg and Utrecht, serious European universities, maintained a reserved opinion of American higher education but listened politely to what its alumni had to say.

The meeting's first half hour had been taken up with nitpicking changes in punctuation and semantic substitutions, but so far none of the conferees had challenged the thrust of the estimate, and Ramey felt greatly relieved. He glanced at the wall clock, hoping everyone would sign off in another half hour and he could get down to Fort Belvoir for the next segment of General Berlikov's interrogation.

"What we're saying here," Ramey reprised, "bottom line—is that sooner or later Red China and the Soviet Union are going to reconcile. When that takes place the Soviet Union will feel less threatened militarily and able to invest military savings in the production of deficit consumer goods. That will appease the population and enable the leadership to calculate the benefits of relaxing Communist rule."

"Which," countered the Defense Intelligence Agency representative, a white-haired lieutenant colonel wearing a lime green shirt, white-on-white tie, and a loud plaid jacket, "they can't do. Their economy and goods distribution system depends on strong central control, the antithesis of a free-market economy. The solution we should be pressing on the Sovs, like it or not, is abandoning their economic dogma, revoking Communist theory." He looked around belligerently.

Ramey swallowed. "However fruitful such a policy might eventually be," he countered, "it is unrelated to the thrust of this estimate, which is to encourage Sino-Soviet détente."

Jan Abrams declared ponderously, "I believe our colleague has a point. I for one feel it premature to encourage or discourage ideological reconciliation between China and the Soviet Union. The U.S.S.R. is politically exhausted, power centers fragmenting. Meanwhile, China, you may be certain, is watching with glee and anticipation." He blinked and adjusted his heavy glasses. "Whether China takes advantage of that exhaustion is well beyond our powers to influence."

"Fair enough, Jan, as far as analysis goes," Ramey said irritably. "What positive action should we be taking?"

"Well, since you ask, Mark," said Abrams with a reptilian smile, "my opinion is that our best course is to do nothing. The Soviet Union has been heading toward self-destruction since 1917. Let the process continue; let socialism be thoroughly discredited, its pieces fall where they may. Then perhaps we, along with other Western democracies, can combine to rescue the people rather than the system. Ultimately I envision a new alignment whereby a democratic Soviet Union is integrated economically, and, yes, militarily, with Europe and the U.S. That, of course, is not an immediate prospect, but one worth strategic consideration."

The DIA representative said, "But I foresee a point at which the Red Army, frustrated during all this *perestroika* and arms reduction, may attempt a power grab. Whether or not that happens, the Chinese military faction may view the situation as opportune to move against the U.S.S.R. Shouldn't we be sending the PRC an unmistakable signal against intervention?"

The State representative, a former political science professor at Bryn Mawr, sat forward. "A warning?" she asked.

Jan Abrams said mildly, "Let the PRC interpret it as they will. But I am more concerned over the possibility of joint Chinese and Soviet action. Their ideological bonds are strong and will remain so until communism no longer dominates the Kremlin."

The DIA representative pointed out, "That touches on an area of great concern within the Pentagon, the strategic order-of-battle implications should Russia and Red China reach an accommodation. Fifty years ago the Nazi-Soviet Pact allowed Hitler to sweep across Europe. What are the parallel implications if Russia is relieved of pressure of its eastern borders?"

Mark Ramey frowned. "The Agency consensus is that we should accept Sino-Soviet détente—when it comes—as enhancing the prospects for world peace. Naturally, you military people are concerned about—"

"—not only Soviet aggressiveness," the DIA man interjected. "I fought in Korea. We didn't expect Chinese intervention and we paid for that illusion—they damn near whipped our butts."

His Department of Defense superior nodded. "Our position is that any military alliance between Russia and China poses a tremendous threat to the West. I can't sign off on this for the secretary. Sorry, folks."

Mark Ramey blinked. The whole estimate was coming apart as he sat there. "Doesn't anyone feel it's worthwhile giving peace a chance?" he pleaded.

Jan Abrams said, "Neville Chamberlain tried that with results so horrible the world can never forget. Again, I think more attention has to be paid to Soviet intentions. What are they likely to do vis-à-vis the West if their eastern frontier is secured by treaty?"

"Well," said Ramey, feeling betrayed by a onetime CIA colleague, "we don't know that, of course. But this is an all-source estimate, Jan. Everything we have has gone into it. The estimate is as comprehensive as possible."

Abrams eyed him coolly. "All-source? It included Sachem material?"

Ramey felt his throat go dry. "I'm not authorized to discuss Sachem," he muttered. "Anyway, how did you—?" He broke off.

Abrams said, "In this forum we shouldn't discuss sensitive clearance levels, but until I'm convinced that the estimate includes Sachem-derived intelligence, I recommend the draft be put on hold. Failing that, I have to withhold concurrence in the NIE as drafted."

The State representative complained, "I've got sky-high clearances and I've never heard of Sachem." She glared at Ramey and tapped her fountain pen irritably on the mahogany table.

"Neither have I," said the Defense representative, "but Mr. Abrams's reservations sound valid to me."

"Likewise," said the DIA man. "There's no rush anyway. I don't know of any moves toward Sino-Soviet rapprochement—though I may be uninformed."

Mark Ramey looked around the table. NSA hadn't said anything pro or con, and the FBI had no vote anyway. Nor had he. Three negatives and the NIE was torpedoed. Damn Abrams, he thought, who the hell told *him* about Sachem? Reluctantly, he said, "That being the consensus, I withdraw the NIE from current consideration. Leave your copies with me and my people will have another go at it. Thanks for attending."

Panel members rose and piled their drafts on the table beside Ramey. Abrams was the last to surrender his copy, and when the two of them were alone in the room Ramey said, "That was tacky, Jan."

"Not when the Agency's withholding evidence," Abrams returned pleasantly.

"But Sachem material won't be available to the estimate process for . . . months anyway. A lot of work went into this estimate and it's useless now."

Abrams said, "A lot of work went into the Maginot Line. Take our consensus to heart, Mark, and next time you say *all-source* make sure it's the truth." Briefcase in hand, Abrams left the conference room.

At noon Abrams went over to the White House mess, drank a chilled manhattan and ordered the chef's low-cal special—cottage cheese and broiled lamb chop. He drank a glass of skim milk and ordered a pool car to take him to the Smithsonian's Air and Space Museum on Independence Avenue. At one o'clock he reached the lunar landing module and waited there until he saw Harold Josephson coming toward him. A short, plump, balding man, Josephson was a senior editor of the *Washington Times,* had been deputy USIA director in the prior administration, and was an old friend of Abrams. They shook hands as if meeting by coincidence and strolled down one of the galleries to a corner, where they halted as though to admire the glassed-in exhibit of lunar rocks. "What's the mystery, Jan?" asked Josephson. "I was all set to buy you a power lunch at the Ebbitt Grill, but no go."

"I'm about to become a confidential source—if you'll have me."

"Hell yes. On what subject? Cabinet changes?"

Abrams said, "Occasionally there come times when the interests of government and the rights of an individual collide. In such instances, Harold, where does morality lie?"

"Why, with the individual, of course." Josephson's eyes narrowed. "Jan, you're not in trouble—victimized by some scurvy intrigue?"

"Not yet," he replied, "though a friend of mine is. I'm sure the murder of Pavel Sosnowski is fresh in your mind?"

Josephson nodded. "Your friend, then, would be Quentin Chance. Should I be taking notes, Jan?"

"Let me tell you the story; then you decide what to do with it." As they strolled into the courtyard he told the newspaperman all he knew and, unobserved, passed him several typed sheets.

"Berlikov's recordings?" Josephson asked.

"A bootleg copy of the transcript. No classification on it as on the original. Justice, CIA, and FBI propose to suppress this information while they figure out how useful it might be against General Sobatkin and Marshal Yaroshenko. They may never reach a consensus—or if they do, figure the time's not right." He paused.

343

"Meanwhile, Chance remains a fugitive from justice, as well as from the Russians and the Chinese."

"What about Berlikov?"

"He's in safe hands. The Russians know he's telling us everything he knows, so there's no compromise problem. Sobatkin, of course, doesn't know about the clandestine recording, nor does Marshal Yaroshenko. But as leverage against them its value is considerably reduced because covert negotiations between Russian and Chinese Liberal factions were broken off. Not a bad development, really, because it's clear Yaroshenko is playing some kind of convoluted double game using Sobatkin to smoke out the opposition."

"Huh?" Josephson scratched his head. "Could you clarify, please?"

"When Yaroshenko has identified the Liberal ministers, he can evaluate their strength and decide whether to join them or stay put. An old hand as crafty as Yaroshenko is always going to have a fallback position prepared. Basic military strategy."

"Making Sobatkin expendable."

"He always was."

They walked farther around the perimeter until Josephson said, "Jan, obviously you've given all this a lot of thought. Any suggestions?"

"You could write a general story, attributing it to a highly placed Soviet source. Leave out Sobatkin and Yaroshenko's names and take it to Justice for comment."

"Just comment?"

"Well, you might tell Tom Levitt you'll publish it with agonizing details unless Chance is publicly cleared."

"Levitt, huh? I could do that. Of course he'll be outraged, give me a red-faced lecture on media responsibility to national security. Then I'll ask him what my story reveals that the Soviets don't already know."

"Exactly," Abrams said approvingly, patting him on the back. "And what you'll get out of it is an exclusive on Chance's rehabilitation. File related information away for future background use."

They left the building together and walked along Independence

Avenue. Josephson said, "I'll work it out, Jan; leave it to me to see justice served. But what if suspicion falls on you?"

Abrams shrugged. "I'm expendable. If I have to leave before I'm ready, that's a worthwhile trade-off."

Josephson smiled. "Thought that's what you'd say. But they'll never hear your name from me."

"That's why I came to you."

Josephson looked at his watch. "Okay, confidential source, I want to start working on this while everything's fresh. And I'll get an appointment with Assistant Attorney General Levitt in the next couple of days. The story'll hit him like a megabomb."

"That's the idea," Abrams said. They shook hands and took separate taxis back to their offices.

At two o'clock Abrams went in to the national security adviser and told him in general terms why the NFIB panel had declined to concur in the Agency's latest NIE. On the way back to his office Abrams thought about Quentin Chance, hoping he'd be alive to hear the good news when it came.

FIFTY-EIGHT

As Chance hoped, Wolf turned out to be a good companion. After removing burrs and ticks from the dog's coat, Chance cut away matted patches, bathed the Alsatian, and accepted a thorough face-licking in the same spirit.

The stream-fed pool proved home to a reliable supply of one- to two-pound trout, and Chance fished each day, freezing what he did not cook for lunch or dinner. As autumn deepened, snow crept down the slopes of El Tronador, the mountain looming majestically to the west, its saddle peak twelve thousand feet above the level of the lake. Wolf fattened and his coat thickened and grew sleek. Chance took him regularly into the hillside forests where the big Alsatian chased ground squirrels, field mice, and hares. When Chance carried his Mauser they hunted together, Chance improving his marksmanship on large ravens perched in distant trees, thinking that one day—or night—he might have to steady the cross hairs on a human figure.

Early one morning, as they went up the hill, Wolf picked up a scent and bounded off, disappearing through high grass into aspens at the forest edge. Presently, Chance heard Wolf barking, halted, and saw a deer bound over windfall and pause to sniff the wind. Shouldering the Mauser, Chance dropped the buck with a single bullet through the neck, and as he walked toward the deer Wolf appeared, barking approvingly. The dog settled down to watch Chance gut the young buck and to devour his share of liver, heart and warm entrails.

Chance hung the carcass on the rear porch and skinned it. Then he scraped flesh, fat, and sinew from the soft hide, and salted and stretched the skin against the cabin wall to cure in wind and sun. Dressed, the carcass yielded more than forty pounds of loins, steaks, chops, and haunches. Chance, who had learned early in life to appreciate the delicate flavor of wine-marinated venison, considered the buck a gift from the mountain gods.

For five weeks Chance let his beard grow, to protect his face from sun and wind and so he would look more like Ruprecht's passport photo. Chopping wood and climbing the steep foothills restored muscle tone, and he felt more physically alive than he had in years.

Twice a week he hiked into Bariloche for supplies, to buy reading material, and to telephone Buenos Aires to see if Toni had replied. He left Wolf to guard the cabin, confident that his dog was up to the job. As his sixth week of isolation began, Chance bought fresh vegetables at the town market and walked over to the *Telégrafos y Teléfonos* office to place his customary call to *La Nación*. The connection was poor, but he was able to hear the ad clerk saying that, yes, a letter had been received for him. Almost incredulous, Chance said, "Mailed from where?"

"Buenos Aires, señor."

"Please open it and read it to me." His heart was pounding as he waited.

The clerk read: " 'I don't usually pray, but I am praying you will receive this. Until I hear from you I'll wait at the Hotel Palacio. All my love. Toni.' "

"Thank you," Chance said. "Thank you very much. Now, could you give me the telephone number of the Palacio?"

"Certainly, señor, one moment." Chance wrote down the number, thanked the clerk again, and had the operator place the call.

A maid answered the phone in Toni's suite. Chance identified himself as Señor Duroc, and in a few moments heard Toni's excited voice. "Darling, this is the most wonderful day of my life! Where *are* you?"

He thought quickly. "Go down to the hotel telephone office and I'll call you there in ten minutes."

"But why, *chéri?*"

"In case your room phone is tapped. They can't cover an entire

347

switchboard. Tip the head operator and stand by. Ten minutes?"

"Less, oh, much less."

Ten minutes later Chance instructed, "Listen carefully, I want you to buy walking boots and cold-weather clothing, light but very warm. From your room take only a small bag of essentials—a purse would be better—and leave the hotel without checking out. Go to a travel agency—not the hotel's—and buy a ticket on the afternoon flight to Bariloche in some other name. Change taxis a couple of times and get to Ezeiza in time for the flight. I'll meet you here."

"But my baggage?"

"We'll take care of it later."

"I'll do everything you say, and I can't wait to see you."

"I've missed you," he said, throat tight. "Be on the plane."

He broke the connection and paid for his calls. Then he walked back to his cabin and began cleaning it. If her flight came in on time, she would be landing in just six hours.

At the airport, Chance felt his pulse racing as though he were waiting for his first date. The flight was delayed half an hour and landed on the bleak airstrip just before dark. Five passengers deplaned, Toni one of them. She rushed into his arms and they embraced as an oriental man walked by, noticeable because he was wearing a gray topcoat and a black astrakhan. Chokingly, she said, "I've missed you so. I was in Rio when I saw your ad and came to B.A. immediately." She drew back and scanned his face. "You look marvelous, Quinn."

"You know my name. Paul?"

"Natalya. We had a long talk that morning. . . . It seemed so strange to learn about the man I love from a . . . a near stranger."

"Thank God I can drop the pretense," he said. "And no more secrets from you."

"Ever?" She snuggled against him.

"Ever," he said, and they walked to where the baggage was arriving. Toni had a single Adidas bag that Chance carried to his waiting taxi.

As they were getting into the taxi the oriental passenger came up to them and asked, "Pardon me, could you recommend a good hotel in Bariloche?"

"The Edelweiss is quite good," Chance replied, "and the Ansonia a notch down."

"Thank you." He looked around the deserted drive. "There seem to be no taxis available. Would you mind letting me ride into town?"

"Of course. Get in." The man's face was round, his skin the shade of old vellum.

Chance sat between Toni and the Oriental, wondering how the man knew he spoke English and what an Oriental was doing in this remote part of the world. Was he Japanese, Korean . . . Chinese? Chance's left elbow pressed his shoulder-holstered pistol, whose hardness reassured him. He removed his right arm from around Toni's quilted après-ski jacket, but as the taxi drove west over the dark lakeside road he wondered if he wasn't overly apprehensive. As Bariloche's scant lighting came into view the man spoke again. "You chose an excellent place to hide, Mr. Chance."

Chance turned to face him. "You must be mistaken," he said, feeling his stomach freeze.

"No, I think I am quite correct, having followed Madame Valcour from Geneva." His bland expression was unrevealing.

Toni gasped and Chance said, "You've come a long way. I suppose you'll tell me why."

The man nodded. "Despite your abrupt and somewhat violent departure from Geneva, Hsiao Kuan-hua felt you had acted in good faith, and, no, don't reach for your gun if that's what you're doing. I mean you no harm." He showed Chance empty hands. "Now, if you will permit me to give you something, my mission will come to a close."

"What is it?"

"Hsiao instructed me to give it only to you. A tape recording of General Nikolai Berlikov confessing his role in the murder of Pavel Sosnowski. Ah, may I?"

"Slowly," Chance said. "Very slowly."

One hand reached inside the man's coat pocket and brought out a small envelope. Giving it to Chance, the man said, "Compliments of Hsiao Kuan-hua and the People's Republic of China."

Taking it, Chance said, "My thanks to Mr. Hsiao," and passed it to Toni. The taxi drove around behind the civic center and pulled up in front of the Hotel Edelweiss. The Chinese agent got out, took his bag from the front seat, and said politely, "Good night, then, to both of you."

"Good night." They watched him walk into the hotel, and Toni sighed in relief.

Chance told the driver where next to go and kissed Toni. "To think I had no idea I was being followed all this way," she said, "but now I remember noticing him on the flight from Geneva."

"Hsiao's people are very competent," Chance said. "For a moment, though, I thought the gift might be a bullet."

"So did I."

"Fortunately for us, Hsiao follows the Celestial Way."

The taxi drove up the graveled road to the cabin, which Chance had left lighted inside and out. As he paid the driver he heard Wolf barking furiously inside. Toni said, "You have a dog?"

"He's a good pooch and a good companion. You'll like him." He carried her bag to the porch and unlocked the door. Wolf bounded out, prancing on hind legs as he tried to lick Chance's face. Toni knelt and beckoned the Alsatian to her, stroking his muzzle and speaking softly until Wolf calmed down and began licking her gloved hand. Then they all went into the cabin.

Chance lighted the log fire and showed Toni the bedroom. While she was unpacking he daubed garlic oil on two trout and set them under the broiler, then filled two glasses with chilled Riesling.

When Toni appeared she was wearing a black jogging suit with red stripes. He said, "I hope you like this place because we're going to be here awhile."

She looked around appreciatively. "I'm sure I'll love it." She took his hands and pressed them. "Quinn—I must get used to your name—do you realize this is the first time we've been alone in . . . months? And in our own place for the first time, too. No Paul, no Sam and Lao-li, just us." He kissed her lips, gave her a glass of wine, and drew her to a rustic poncho-covered sofa facing the fire.

"Just us," he echoed.

"And Wolf."

He nodded. "Our trusty watchdog." They were sitting side by side, feeling the fire's warmth, sipping wine and communicating silently, finally secure after flight and separation, the stress of their unexpected encounter with the Chinese agent. Moodily, Toni asked, "Won't Berlikov's confession clear you, let you go home whenever you want?"

He glanced over at Wolf curled contentedly on his pad. "The Soviets," he said matter-of-factly, "aren't as indulgent as the Chinese, and they never give up."

"I see." She walked to the fireplace, face troubled. "I thought . . . hoped," she sighed, "but I'm not going to worry about that, not now that I've finally found you. If necessary, we'll stay here forever." Her nose wrinkled. "Smells good. You can even cook. I *knew* you were a find."

"I was a bachelor for a long time," he said, and sipped the dry wine. "My wife . . ."

"I know. Paul told me about Carla. I—I'm so sorry, Quinn." She kissed the side of his face. "You've gone through so much."

"I loved her," he said simply, and left to turn the trout. He showed her the vegetable bin and suggested she make salad. Hesitantly, Toni said, "Will you show me how? Truth is I know nothing about kitchens or how to prepare food." Her face brightened. "But I learn fast."

"No big thing," he replied, scraped carrots and cucumbers, and sliced them with tomatoes and crisped lettuce. Toni's eyes crinkled. "That's all there is to it?"

"Oil and lemon in the fridge."

After they sat at the round, Formica-topped table Chance asked, "How long ago did you talk to Paul?"

"From the airport. Ezeiza."

"Today?"

She nodded. "I knew he'd be anxious about you. Quinn, you look so *grim*. Did I do wrong? Surely we can trust my brother."

"I hope so," he said slowly, "but he's an odd bird, with some strange associations."

"But you two were friends for years."

"Friendships can change." He looked away.

"I refuse to worry about Paul betraying us," Toni said lightly,

"God, you saved his life. So, let's put it aside—at least for tonight."

Chance smiled. "We'll do that, for tonight."

"And you'll tell me everything that's happened since Geneva? Everywhere you've been?"

"Of course."

"Having our future in mind, I found a place in Cuernavaca and optioned it subject to your approval. And a rather nice condo in Cancún, on the beach."

"Any more trouble from Mohammed?"

She shook her head. "I read he's remarried, an Italian actress this time."

He raised her hand and kissed her fingertips. "I want you to marry me, but in Latin America it's not easy. You need birth certificates, lots of documentation I don't have. So if you can be patient . . ."

"I can wait forever, so long as we're together."

After dinner they sat arm in arm before the fireplace and Toni said softly, "I feel whole again, being with you, Quinn. Before you I never knew what it was to love someone."

He stroked her hair and gazed into the fire. "I want to cherish you and protect you, and for that we're going to have to take precautions—be alert to strangers, limit our trips to the village." He gestured at Wolf nodding on his carpet. "He'll warn us of prowlers."

"Then you're serious about Paul—I mean—"

"I admired him for a long time, then he became—corrupt. In a given situation I don't know what he'd do. . . . Bottom line, I can't trust him."

"Well, I think you're wrong about my brother, but it's your judgment I trust." She sighed. "I've been thinking about Natalya. Have you heard from her? Know where she is?"

He shook his head. "Why?"

"Mainly because she saved our lives that dreadful night, and—"

"Hey, you did plenty, too."

She shrugged. "Inspired, I guess. She told me she might have to leave Russia but wanted to stay as long as she could."

"She shouldn't wait too long," he said soberly. "Too many have lost their lives delaying—hoping for change that never comes."

"I know. And I told Talya I'd help her however I could."

"How will she let you know?"

"She'll send a postcard showing Moscow University, then go to Leningrad and wait." She kissed him. "Don't you agree we should help if she needs it?"

"I do. She's safe as long as Ligachev has power. But when he goes, watch for that postcard."

"She said as much, and that the CIA would be glad to have her."

"No question about it. She'd be a valuable asset to any intelligence service. And she knows ours pays better."

"Well, I'm glad you agree. Now tell me how you left Geneva and where you've been all this time. Including your Chinese connection."

Their lovemaking was tentative at first as they explored each other's bodies, renewing familiarity and gaining confidence in the fullness of love. Toni fell asleep almost at once, and as he looked at her calm face he tried to accept her equanimity about their future together.

His head turned on the pillow until he was facing the window. A horned moon rose above the foothills, and as he watched the wind-stirred trees he thought that he would have to make a stand sometime, someplace. He was tired of running, so it might as well be here.

On his terms, not theirs.

FIFTY-NINE

In the morning Chance built another fire to warm the cabin and made coffee. He fed Wolf and let him out to roam the hillside. When Toni appeared Chance fried eggs and bacon and they breakfasted before the fire. Afterward he watched Toni trying to clean dishes, cutlery, and frying pan with a bar of hand soap; then he intervened. From the fireplace he scooped ashes into the pan, scoured away the fat, and rinsed the skillet. He partly filled the sink with hot water and sprinkled it with soap flakes, stirring into foam, then finished the job. As he dried his hands Toni said ruefully, "I'm just no help at all."

"Tricks to every trade," he said gently, and while she refilled their coffee cups he said, "I think you should settle on the Cuernavaca house and the Cancún condo."

She eyed him. "So we can have servants?"

"That, but I'd rather spend the winter in sunny Mexico than snowbound in Bariloche, wouldn't you?"

"All things being equal, yes—but they're not. Oh, you're so transparent, Quinn. You think there's danger and you want me safely away, isn't that it?"

Chagrined, he thought for a moment. "I'm reasonably sure I can take care of myself but not so confident I can protect you, too. I'll join you in Mexico."

She shook her head. "Uh-uh. I'd go crazy worrying about you. No, absolutely not. If there's danger, we'll face it together. This is where I belong—with you."

He gazed at the leaping flames. "Remember what happened to

Paul and Maurice? Two specialists killed three men and two dogs and walked away without a scratch. Suppose *spetznialniy* start shooting up this cabin? Or lie up in the woods and pick us off?" He shook his head. "We've seen what they can do, we know it's possible."

"Even so, I know how to shoot."

"What have you shot?"

"Pigeons, quail. . . ."

"With what?"

"A four-ten and a twenty gauge."

"That's shotgunning and we don't have a scattergun. What I have is a scope-mounted rifle and a semiautomatic pistol."

"You can't use both simultaneously. That leaves one for me."

He drank the last of his coffee and looked at her. "There's a noon flight to Buenos Aires."

"I won't be on it. Quinn, you're four kinds of bastard even to think I'd go. Suppose I went and something happened to you—could I ever forgive myself? Besides, I want you to teach me how to cook, and there'll never be a better opportunity."

"That's the clincher," said Chance with a grin. "But before culinary class comes pistol drill." Using fireplace charcoal, Chance outlined a man-size figure on a sheet and tacked it to the side of the cabin. Then on the porch table he field-stripped the Walther, explaining its features and showing her how to insert the magazine and chamber a shell.

After pacing fifty feet from the target, Chance demonstrated standing and kneeling fire and refilled the magazine. "Snap shooting is for the movies," he told her. "You should grip the pistol firmly in your right hand, support the butt with your left, and sight on the target. Squeeze the trigger slowly, without jerking and ruining the sight picture. Resight and fire again. When the magazine's empty the slide stays back exposing the barrel as I showed you. Okay?"

He stood behind her, steadying her arms while she slowly emptied the magazine at the target. Checking it, he said, "Out of nine shots, you hit four vital zones. The last five went over his head because recoil lifts the weapon with each shot. So make the first two count. Reload and try again. Aim for belly and chest."

"This pistol kicks like a camel," she complained, licking her right hand.

"The cartridges are high-power. It's a killing machine, Toni, not a backyard toy. Now load the magazine."

He kept her at it for two hours, then said, "Enough for lesson one. Let's go catch some trout."

"I'm not sure I can hold a rod."

"Try." He shouldered the Mauser by its leather sling and took her down to the shaded pool.

In the afternoon Chance and Toni went to the town telephone office, where she placed a call to the Palacio desk and asked the hotel concierge to pack her clothing and store the bags. She would retrieve them and pay her bill on returning from a friend's *estancia* near Córdoba.

Chance bought more ammunition while Toni shopped for supplies, and then they took a taxi back to the cabin.

They made love in the quiet bedroom, slept until evening, and then Chance showed Toni how to prepare and broil trout they had caught that morning. She peeled and sliced potatoes for frying, and competently made salad. Chance cooled and opened their wine, and they dined by the fireplace.

Each day began with pistol instruction, and after a week Toni could handle the weapon safely and with reasonable accuracy. Living together deepened their intimacy and soon he told her of his youth, his life with CIA and Carla, the love he felt for his parents and brother and the shattering impact of their deaths on his life.

"You'll want to go back to Charlottesville, won't you?" she said as they headed to the cabin with the day's catch.

"I'm not sure. Studying, teaching were palliatives for me. Perhaps I've outgrown the need. Anyway, I can't quite picture you as a faculty wife."

"I'll be whatever you want me to be, Quinn. You know that."

"I think a month of watching me prepare lectures and mark exams would drive you up the wall."

"You don't want to return to CIA?"

"Not after being disavowed—I'll always be bitter about that."

"And have every right to be. They never gave you a chance to explain about Sosnowski."

"They didn't want to hear it—simple as that."

For a while she was silent; then she said, "Please tell me the truth. Was Paul wrongly accused of killing those blacks and stealing the gold?"

"The truth," he said, "is I don't know. I know what my findings were and what Paul told me, but there's no way to reconcile the two. There's insufficient evidence for the Agency to press charges, go into court against him. Paul's always known that."

"Then you don't mind if I give my brother the benefit of the doubt?"

"You're entitled to."

"Even if you won't?"

He kissed her. "We've exhausted the topic. Now, let's marinate some venison and grill it on a stake the way gauchos do."

"How's that?"

"Watch."

Later that evening, while Toni was washing dinner dishes, Chance heard Wolf growling and barking furiously outside. He went to a frosted window, looked out, and saw Paul Valcour walking slowly up the drive.

SIXTY

Toni asked, "Who is it?"

Chance closed the window blind. "Your brother."

"Paul? How wonderful!" She put down her pistol and started for the door, but Chance held her back. "I'll handle this."

"You mean—? I don't understand. Surely he can come in."

Chance strapped on his sheath knife and picked up his Mauser. He drew the bolt and chambered a shell. "Get the pistol," he told her.

"What *is* it with you? That's my brother out there, not some assassin!"

"Get the pistol," he repeated, and opened the door a crack.

Valcour was wearing a short camel-hair coat, gloves, a muffler, and a tweed cap. Wind flapped flannels around his legs. He halted, held at bay by the menacing Alsatian. Cupping his hands, he shouted, "Hello, there. Anyone home?"

"State your business," Chance called back.

"Business? Why, I want to see you two lovebirds. Call off your dog—it's cold out here."

"Go back, Paul. The altitude's bad for your lung."

"Oh, I feel fine, just damn cold. Toni there?"

"She's knitting. Too busy to see you but sends her love." Behind him Toni exploded. "Damn you! If you won't let Paul in, I'm going out there!"

Turning, Chance said, "Keep going, then. It's him or me, babe. Decision time."

"I can't believe you're afraid of my brother."

"I'm not—just of his friends."

She peered around Chance's shoulder. "He's alone."

"I don't expect them to come marching up four abreast for inspection. Going or staying?"

She backed away. "I'll get the pistol."

Cupping gloved hands again, Valcour shouted, "What's the problem, Quinn?"

"You know the problem, Paul, known it all along."

"I can't believe this is the same old Quinn Chance I knew."

"It's the same Quinn—not the same Paul Valcour. Go back, Paul, you're not well. Get out of it while you can."

Valcour's arms dropped weakly to his sides. "Let Toni come out."

"She prefers my company."

"So you've been telling her about me, have you? Lying about me? Hell of a thing, Quinn, not gentlemanly at all."

"I've told her nothing," Chance called back. "Go away, Paul, back to Geneva."

Tautly, Toni said, *"What* haven't you told me?"

Chance set his teeth. "Paul's been a Soviet agent for fucking years—*that's* what he doesn't want you to know."

"I don't believe it!"

"Well, he forced it out of me. You think he came alone?"

"Yes!"

"Stand clear." He pushed her aside, stood behind the jamb, and flung the door open.

Within two seconds a bullet whined in followed by a distant *crack*. Toni gasped. A second bullet whistled in and another sharp *crack* echoed. Chance kicked the door shut and locked it. "That should answer some questions," he said. "Now, turn off all inside lights and put on the outside floods. Hurry."

He was sitting beside the door, rifle between his knees, when she came back through the firelight. Another rifle shot, but Chance heard no impact. He peered through a window and saw Wolf lying motionless on the drive. *"Damn them!"* he groaned as Paul cut slowly across the field toward the cover of trees. "That dog was worth more than any of them."

Toni was sobbing. Chance said, "Time for that later. They may

359

try to get in, so cover the back of the house. I'll take this section." In the kitchen he filled a pot and doused the fire. Toni was walking between the bedrooms, pistol in hand.

He went to the kitchen door and pushed it open. No rifle fire. He closed the door and locked it.

Out there was one rifleman he knew of. How many more? Even if Valcour couldn't move fast, he could shoot. Two enemies, minimum.

Chance went into a bedroom, lay on the floor, and with the rifle muzzle poked on the room light. A bullet shattered the windowpane, slammed into the wall above his head. He cut off the light and got up. Same marksman? Could have shifted position, he told himself; that's what I'd do. He went quickly to the front door and opened it.

No answering shot.

Was the movement unseen or was the shooter holding fire, having been suckered thrice before? How the hell many out there? The cabin was getting cold, but outside it was one hell of a lot colder. Would they go back to Bariloche and come back before dawn to get in position? Wolf couldn't warn him. His throat tightened.

The lighted zone around the cabin extended about fifty feet in all directions. They couldn't enter it and he couldn't leave without making a splendid target.

Shit!

He pulled on his anorak and gloves, went to Toni, and said, "Stalemate, honey. Turn off the outside lights for five minutes, then turn them on."

She stared at him. "What are you going to do?"

"Inside I'm helpless. So I'm going out and reconnoiter."

"Why?"

"Don't know how many there are. Maybe I can find out."

"And get killed!" Her lips trembled.

"Look, I'm counting on you. While I'm gone, shoot anything that tries to get in. Now, shut off the damn lights!" He went to the kitchen door and unlocked it, and when the lights went off he crawled out on his belly.

Wind slashed at his face and he was thankful for his beard. He

360

slithered off the porch and in a crouch began running up the hillside toward the woods. He ran confidently, knowing every square yard of the surroundings, staying low, rifle slung across his back as he moved through what was by now almost complete darkness.

Near the edge of the pines he reached a knoll, dropped behind it, and readied his rifle. Resting it on the brow of the knoll, Chance sighted through the scope at the woods below, where Valcour had disappeared.

By now the rifleman who fired through the open door would have moved around, probably in a hillside arc to cover the cabin from high ground. Chance scope-searched the tree fringe, hoping to see movement, a metallic glint, a glimpse of something that could be clothing, but saw nothing useful.

The cabin's outside lights went on.

He had hoped he might spot the enemy approaching through the lighted zone, but it was bare. He wondered what they would be thinking. Chance could see three sides of the cabin but not the front. To survey all sides equally he would have needed a helicopter. He listened for a cracking twig, the scrape of a boot on hard ground, while he watched the cabin. Looking beyond the roof, he could make out the pebbled drive and the dark motionless bulk that was Wolf's body, and his hands gripped the rifle more tightly.

He couldn't blame Toni for her naïveté. The same boarding schools that hadn't taught her cooking hadn't taught her about intrigue, betrayal, and violent death—but she was learning now. Her postgraduate course. Accelerated.

Chance drew up the anorak hood to cover his head, and shifted position. Cold from the earth was beginning to seep into his body. Well, the enemy was even colder.

He recognized Valcour's coat as a civilian copy of the British officer's coat, the traditional British warm, probably tailored by Gieves. But would the others be as well clad? Chance doubted that the murder party had come prepared for a prolonged stay on the mountainside. Valcour had been sent to lure him out so the sniper could do his deadly work, speedily.

So they must be conferring, deciding what to do next to bring on the denouement. Torch the cabin? Possibly.

By now, he thought, they must realize one of us is outside. That would make them cautious.

Maybe they'll withdraw and try again.

Maybe not.

He had to break the standoff. Like with a couple of parachute flares and a satchel of hand grenades, none of which he had. Time for the marines.

No marines.

Slowly he scoped the woods' fringe below and stopped, sucking in breath. A tiny ruby light showed and Chance ducked below the knoll as a bullet plowed into earth where his head had been.

Damn—they had a night scope!

Rolling sideways, he poked the rifle over the crest and fired three quick shots at where the ruby glow had been. No yells of pain, no body crashing into underbrush. Just a sardonic yell from Paul Valcour. "We know where you are, Chance. Be reasonable, let Toni go."

"Bastard!" Chance shouted. "Come get me!"

"Quinn, you've been extraordinarily lucky." Valcour's smooth voice pierced the wind. "But your luck's run out. Be realistic. Give up and Toni won't be harmed."

Chance began moving down the slope toward Valcour's voice, rifle in both hands, ready to fire. Valcour was too weak to be fully mobile, so his companion would be making the sweep-search.

The moon was rising above the mountain barrier, filtering pale light into the forest, giving Chance more visibility. He picked his way from tree to tree, confident that he would come upon Valcour at any moment.

Then from the cabin came a shot. A scream.

Toni! He froze in his tracks.

While he'd been blundering about in the woods an enemy had entered from the front. Who had fired?

Chance moved to the edge of the trees, stared at the cabin. Inside, a light went on. Helplessly, he gripped his rifle. Then from around the cabin's far corner two figures emerged. Toni first, a man close behind her, pistol in hand, using her as a shield. Chance steadied the rifle against a tree and sighted on her captor as they moved into the floodlit zone. He estimated the range at about ninety yards, but the wind was too gusty to risk a shot. He clicked the cross hairs down—in case the wind dropped—and kept them on the gunman.

The man wore a heavy coat and a fur cap. He had a thin, weathered face and a hooked nose. Toni's face was white, drawn. Her hands formed tight fists as the gunman shoved her forward.

Then from bracken cover came Paul Valcour, a rifle looped over one shoulder, light glinting from the bulky night vision scope. Turning to face uphill, Valcour shouted, "Toni's going with me, Chance. You and Sobatkin can shoot it out. Good night, and good-bye."

Sobatkin! Berlikov's boss? The man who planned Sosnowski's murder? Chance's cross hairs held on the fur cap and his trigger finger began to tighten, but Sobatkin's head moved behind Toni's.

Valcour was walking toward them—slowly, as though each step were a painful effort. Chance saw his lips moving, but wind covered his words. Sobatkin shook his head. Valcour beckoned at his sister, but Sobatkin gripped her arm.

Valcour was only a few yards from Sobatkin and moving closer. His face was angry, his voice loud. Sobatkin shook his head again and pulled Toni against his body.

In that moment Chance stepped out of the woods and yelled, *"Let her go!"*

Sobatkin whirled and fired three pistol shots at Chance, but the range was too great. Chance saw Valcour unlimber the rifle and start raising it to point on Sobatkin. But the Russian saw the movement and swung his pistol around. Before Valcour could ready the rifle, Sobatkin fired. Valcour crumpled before the sound reached Chance.

Toni screamed and rushed to her brother, covered him with her body, and fought off Sobatkin, who was trying to drag her away.

Chance fired at the Russian, missed narrowly, and sighted again. But in a crouch Sobatkin snatched up the fallen rifle and dodged into the woods.

Chance yelled, "Toni, get into the cabin, or he'll kill you. Take the pistol. Run."

She hesitated, looking at her brother, grabbed Paul's shoulders, and tried to drag him with her.

Chance shouted, *"Don't wait, take cover!"* and as Toni started running back toward the cabin, he scanned the woods for Sobatkin. But the Russian had disappeared.

Valcour lay motionless in the thin moonlight.

Chance backed into the woods, moved downhill a few yards, and squatted at the base of a tree. Sobatkin was somewhere down there, furious and vengeful. After hunting Chance down, he would murder Toni.

Sobatkin had the night-vision scope, but he didn't know the surroundings as Chance did, slightly evening the odds. Chance blanked Paul and Toni from his mind to concentrate on the Russian general, listening for anomalous sounds, trying to pierce the dark forest with his eyes.

Daylight would reveal them to each other, but Chance thought Sobatkin would try to force a finish before dawn so he could leave under cover of darkness. And Sobatkin would become increasingly desperate. If he tried to reach the cabin and take Toni hostage again, Sobatkin would expose himself to Chance's fire.

Chance left the tree's shelter and moved farther downhill. Squatted, listening. He glanced at the cabin and saw that it was dark again. Wisely, Toni had turned off the inside light. Had she recovered the pistol? He hadn't seen it in her hand.

Subconsciously it relieved him that he faced only Sobatkin, that no *spetznialniy* had come. But so far Sobatkin had done all the right things, keeping Chance diverted with Valcour while he ranged wide and entered the cabin. Unquestionably, Sobatkin was a skilled and dangerous enemy.

Chance was staring downhill when he heard a branch crack uphill to his left. He focused in that direction while quietly dismounting the Zeiss scope; if Sobatkin was that close, the scope was useless. He moved his body behind the tree and held the rifle ready, pointing in the direction of the branch sound. Waiting for a glimpse of something to shoot at twenty or thirty yards away.

His left hand scraped at pine-needle ground cover, felt stone, dug it out. After listening a few moments, Chance heaved the stone to his right, and as it crashed he was rewarded with a rifle shot.

The brief red-orange muzzle blast oriented him and Chance

fired twice. The second shot brought a yelp of pain, the sound of a body plunging away through thick cover.

He stood up and moved from the tree, began trailing the sounds. Suddenly they stopped, and Chance trod carefully, every nerve on edge, realizing he had given away his location just as Sobatkin had.

He was close to a broad tree trunk when the hidden Russian fired. The bullet hit Chance's left forearm and jerked him sideways. Despite spears of pain Chance set his teeth and stayed silent. He knelt and steadied the rifle barrel on his left knee, finger on the trigger.

No movement from the Russian. How badly was he wounded? Not so badly he couldn't shoot. Chance forced his left arm to grip the barrel while his right hand searched for another stone.

Found none.

As his hand withdrew, it brushed the leather sheath. Chance pulled out the heavy knife and hurled it hard to the right. It hit a tree trunk and gave off a sharp metallic *ping*. From less than thirty feet away Sobatkin fired at the sound. Chance swung his rifle toward the muzzle flash and fired, awkwardly drew back the bolt and homed his final shell. He saw Sobatkin limp into a clearing, head turning from side to side as his eyes searched the thicket. Chance's finger was on the trigger when the Russian saw him and pointed his rifle.

Chance pulled the trigger.

The bullet caught Sobatkin; he staggered back, firing once. The bullet zinged above Chance, whacked into a tree as Sobatkin fell forward.

Cautiously, Chance approached him and saw he was still breathing despite a baseball-size exit hole between his shoulder blades. Chance dropped his Mauser and picked up Sobatkin's rifle. A Mannlicher, he thought irrelevantly as he chambered a cartridge.

With his foot he turned over the Russian, saw his bald head and vulpine face. The mouth opened and closed; breath rattled in his throat. Chance thrust the muzzle into Sobatkin's mouth, saw horror freeze his features, and rasped, "Eat it, motherfucker."

Pulled the trigger.

Eyeballs bulged from Sobatkin's head. His body jumped, arched, went limp. It was over.

Breathing heavily, Chance stared down at Sobatkin. This was the grand master, originator of all the plots and schemes, his would-be nemesis. And it came to Chance that this was the first time they had ever looked on each other's faces.

Now Sobatkin was dead as the dog he had slain.

Carrying both rifles by their slings, Chance left the woods. As he reached the lighted zone Toni came running out of the cabin. She clung to him, then saw his bloodied sleeve. "Oh, God," she gasped, "how bad is it?"

"I'm in better shape than Paul," he said, and walked with her to where her brother lay.

The tweed cap had fallen away, revealing Valcour's white, silken hair. In the moonlight his face was pale, bloodless, ghostly.

Toni was sobbing. Chance pressed the carotid and found a pulse so faint and slow that it was barely palpable.

Valcour's lips opened. Gutturally, he murmured, "Sobatkin forced me to come—I told him it would kill me." The lips tried to form a smile. "It did."

Toni covered his face with kisses, sobbing hysterically. Chance left her and went into the cabin, aware of blood dripping down his arm, drenching palm and fingers. Pain came in stabbing bursts and he felt nauseated.

With his right hand he pulled a blanket from the bed and went back to Valcour and Toni. Together they bundled Paul's body, and as Toni knelt beside her brother she cried, "I don't know what to do."

Faintly, Valcour said, "Nothing to be done. Killed Sobatkin, did you, Quinn? I told him he underestimated you. Now he knows." His hand clawed for Toni's, found it, and held tight. In a somewhat stronger voice he said, "I don't expect Quinn to forgive me. Will you?"

"Of course, of course—I don't care what you've done. You're my brother. And you saved me from the Russian. I love you, Paul."

"That's good to know," he murmured. "I'll take the memory with me." For a while his lips were motionless. When they moved again his voice was a thin whisper. "Wherever I go."

Breath caught in his throat. His body tensed and went slack. Toni gasped, then burst into wrenching sobs. Chance probed the carotid again, but this time there was no pulse. He looked at the dull, staring eyes and closed the eyelids.

Tears streaming, Toni rose, and together they went into the cabin. In the kitchen he uncorked the Old Smuggler bottle and drank deeply, feeling the liquor course down his gullet like liquid fire.

He sat at the kitchen table and told Toni to slit his left sleeve. He needed help, and he hoped it would draw her thoughts from her brother.

Exposed, the wound ran across the thick forearm muscle, about three inches below the elbow joint.

She swabbed away congealing blood, tied a tourniquet above his elbow, and waited while Chance poured whiskey into the wound. The raw pain made him gasp until he was able to tell her how to fashion a cloth compress and bind it tightly over the bullet wound. His head throbbed, and to fight off nausea he lay on the couch while Toni got a fire going in the fireplace. Sitting beside him, she said, "We have to do something about Paul . . . his body." Her lips trembled.

Slowly, he said, "I'll think of something."

"And there's the other man, the Russian."

"General Yevgeni Sobatkin," Chance said. "He killed Wolf, killed your brother, and tried to kill us both. Let him rot."

"But he'll be missed, Quinn. Won't others come looking for him?"

"Let's not wait around to find out."

The fire warmed him, pain stabilized. Reaction from the long manhunt, loss of blood, gripped him with exhaustion. Toni held his hand, kissed his forehead.

He slept.

When he woke, light streamed through the windows. He smelled bacon and was hungry.

Toni brought him coffee and bacon and eggs. She helped him devour the burned bacon and gooey eggs, then made a sling for his left arm. He got unsteadily from the couch, but outside air cleared his head. He drew in deep lungfuls and gained strength.

Together they rolled Paul's body on the blanket and dragged it around to the rear porch. Chance said, "He died here, I think he should be buried here. If we bring an undertaker from Bariloche, he'll assume I killed your brother." He touched his wounded arm. "I don't want to be arrested again for something I didn't do."

Slowly, she nodded. "Paul brought death with him. I wish I could give him a proper funeral, but I know it's not possible. And I can't lose you again."

Where sun warmed meadow earth by the forest's edge they dug a grave for Paul Valcour, Chance shoveling awkwardly with one arm, Toni taking turns, hands blistering. Before they interred the body, Chance removed Valcour's passport, billfold, and clothing labels. Soon the mound would be invisible under snow, settle under spring rains. Earth to earth.

Chance carried the scope-mounted Mannlicher into the woods and left it near Sobatkin's body. He burned the Russian's identification in the cabin fireplace.

Then he and Toni hitchhiked into Bariloche, where a doctor stitched Chance's wound and gave him antibiotic capsules. Chance said he'd burned his arm with a fireplace poker, not caring whether the doctor believed him.

They buried Wolf behind the cabin, where Chance had first seen the starved Alsatian baying in the moonlight. His eyes filled with tears as earth covered the dog's body, and he realized that he cared far more for Wolf than for Paul, his onetime friend.

Before leaving the cabin, Chance worked on his passport and Paul's, replacing Paul's photo with Ruprecht's, while Toni watched with streaming eyes. When the paste dried Chance said, "We'll travel as brother and sister; it'll be easier that way."

They packed their belongings, locked the cabin, and got into the waiting taxi that took them to the airport for the flight to Buenos Aires.

SIXTY-ONE

Minister of Defense Yaroshenko sat at his desk, sipping a glass of vodka. There were no papers on his desk, only a vodka bottle. He gazed moodily through the window at the onion domes of Saint Basil, beyond the Kremlin wall in Red Square.

After a while there was a knock on his office door. "Come in," he called. The door opened and the senior colonel of the Kremlin Guard entered with two sergeants. One closed the door and took up position before it.

Yaroshenko said, "I've been expecting you. Let's get it over with."

Formally, the guard colonel said, "It is the premier's desire that you resign from the office of minister, Comrade Marshal."

Yaroshenko nodded, gestured at the bottle. "Have a drink with an old man, Colonel. I was fighting Nazis when your mother was still a virgin." He took a glass from a desk drawer, partly filled it, and held it toward the colonel. "As a favor."

The guard colonel hesitated, then took the glass and raised it to his lips. "I salute your history and your courage, Comrade Marshal." He emptied the glass in a single swallow and set it on the desk.

Yaroshenko nodded thoughtfully. "Ah, I could tell you stories you'd find incredible . . . but there's not much time." He lifted his glass and drained it.

The colonel said, "At your convenience, Comrade Marshal." His arm extended across the desk. Yaroshenko unsnapped his holster and handed the service revolver to the colonel, butt first.

The colonel took the revolver, emptied the cylinder, and replaced one cartridge. He handed the revolver to Yaroshenko and saluted.

Yaroshenko returned the salute and placed the revolver before him, on the desk.

"With permission, Comrade Marshal," the colonel said, and did an about-face, then turned back. "I am only carrying out orders, Comrade Marshal, you understand."

"I understand, Colonel. It was so in my day, too."

"And I will always admire your fortitude and bravery."

"Thank you," Yaroshenko said. "That's good to hear."

The guards opened the door and followed their colonel outside. The door closed and Yaroshenko was alone.

So it happens, he thought, as it's happened to better men than me. Sobatkin was too old, too blindly zealous for something so delicate. But in the end it's my fault for having chosen him.

Briefly he thought back to the bleak collective farm where he was born, the battles he had fought, the bravery of comrades. . . .

He had always known that the other ministers in the conspiracy—Gordievsky, Bragovitch, Glazunov, and Fotov—would disavow him as they had. Yet had he been able to conclude a fraternal alliance with the Chinese military, the others would have wanted to share power with him.

What egotists, he thought, what simpleminded fools. Rodina—the Motherland—requires a single strong leader; another Lenin or Stalin, not a council of compromisers. Had I overthrown the premier, I could have ruled Russia and been buried in the Kremlin wall. Was that love of Motherland . . . or vain ambition?

He left his chair and walked to the window. Outside, life would always go on whether he lived or died. His fate had nothing to do with the destiny of Mother Russia. For a time, perhaps years, his Rodina would face cataclysms, hardships unequaled since the Great Patriotic War, until men of steel rose from the chaos to take his place and fulfill the Motherland's destiny. His time, he mused, had drawn to a close. So let me die as bravely as I lived, he thought, and picked up his revolver.

Outside the door the Guard colonel and his men heard the shot. The youngest guard paled, but the colonel placed a hand on his shoulder. "Do your duty, comrade," he said, and walked slowly away.

Farther down the corridor the guard colonel turned into a dim alcove, where a gray-uniformed KGB colonel waited. The guard colonel saluted the KGB officer, who said, "It's done?"

"Yes, Comrade Colonel."

"Good." The colonel handed him an embossed document. "Sign, please, to confirm that the premier's order was carried out."

As the colonel reached for a pen he said, "Will this be held against me?"

"For your sake, let us hope not."

He signed the document and returned it. The KGB colonel put it away and said, "In the morning I'm flying to Leningrad. Please see that there is transportation to Sheremeteyvo at ten."

"Of course, Colonel Yegorova. It will be done as you desire." He saluted; the KGB colonel returned his salute and strode away.

As she neared her office, Natalya Yegorova felt deeply satisfied. If the Motherland was ever to find peace and contentment, old warmongers like the late marshal had to be purged. Even so, she reflected as she opened her office door, Deputy Premier Ligachev was fast losing power and her own enemies were closing in. KGB chairman Kryuchkov—old Vlad, the careful, vicious bureaucrat—had long resented her special relationship with the deputy premier. She might last a few more weeks in the Kremlin, but having performed a final patriotic act for the Motherland, Natalya believed it was better to go now when she could leave unhurriedly.

She unbuttoned her uniform blouse and hung it neatly on the stand, then sat behind her desk. Last week she had mailed the trigger postcard to Antoinette Valcour's Geneva address, and she wondered how long it would take to reach Toni, wherever she might be.

She was prepared to wait two weeks in Leningrad, then if Toni or Chance didn't come, she would leave Russia on her own. Whatever happened she would accept philosophically.

Sudba—fate—would decide.

She was selecting files for destruction when she heard voices and pounding feet along the corridor outside her door. Leaving files by her shredder, Natalya went to a window and looked down. Red Square was filling rapidly with people, not as in an organized demonstration but haphazardly. She counted four army personnel carriers speeding past Lenin's tomb. Each was crowded with soldiers, but their weapons were not pointed at the growing mob.

Confused, Natalya unlocked her door and peered into the corridor, saw the guard colonel striding rapidly in her direction. Glimpsing her, he stopped, and she saw that his face was flushed and angry. "What's happening?" she asked anxiously. "Is it war?"

"No, no, Colonel Yegorova, it's a coup."

"A coup?" she said disbelievingly. Her throat felt tightly clamped. As he started moving on, she caught his sleeve. "Wait—who are the plotters? I must know. Is—Ligachev . . . ?"

"No, not your patron, Natalya Yegorova. The KGB chairman himself is one of the plotters. With Kryuchkov are Yanayev, Pavlov, and Minister Pugo." He wiped perspiration from his forehead. "Please, I must go, position guard units. . . ." He looked at her unhappily. "Gorbachev has been arrested, a prisoner somewhere." His eyes were wild. "The Emergency State Committee says he's too ill to continue."

"I don't believe that," she said coldly. "Do you?"

"I—I have no opinion." He swallowed. "But it's a bad time for me, for you, for many others." Pulling his sleeve from her grasp, he said in a lower voice, "Hide while you can."

"And you?"

"I don't know. Wait to see what happens."

"Then you're a fool," she snapped, "but I thank you."

As he hurried away she saw that the corridor had become a concourse of fast-moving bodies, some uniformed. Everywhere there was confused shouting. She went back to the window. Soon Red Square would be filled. If the army was going to disperse the people, it should have acted by now. No gunshots, not even water cannon. Strange.

Methodically, she fed files into the shredder, then put on her uniform blouse and undid the holster flap for access to her pistol.

Events had overtaken her, she reflected as she scanned her office for the last time. She had no confidence in the Emergency State Committee, and she feared KGB chairman Kryuchkov. Instead of leaving tomorrow she must leave Moscow now. The general confusion, she hoped, would help her get safely away. She breathed deeply to slow her pulse and remembered something.

From her safe she withdrew a thick envelope of hard currencies: dollars, Swiss francs, German marks. It would be foolish to linger in Leningrad, she told herself, when she could bluff or bribe border guards into letting her ride the hydrofoil to Helsinki.

She distributed the bills among her pockets to avoid a single suspicious bulge and unlocked her door. From Helsinki she could begin the search for Chance and Toni; she did not think it would take very long. A few weeks at most.

Outside her door she was swept along by the moving throng, barely able to stay upright as she was shoved and buffeted by the mob. For almost the first time in her life she realized she was on her own, free to choose, free to go. That her feet were being painfully trampled, her breasts and body mauled, was unimportant. After the massed bodies half carried her down the staircase and beyond the Kremlin wall she managed to detach herself and stand aside. Gulping air, she steadied herself a few moments, then began walking toward the nearest Metro entrance. The subway would take her to Sheremeteyvo Airport. Natalya touched her pistol, drew back her shoulders, and quickened her stride.

SIXTY-TWO

In contrast to Bariloche's cold, the terraced Cuernavaca garden was sunnily warm and filled with August flowers. Purple hummingbirds darted from blossom to blossom; butterflies hovered by roses and bougainvillea, and a small stream bubbled down volcanic rock into a crystal pool.

Toni was floating in it while Chance read the *Washington Times* at poolside.

The story was there—not all of it but enough to vindicate him after so many months of flight. He called, "I never heard of this Josephson, have you?"

"No, but obviously he's got high-level contacts, and he's a friend. I think you ought to write him a note."

Chance sipped iced tea and put aside the paper. Soviet defense minister Yaroshenko was dead, too—of a heart attack, if Kremlin reports could be believed. Perhaps Sobatkin's disappearance had something to do with the marshal's demise, but he would never know.

The month's tumultuous events in Moscow—the coup defeated, Gorbachev subdued, Yeltsin triumphant—had gripped the world's attention, but Chance and Toni had focused on Natalya's chances of survival. Chance had said, "I think they're better, much better with Kryuchkov gone." And she had said, worriedly, "Then you think she may not leave?"

"I think she will if she can, darling. The only question is when."

Later Toni had asked when he thought it would be safe to go back to Washington. To that, Chance replied, "When Wilson Jones says so—but why should I? Aren't we comfortable here?"

"I am. But, won't the KGB keep looking for you?"

"Doubt it. Sobatkin was behind all that—and you know where he is. Unfortunately I'll never have complete confidence in my government again, so if I go back to the States, it will be to collect my books and other things. Bring them here."

"That pleases me." She'd smiled, and the subject did not come up again.

Besides, Chance knew that he would never be allowed access to General Berlikov, whose defection had recently been announced. The government would guard and protect him for a very long time.

So, he thought, I'll settle for two out of three. Or, counting Paul, three out of four.

He would never fully understand Valcour's motivations, and Paul had taken the answers to his grave.

Enough thinking of death, he told himself, with life all around me.

When Toni's float drifted nearby, Chance knelt at the pool edge, kissed his wife's lips, and touched her breasts.

Drowsily she murmured, "That feels nice. Please put more oil on my tummy, dear. Don't want stretch marks, do we?"

His left hand steadied the float while he smoothed sun oil over her rounding belly, thinking with awe and gratitude of the new life within; a new life to nurture and cherish, as they would love and cherish each other to the end of their days.